M000080288

NO
TURNING
BACK

NO TURNING BACK

a novel

JOANNE WILSON MEUSBURGER

AMBASSADOR INTERNATIONAL
GREENVILLE, SOUTH CAROLINA & BELFAST, NORTHERN IRELAND

www.ambassador-international.com

NO TURNING BACK

This is a fictional work. Names, characters, places and incidents either are the product of the author's imagination or are used fictitiously. Any resemblance to actual persons, living or dead, events or locations is entirely coincidental.

© 2013 by Joanne Wilson Meusburger

All rights reserved. Printed in the United States of America. Except as permitted under the United States Copyright Act of 1976, no part of this publication may be reproduced or distributed in any form or by any means, or stored in a data base or retrieval system, without the prior written permission of the publisher.

ISBN: 978-1-62020-243-2
eISBN: 978-1-62020-342-2

Cover design and typesetting: Matthew Mulder
E-book conversion: Anna Riebe

AMBASSADOR INTERNATIONAL
Emerald House
427 Wade Hampton Blvd.
Greenville, SC 29609, USA
www.ambassador-international.com

AMBASSADOR BOOKS
The Mount
2 Woodstock Link
Belfast, BT6 8DD, Northern Ireland, UK
www.ambassador-international.com

The colophon is a trademark of Ambassador

To Bill, whose book this is as much as mine

ACKNOWLEDGEMENTS

My heartfelt thanks to Tim Lowry for taking my manuscript to the publisher at Ambassador International. I'm deeply grateful to Barbara Lawing for her first edits, to Kathleen Freeman and Beth Steury who faithfully critiqued it online at American Christian Fiction Writers and to Vanessa Suggs Wallace who polished the final version. Finally, thanks to my family who never told me I was too old.

PART ONE

CHAPTER 1

Bregenz, Austria

Summer, 1898

Her daughter's voice interrupted Helga Thannen as she swept her employer's porch with quiet strokes of the broom.

"Mutter! Mutter!"

Helga shook her head as she shaded her eyes with one hand. Katy seemed to snatch life like a babe at its mother's breast—she had no patience with patience.

The genteel neighborhood slumbered through a quiet afternoon, but Katy's excitement overrode any need to honor tradition. Her sturdy shoes clattered over the rough cobblestones.

"Mutter!" her voice echoed back down the hillside. "I got it . . . I got the job. I start Monday."

Helga stilled her broom on the porch, and shaded her eyes with her hand. A frown creased her brow.

"Katy, Katy," she scolded. "Will you ever act the lady? People here like their quiet."

Katy sank on the stone steps, tugged at a hairpin to whip off the starched white cap of her school uniform, and fanned her rosy cheeks. Her raven locks loosened from the braided coil she wore and cascaded down her back.

"It's just for the summer," she said, "but it means I'll earn my own money. I won't have to beg you for every schilling."

Helga frowned, lifted the broom, and set it down hard.

"Fourteen years I've worked here at the Schwartzler's so you could have advantages I never had."

Using both hands, Katy lifted the curls off her neck, and then freed them again with a toss of her head.

"I know that. I'm grateful, Mutter, I truly am. For now, I'll be a household maid like you. I'll save up money, so when I graduate next spring I can find my own way. Innsbruck maybe, even Vienna."

Fierce strokes of the broom punished the wide-planked porch.

"I'm a cook and housekeeper, not a maid," she corrected without looking up. "I pray you'll give a good account of yourself, the way I've taught you."

"I will. It's only doing more of what I do at home, only taking orders from Frau Meisen."

Katy replaced her cap in haphazard fashion.

Helga heaved a deep sigh of resignation. She had raised her beautiful daughter to reach higher than other girls of her station. She knew Katy's looks were a definite advantage. *Have I gone too far, turned Katy's head?*

She pressed her hand against the small of her back and argued, "You should count it an honor to work for the governor's family."

Katy stood and smoothed her apron. She gazed toward the afternoon haze on the distant mountain peaks.

"I do, Mutter. For me, though, it's new shoes and a pretty dress—or two—instead of this frumpy uniform. I'll save the rest of what I earn for beginning a new life somewhere else."

"You hurt me by saying such things, Katharina Elisabeth. What's wrong with Bregenz?"

"Nothing, but you're the one who sent me to convent school, saying you wanted something better for me. Besides, haven't I always made good marks?"

Helga paused her sweeping, again.

"Your brothers learned their father's blacksmith trade. Yet, you always ask questions, wonder 'bout things. Same as I did your age."

Katy hopped off the step, and scattered the youthful scent of salty sweat mixed with the sweet rainwater she used to wash her hair.

"There, you see?"

She swung one arm in an arc toward the distant Alps.

"The world's bigger than our little town of Bregenz."

Her cheekbones flushed against her milky skin as she hoisted her book bag onto her hip.

"I'd better go before the neighbors start peeking through the curtains."

Katy blew her mother a kiss and turned to leave. A smile hovered on Helga's lips as she watched her daughter disappear back down the cobbled street, and around the corner. Then, she hoisted the broom and went into her employer's house, closing the door with care.

• • •

Katy slowed her pace to a stroll as she made her way down the wooded slope. The street led to the shore of Lake Bodensee, a wide expanse separating Austrian soil from the Swiss frontier.

More than she often admitted, Katy loved her birthplace. The mountains of the Bregenzerwald extended to the east, and on many Sunday outings she devoured the lunch her mother had laid out on a checkered tablecloth, and then scampered away to play in alpine fields massed with wildflowers.

The highlands formed a natural barrier. As she grew older, Katy often wondered what lay beyond them. Without prodding from watchful nuns, she pored over geography books and eventually viewed the water to the west and the mountains to the east as bookends which restrained her from whatever lay beyond.

She determined to see beyond, even if it meant doing without sweets and store trinkets to save up money. She had made up her mind.

"*Just wait,*" her brothers teased. "*Soon, some fella will catch your fancy. Then, you'll forget your silly plans and start birthing babies, proper-like.*"

Their taunts only served to stiffen her resolve.

Katy slowed her steps as she, again, neared the imposing three-story residence of her new employer, a house befitting a regional governor. It sat back from the street on a slight rise of ground, its white stone exterior reflecting the afternoon sunlight. Grillwork graced the balcony where a slender young man with blond hair leaned against the railing.

When he smiled in Katy's direction, her cheeks grew warm; yet, she pretended not to see him. He must be the governor's son, home for the summer. The Meisens had three offspring—two daughters who also attended the convent school and a son who was enrolled at the university, likely the heir to his father's important position.

Katy never lacked for male attention. She had perfected the little ritual—a delicate half-smile, half-pout accomplished with a sidewise glance of her eyes, and a slight downward slant of her lips followed by a demure lowering of her long, black eyelashes.

During Mass on Sundays, she memorized the blissful smile of Mary beside the altar and practiced the innocent gaze in her small hand mirror. How she loved the Blessed Virgin. The nuns taught her to greatly fear God, but Mary was to be loved, and imitated.

She knew the Sisters meant for her to emulate the Virgin Mary's qualities, not her looks, but a smile like the Blessed Virgin's melted any heart. When she glanced over her shoulder to bestow it toward the young man on the balcony, she saw him smile back.

As she proceeded on down the hill toward home, Katy thought back on the scene with her mother and felt a twinge of guilt. It had, however, always been that way. They seldom talked without somehow disagreeing.

After she left home, there was no longer a need for her mother to work so hard. The thought made her feel pure of heart, like Mary.

CHAPTER 2

Katy shook the airy featherbed out the open window and bunched it to air atop the balcony rail. Although she had been at work in the Meisen household for a week, she had yet to meet the young man she had seen on the balcony who she assumed was the Meisen son and heir.

"Now that he's home from the university, I suppose he shadows his father all day," she told her friend, Sofie. "What a bore that must be."

"Well, his looks certainly aren't boring," Sofie replied.

"How would you know?"

"He brought a ring to my father's shop for cleaning last week. I couldn't believe it when he gave his name. He's terribly handsome."

Katy tucked the feather duster under her arm and toyed with a ring laid on the starched scarf atop the dresser. She held it up to the light from the window and studied the rugged profile of a helmeted knight wrought in silver. *Is this the same ring?*

In the mirror above the dresser, a likeness of the knight appeared. Katy stared in surprise as wide-spaced brown eyes twinkled with hazel highlights, and nose and chin sharply defined beneath high cheekbones.

As her cheeks flamed, Katy dropped the ring atop the dresser and whirled around, afraid he might think she was a thief. He was not dressed in knight's armor, but wore gray lederhosen and a white muslin shirt. His blond hair sprouted at the open collar. His brilliant blue eyes held a questioning look rather than the obvious message many boys sent her way.

"My apologies, Herr Meisen, Frau Meisen told me to dust this room. I didn't know anyone would be here."

Alex backed away and countered, "No, I'm the one intruding. I started off on a hike to the highlands, but came back for something I left behind. Silly, but I don't feel dressed without it."

His eyes rested on the ring.

"I see you found it."

Katy felt the hated heat in her neck and stammered, "It's my job to tidy the room, sir."

"Of course," Alex blushed in turn. "What I meant—I'm glad it's here. You see, my grandfather fashioned it for me and . . ."

"Used you for the model," Katy interjected as she smiled and circled past him toward the open door. "I'll just go on with my work."

• • •

Alex hated the way he stumbled over his words instead of talking to girls the way other men did. He was pleased she recognized the ring's likeness and thought he should have told her so.

"I meant no offense," he hurried to add as he followed her out of the bedroom.

He ran his fingers through his hair to push it back from his forehead.

"I'm sorry I startled you."

As she started down the staircase and swished the duster along the railing, he noticed her hands. They were soft and white, the knuckles smooth, unlike the rough, nail-bitten hands of most servant girls. The sleeves of her cotton dress were pushed up to her elbows and faint freckles sprinkled her forearms.

"My name is Alex and you are . . . ?"

"Katharina, Katharina Thannen. Everyone calls me Katy."

Katharina. What a beautiful name. Do I say so?

"Nice to meet you."

"Thank you, Herr Meisen."

She made a little curtsy and flipped the thickly-plaited braid back over her shoulder.

"My name's Alex. Remember?"

"I'll remember."

"Good."

Alex hesitated, and then hurried on down the stairs and out the front door. As he climbed the hill, he berated himself for his awkward way with girls. *Why didn't I start a conversation to set Katy at ease after bursting in on her like that? Now, she probably thinks I'm condescending, even pompous.*

He felt he always walked a tightrope between the gentle sphere of his mother's influence and the stern, uncompromising approach of his father. His strict upbringing in the Roman Catholic Church taught him to honor his father and mother. He tried hard to achieve a balance, but found it increasingly difficult. Whichever way he leaned caused him to feel vulnerable and unsure.

I'm twenty years old, he chastened himself. *When will I act like it?*

The night before, he had summoned courage after dinner to tell his father he planned to take the following day off to hike in the mountains. His father disapproved, as Alex had expected.

"You have the privilege of learning the workings of government," Herr Meisen lectured.

He paused to pack his pipe before continuing.

"You must take every advantage of the opportunity."

His mother intervened.

Surely, Anna thought, *Alex deserves a little time to himself before starting work.*

When she leaned to place her hand over her son's hand, Alex noted their similar coloring as opposed to his father's darker complexion. Herr Meisen waved a hand in dismissal and got up to leave the room.

Alex tried not to dwell on the future laid out for him. He preferred courses in history as opposed to political science. He longed to emulate those who fostered a vision and let nothing stand in their way.

Certainly, he harbored no ambition to govern the masses: uphold and facilitate laws regardless of their value solely because they were written on dusty parchment. Besides, he lacked the necessary bravado and bluster to prevent people from questioning the requirements of power.

He knew his failure was inevitable from his father's impatient gestures and disdainful attitude toward everything he did. He admired his mother's example—the way she laughed and talked with the household staff. His father, however, saw them as no more than servants to do his bidding.

One day he heard his father scold her.

"You're no longer a painter's daughter. Such behavior is below your station and reflects on my position."

"Nonsense," his mother had replied. *"There's no shame in being a painter, Thomas; nor a farmer for that matter. We are who we are."*

Alex had yearned to take his mother's side. He knew the populace respected his father as a tough administrator, one who achieved his position through civil service ranks rather than aristocratic privilege. Yet, Alex perceived another side to him—intolerance toward the peasant classes and condescension toward his wife.

Later that same week, he came downstairs dressed to work at his father's office and discovered Katy as she stood on the front stoop shaking one of the patterned woven mats laid atop the parquet floor of the front hallway. He hurriedly took off his suit coat, folded it, and laid it on the granite bench which bordered the porch.

"Let me," he said as he picked up another mat.

"Thank you, but I can manage," Katy told him.

Alex persisted, "They're heavy. Mother and Father sent them back from the Orient; Father said the freight cost a fortune."

He took the mat from her hands and shook it out over the porch railing. Alex was pleased to do something for her. As a member of the bobsled team, actions came easier than words.

He helped Katy replace the mats, and laughed with her when he laid them in the wrong places. Then, he saw his mother approach as she came home from morning Mass which she never missed. A handsome woman, she wore her dark hair in a tight coil at the back of her head.

He stepped to her side, and leaned down to kiss her cheek.

"I thought Katy could use some help. I'll only be a few minutes late. The wheels of government turn very well without me."

"Well, I'm sure your father values your assistance."

She smiled, turned to Katy, and instructed her, "It's time to set the noon-time table."

Katy made a small curtsey and followed her mistress. However, not before she gave Alex one of her over the shoulder smiles that intrigued him so.

It made Alex feel good. He hoped Katy regarded him as a friend and fellow citizen instead of the aloof son of her wealthy employer. Her lovely smile lingered in his thoughts.

• • •

As she prepared for bed, Katy massaged her hands with sheep's fat. Her mother scoffed at the vanity of spending hard-earned money for such extravagance.

Katy told her, "I've not asked you for anything since I started working for Frau Meisen last month. I've even money left to buy a pastry at the festival next week."

All of Bregenz suffered festival fever. Hammers banged day and night constructing the floating stage which linked the platform to the shore of Lake Bodensee by ropes and a long wooden pier. From towns and hamlets near and far, the music festival attracted nobility and simple peasants alike. Besides the stage production, many came for the sole purpose of dancing country waltzes on the cobblestone streets, especially to the popular strains of Johann Strauss, the recently famous composer.

Katy and Sofie discussed little else. Helga sewed Katy a bright green dirndl which set off her lustrous dark hair. Even though Katy showed little interest in boys her age, their clumsy compliments gained her extra favors.

She knew she was certain to be among the first asked to dance, and the source of arguments over who was to buy her pastries. She might even see Alex Meisen there, although it was unlikely.

Opening day dawned bright and breezy. Rippling waves bobbed the huge stage up and down, as if it also found waiting difficult. Stores and government offices were closed, but cafes and pastry shop owners awaited the clang of their cash registers.

Anna Meisen had given Katy the day off. She said she believed all young people should enjoy the festival atmosphere.

Katy and Sofie sauntered along the board sidewalks, and took inventory of the enticing tortes and strudels. The tantalizing aromas of crisp-fried Wiener schnitzel and beef soup with potato dumplings wafted out open doors.

Sofie's thick braids wrapped round her head in a neat coil, and silver buckles graced her shoes in place of sturdy laces. Her plump figure testified to her love of food as she gazed longingly at each enticement. When Katy, at last, bought some wiener schnitzel and a cake to take home to her mother, Sofie purchased a cake topped with apricot jam and chopped almonds.

Crowds began to fill the streets and the *oompah* of gleaming tubas lured people to the floating stage for the afternoon performance of a popular operetta. Then, at last, the lamplighters began their rounds. Excitement built as the metallic strum of a zither broke through the gathering dusk.

Boys lined one side of the cobblestones and eyed the girls on the opposite side to size them up. Soon, skirts began to whirl and men slapped thighs, knees, and the soles of shoes in a fast-moving folk dance designed to break the ice before couples paired off.

Katy spun past familiar faces, and then saw Alex Meisen. His attendance surprised her because street dances attracted mostly common folk like her. He stood to one side and watched the dancers.

The tempo of the music increased as the dancers caught a hand, and then released it to catch another. Katy knew she was sure to have her choice of partners as the dancers paired off.

One minute she twirled with confidence. The next instant her shoe caught between two stones; she fell and twisted her foot as it wedged between two cobblestones. As she cried out in panic and pain, strong arms caught her—she turned to realize with surprise it was Alex Meisen who had come to her rescue.

He bent down to free her foot. Then, he swept her into his arms and took several swift strides away from the whirling figures to place her atop an upturned barrel in a narrow alley between two shops. As sharp pain throbbed through her ankle, she bent over to clasp it with her hands.

"I've twisted it or something," she cried as frustration and pain pinched her voice.

• • •

Alex concentrated on Katy's injury. In the brief contact of their bodies, he observed the rounded shapes above the laced bodice. His heart pounded as he inspected the ankle and gingerly flexed her foot.

"Does this hurt?"

Katy winced, took in a sharp breath, and replied, "How stupid of me."

Alex grasped for something to say.

"Cobblestones make dangerous footing. Someone is always falling. You need to bathe your ankle in salts to prevent it from swelling. Do you think you can walk?"

"I don't know."

Katy gazed toward the crowded street. Violins had replaced the zither, and couples swayed in rhythm to the haunting strains of the Blue Danube Waltz.

"Just when the fun started," she said. "What rotten luck."

She was beautiful even with her lower lip turned down in a pout. Alex lifted her down from the barrel.

"Easy now."

She ventured a step, gasped, and reached out to grab hold of his arm. Alex felt strong and protective.

"Lean on me," he told her. "You'll have to tell me how to find your house."

He placed her arm across his shoulder to act as her crutch. Thus, they made slow progress through the crowd and began a careful climb up less-crowded streets.

Alex drank in the warm scent of her body; her soft flesh pressed against his thigh as they moved in awkward tandem over the cobblestones. He stopped beside a low stone wall and offered to let her rest.

"Perhaps, it'd be best if you waited here while I fetch the carriage."

"It's not that far," she told him, "just one advantage of living near the town square."

In the gathering darkness, Alex studied her face and wondered if she meant the remark to point out their differences. Her expression told him nothing. Her soft cheek close to his, its roundness as well as the curve of her throat beneath made his chest ache.

In front of a plain clapboard cottage with darkened windows, Katy stopped.

"This is where I live," she said. "Everyone's at the festival."

"Will you be able to manage?" Alex asked in a husky voice.

He barely made out her profile in the gathering dusk.

"I'll be fine. I need to light a lamp and find the salts to soak it."

As she reached out to lift the iron latch, Katy dropped her arm from his and turned toward him.

"It was kind of you to help me. Really, it was."

Her face was so close to his the tongue moistening her lower lip enticed him as a tasty morsel to devour.

"I'm afraid I've spoiled your evening."

"Not at all. I'm not a good dancer, anyway."

Alex had never been this alone with a girl. His inherent shyness battled fierce longing and caused him to instinctively retreat a little. Then, to his deep delight and disbelief, Katy's hand encircled the back of his neck and pulled his mouth down on hers for a long kiss.

"Good night, Sir Meisen," she whispered.

Then, she lifted the latch, pushed the door open, hobbled inside, and pulled it shut behind her.

Alex did not move. Candlelight flickered behind the wood shutters and, at last, he turned away to continue the climb up the hill. His heart still throbbing in his ears, he was no longer drawn to the strains of merriment below. From that moment, he thought himself to be in love.

CHAPTER 3

Alex began a careful courtship, desperate not to frighten her away. He did not presume too much upon the kiss; yet, he agonized over every moment. He told himself the kiss resulted from a sudden impulse of gratitude for his assistance; he dared not presume more. Also, he had to be discreet to safeguard her position in his household.

He regretted their need for deception, especially with his mother. However, he was not yet ready to risk her knowing the extent of his feelings. After she knew Katy better, she had to understand his feelings for her. He was sure of it.

One day Anna scolded him, "Alex, I'm surprised to see you be so distant with Katharina. Just a few weeks ago, you laughed together like friends. Now, you only speak to her when necessary. It's not like you to be so distant."

From the next room where she was dusting furniture, Katy turned and gave him her sweet smile—the one he adored.

"I'm sorry, Mother," he answered. "I don't mean to be rude. It's just that I have other things on my mind, this being my last term, and Father pressuring me to go ahead and study law. I'll be more considerate."

"You're never unkind, my son," his mother replied. "It's not in you."

• • •

After dinner, Katy's duties were complete, so she then left for home. She often met Alex by prearranged signal in the nearby woods. One night as they sat together on a fallen log, he held her hand, and sometimes pressed it against his lips. He talked about art, architecture, and faraway places.

Katy did not pay close attention, but she made sure Alex did not know. She longed to see the world, but art and architecture failed to interest her the way they did him.

She broke in to say, "I love our hills, but I long to see what's on the other side of them."

Alex squeezed her hand and gazed upon her face.

"You're so unusual, Katy. You have goals for yourself. Things you want to experience. It's why I want to teach history—to encourage youth to expand their interests beyond what they experience—, but my father insists I study law."

Katy found it flattering when Alex talked to her as an equal. When he kissed her before they parted, his lips lingered on hers a little longer each time. She found it thrilling, but the end of summer approached before he poured out his heart.

One evening as dusk gathered around them, Katy got up from the log, brushed off the back of her skirt, and said, "Mother will be watching for me."

In a rush, he grabbed her hands.

"You're so beautiful," he told her, "and smart. You have a child-like innocence I struggle to preserve. Each week I visit the confessional to make penance for my carnal thoughts."

Katy stood on tiptoe to give him a quick kiss. She was hardly able to wait to tell Sophie.

Alex hurried on and told her, "I intend to speak to Father. Our courtship has been entirely proper and he must see by now what a fine person you are. As for my mother, I have no doubts concerning her approval."

What does he mean by "speak to Father?" Katy thought. *As for courtship, Alex is leaving in just a few weeks.*

"I've studied hard," Alex continued. "In fact, my marks exceed my father's expectations and I've received acceptance into law school. Timing is crucial. I mean to state my intentions in all areas concerning our future together. No matter what he says, I have no desire to enter provincial government, even if my doing so led to the court in Vienna, as he hopes it will."

Katy had stopped listening. She did not know what Alex was talking about, and she needed to get home to avoid her mother's questions.

• • •

When Alex walked into the government building with his rehearsed speech in mind, the clusters of gossiping secretaries in the hallway should have alerted him. He should have noticed the bespectacled woman who guarded the outer office was absent from her desk. Instead, he rehearsed his speech, again, as he walked into his father's office to find him pacing the floor.

His father asked without stopping, "What brings you here?"

Alex appraised his father. Though tall and thin like he was, Thomas Meisen wore his expensive clothes without an iota of style. The slight stoop of his shoulders caused the fabric of his vest to droop inward and swung the gold watch chain out away from the cloth.

In back, his coat pleated in the middle and protruded slightly, like a rudder. Alex tensed as he sensed the air of rigid intensity which marked his stern countenance.

He cringed at the strong scent of his father's cologne, and found it loathsome. He wondered how others stood it. His father's underlings must steel themselves to it, as they did the bushy eyebrows and swooping mustache that gave their employer an air of constant reproach.

With a curt nod, Thomas Meisen waved his son toward a chair. He seated himself at the walnut desk in front of the framed portrait of Franz Joseph, emperor of Austria.

When Alex extended the crisp envelope embossed with the university insignia, his father took it from him, slit it open, and scanned its contents. Then, he stuffed the paper back in the envelope.

"Splendid," he commented. "I expected nothing less."

He opened a drawer of his desk and dropped the envelope inside which provided Alex's first clue of something amiss. Above all, his father was fastidious.

"I'm sure you'll continue to do well," his father told him.

He shut the drawer and stood.

"Now, I must get back to work. I'm sure you understand."

Alex twisted the ring on his finger and contemplated his father's orderly desk.

"But Father . . ."

"What is it?"

Herr Meisen fiddled with his watch chain, another action entirely out of character.

Alex hesitated, confused. Armed with courage he might never again find, he forgot the prepared speech so carefully constructed.

"I'm in love with Katharina Thannen," he blurted out. "I intend to marry her."

Muscles twitched at the corners of the dove-gray mustache.

"And just who is Katharina Thannen?"

"Katy? She's worked in our household for months now. Surely, you must—"

"The maid?"

Relieved his father appeared more perplexed than angry, Alex continued.

"Katy's a wonderful person, very intelligent and from a hard-working family. Her father owns a blacksmith's shop and her mother—"

Thomas Meisen's fist struck the oak desktop so hard the inkwell rattled.

"That qualifies her as a barrister's wife? She's what . . . Sixteen? Have you lost your mind, Alex?"

Alex's cheeks burned. His voice rose in volume as he fought to control it.

"Katy's well educated, mature for her age. She attends the convent school."

Herr Meisen's spinster secretary, pencil stuck behind her ear like an exclamation mark, opened the office door and poked her head inside. Then, she quickly pulled the door shut again.

"That's commendable," Thomas Meisen continued as he ignored the interruption, "but the indisputable fact remains: she's beneath you and, therefore, altogether unsuitable."

"But Father—"

Thomas Meisen slammed his fist down, again. This time ink splashed on nearby papers.

"I forbid it, Alex. Do you hear me? For many reasons . . . All of which common sense should reveal to you. If nothing else, you of all people should be warned by the lesson of this infamous day."

"What are you talking about?" Alex asked, furious he was at some added disadvantage he knew nothing about.

It was bad enough to have his father dismiss his feelings as meaningless and trivial, but now he felt an ignorant fool as well.

"How's it possible you haven't heard? You must be the only person in Austria who hasn't, even with word traveling as slow as it does from Vienna."

His father's voice thickened with bitterness.

"It took until noon for the official telegram to reach my desk."

Alex stared at him, as if being addressed by a lunatic. *Perhaps, this is all a dream.*

"The emperor's wife has been assassinated," Thomas Meisen spat out in disgust. "While away from her duties—naturally roaming across Europe since her son committed suicide. Something else to tear the empire apart, yet added proof of what I'm saying, Alex. Only tragedy can result from a bad marriage. Perhaps, this conversation is timely after all."

Alex recognized the utter uselessness of further conversation. His shoulders slumped in defeat.

"Go on home, now, and tell your mother I'll be late for supper," Thomas Meisen instructed, as if to a child. "Meanwhile, think this through. Dally a bit if you must, but don't throw away your future. Married love matures out of commitment and shared goals, not a bellyful of lust."

Alex walked out of the office and down the steps of the government building. His neck burned hot, but he concentrated on avoiding the sympathetic stares.

He walked toward the lake—his head hung down and hands inside his pockets. Furious and humiliated, he thought about not going home at all, but where else was he to go?

At last, he turned toward home where he found Anna in the kitchen. He poured out the story to her. Surely, he counted on his mother to understand.

"Oh, Alex, I wish you had confided in me!"

Anna untied her apron, and then absently tied it back on. Her cheeks were flushed.

"I could've predicted your father's reaction and saved you the embarrassment. Katy's a lovely girl, but you've always been shy around women, allowing you no basis for comparison. I could arrange some introductions—"

"With someone more suitable," Alex interrupted. "Is that what you mean, Mother? I don't believe it. You sound like Father."

"But darling, what's the hurry? Your whole life is before you, and Katy's so young. Sixteen, if memory serves me."

"Almost seventeen, but it isn't age that matters, Mother. I believe she's fond of me and I know I love her. I thought you'd be happy for me. Many girls marry young with the blessing of their family."

"Oh, Alex, Katy's background makes no difference to me. I like Katy. She's intelligent; better schooled than many girls from wealthy families, but is she right for you? As a wife, I mean. Please, Alex, don't hurry into something you'll regret."

Alex left the room and his mother let him go.

• • •

"We need to talk," Anna told her husband as she met him at the door.

She had fought her emotions through a long afternoon.

"About Alex."

Without waiting for a response, she motioned toward the library. Herr Meisen placed his hat on the hall table and followed her down the hallway; his footsteps were heavy on the woven mats. Anna shut the paneled door behind them, but he spoke first.

"I've had an exhausting day, Anna. I was forced to spend much of it diffusing hysterical rumors and attempting to get work out of clerks gossiping over the act of a lunatic. Now, I come home and find you wanting to talk about some equally insane notion on the part of my son. No, Anna. It's very simple. I absolutely forbid him to marry the girl."

Anna bristled.

"I can't believe I'm hearing you compare your son to the senseless act of a total stranger," she snapped as her dark eyes flashed. "Alex isn't a child, Thomas. If you issue an ultimatum, you'll simply force him to oppose it. Give him the opportunity to reconsider. I believe he'll come to his senses."

"I won't be party to your coddling, Anna," Thomas replied as he ran a hand through his receding shock of bushy hair. "And I won't abide them here together under my roof all summer, flaunting their contempt for my authority."

"How can you say such a thing, Thomas? You know Alex is decent and principled. He respects you deeply. If you'll only listen, I have an idea that might solve things. I've been pondering it all afternoon."

● ● ●

Alex intended to ask the same question as soon as he walked into the dining room, but his sister, Rosa, beat him to it.

She asked, "What happened to the maid?"

She poked at the pins which held her elaborate hairdo. Then, she wet her little finger to smooth an eyebrow.

"Katy? I sent her on home," Anna said.

"Did you let her go?" Maria asked.

She was the prettier of the two sisters, shorter and shapelier.

"Of course not; it's just a simple meal. No need for her to stay."

The girls whispered behind their hands as they took their seats side-by-side. Each used a dainty forefinger to cross herself as their father pronounced the usual blessing. Anna placed a white ceramic tureen in front of her husband, and the two girls smiled and passed their bowls for him to dish out the hearty Hungarian beef soup laced with paprika, peppers, tomato, potatoes, and onions.

Alex cleared his throat and asked "Did you have further contact with Vienna, Father?"

"Vienna?" Thomas Meisen asked with scorn. "Where's that, pray tell? Does anyone at the palace know Vorarlberg is part of the empire? No, of course not; they still think Austria belongs to France. Why should today be any different?"

"The summer will soon be over," Anna interjected. "We should plan a picnic in the mountains. Perhaps, this Sunday after church; I long for a bouquet of edelweiss before they're gone."

Where's Katy? Alex thought.

He had not seen her all afternoon and now she was absent from her usual duty of serving the meal. He tried once more to direct the conversation to prove to his father he was able to discuss matters in a reasonable manner.

"I apologize for my ignorance of the situation today, Father."

As though his son had not spoken, Thomas responded to Anna's comment.

"Speaking of mountains . . . ,"

Anna's hand fluttered to her throat at her husband's dismissal of their son's extended olive branch.

"We might as well get this said."

Thomas put down his spoon and turned to Alex and announced "Your mother and I have arrived at a decision."

Alex turned to look at his mother. She busied herself buttering a roll. When his father continued to speak, his voice dripped with sarcasm.

"By now you're well-versed in my limited vistas of power. It's well for you to acquire some practical business experience before pursuing your law degree. Therefore, I plan to contact my cousin in the valley of Egg. You'll live with his family for a time and learn the family cheese business. I'm sure Cousin Alois will welcome the additional money I'll pay him to house and train you."

Rosa and Maria sat stone still. Their mouths were agape.

Thomas Meisen consumed a mouthful of soup, and then placed the spoon into his bowl and took deep swallows of wine from the crystal goblet. The pendulum on the heavy wall clock swung in its slow, steady arc. The ponderous sound filled the room.

Alex sought to remember his cousin. It had been years since he had visited Egg as a child, though the village was not too far away.

He began, "Father, I—"

"It's settled, Alex."

"—and if I refuse to go?"

Rage trembled along the edges of his words.

Anna's eyes were focused on her plate, but she instantly raised them like a doe alert to danger in a meadow of hunters. The unruffled bureaucrat continued to spoon his soup, not once did he look up.

"How do you propose to support yourself? You have no means of your own."

With sudden clarity, Alex realized he hated his father. This knowledge frightened and empowered him.

"I'll teach history somewhere. It's what I want to do, anyway."

"By now," his father stated matter-of-factly, "positions for the fall term have been filled."

Rosa and Maria remained silent and still as if unwilling to draw their father's attention to them in any way. They kept their heads down, sipped their soup, and stole furtive glances at their older brother.

When Alex stood, his chair scraped the oak floor; they each flinched. The violent motion splashed Alex's soup from the bowl into the saucer, some stained the tablecloth.

"Excuse me," he said stiffly. "I won't be eating at this table, again."

Anna stood as well.

"Please, Alex," she begged. "We can talk about this. I've made your favorite strudel for dessert."

"Let him go, Anna," Thomas ordered. "The subject is closed."

Anna continued to beg, but her words were smothered by sobs. Her husband and daughters bent over their soup bowls as Alex strode from the room. His heavy hiking boots thudded loudly until his footsteps faded onto the carpeted staircase.

CHAPTER 4

Letters from his mother arrived weekly, but Alex waited in vain for one from Katy. Nestled at a juncture of the Alps, the valley of Egg was only a few kilometers from Bregenz, but to Alex it seemed farther away from Katy than Innsbruck ever had.

He found himself effectively cut off from her. Although he wrote every day, and mailed the letters once a week, he never received a reply. Not that he blamed her.

Cousin Alois and his wife, Therese, were kind, hard-working people. Their two sons—Albert, eight, and Bernard, six; a newborn baby girl; and Alois' mother lived with them. They did their best to make him feel at home. With little warning of his arrival, they made room for him and included him as one of the family.

When Grandfather Meisen died, Alex's father, Thomas, and his nephew, Alois, became joint heirs of the cheese factory. Alois, who had lived in Egg all his life, ran the operation while Thomas served in an advisory capacity.

Both men shared in the profits, with Alois receiving the larger share for undertaking the daily responsibility. Although Cousin Alois did not farm land like other villagers, his stone house was no different from most others in Egg; it was built above the barn.

Alex's bedroom overlooked a stone wall. He woke each morning to the faint smell of animals and the sound of Therese clucking to the hens as she scattered corn beyond the stone wall beneath his window. They also kept a few chickens, some hogs, a cow for the family's use, and a goat.

Plump and cheerful, Therese rose before dawn; put on the starched, pleated black dress and white apron of her ancestors; tended to the baby girl; and set out a light breakfast of bread and butter, cheese or sausage, with coffee or milk for her husband and two young sons. At mid-morning she mixed cornmeal with fat and stirred it into hot milk which formed a fluffy paste she fried for the noon meal.

Grandmother Meisen, frail, bent, and well into her nineties, helped with the mending and laundry. In addition, Albert and Bernard had their chores—at home and the cheese factory.

The day of his arrival, Cousin Alois gave Alex a tour of the cheese factory. Alex knew the situation was awkward for everyone and appreciated the earnest manner in which his cousin sought to mitigate it. His abrupt arrival must have caused a considerable amount of curiosity and consternation.

"Making cheese isn't that different from my great-grandfather's time," Cousin Alois had told him.

He pointed to a cream separator.

"Your father purchased that machine. It parts the milk from the cream—lots faster than waiting for the cream to come to the top. Also takes the guesswork out of how much to skim off. Mama Meisen called it a foolish contraption—said we'd managed fine without it for years. But Uncle Thomas keeps up on such things . . ."

His voice trailed off. Then, he mopped his round face with his handkerchief.

"Gonna be hot today."

He showed Alex the corner desk that served as his office. It did not take long for Alex to discover the simple bookkeeping tasks assigned to him consumed only a few hours of each day. It left him time to wander about the cheese factory to observe the way it operated.

At least that kept his mind from dwelling endlessly on Katy— no easy task. Her beloved face remained fixed in his memory.

The grasses of the high meadows combined with the careful breeding of Brown Swiss cows to produce the unique flavor of cheese for which the factory was known. Other factors entered in as well. Alois explained: the quality of the rennet, the starter used to firm up the curd, the amount of salt used, and the length of cure— variables which remained a carefully guarded formula.

"I never appreciated cheese-making as an art before," Alex admitted.

"Never thought of it like that," Alois replied as he bent over one of the large vats to scrub it out with a stiff brush. "We're still behind the times in some ways. Still make our own rennet, for example."

His short, stout cousin was devoid of pretense. *He couldn't be more different from Father*, Alex thought.

"I'm sorry, Cousin," he said. "You'll have to explain rennet to me."

Alois chuckled.

"Glad to. I like a man who'll ask questions. Don't mean any disrespect, but I swear your father would choke at times rather than admit what he doesn't know. Anyhow, rennet comes from the stomach of milk-fed calves. We salt and soak it in sour whey to curdle it. Lots of the bigger factories buy commercial extract from a laboratory in Denmark, but change comes slow to these valleys."

A workman raked the curd into a groove lining on one side of the vat. The strong odor pervaded the barn-like shed. At one end, the whey strained through a filter into another container. At noon, Alex was surprised when village children came with kettles or pails, and collected it to take home for their mothers to use to make soups or baking bread.

Alex followed his cousin down to the cellar where the blocks of cheese were stored.

"The cheese really belongs to the whole valley, doesn't it?"

Alois smiled and confirmed, "You catch on fast. Yes, the people of Bregenzerwald feel they own the cheese in the same way they do the mountains and old traditions. It binds us together, makes us feel safe knowing life goes on no matter what happens in Vienna or the rest of the world."

Alex gazed at the rows of shelves which reached from floor to ceiling. Each row was filled with pressed and shaped blocks of cheese resting in various stages of the curing process.

"I envy you, Cousin. What you do matters. It's a trust the people have given you."

His cousin's face flushed red.

"But you have an education," he protested. "Your family has money. You'll be an important man someday."

Alex heard the distant tinkle and clank of cowbells which heralded the arrival of cows for afternoon milking. He pictured himself behind a desk doing a job like his father's.

"Importance takes different forms," he said. "Somehow, I like your kind better."

• • •

Eventually, Alex told his cousin about Katy—his feelings for her and the real reason for his abrupt arrival in Egg. Alois was a good listener, but he refrained from taking sides.

One warm night in late September, Alois carried the wooden table outside after supper and placed a wooden bench beside it. Then, he placed a bottle of lager between them while his sons chased each other about the yard in a boisterous game of tag. Alex toyed with his foaming mug while Alois whittled on a piece of wood. Inside the house, a lamp had been lit and Frau Meisen rocked the baby to sleep.

"I know I'm moody at times," Alex confessed. "I'm sorry. It's so beautiful here, and you and Therese make me feel welcome, but I resent having to leave Bregenz the way I did. I resent my mother and father for treating me like a child."

For several moments his cousin sat without speaking; he drew on his beer.

"Egg has always been my home."

He picked up the short knife to chip away at the soft wood, again.

"I don't know what it's like to be gone from someone you love. But I know you're hurting. I also know your father can be as hard-headed as they come. It's not easy being a father. At times, I fear my boys taking a wrong turn and I come down hard, and then wish I hadn't. I guess every father wants to see his kinder turn out right."

"His kinder, yes, but I'm hardly a child. I'm twenty-one years old with no money of my own, for which I have no one to blame, but myself."

Alois laid down the whittling knife and took a swig from his glass. He traced circles with its wet bottom on the wood surface.

Alex stretched out his hand and continued, "See this ring? My Grandfather Geist fashioned it for me. He died when I was twelve, but I admired him very much. He fought against Napoleon, but he was also a painter and a silversmith."

"I've noticed it," Alois replied as he bent over to examine the intricate design in the fading light. "Unusual. A knight, isn't it?"

"Yes. A crusader actually. My grandfather loved history and was fascinated by the First Crusade in 1096—the one which came across Austria on its way toward Jerusalem. He modeled the likeness on this stone after Godfrey of Bouillon who had led the knights and their followers to redeem the Holy Land for Christendom."

Alex chuckled self-consciously.

"I've been told the likeness favors me."

"You know, it does."

Alois drained his beer and poured more.

"I'm afraid I'm not much of a student. I never could understand all those crusades. Seemed like a bunch of bloody battles that didn't amount to much in the end."

Alex played with the ring, and then looked up to answer his cousin.

"I guess that could be said of the others. But the thing which impressed Grandfather was the religious fervor that inspired Godfrey's belief he was doing God's will. He told me, 'Wear this ring to remind yourself to pray for the courage and strength to hold to your convictions. Be your own man.' I'm afraid he'd be disappointed in me now. I'm not sure I even have convictions at this point. Katy must think me a pitiful weakling, doing exactly as my father says."

"You don't know that for a fact."

Alois stood from the table, placed the knife and carving in his pocket, and called to his boys.

"If she loves you, she's waiting. If not, you're better off. Takes a brave man to find out which. Sleep on it, Cousin."

• • •

"Alex left without even saying good-bye," Katy complained to Sofie as they strolled among the fruit and vegetable stands in the market square. "He writes that his father's decision left him no choice, but Alex had never mentioned anything about a cheese factory. It's all very confusing. I was so embarrassed when Herr Meisen told me they no longer needed me. He said he had put in a good word with Frau Dolph, the banker's wife, and she would hire me part-time after school starts. None of it made sense. Frau Meisen was crying and I've never been so humiliated."

Sofie clucked her tongue and said, "Poor Alex."

"And Egg of all places. I've heard the people are very backward, not at all up with the times. The women still wear those black, starched dresses with their hair braided under pleated caps. Can you believe it?"

Katy stopped to purchase a handful of cherries and offered some to Sofie. A group of boys circled past; they laughed and pushed each other as they glanced her way. Katy paid them no mind, and used a finger to toy with a ringlet of hair straying from her braid.

"Alex told me he had plans for us," she continued. "He never said what, but he ruined everything by telling his father he planned to marry me. He never said anything to me about marriage, or I would've told him it would never work."

"But Katy, he loves you. You get letters from him almost every day. It's all so romantic."

Katy shrugged and muttered, "What's the point? He'll be going back to the university, and I'll be leaving Bregenz after this next school term."

"I wish you wouldn't talk like that." Sofie said as her voice trembled. "I thought we were best friends."

"We are, you silly goose."

Katy ate a cherry and deposited the seed in a nearby bush.

"You know what I mean. Hearing Alex say he was in love with me was exciting. He's handsome. Smart, too. Not to mention his kisses. By now, he's probably taken up with some milkmaid in Egg."

"Katy Thannen! What would the nuns say?"

"The nuns . . . What do they know? They're just jealous 'cause they've taken vows and aren't allowed."

Sofie took a deep breath, and then spoke in a rush.

"I have an idea. My father made a watch for a nobleman who lives in an old castle near Lingenau. My brother plans to drive up to deliver it to him next Sunday. Maybe we could ride with him, and take along a picnic lunch to celebrate your birthday somewhere nice along the way."

Katy turned to hug her and said with glee, "You remembered! And here I was thinking I'd be turning seventeen all alone."

She plucked two cherries from her pocket and gave one to Sofie. Then, she sucked the juice from hers.

"Isn't Lingenau the village just a short distance from Egg? Wouldn't it be something if we saw Alex? I could tell for myself if he truly means what he says in his letters. It's so thoughtful of you, Sofie, remembering my birthday like that. We'll have great fun."

• • •

The autumn day dawned warm and bright. Katy and Sofie sat on the floor of the wooden cart and swung their feet off the back as they passed through the lower reaches of the Bregenzerwald. The day was so clear, and the sun so brilliant, Katy threw her head back and yodeled.

The plodding horse picked up his ears and flicked his head. Sofie's brother laughed as the melodious sound echoed through the treetops.

"I'll meet you here at three o'clock," he told them as he stopped the cart at the bend of the road which curved toward the castle.

"Don't be late. I'll complete Father's business, eat my lunch, and be back for you. Remember, Father thinks you're going to be with me all day, and I'll catch it for sure if anything happens."

"Don't worry. We'll be here," Sofie told him.

Katy skipped down the road leading east. She swung the picnic basket in one hand and her wide-brimmed hat in the other.

"Come on, Sofie. I haven't skipped since I was a little girl, but who's to see? No work, no nuns, no one to tell us what to do or not to do . . . just a big surprise in store for Alex if we happen to see him."

Sofie panted as she ran to catch up. Her face was flushed red from the effort.

"What am I supposed to do if we find him? I'll only be in the way."

Katy knew Sofie always wanted to do anything for her, but her clinging ways were trying at times.

"Nonsense . . . We came here to have our picnic, didn't we? If we see him—which we probably won't—it's not like I'm going to spend the day with him. In fact, it'll serve him right if he wants to get me off by myself. I hope he burns up in the trying."

"Katy Thannen! How you talk!"

"Why not say it? You think such thoughts. I know you do. Why else do you fuss your hair and bite your lips when Johann Schwartzler looks your way?"

Sofie blushed, but Katy paid her reaction no mind. She pinched her cheeks for color, bit her lips, and tied her apron tighter.

In truth, she had been wondering all week how to arrange to be alone with him if she did, by chance, find Alex. She wanted him to know just how humiliating it had been when he left so suddenly, and Herr Meisen had personally dismissed her from the Meissen household.

Alex's letters flattered her. She wanted to see him face-to-face, however, to truly judge if he missed her as much as he said he did.

Their steps slowed as they looked about for a place to picnic. Then, the tall figure of a man appeared over the next hill. They stared as he walked directly toward them.

Katy stopped, clutched Sofie's arm, and gasped, "Can it be?"

Alex had attended morning mass as a courtesy to his host and hostess. His Catholic faith became less important to him after he went away to the university. Additionally, after what had happened, he was angry with God. After all, he had made it a point to attend morning mass on the way to talk with his father on that fateful day. *Where did that get me?*

Today, his thoughts strayed far away. After the service ended, he asked Alois to excuse him to walk among the headstones in the adjoining graveyard. He suspected the parishioners, though respectful, eyed him with curiosity and a measure of distrust. After all, their loyalties lay with Alois, not the son of his aristocratic, but absent partner.

Markers bearing the Meisen name stood near the church as a testimony to the largess bestowed by one of the valley's more prosperous families. Alex found his grandfather's carefully tended gravestone, and then strolled on out the gate and down the road. When he arrived at the fork which veered toward Lingenau, he walked in that direction.

At last, he had received a short note from Katy. She mentioned a picnic she and Sofie had planned in a nearby valley to celebrate her seventeenth birthday. She made no mention of seeing him, but he was certain he was on the path they most likely took.

• • •

For a moment, Alex thought he had conjured up her image. With skirts hiked up in both hands, Katy began to run. He disbelieved his eyes until the moment she ran into his arms.

"Katy! Oh Katy!"

He embraced her and all his doubts vanished. Her presence was proof of all he needed to know.

"My darling, I can't believe it. You're actually here."

Katy pushed him away and took a deep breath.

"You don't understand. Meeting you here is pure coincidence. As I said in my letter, Sofie and I had planned a picnic for my birthday, but we had no idea we'd see you."

"Is that so? All the places you might have chosen and you came here. And no, I haven't forgotten your birthday."

His eyes roamed over her hair, lips, and slim neck, as if he needed confirmation of her actual presence.

"Now, I can explain everything; answer your questions so you can understand what happened. You don't know how I've longed to do it face-to-face."

Katy tossed her head. The red ribbon atop the thick coil of braids bobbed prettily.

"What questions? I've put you completely out of my mind. We just happened to have a ride with Sophie's brother on his way to Lingenau, and thought this valley would be a pretty spot for our picnic. Isn't that right, Sofie?"

Sofie approached. She nodded to Alex, but looked none too happy.

"Hello, Sofie," Alex muttered.

He wished her far away.

"I know the perfect place," he said as he turned back to Katy. "Mind if I tag along? If you have anything to spare, I'm starved and I've already missed dinner with the family."

"Well . . . Actually, we do have plenty of food."

Katy gave him just the hint of a smile—she asked, "Do you mind, Sofie?"

Sofie shook her head, but her eyes mirrored her disappointment if they had even looked to see.

Alex led the way to the secluded glen he discovered one day on an afternoon walk. Tall beeches bunched together, their gray trunks smoothed beneath the tender foliage, the sockets of their branches adorned with rich green moss. To one side, a stand of lofty pines spread their green lace-work to the sky and carpeted the ground with fragrant needles.

The woodland had never smelled fresher or purer. A tiny water-fall spanned a short drop in the small stream, and then pooled into an azure pond surrounded by hepaticas and anemones. Sweet-smelling cyclamen balanced gracefully on fragile stems; a wayward breeze revealed the undersides of their green leaves in resplendent red.

"It's a fairyland," Katy gasped. "Prettier than any place we met before. If you remember, that is."

She knelt to open the picnic basket, pulled out a white cloth, and spread it over the ground. As she reached to smooth the opposite corners, her movements stretched the fabric which covered her bosom, and Alex felt his stomach tighten. His heart raced.

"Katy, you know I haven't forgotten one minute we spent together," he said as his voice caught in his throat.

"How would I know any such thing?"

Katy's lower lip protruded in a pretty pout. She removed the fruit and cheese from the basket, and purposely did not look his way.

"Here, Sofie," she demanded and handed her the bottle of wine, "do something useful."

Alex sprang forward and asserted, "I'll do that."

"I . . . I'm not very hungry," Sofie stammered, her voice small. "If you don't mind, I think I'll look around a bit."

"Suit yourself," Katy replied without looking up. "I'll see you back at the crossroads."

She did not see Sofie's shoulders sag as she disappeared behind the low-hanging tree branches. Meanwhile, Alex had dropped to his knees beside her.

"Oh, my love, how very beautiful you are. I've missed you so terribly, and how desperately I've wanted the chance to tell you in person."

As Katy busily laid the food out, a smile hovered round her lips. She spoke so softly Alex had to lean closer to hear.

"Some men believe actions speak louder than words."

With her face only inches from his, Alex reached for the pins which held the coiled braid, and gently separated the silky strands of hair with his fingers as his eyes found and held hers. The lustrous black cloud cascaded round her shoulders.

Her questioning gaze appeared to mock him, and for a moment he hesitated. Then, her lips began to tremble. He pushed her shoulders gently back until they rested on the velvet grass.

The lush aroma of her firm young flesh mingled with the perfume of the forget-me-nots crushed beneath her. The pounding in Alex's ears shut out the trickle of the brook and the melodious songs of many birds. The glen belonged to them, so secret surely God forgot their presence there.

CHAPTER 5

When Alex climbed the steps and entered the house through the back door, Therese and Mama Meisen were still in the kitchen. The old lady looked up from her mending.

"In my day, folks excused themselves if they weren't showing up for dinner," she scolded.

Therese blushed, ducked her head, and pleaded, "Hush, Mama. It doesn't matter. Alex is our guest."

Alex deferred to the elder.

"No, she's right. After Mass I decided to walk home by a different route while you visited with your friends. I took a wrong turn. I apologize."

Mama Meisen nodded. Therese started toward the cupboard; she said, "I'll fix you something."

Alex put up a hand, acutely aware of his crumpled clothes.

"No, please. I'm not hungry. If you'll excuse me, I have a letter to write."

The room suited him—square and neat with a bed, wardrobe, desk, and chair. Today, however, it pushed in on him, suddenly small and stifling hot. He crossed it to fling the shutters open wide.

Did Katy meet Sofie for the ride back to Bregenz? How will she explain the uneaten food or the lost pins from her braid?

He smiled to himself and whispered, "Knowing Katy, she'll think of something."

He stretched out on the bed, arms crossed behind his head. Thoughts of Katy obsessed him as he recalled the time they spent together.

• • •

Anna Meisen decided she had never lived through a longer month. She felt almost giddy as Thomas handed her into the carriage.

Rosa and Maria sat on the seat behind her as Thomas climbed in from the other side, and took up the reins. After she placed the picnic basket by her feet, Anna settled back and smiled up at the cloudless sky.

"It'll be so wonderful to see him," she said aloud.

Thomas cracked the whip, and started the horses off at a fast clip. Anna took this as a positive sign her husband also looked forward to their destination.

She turned toward him and said, "It seems he's been gone a long time, doesn't it?"

"Only a month; he'll be coming home at Christmas. This outing would be pointless, except it's my usual practice to pay Alois a visit at the end of the fiscal year. It allows me to judge if he's keeping up with the times, the equipment is maintained, and the books are in order. Reminds him I'm keeping an eye on business."

"I'm sure everything will be fine."

Anna turned to the girls.

"Aren't you excited?"

Rosa had pulled off her bonnet to fan her face with it.

"The sun's in my eyes and the day's already hot."

"If Mama lived in Egg," Maria remarked, "she'd have to wear black all the time."

She smoothed the skirt of her bright dirndl and smiled a prim smile.

"All the old women do."

Her father flicked the reins.

"Hush, Maria. What nonsense. I hope Alex has made a satisfactory contribution. I don't expect reports from Alois. He never went far in school you know, but Alex has made no attempts to keep us informed."

For many days, Anna had searched the mailbox for a letter, only to be disappointed. Alex had sent a brief greeting on her birthday. That was all. Well, she meant this reunion to mend the rift.

Alex had always been levelheaded. She hoped he had recognized his feelings for Katy as infatuation—even if he was too proud to admit it—and the picnic would help put all that behind them. When he returned home, she planned to have a social event to make sure plenty of young people his age attended.

"Will we never get there?" Rosa questioned. "I'm so hot I'm sticking to this seat."

"You can stop your whining," her father answered, "Egg is around the next bend in the road."

• • •

Alex stood outside the house with Alois and the rest of the family. He soberly strode to help his mother down from the carriage, and kiss her on the cheek.

"Hello, Mother," he said. "I trust you're well?"

"Thank you, son, I am now that we're here. It's so good to see you. You look wonderful."

"Frau Meisen feeds me well."

Grandmother Meisen and Therese stood in the doorway. Anna greeted them.

"Therese, Aunt Emma! How nice see you, again. We've been looking forward to it."

Grandmother nodded; Therese smiled and made a small curtsey. Thomas tied the reins to the stone post, and then took Alois' outstretched hand.

"Hello, Cousin. Since you've granted our son your usual hospitality, I expect to hear he's pulling his weight."

"No doubt about that. Alex has taught me more than I've taught him. We're disappointed you won't be eating at our table, but, at least, come in and share some schnapps with us."

"That would be nice," Anna said, "but we can't stay long. I have my heart set on a picnic in your beautiful valley."

They filed into the cool interior of the stone house and crossed the plank floor past the huge ceramic stove to the small parlor. Alex had not spoken, except during the first brief exchange.

"I trust the cheese business is doing well?" Thomas asked.

"Yes, Father." Alex answered as he strived to keep his tone carefully correct. "I believe you'll be pleased with the profits. You can thank Alois for that. As for the books, they're in order, as I'm sure they are every summer."

"Splendid. Then, I trust everything else concerning the operation is acceptable as well?"

"It is, Father. Cousin Alois sees to that."

An awkward silence followed while Alois measured schnapps into small glasses and handed them out. Anna sipped the bitter spirits.

"My, what a sweet baby," she remarked. "May I hold her?"

Therese transferred the child to Anna's arms. The two women chatted concerning the raising of children, the warmth of the day, and other mundane subjects. Rosa and Maria stared at their boy cousins who stared back.

Alois reported on the merits of the new separator, and the volume of cheese ready for market. After a proper interval, Thomas stood.

"We need to be going. Thank you for your hospitality—to us and Alex."

"Alex pulls his own weight," Alois replied. "We enjoy having him here."

• • •

Alex squeezed into the carriage seat beside Rosa and Maria. As soon as they pulled out of the yard, his sisters began their chatter. Alex remained silent while Anna directed her husband to the clearing she had in mind.

She found it as charming as she had remembered, and was determined to recapture the holiday mood. Butterflies darted about and a red squirrel with pointed ears scurried up a tree. Anna named the wildflowers for her daughters, and then opened the picnic basket to spread a blue and white checkered tablecloth on the ground.

Maria took a seat, spread out her skirts, and reached for a juicy apricot.

"I'm glad we brought our lunch. Can you just imagine what food Cousin Therese would have served?"

"Good, wholesome fare, that's what," Alex retorted.

"Not to my liking," Rosa returned.

"Enough!" their father thundered. "I'll not have my kinder bickering like undisciplined brats."

"Father," Alex replied. "You continue to treat me like a child. I had hoped things had changed."

"Show your father respect, Alex." Anna heard the desperation in her voice.

Then, she wished to take the words back. After all, what Alex said was true. Thomas always treated his children with condescension. Alex was an adult with every right to confront him. *But why now?*

She so wanted the day to go right, and hurried to fill the air with talk of the valley and its traditions. To her horror, when she cut the block of cheese, Anna failed to keep her hands from shaking. Alex reached over to lay his hand atop hers.

"I'm sorry, Mutter, but there's something I must say. This month has changed nothing. My intentions remain firm. I plan to marry Katy Thannen and I hope you'll accept her as my wife and be happy for us. If not, I plan to marry her, anyway."

Thomas Meisen threw down his plate and upset the bottle of wine. A red stain spread over the cloth and mingled the checkered squares.

"You do and you're no longer my son," he raged.

"Oh, Thomas. No!"

"Hush, Anna. I've toiled all my life to bring respect to the family name. I refuse to accept the humiliation of my only son marrying a common housemaid."

"So be it."

As Alex stumbled to his feet, his face was chalky white.

"I'm sorry to spoil your picnic, Mother, but its best I leave now. I'll walk back."

With that, he turned and strode back toward the road. Anna stumbled to her knees.

"Thomas," she pleaded. "Do something."

"Let him go," he declared and righted the wine bottle. "I've said what had to be said."

• • •

Katy found the letter when she returned home from work. The day was hot for early October and, her new mistress had been testy. She was supposed to start dinner, but her mother was not home yet. So, Katy decided to walk down the hill to the lake.

She tucked the fat envelope into the deep pocket of her apron. After what happened in the forest, what Alex had to say was bound to be delicious. Oh, she knew they had sinned, but she had gone to confession. No one else ever had to know, not even Sofie.

Maybe she would find a job in Innsbruck after she graduated from the convent school next spring. She had been mulling the idea over in her mind.

When Alex returned to law school, she anticipated being near him, again. *Herr Meisen wouldn't keep Alex in Egg forever.*

The thought sent shivers down her back. She had never intended things to go as far as they had. She knew Alex had not either—he had said so. Yet, things were bound to definitely be more romantic from now on.

She gazed out over the lake. Someday she wanted to sail the ocean on a really big ship.

She walked to the end of the pier, balanced herself on one of the posts, and spread out her skirt in one last agony of self-restraint. Then, she ripped open the envelope and began to read:

Dearest Katy,

I had hoped with all my heart to come back to Bregenz to marry you. Not because of what happened between us, but because of my deep love and respect for you. I haven't forgiven myself for what happened, but I think of you only in terms as pure as I did before. You're forever sweet and innocent.

Katy squirmed as she remembered, all too well, her willing passion.

As you know, my father disapproved of my feelings for you and sent me away, believing I'd forget you. Although angry, I bided my time—doing my job well—so when I brought up the subject, again, I might receive a more favorable response. I still hoped to have my father's blessing, or, at least, the encouragement of my mother. Sadly, neither came to pass.

Katy's lips tightened, and then she mused: *why do mothers insist on keeping their kinder from living their lives?*
The letter continued:

Therefore, my beloved, I'm forced to take drastic measures to ensure our future happiness. You'll find another envelope enclosed.

Katy fumbled among the pages; it was there. She read on:

I must risk two things. First, I must dare to believe you feel as I do and will agree to my plan. If you don't, I'll have gone too far to turn back and will never see you, again.

Katy stopped and read the sentence once more.
"What does he mean?" she whispered.
Alex's words continued:

The second risk is mine alone, and I won't burden you with those details. All you need to know is I'm sending you money for travel to America where we can be married and accepted as man and wife, separate from our family backgrounds.

Katy gasped and steadied herself.

Just a few months ago, Theodore Roosevelt, the great cavalry colonel of the Spanish-American War, who will probably one day run for President of the United States, said, "I wish to preach, not the doctrine of ignoble ease, but the doctrine of the strenuous life."

Katy paused, again, and reread the sentence. She hated it when Alex talked in circles and did not come to the point.

Think what it'll be like to live in a country where a man can cast his vote for such a statesman. Opportunity abounds for anyone willing to work. You may be sure I'll provide for you always.

I realize my plan to leave Austria and go so far away will come as a shock and cause you great pain as you think of leaving your family behind. If we're to be together, it's the only way. I know my father; he'll never accept you, nor will he allow me to remain his son and heir if I marry you.

Therefore, we must make a new life for ourselves. America will be the best place to do so. It's our gateway to freedom, my darling.

Katy rubbed her forehead and dropped the letter in her lap. "America?"

She, who had never left the province of Voralberg and had dared to only dream of a journey across the Alps, to Innsbruck, or perhaps, as far away as Salzburg . . . , but *America?*

She recalled smatterings of information from her history books about the Indians, Boston Tea Party, and War Between the States. Yet, the continent of North America remained to Katy another world as unknown as Asia or Africa.

The letter continued:

It'll take great courage, Katy, courage that comes from conviction we truly love each other, and can face any hardship together.

Katy had never given much thought to courage. Courage was a simple matter of making up ones mind to go after something.

"What does Alex mean by 'conviction'?"

The priest talked about the conviction of sin. *Does our sin compel us to now run away together? Won't God punish us, anyway?*

And as for love, what's love?

The priest said people were to love one another. She loved Sofie because she was a faithful friend who never let her down. She loved her mother because she had raised her and provided the things she needed and wanted. She loved the mountain meadows because of their beauty; pastries because they tasted good. *But Alex . . . Do I love him, or the excitement of our unlikely relationship?*

She admired how he talked about many different subjects, and the way his good manners made her feel special, as if she had come from a rich family. Since that afternoon in the forest glen . . . She ached because she wanted to be with him, again, in the same way.

"Is this love?" she wondered aloud.

Regardless, she was certain going to America was an incredible adventure. She ripped open the enclosed envelope, and took out a bank note and several other pages. The bank note was for an amount larger than she ever expected to earn in her lifetime. She held onto it as if the paper might disintegrate and continued to read:

> *If you agree to my plan, you'll take the Arlberg railway to Bludenz on September 7 and transfer there on the northern route into Germany. Several rail changes will be necessary to reach Wiesbaden, our mutual destination. I have made careful inquiries and included all the instructions.*

Detailed information followed concerning schedules, fares, and times of departure.

> *I wish we could travel to Wiesbaden together, but I dare not risk meeting you in Egg. Instead, I promise to join you on the dock in Wiesbaden at the time and date I have noted. There we'll board a steamer ship to travel up the Rhine to the Port of Rotterdam in Holland. Wait until you see the river scenery—the vineyards and quaint houses, ancient stone bridges, and fabulous castles perched high on the hills. It'll be a trip you'll never forget.*

Katy gazed into the far distance where the Bodensee narrowed into the Untersee. She recalled the time her brothers rented a small sailboat and took her with them as far as the channel had allowed. When the way became shallow and full of reeds, they turned back, but she recalled a picture in her geography book of a castle on the Upper Rhine. She had been disappointed when they were not able to navigate the sailboat further.

A sea gull landed at her feet and interrupted her reverie. She returned to the letter:

> *At Rotterdam, we'll sail together to America. The ship's captain can marry us which I think you'll agree will be incredibly romantic.*

"The ship's captain?" Katy questioned his suggestion. "Surely, only a priest can perform a marriage ceremony."

Alex further wrote:

> *The amount enclosed should also cover meals and unforeseen emergencies. The appointed date allows you enough time to make arrangements. I've tried to think of everything, but I know you won't be afraid to ask questions of people along the way if the need arises. Your boldness and determination are qualities I love in you. With the exception of my mother, most women act helpless and weak, but you're different. You can do it.*

Katy smiled and said, "Yes, I can do it."

Whether she chose to do so remained to be seen, but the compliment pleased her.

> *Secrecy, my darling, will be of utmost importance to the success of this tremendous adventure. You must tell no one in advance.*

A small frown creased the bridge of her nose. If she did go— and she certainly had not decided, yet—

She blurted, "How can I *not* share this with Sofie!"

The letter continued:

> *If you don't meet me in Wiesbaden, I'll know you've decided for good reasons not to come. Although my heart will*

break, and I'll have to continue the journey alone, I'll never forget our love which will help to sustain me.

Her head was spinning with the enormity of what Alex proposed. *Why does Alex insist I love him? Yes, I'm attracted to him, but love? Isn't it enough we want an exciting new life and marriage allows us to be together as we were in the glen without feeling guilty? And why would he have to continue on without me if I don't go? Why couldn't he just come back to Bregenz and make up with his father?*

She refocused to finish his letter:

The money is yours to keep regardless of your decision. It's little enough for the happiness you've already given me. But I plead with you, darling, let your answer be aye. I'd kill myself rather than let you regret it.

Forever, Alex.

Katy stared out over the huge lake, its expanse wider than anything else she was able to imagine.

"Is it possible I, Katharina Thannen, can cross an ocean to the other side of the world?"

Streaks of red filtered the sky as she walked home. Her thoughts were far away, the letter tucked deep inside her pocket.

CHAPTER 6

Alex felt his chest tighten and a lump form in his throat as he bid farewell to Alois and Theresa. Their friendship and goodness toward him was genuine; the valley of Egg symbolized the beauty of his homeland he was about to leave behind.

He wanted to tell Alois of his plans—grant his cousin a face-to-face explanation for his actions—, but he dared not take the chance. They were going to find the letter later, when he was well on his way. He prayed for their forgiveness.

He also declined his cousin's offer to drive him to the train station at Bludenz. He was not headed to Innsbruck, as Alois supposed. Instead he found an old man who was willing to take him over the Alps—not east to Bludenz, but north into Germany.

The wagon showed hard use, but looked sturdy. The old man's head nodded as his gnarled hand kept a loose hold on the reins which rested on his knee. When his head lowered to his chest, the horses took their lead—the stilted conversation ceased and Alex was grateful.

Katy should've left Bregenz several hours ago. How far has she traveled by now? How painful was it for her to leave without saying goodbye?

The possibility she might change her mind was something he refused to contemplate. She had answered his letter to say she agreed to come. He held to that belief. In just one more day, they were to be together forever.

He had rehearsed the moment of reunion repeatedly. He planned to swing Katy off her feet, and then set her back down for a passionate embrace—not knowing or caring who saw them.

Katy's dark eyes would snap with excitement as they traveled to Rotterdam, and then on to America where they would begin their new life together. He would be so proud to have her at his side.

Thousands of others had made the trip before them. It could not be too hard, although it did worry him some. His role was to take charge, and make wise decisions to ensure Katy's well-being. More than anything, he wanted her to see him as the one to lean on, one who not only loved her, but also protected her always.

The old man roused himself and shifted his bony frame on the hard plank seat. His watery eyes focused on Alex from a deeply lined face. Beneath the short-billed cap, he looked rather like a gnome.

"Talk has it you hail from Bregenz."

"I do," Alex answered. "I'm taking a holiday in Germany."

"Ah."

His curiosity and conversation ended there; soon the old man dozed once more as the horses plodded on.

Mention of Bregenz stabbed his conscience as Alex thought of his mother. If it was not for her, leaving would be hard, but without regret. Her collusion with his father to send him off to Egg still rankled, but he loved her as much as he ever had. He vowed to do well in the new world in order to return one day and somehow make up for the heartbreak his departure would cause her.

His mother's face frequented his restless sleep. The previous night's dream found him under the street lamp in front of his family's house. She appeared in the rain-streaked window, and he stepped forward expecting her to hurry to the door to greet him. However, when she stayed in place at the window, he realized she was very old.

Deep creases framed her mouth, and her eyes were vacant. Then, the street lamp became a bright, shining moon and the raindrops on the window turned into his mother's tears.

• • •

Katy paced back and forth on the platform with an ear cocked to hear the train whistle. The actual moment of departure was upon her and proved more painful than she had anticipated. She wanted it to be over.

Sofie shed many tears as she trailed behind Katy. She told Katy between sobs how thrilling she found it to play a part in the secret plan—it was more romantic than the plot of any novel she had ever read. As she tugged her cloak closer against the early morning chill, Katy, at last, faced the reality of perhaps never seeing Sofie, her mother, or her homeland, again.

"Oh, Katy," Sofie exclaimed, "it's so daring—like you're being carried off by a knight in shining armor."

The tremor in her voice revealed Sofie's losing battle to hold back the tears.

"I think that's exactly the way Alex sees himself," Katy murmured. "Like the knight on that ring he prizes so much. It's a real dare all right, not knowing what lies beyond. I've never sailed in anything, but a sailboat. Now, I'm about to cross an ocean."

"It gives me goose bumps," Sofie shivered. "I could never do it, but you're always so brave. You can do anything . . . especially for love."

Katy frowned and said, "Sofie, how many times must I say it? I'm fond of Alex, but I'm not in love with him. But it's an opportunity most people only dream of and never carry out. I love my family and I know this will hurt them, especially my mother, but now she won't have to work so hard to pay for my schooling."

"I still don't understand. You always said Alex lived off his father. Where did he get that much money?"

Katy looked down the track and felt almost desperate since the train might appear at any moment.

"I don't know, but he said I could keep it even if I didn't go. At first, I thought about saving it for when I could go to Salzburg and pay for a nice flat. After all, I never asked him for the money, and he said it was mine to keep. But then I got to thinking. Suppose Alex stole it and admits sending some of it to me. Then, I'd be in trouble and out the money as well. So, I'm following his plan."

"And you'll marry him?" Sofie asked breathlessly.

"Probably . . . I wouldn't mind. But we'll see. A lot could happen between here and America."

"What does that mean?"

"Oh, don't look so worried," Katy said. "I'm not going to push Alex overboard. I just meant it's the start of a whole new life and who knows what will happen along the way."

Sofie swallowed hard and whimpered, "The worst part is that I'll probably never see you again."

"Now, don't cry, Sofie," Katy demanded as she swallowed the lump in her throat. "I agreed you could come to see me off only if you promised not to make it hard for me."

Katy had recruited Sofie to hide one of her suitcases and bring it to the station. However, she began to regret her decision. The sight of her best friend fighting back tears made the actual departure suddenly real.

She wanted to put the scene with her mother out of her mind. *Why had things changed between us?*

• • •

As a child she adored her mother. She hung on Helga's skirts, plied her with questions, and believed her mother knew all the answers. In the past year, however, they frequently disagreed and Katy often sensed her mother's disapproval.

The previous week proved no different. After she spent the day with Sofie, Katy came home to find Helga waiting with her arms crossed across her chest.

"Well, I know where you've been," her mother accused.

Katy waited. She knew silence infuriated her mother more than any other response.

"You don't have to tell me," Helga continued. "Frau Dolph did that. Isn't it bad enough you were dismissed from the Meisen household? Now, you've quit this job as well."

"I need a little vacation before school starts."

"That's the least of it. I wanted to tell you some important news, so I stopped and waited outside Frau Dolph's house on my way home from the Schwartzler's. Who should come along, but Herr Meisen."

Katy did not react. She felt her heart beat in her chest.

Helga continued, "I found the courage to ask him why you lost your position. It brought such disgrace to our family and you've never given a real explanation. Seems he sent his son away because the two of you were 'too cozy.' When he told me I nearly died of embarrassment—my daughter not knowing her place. He sees the two of you as an unsuitable match and, of course, I agreed. But that isn't all. He thinks you've continued to meet Alex behind his back. Have you?"

"How dare he?"

Katy summoned indignation into her voice, but she failed to meet her mother's eyes.

"Katy," Helga sighed as she collapsed on a nearby chair, "all I want is what's best for you. You're only seventeen—a child in a woman's body."

"Oh, Mutter, a lot of girls marry and have babies by my age. I'm capable of making my own decisions."

"Of course, you are. But planning to marry Alex Meisen shouldn't be one of them."

"Who said anything about marriage? Is that what this is all about?"

Helga stood and jerked her apron from a peg on the wall.

"Go pump me some water to boil potatoes. I just don't want you to do something too sudden. Wait 'til you understand what it means to share interests with a man, be accepted into his family, and plan your future together. Have some patience."

"Patience?"

Katy felt the hated purplish blotches spread over the skin of her neck.

"Patience is for people who are satisfied with what they have. Father spends all day making horseshoes over a hot fire, and then returns home to fall asleep over his supper. Well, I won't settle for such."

Katy had not meant to go so far. Fury ripped the words from her she could not take back. Tears streaked her cheeks as she fled the room.

At supper, her mother's eyes were red-rimmed. Silence stretched tight between mother and daughter. Katy's father and brothers talked as usual and appeared not to notice.

Katy slept very little. The next morning when the others left the house, she tugged her suitcase from beneath the bed, and took a final look around the house before she left. *Will I ever return?*

• • •

"Remember," she reminded Sofie, "wait two days before taking the letter to my mother. That's very important. It'll give us a head start, so no one can catch up with us. I'll never forget your help. You're the best friend in the world."

Tears streamed down Sofie's face. As the big engine chugged by, the two girls clutched each other until Katy broke away. The porter helped her up the steps to the back platform.

Katy's gloved hand clutched the platform railing as the train lurched. Then, she entered the car without looking back.

• • •

Sofie had dreaded the moment so much; Helga's wrath came almost as a relief.

"I'm sorry, Mrs. Thannen," she said fervently. "I couldn't tell you. I promised Katy."

"You had no right . . . no right, do you hear?"

The shrill pitch rose higher.

"Now, it's too late. She doesn't even know she's to have a baby brother or sister next spring. She's gone and what will become of her?"

Across town in the Meisen household, a different drama no less traumatic unfolded. Thomas answered the knock to find his cousin standing on the doorstep. Alois constantly turned the brim of his hat around and shifted from one foot to the other.

"What is it, Cousin? Come in, come in. What brings you?"

Alois stammered so bad Thomas Meissen stopped him with a gesture of impatience.

"For God's sake, man. Sit down and calm yourself."

Anna appeared in the hallway behind her husband. When she saw Alois, she reached out to steady herself on one of the foyer chairs.

"I don't know how to tell you this, Uncle."

"Is it Alex?" Anna inquired of Alois. "Has he had an accident?"

"No . . . Nothing like that."

Anna let go of the breath she held.

"Then what is it?"

"It's so unlike him. I would've trusted him with my house, children, even my wife—"

Thomas Meisen scowled and reached out to shake his cousin's arm.

"In the name of God, man, stop rambling. Just tell us."

The fierce tone served to help Alois steel himself, collect his thoughts, and start from the beginning.

"Alex left last Saturday morning and headed to Innsbruck—we assumed—as he had told us. I wanted to drive him to the train, but he insisted on hiring a driver."

Thomas frowned. He nodded and encouraged Alois to go on.

"Yesterday was Sunday—the Lord's day, so I didn't go to the factory. I didn't find the letter until this morning, on my desk."

"What letter?" Thomas grilled; his face was inches away from his cousin's.

Anna concentrated on the Adam's apple which bobbed up and down Alois' neck. At last, it stayed in place.

"He took it," Alois blurted.

"Took what?"

Thomas measured out the words as if speaking to a slow-witted child.

"The money. Your money. Your profit from the cheese."

"Oh, there must be some mistake," Anna protested. "Alex would never do such a thing."

"I've been over and over the books, Frau Meisen. I'm not as fast at them as Alex, but I know when a large sum has been withdrawn, and there's a check stub showing who got the money."

"But why?" Thomas probed; his tone harsh.

Alois ventured in another direction.

"There's something else. I found the driver who took him. He likes trains . . . waited around to see Alex leave. The train Alex took left on a track headed north which didn't surprise the old man since Alex told him he was taking a holiday in Germany."

"Germany? Why would he be going to Germany?"

Anna sat down hard on one of the hallway sofas.

"Thomas, don't you see?"

Her voice wavered and she began to sob.

"I had a premonition that day in the mountains. I kept telling myself I had to be wrong."

She fumbled for the handkerchief in her pocket and buried her face in it.

"Now, I know I wasn't. Alex isn't coming home."

"Nonsense . . . He'll be back and return every cent he owes. No son of mine would dishonor our name like that."

Herr Meisen reached out to pat Alois on the shoulder.

"Not a word of this to anyone, understand? I'll be in touch. There's an explanation. You'll see."

• • •

The explanation came in the next day's mail. Alex's letter bore the address of both parents so the envelope remained on the hall table throughout the day. Anna fingered it many times and examined the handwriting for clues. She held it in her hand when, at last, she heard her husband's heavy step on the porch.

He took the envelope and glanced at the writing. Then, he took out his pocket knife, slit open the flap, and scanned the contents.

"Thomas . . . Please!" Anna begged.

His voice showed no emotion as he read the letter aloud. Anna wept bitter tears. Thomas Meisen shed no tears at all. His words dropped like stones so his daughters, who stood on the staircase, drew back.

"Alex Meisen is no longer my son," he proclaimed and laid the letter back down on the table. "No such person will be mentioned ever in my presence again."

He glared at his wife and daughters.

"Do you hear me? The name will be stricken from all family records, omitted from the graveyard tombstone. My son is dead."

Anna Meisen fainted.

CHAPTER 7

Katy kept her face close to the window to not miss the magnificent views of her alpine homeland. Hewed out of the mountainsides only twenty years earlier, the Arlway railroad line remained a marvel of engineering. It only ran west to east and necessitated a change of trains in Bludenz.

Katy consulted Alex's directions. She almost had them memorized. *Strange to be in Bludenz,* she thought.

She knew it as the birthplace of her parents, but she had never been there. She was hungry and might find a croissant in the nearby shops, but she was afraid she might encounter a relative. Some of them traveled to Bregenz for the festival. Instead, she waited on a wooden bench, edged away from a rancid-smelling spittoon at the end of it.

The next train was older and had more sway. As it curved north, it left the womb of her beloved Bregenzerwald and headed toward the border of Germany. Katy shed some tears, birthed by trepidation and sudden sadness as she left the only world she knew.

A bewildering schedule of connections was ahead, but Alex had done his homework. She missed a train only once, at Munich. Even then, Katy did not worry much because she had an overnight reservation in Frankfort. She would not meet Alex in Wiesbaden until the next morning. Besides, it gave her time to purchase some bread and cheese while she waited.

As she entered the station, the odors from the food stand made her queasy—probably due to the motion of the train. *Eating will settle my stomach.*

She had removed the cheese from its wrapping when two well-groomed women sat beside her on the bench. The first—dressed in lavender with a matching felt hat—appeared middle-aged. The other—face more lined and gown a somber blue—leaned heavily on a black cane. She smiled pleasantly at Katy.

"A warm day for September, isn't it?"

Katy smiled and nodded. She would not mind a little company. No one had spoken to her since the train left Bregenz, except the conductor who asked to see her ticket.

The older woman inquired, "Traveling alone, dear?"

"I'm meeting someone in Wiesbaden," Katy replied.

"How nice, we're also traveling to Wiesbaden . . . for the baths."

Without warning, Katy felt the urge to vomit. She stood, the food on her lap spilled across the floor, and she ran for a door marked: LAVATORY – WOMEN. Inside, she lunged for a stall, fell to her knees, and retched into the stained toilet bowl.

When her stomach felt empty, and she was able to stand again, she brushed the grime off her skirt with great distaste. As she clutched the wash basin, she splashed cold water on her face. The ashen features which stared back at her from the mirror were those of a stranger.

When she re-entered the lobby, the two women jumped up and rushed to meet her. The younger still held her purse. The spilled food had been swept from the floor.

"My goodness, we were so worried."

The older woman took Katy's arm and guided her back to the bench as her cane tapped against the floor.

"I'll be fine, thank you."

Katy sat back down on the bench. Her insides still quaked.

"You see," she continued, "I boarded without breakfast this morning and I'm afraid the train ride, plus the heat—"

"Oh, dear, one should never travel on an empty stomach."

The older woman handed Katy the purse.

"Please let us buy you something else to eat."

Their concern, so obviously genuine, brought unwilling tears to Katy's eyes. She missed her mother's touch—a hand to her forehead, the other on her back.

"My stomach's been upset the last few mornings," she heard herself say. "Excitement of the trip, I guess."

The two women exchanged glances.

"I'm sure that's it," the younger said in a soothing voice. "Oh, please forgive us. We've been very rude. I'm Frau Renner and this is my mother, Frau Freurstein."

"Katy Thannen."

The older woman reached out to pat Katy's arm. Katy drew back. She did not need their sympathy. She would be reunited with Alex soon. Then, he would take over and everything would be fine.

"You mustn't be embarrassed," Frau Freurstein soothed. "We all suffer ill health at times. At my age, I'm often dependent on the patience of others. Did you say someone is meeting you in Wiesbaden?"

"My fiancé; we're traveling to America."

Katy wondered why she shared this information with total strangers. For some reason it seemed important to redeem herself, to appear mature and responsible.

"You're leaving home so young . . . to go so far away? Oh, dear, your poor mother. "

Katy heard the conductor call her train. With a rush of relief, she jumped to her feet.

Why had I babbled on so, like a common peasant girl?

"Thank you, again," she said. "I'll be fine, now."

She then hurried toward the exit to the train platform.

The two women followed and boarded the same car; they sat across the aisle from Katy. The whine of the wheels gave Katy an excuse to close her eyes and pretend to sleep.

At the next stop, Frau Renner laid a hand on her shoulder.

"Still feeling poorly, my dear? You're quite pale. Can we get you something? Some water perhaps? A headache remedy?"

"No, thank you. I'll be fine."

Katy gathered her things and stood to follow them down the aisle. Bright sunshine flooded the platform and Frau Renner raised a parasol to shield her mother. The women lingered near Katy as she waited to board the next train.

"What a tedious ordeal," Frau Renner sighed. "Are you going all the way to Wiesbaden tonight, Miss Thannen?"

"I'm stopping in Frankfurt."

She hoped the brevity of her reply had stemmed the flow of conversation. Frau Renner seemed to not notice.

"That's wise. We're spending the night here in Nuremberg, thank heavens. Mother never complains."

She rubbed her mother's arm.

"Why should I?" Frau Freurstein asked. "You're always so good to me, dear."

Frau Renner continued, "Tomorrow we plan to visit a museum and perhaps one of the beautiful cathedrals as well."

"You're Catholic?" Katy asked.

"No, Lutheran, but the Renaissance sculptures and wood carvings in the old cathedrals are truly exceptional."

Katy had never met any Lutherans. Almost everyone in Austria was Catholic. She never gave another faith more than a passing thought.

The train whistle blew and Frau Renner put her hand on Katy's shoulder.

"I pray God will grant you a safe journey, my dear, one you'll continue in good health."

Katy remembered her manners, then said, "Thank you for your concern, but I'm sure I'll be fine. I hope you also have a pleasant holiday."

The women started to leave, but then the older woman stopped and turned back.

"Forgive me, my dear," she said, her voice hurried, but urgent. "I don't mean to meddle, but it's a privilege of age perhaps. Don't act in haste. Consider going back home. At certain times a young girl needs her mother, even when she fears reproof."

Katy stared at the old woman. How could she know anything about Katy's argument with her mother? She tipped her chin up and made her tone stiff.

"I can take care of myself."

The old woman sighed, leaned more heavily on her cane, and then said, "Then, let me pass on some small advice in your mother's place. Sometimes it relieves morning sickness to eat a cracker or an apple before you get out of bed in the morning."

Katy jerked back and stammered, "But I'm not . . . You misunderstand . . . It's only—"

"You needn't explain, dear. It's not my place to judge. Just remember God is our Mighty Fortress. He promised never to leave nor forsake those who trust Him. Whatever you decide, hold tight to your faith. God will never fail you."

What's she babbling about?

Katy hurried to board the train and pull down the shade on the window so she would not chance seeing the women again.

By the time the train arrived in Frankfurt, Katy felt physically and emotionally exhausted. The oil lamps had been lit and the sooty smoke gave her a headache.

As she left the train, she asked the porter for directions to the hotel Alex had listed in his instructions. The porter directed her to where taxis waited, but she had difficulty making her way across the platform because of all the activity.

She had never seen such a hubbub—something about a train wreck, she overheard a man say. Men shouted orders as others hurried by with stretchers and loaded injured passengers into horse-drawn ambulances.

With a shudder she hurried off to find a driver to take her to the hotel. After a trying day, she wanted to be spared the details.

CHAPTER 8

At the border into Germany, Alex changed trains to ride in a fourth class carriage. The stark interior had bench seats around the sides. He did not complain when he found all the seats were taken even though it forced him to stand and clutch one of the brass poles for balance.

As long as Katy enjoyed comfortable accommodations, nothing else mattered. The cheaper fare saved money for a better cabin on the ocean crossing.

The route through the Bavarian Alps traversed some of the most beautiful countryside in Europe, but Alex saw little more than the ground rush by. The side-to-side sway and frequent jolts over the uneven rails and ill-adjusted points made balance a delicate matter. Alex braced his feet; he planted them wide apart.

The train made few stops; therefore, it proceeded in good time. Alex relaxed; confident of his arrival in Wiesbaden in plenty of time to meet Katy at the boat dock. He planned to arrive early with a bouquet of daisies in hand and choose the most picturesque spot to meet her. Every detail must be just as he envisioned it.

He studied the faces silhouetted against the gray walls of the rail car and wondered idly who the people might be and where they were going. The passengers talked little among themselves, perhaps wearied by the noise or lost in their thoughts. Alex aligned his body to the rhythmic sway and allowed his thoughts to wander.

He pictured Katy aboard a comfortable coach, rapturous with each scenic view. He wanted to encourage her to describe the trip and seize the opportunity to gaze upon her face which he recalled in detail. Alex lost himself in longing.

The hours slipped by. Although Alex was cramped and weary, he had no sense of impending disaster, nor could have prepared himself if he had known.

When the engine plowed into the dense underbrush, cars jumped the tracks in rapid succession. Brief, but violent, the crash shattered more than the windows. It demolished the fragile order within the cars and replaced it with immense confusion.

Flailing bodies assailed Alex from all directions and rising dust choked him as he struggled to extricate himself. As he pushed with his hands to raise his torso from the floor, he felt a weight shift sideways and fall off his back.

When he turned his head, he stared into the sightless eyes of a young girl, her head pierced by a shard of glass. Horrified, he felt warmth spread across the back of his neck and reached up—he withdrew a red hand covered with blood.

The car had come to rest against the slope of a hill. As he stood, Alex had to scramble to regain his balance.

"Help me, please help me!"

A woman in the aisle clutched her thigh. Alex saw her ankle caught under a bench, her leg twisted in a grotesque position. He freed her ankle, but the woman screamed in pain.

"Lay still, fraulein. I'm afraid your leg might be broken."

He removed his suit coat and spread it over her.

"Help will be here soon."

Alex hoped he sounded more confident than he felt.

People pushed toward the exit at the rear of the car. Thankful he had only minor complaints Alex offered aid and reassurance wherever possible and ignored the pounding headache at the base of his skull. If help arrived soon, he had a chance to board another train and still reach Wiesbaden in plenty of time.

As the thought came to him, a white-coated figure appeared at the edge of the upturned rear door.

"I'm a doctor," the man announced. "If your injuries aren't serious, please get out so we can attend to those needing help."

Alex went weak with relief and made his way out by hanging onto bolted benches. He accepted a helping hand at the threshold.

His rescuer asked, "Are you injured?"

"No, thank God. I'm fine."

Alex jumped to the ground, and then collapsed, unconscious.

CHAPTER 9

Katy had slept a deep sleep and awoke refreshed. Her stomach felt a bit queasy again, but she managed to drink some tea and eat a croissant in the hotel dining room before boarding the train for the last few kilometers to Wiesbaden. The Frankfort train depot displayed business as usual; the frenzy of the previous afternoon had gone away.

Wiesbaden bordered the Rhine at the base of wooded hills. It reminded her of Bregenz, and she felt a stab of longing before she reminded herself about meeting Alex to start a new, exciting life. The thought of his hard, lean body made her throat contract and her ears throb.

She asked for directions to the boat dock and paid a driver to load her luggage and take her there. The first sight of the double-decked steamer took away her breath. Black and white smoke stacks—lettered with the words: NETHERLANDS STEAM SHIP CO.—belched smoke into the clear morning sky, and colored flags flew gaily from the masts. The flow of the river made the ship rock in a gentle rhythm, as if beckoning her.

It was just like Alex to surprise her, to steal up from behind and grasp her elbow or kiss her neck. Perhaps, he would bring her a bouquet of wildflowers. He remembered little things like that. She set her suitcases down, turned in circles, and searched for him in every direction.

Passengers crossed the walkway to board the ship. As the sun rose higher in the sky, ticket-taking grew brisk.

A man removed his coat and revealed striped suspenders which matched his bow tie. A lady in a soft print dress with a ruffled skirt opened her parasol. Young children chased each other about the promenade until called by their parents to board.

Everyone was with someone. Katy felt conspicuous and out-of-place. *What's keeping Alex?*

The thought he might not be there had never occurred to her. He should be the one relieved to find her, not the other way around. *What should I do?*

Her palms began to perspire. She swiped first one, and then the other on her skirt. *Maybe I should buy my ticket and wait on deck. Proper young women don't take pleasure trips alone.*

She felt as if everyone stared at her.

The ticket agent asked, "Traveling alone, fraulein?"

He motioned to a porter to take her bags.

"I'm meeting someone on board."

She fought to keep her tone casual, matter-of-fact. *How can Alex do this to me?*

The porter stowed her luggage. She dug in her purse and paid him a sum that seemed plenty to her, but which he frowned upon. She found a place at the rail which viewed the length of the promenade, and she fought to control her panic.

Had Herr Meisen discovered the plan and prevented Alex from leaving? Surely, he would've found a way to let me know.

The boat hands prepared to lift the anchor. *Should I get off? Take a train back to Bregenz?*

She could not do that. The imagined shame was too great. She felt faint and clutched the rail for balance.

The stately steamer began a slow slide away from the pier. This was her last chance. If she did not get off, it would be too late.

Frantic, she tried to pull her thoughts together. In desperation, a solution came to mind. She would continue on to Rotterdam. *Why not? If Alex still doesn't show, I'll purchase a train ticket to Innsbruck or Salzburg and find work.*

After all, that had been her first plan before this grand scheme Alex had set before her. So, she turned from the rail, chin high. If Alex Meisen had truly abandoned her, she did not need him—she had looks and money.

"I can make it on my own," she resolved.

She stayed to herself and found a bench on deck apart from

other passengers. Deep inside a strange inner trembling had taken hold of her. It required her full concentration to keep it hidden.

The panorama of changing scenery enchanted her. The boat passed under handsome stone bridges and others of ornately-carved wood. Vineyards mounted steep hills, trellis by trellis, and fierce-looking castles topped the rugged crags.

• • •

Father Kaspar watched the pretty young woman's pinched face for some time before he approached her. He had encountered many desperate souls in his time.

Every year he took his vacation in Wiesbaden to visit his sister and relax at the famous baths. It served as a time of renewal and reflection. Perhaps, it explained his heightened awareness of this young woman—her rigid posture and controlled countenance.

Without fanfare, Father Kaspar seated himself on the bench beside her. Katy looked up, her eyes widened to see the white collar of a priest.

"Forgive me, my child. I didn't mean to startle you."

He leaned back to stretch out his legs and cross them at the ankles.

"I'm Father Kaspar. Just wanted a place to sit and admire the view. Do you mind?"

"No, of course not, Father. I'm Katy Thannen."

She offered her hand.

"Pleased to meet you," he said as he shook it.

They sat in silence. Katy studied him from the corners of her eyes. His thatch of white hair ruffled in the breeze. Tanned and weathered, he had the complexion of someone who spent much of his time outdoors. Except for his attire, he could have been a field laborer of some sort, his hands calloused and rough.

"I never tire of watching the water," the priest mused aloud. "Sailing is my passion, you see. I've discovered water isn't just water, as most people think of it. Water possesses many moods and takes on a variety of characteristics."

"I'm from Bregenz, on the Bodensee. The lake has many sailboats."

"Ah, the Bodensee, I know it—such a vast lake. Rather like the Galilee, as I remember: placid one day, violent the next. If you remember, the disciples feared that lake. They woke Jesus to save them from its storm. I'm from Holland myself. In winter, I sail the canals; and in summer, the Zuider Zee."

"The Zuider Zee?"

"Yes, a large inlet from the North Sea: the source of water for our canals. Unless there's a storm out at sea, the canal waters are calm and peaceful. We use them to irrigate our crops. But the sea can also be an angry enemy—breaking through the dikes, flooding the land, threatening the lives of animals, even people. Much like life itself, I think."

Katy furrowed her brow and admitted, "I don't understand."

Father Kaspar pointed upstream and asked, "Do you see that massive cliff coming up on the left? Legend has it the sound of the wind circling the rock is the singing of Lorelei, a nymph who lures boats and fishermen to come closer so they'll shipwreck on her rock as they try to reach her."

Katy craned for a better view as the boat slid nearer the stony crag.

Father Kaspar continued, "Life is like that, I think. It deceives us with its plentiful provision, its peaceful appearance. Then, an unexpected storm comes along or something lures us into making a wrong decision. We're tempted to turn in the wrong direction and risk shipwreck."

Katy shifted on her seat, but kept her eyes on the river. The rock passed without incident.

"You make sin sound inevitable. I didn't know priests believed in fate."

Father Kaspar turned to look straight into her troubled eyes, and then said, "Not fate, my child, but the predictability of man's nature without God."

Katy's mouth pinched and she turned away.

"Forgive me," he hurried on. "I meant no offense. I'm a priest, but I'm also a man. It was my shipwreck to which I referred."

"You did something bad?" Katy blurted, suddenly curious. "But you're a priest!"

Father Kaspar's throaty laugh proved infectious. Katy smiled in spite of herself.

"Also a man," he reminded her. "Yes, I did something quite bad, in fact. I drifted away from my childhood faith . . . allowed myself to be lured into wild living. I became an angry person, lost all self-control, and beat a man so badly I went to prison for a time."

A frown creased his forehead, and then disappeared.

"It was only as I came back to the Roman Catholic Church and received God's forgiveness when I found peace and direction for my life. It granted me the desire to serve Him the rest of my life. I'm German, but a kind archbishop sent me to Holland, where no one knew me, and I'm well content in my adopted country of windmills and wooden shoes."

Katy felt deflated somehow. She longed for the sense of peace Father Kaspar described, but she was not about to become a nun to find it. Still, this man knew what it was like to be in a bad predicament. Perhaps, he was able to understand the uproar raging inside her.

She found herself telling him about Alex, and the plans gone awry. She omitted any mention of their afternoon in the forest glen. After all, the bench was not a confessional, and Father Kaspar was not her priest. Besides, he might judge her sin as even worse than his. The nuns always lectured long and hard about immoral behavior.

Katy told him about her dreams for the future and her mother's lack of understanding. As Father Kaspar listened, she painted a glowing picture of Alex, their plans for marriage, and his love for her.

"If he's not in Rotterdam, I'll have to decide between sailing to America alone or going elsewhere to find a job to support myself."

"Why not go home? I realize it wouldn't be easy, but I'm sure your parents would be relieved to welcome you back."

"Oh no, I can't. My mother might forgive me, but she'd do everything to keep me there, and I won't settle for that."

Father Kaspar sighed, "America is a long ways away. You might never return, might never see your homeland or your parents again."

"I know."

Katy struggled to keep the quaver from her voice.

"Still, it could be exciting—a new beginning."

"But a frightening thing to do alone."

Katy began to regret confiding in him after all. He voiced everything she had been trying not to think about. She jutted her chin upward.

"I could do it," she told him.

Father Kaspar chuckled.

"I'm sure you could, but there are rules, you know. So many people want to go to America these days, for a wide variety of reasons: land, jobs . . . A clean slate. Yet, not everyone gets into the country when the boat docks. Each person is questioned: Is he in good health? Does he have money, or a place to stay until he finds a job? How will he make a living? Even in the Land of Opportunity they don't want immigrants who might become an added burden."

Katy had not known of these requirements. She fought to conceal her dismay.

Father Kaspar changed the subject. Soon, the steward announced lunch.

"May I accompany you to the dining room?" Father Kaspar asked.

"No, thank you. The motion of the boat has made my stomach queasy."

"You'll feel better if you eat. It's been a long time since breakfast and I'm starved."

• • •

The meal was served in grand style, as one might expect dining in a luxury hotel. Katy picked at her food; nonetheless, grateful to be in the good priest's company.

As he accompanied her back on deck, Father Kaspar remarked, "The current of the river will be nothing compared with the ocean tides. If you have a weak stomach, it'll be difficult."

"Oh, I'm better now," she assured him. "It's the upset of not meeting Alex, I expect. Once I find out what's happened to him, my nerves will settle. I'm sure of it, although it's kind of you to be concerned."

At the fork of the river that branched off to Amsterdam, Father Kaspar collected his things for transfer to a different vessel. Then, he took a small notebook and a pen from his pocket, opened the notebook, and scribbled something in it.

When the time came for him to depart, Father Kaspar took Katy's hand, turned her palm upward, and pressed a folded paper down upon it.

"Don't lose this. If you decide to make the ocean crossing alone, which I pray for your sake you won't, this is a note I've penned to a good woman in New York City, a former parishioner who runs a boarding house there. She'll give you a place to stay and help you find work."

Katy flung her arms around his neck and cried, "Oh, thank you, Father. You've been so very kind."

"It's our Father in heaven who's kind, Katy. Remember your prayers."

"Of course, Father. I will."

He stood at the rail of the other ship and waved until the triangle of land between the forks in the river grew too far across.

"Dear God," he prayed aloud. "Please go with Katy Thannen. Guard and keep her safe wherever her path leads. Let not stubborn pride stand in her way, but bring others to help her recognize the height and breadth of Your great love."

CHAPTER 10

As the steamer approached the landing, the scene overwhelmed Katy. Her mind rushed to find a known comparison, but found none for the maze of canals and drawbridges converging upon the wide channel leading into the North Sea. According to the captain, each year five thousand sea-going vessels entered and left the port.

Multitudes bustled about the docks. Tall ship masts loomed ahead and the tall buildings of the city poked into the sky behind them. All sights and sounds of nature stilled, replaced by resounding ship horns and the ringing of bicycle bells.

Amazement came over Katy. For the moments it took the ship to dock, she forgot it was the face of Alex she sought in the milling crowd.

The steamer captain raised his bullhorn again.

"Ladies and gentlemen, we're about to dock at Rotterdam! If you're booking passage to America, you'll find steam line representatives waiting to accommodate you. Look for a sign printed with the language you speak and the destination you're seeking."

Katy searched among the many faces which lined the pier below her, careful not to miss a single one. Somehow she already knew Alex would not be there. Nor did anyone inquire of her with a message.

She had to face facts, she had no choice. She was going to sail for America. Besides the nausea, she had missed her second monthly. Without a doubt she was as it had been said of Mary "with child." *How dare Alex leave me in this predicament?*

As the captain had announced, men brandishing signs attached to long poles walked the pier. One sign read: DEUTSCHE SPRECKEN. NEW YORK. It was the only city she knew in the New World.

She joined the large group which gathered in front of the man and listened as he explained the different fares, their equivalents in schillings, and where to go to change money into American currency. He announced when the ship departed, and told them where to find accommodations for the night. Then, he began to take reservations.

Katy mulled over which ticket to purchase. The man called it "third class," but she knew it meant steerage—a word with dreaded meaning throughout Europe. A Thannen cousin wrote home of its horrors. The relatives discussed them in detail with much clucking of their tongues.

Already, Katy associated steerage class with the smells pressing in on her: perspiring bodies in front of and behind her, and dead fish bumping against the posts of the pier. She looked westward toward the open sea as a violent shiver passed through her body.

She had money to pay for better quarters, but the cost required almost all she had left. Bitterness enveloped her as she stepped up next in line. Her lip curled with contempt.

"Put me down with the other livestock," she spat.

The ship representative did not look up nor change expression.

"If you mean third class, ma'am, the fare will be twelve American dollars, to include a passport. Bring your luggage to Dock 12 at nine o'clock tomorrow morning . . . and be prompt. The ship sails on time."

He took down her name, collected her money, and turned to the next person in line.

Having spent her rage, Katy felt empty of all feeling. She followed others to a cart provided by the steamship line where the driver loaded suitcases on the back, and let passengers climb into the cart unassisted.

They bounced over rough cobblestones to the long dormitory building a few blocks away. Once inside, men were directed to the left, women to the right.

"Just five more schillings for a blanket," the desk clerk told her. "You can take it with you on the boat."

Katy tilted her chin to show she knew a thing or two.

"Isn't bedding provided?"

The clerk laughed and said, "Never enough, ma'am. Never enough."

Although he probably tried to cheat her, the blanket seemed a prudent purchase. She tucked it under her arm, entered the dormitory where she pushed her belongings beneath her assigned bunk, and fell onto the thin mattress.

A supper of soup and bread was announced, but Katy was not interested. She slept little and made her way back to the dock in plenty of time to exchange her money for American dollars and receive directions to the ship.

As she neared the pier, she searched for Alex one last time.

"No more," she scolded herself.

Katy pushed the hurt and rejection she felt deep inside.

• • •

The Holland America steamship loomed huge and sinister above water lapping against its hull. It reminded Katy of a gigantic black-tarred watering trough, like those from which cattle drank in her beloved Alps. She felt like Jonah, about to be swallowed.

"Thousands have done this before you," she lectured herself.

If only she was not so alone.

A ship's officer stood at the top of the gangplank to divide the long line of steerage passengers down steps which led to the lower deck—women to the left, men to the right. In the square windowless cabin for women, tiers of narrow wood bunks lined the walls. At the far end an open door revealed a latrine with a wash basin and toilet.

Katy claimed a lower bunk near the outside door. She tucked her extra blanket out of sight beneath the straw mattress and placed her satchel beside the tin cup, soup plate, and metal utensils nestled in the center of her berth. Each bunk held similar provisions.

Having expected the worst from the cousin's reports of overflowing chamber pots and intolerable filth, Katy felt somewhat encouraged. The cabin was plain, but clean. She left it and went back on deck.

Uniformed sailors barked out a stream of instructions. They addressed passengers directed to the upper decks as ma'am and sir. A man wearing a bowler hat carried a fancy cane and accompanied a woman dressed in silk. They stared at her over the railing. Katy gave them a haughty look and a toss of her head in return.

A young couple came down the stairs and embraced before parting toward their separate quarters. The woman held an embroidered shawl about her thin shoulders. It failed to conceal the huge mound beneath her muslin skirt. The slight, wiry young man watched until she turned and waved before disappearing inside the women's quarters.

He noticed Katy and greeted her with a friendly smile.

"Guten morgen, fraulein."

"Morgen."

Katy detected an unfamiliar dialect.

Probably from one of the eastern regions, she thought as she eyed the hand-sewn shirt, pants, and white skull cap which rested atop his dark, curly hair.

Amidst a last minute frenzy of activity, the announced departure time approached. Deck hands lowered the last boxes of provisions into the hold and untied the ropes from the pier.

The steerage quarters simmered with anxious confusion as mothers snapped at their children, argued over remaining bunks, and complained about the shrinking space. Katy experienced a sudden wave of claustrophobia. Her forehead beaded with sweat and she swallowed down another wave of nausea.

The young pregnant woman had taken a lower bunk at the opposite end of the cabin.

Good, Katy thought. *At least I'll be spared any intimate disclosures of approaching motherhood.*

An old woman with a black shawl and lace cap planted herself solidly in front of Katy. She pointed back and forth between Katy and the bunk above. Katy knew what she wanted. She supposed she should be respectful and give up her berth. *Is it my fault the old woman had arrived so late?*

Katy pretended not to understand and busied herself with her things. The old woman muttered and hoisted herself into the upper bunk.

Quite nimbly, Katy decided.

Just then, the floor jolted and the cabin grew quiet as the passengers' attention riveted on the surging throb of the steam engines. The noise seemed unbearable.

Will I ever adapt to it? Katy wondered.

She squeezed among her fellow female passengers to reach the ship's deck as it slid from the pier. With a determined pace, the ship plowed between fingers of land toward the open and empty sea to leave behind civilization as she had known it.

• • •

Twice daily, the galley crew carried in iron pots of soup laced with chunks of meat, potatoes, and some thick bread. Pudding appeared on Sundays, and the occasional jam provided mothers with a bribe for good behavior.

Still, portions went uneaten as increasingly more passengers became seasick. Katy was among them. White-capped waves started out two to three feet in height and swelled to well over twenty feet as the autumn sea angered.

After a few days, Katy's stomach stabilized to the point she was able to eat and move around. However, many passengers remained wretched as conditions in the cabin deteriorated.

Footing became dangerous, not only from the pitch of the ship, but because slippery pools of vomit eddied in one direction, and then the other. The accumulating vomit mixed with spilled food, and even urine, as children were not able to wait any longer to use the one latrine.

Crew members swabbed the floor each morning, but it was a futile effort. At last, a bucket was left in the cabin and several times each day, passengers scooped up sea water that washed over the deck and sloshed it across the cabin floor. Passengers with belongings stored underneath bunks complained, of course, but necessity won out.

Each day brought a series of hostile encounters. Vicious arguments commenced over most anything—for example, whether or not to open or shut the deck door. *Which is worse—the foul-smelling air or the chill of the sea?*

As much as possible, Katy wrapped her blanket over her cloak and left the cabin. She preferred the leaden sky and curses of deckhands to the stench and rancor inside.

She often noticed the young couple doing the same—the pregnant wife clutched her husband's arm. Their faces were animated in private conversation.

Katy knew the young woman was often nauseous, as was she. Like her, the woman summoned the strength to leave her bunk. Her husband steadied her as they circled the deck. On several occasions Katy saw them pause and bow their heads, as if in prayer, before they kissed and parted once again.

At night, Katy remembered her promise to Father Kaspar and mumbled the rosary, but the petitions seemed empty and meaningless. She felt embarrassed for the young couple, so public in their private prayer, yet she envied their obvious calm and the warm affection they displayed.

• • •

A week passed, and then the rain came. In a strange paradox, the downpour flattened the waves and the gas lanterns slackened their wild swing to a steady sway. Then, one morning a hazy sun poked through the clouds. Cheers erupted among those strong enough to venture onto deck. That night an almost grim merriment broke out as a group of Hungarians played fiddles and concertinas, and some brave couples ventured to dance on the rolling deck. Others tapped their feet and clapped to the music.

Katy's thoughts went back to the Bregenz festival when she had twisted her ankle and first kissed Alex. It seemed years ago instead of months. If she had not been so bold that night, she probably would not be in her predicament. For several minutes, she lost herself in longing the traditions never to know again.

At last, she became aware of passengers who watched the lower deck from the balcony above. They pointed and laughed as they stood in their expensive clothes unsullied. Katy stepped back underneath the balcony, conscious of her stringy hair and unwashed garments.

When the fiddles stopped, she heard the faint strains of orchestra music.

Underneath her breath she said, "So, the rich had their diversions."

Katy hated them and at the same time wished she were one of them. Most of all, she abhorred the complete lack of privacy.

Since the flimsy lock had broken, she had to brace her foot against the door of the latrine to use the toilet. Every morning she bathed to the best of her ability in the small basin.

She brushed her teeth and combed her hair while others pounded on the door and yelled at her to hurry. She also washed her dishes and utensils, and used the bar of soap to suds up lather.

A few of the women tried to initiate conversation with her, but they gave up and whispered behind their hands as they glanced in her direction. She knew they wanted to hear her story, the way they told theirs, but she stayed aloof and gave them nothing to gossip about.

The children proved the most resilient. Katy watched a fair-haired child weave a string puzzle together, and then unravel and weave it again. The small girl smiled and held the puzzle up for Katy to see, but her mother jerked her back.

"I've told you not to cozy up to strangers," she scolded.

Katy experienced a deep sadness as she thought about Sofie. She could always depend on her friend to listen and sympathize. Now, she had no one.

As the days passed, even a sea gull became a welcome diversion. Katy tried to think, to formulate a plan, but the future remained as obscured as the endless horizon. *Where will I go? What will I do?*

• • •

She awakened from a deep sleep one night to the sounds of a woman in labor. Sweat broke out on Katy's forehead as the sounds transported her back to childhood.

Her mother was summoned to the bedside of a neighbor and took Katy with her. One look at the woman as she thrashed in the bedclothes, and Helga ordered Katy to remain there while she hurried to fetch the midwife. Katy relived the terror of the woman's shrieks. She feared the young Jewish might die any minute.

Other women left their bunks to see what was happening and were eager to offer advice. As lanterns flickered and tossed their shadows against the wall, Katy pulled her blankets over her head. She held rigid every fiber of her body to keep from crying out.

"Please someone," the young woman begged, "my husband!"

"Hush now," a voice rebuked. "You know men aren't allowed in this cabin."

"But I need him. The baby's too soon."

"Babes come when they come. You'll manage. Be a good girl now and pull hard on this here towel I've tied to your bunk . . . This one the first?"

"Yes."

Between sobs she thrust out the words, "I wanted it born free . . . Under God . . . In the new land."

"From the bunk above Katy, the old woman croaked, "Well, dearie, this here ocean's about as wild and free as you can get. If God's not here, we're all goners, anyway."

The cabin silenced as rooms do when people hear truth. The young woman answered, her voice was weak, yet steady, "Yes, oh yes, it's true. Of course, God is present. Thank you, dear lady."

"Push now, push!" the first voice ordered. "I can see the wee head bald as a bowl."

The anguished struggle continued, forever it seemed. Katy clutched the blanket and was desperate to shut out the sounds, yet she strained to hear. Children cried and were shushed. Women wrangled over what to do next.

One woman announced her intention to alert the young husband. Katy recognized the enjoyment some found to bear bad news, borne out when the woman returned to report the young man paced the cold deck. She told them he was sick with worry.

The waiting became almost unbearable. *When will it be over? In spite of anything these silly women do, the young woman will surely die. Had our neighbor woman died?*

Katy could not remember. When Helga arrived with the midwife, she sent Katy home. Soon after, her family moved to a different neighborhood and Helga never told her what had happened.

A brisk rap at the door brought Katy's head from underneath her blanket. She expected the young husband. Instead a woman stood in the doorway. She wore a gray flannel bathrobe underneath a navy cape as she carried a stack of linens in her arms, a doctor's bag balanced on top.

She stood for a brief moment as if adjusting her eyes to the dim light.

"I'm a nurse," she announced. "Word passed someone here needs assistance."

A respectful silence fell over the cabin. Katy felt the same relief she felt when the midwife had arrived all those years ago. The nurse made her way across the cabin and voiced her disgust over its deplorable condition.

When she reached the exhausted young woman, she went right to work. She flung off her cape and scrubbed her hands hard in the wash basin. After the nurse ordered someone to spread clean sheets underneath the woman, she opened the bag and thrust a bottle of rubbing alcohol to another.

"Use it to scrub the bed frame," she commanded.

The strong smell permeated the cabin. Katy sat up to get a better look, and then shrank back from the looming shadows which surrounded the young woman on the bunk.

"There, there," the nurse's voice soothed almost as a lullaby.

She again reached into the bag and removed a different bottle and tipped it to the young woman's lips which bled from being bitten. The woman drank, choked, and pushed the bottle away.

"More," the nurse urged. "You'll need it."

"But it's all, but over," an onlooker insisted. "I seen the head comin' 'fore you got here."

"It's not the head."

The nurse pushed up her sleeves and poured alcohol over her hands.

"What you saw was the babe's bottom. I need to turn it and there's not much time. She's weak as it is, and she's going to tear. So, she'll need all of this she can get down."

The other women moaned and clucked their tongues. Katy started to shiver. *Will it ever end? If You're up there, God, what are You doing? What good are You if You stay away when someone's in such desperate need?*

The cabin was a dank cellar, not an antiseptic hospital with a crucifix above each bed and nuns who knelt to pray by the bedside.

Where will I be in a few months' time when my baby is born? Who will be there to help me?

The nurse barked a stream of orders. All other noise ceased, except for the whimpering sounds coming from the bed. Then, a thin wail broke into Katy's swirling thoughts. She braced herself and believed it to be the woman's dying gasp.

"It's a boy."

The nurse's announcement was met with excited babble. Then, the door flew open and the young husband burst through it.

Others stood back as he made his way to his wife's bunk. He knelt beside it as the nurse used deft hands to cut the cord and place the squalling infant in the crook of its mother's arm. The new father reached to kiss his wife's closed eyelids.

He was seemingly oblivious to the almost reverent hush surrounding the poignant scene. He caressed her wet strands of hair as if they spread across the plumped pillow of a Renoir painting. Sobs shook his body.

"There, there," the nurse patted his shoulder. "She's going to be fine, and so is the babe. You must leave now so I can finish my work and your wife can sleep. Come back in the morning and she'll be awake to help you choose a name."

The young man struggled to his feet and twisted his woolen cap in both hands.

"Bless you, ma'am. Oh, God bless you. We already have a name: Moses. It means: drawn out."

Katy, angry at the tears which coursed down her cheeks, swiped them away with her hands. Moses was a Jewish name.

Appropriate, she supposed as she recalled Pharaoh's daughter had drawn Moses out of the water. *Are these ignorant people too naive to grasp the irony?*

The nurse finished what needed to be done. Then, she turned to the silent group which surrounded her.

"I'll be back in the morning to check on her. Have the steward call me if she needs me sooner. I'm Nurse Pritchard."

She paused, as if reluctant to leave.

"Thank you, each one. Some of you helped and I'm sure others prayed for this brave new mother. Upstairs they told me to not to come down here . . . I'd be in danger of disease."

She busied herself fastening the cape.

"But helping those in need is my calling. I had to come and I'm glad I did. May God be with each of you."

Katy recalled the words of Frau Freurstein: "God promises never to leave nor forsake those who trust in Him."

CHAPTER 11

Alex checked himself out of the hospital on the same day he regained consciousness.

"I'm perfectly all right," he insisted and buttoned his shirt. "I must leave now. My fiancée was to meet me in Wiesbaden. She must be frantic."

The doctor flipped the pages of Alex's chart.

"Can't you send her a message? I'm absolutely opposed to your leaving this soon. You suffered a bad concussion."

"How long have I been here?"

"Three days."

"Three days? That's not possible."

Alex stuffed his watch and other personal items inside his pockets. Then, he turned to the nurse.

He asked, "Where are the rest of my things?"

"Downstairs, where you pay your bill."

"Of course, my bill."

• • •

How ironic it was he had to pay for three days he did not even remember—days which were supposed to be the most important days of his life. He drummed his fingers on the counter as he waited for the clerk to finish her filing. Every moment might be crucial. At last, she turned to him.

"Yes?"

"Name's Alex Meisen. I'm checking out and I need to collect two suitcases brought in with me. They have my name on them."

"Suitcases?"

"Yes, I was in the train wreck—"

"Oh, you're one of the accident patients."

She placed her elbow on the counter and cupped her chin in her hand.

"It's been in all the papers, you know. Reporters are all over the place."

Through thick lenses, her round eyes grew even rounder.

"They still haven't determined what happened."

"Please, fraulein."

The pendulum on the big wall clock seemed to mock the passing minutes.

"I'm in a terrible hurry."

"Well, pardon me!"

She adjusted her spectacles and thumbed through a card file.

"Belongings that come in with patients are kept in the storage room. You can identify yours while I prepare your bill."

She slapped the desk bell twice and a boy ran from the next room.

"Mr. Meisen is in a terrible hurry," she mimicked in a high voice. "Take him to the storage room for his luggage."

Alex found his bags and gave the boy a coin. Everything he had planned so carefully had gone terribly wrong. His mind raced. *Did Katy hear about the accident? Where is she?*

The clerk finished tabulating the bill and swiveled the paper for Alex to see the amount. She smiled with exaggerated sweetness.

"Our best wishes for your complete recovery," she told him.

Alex counted out money he could not afford to spend. Then, he snatched up his suitcases and ran through the hospital lobby and out the front door. For a moment, he was disoriented. When an empty carriage pulled up in front, he ran down the steps and motioned to the driver.

"The train station, please hurry!"

He asked the driver to wait with his suitcases while he bought his ticket, but the train had already left. There was not another train scheduled until the next day. Alex ran back to the carriage.

He asked the driver, "Can you take me to Wiesbaden?"

"If you have the fare."

Alex did not have a choice. He had lost too much time already. He climbed up beside the driver and urged him to get there as fast as possible.

• • •

Alex inquired at the Wiesbaden hotels and searched along the dock for any sign of Katy.

The steamer agent asked, "Name again?"

"Katharina Thannen. She would have purchased a ticket to Rotterdam."

"Ah, here it is. Thannen, November 10."

Alex went weak with relief to learn she had gone on ahead to Rotterdam instead of returning to Bregenz as he had feared she might. Still, disappointment washed over him because she had not waited for him in Wiesbaden.

No, it isn't her fault. She must've been frantic. She can't be blamed for any decision she was forced to make. Had she simply thought me a fool, incompetent to carry out my part of the plan?

He must hasten on to Rotterdam, find her, and explain. He walked to the train station and bought a ticket. The train departed in two hours. He was still scheduled to be at the port city by nightfall.

Choosing a seat at the back of the car, he avoided speaking to any of the other passengers. Thoughts of Katy and her welfare filled his mind.

She was capable of taking care of herself, yet should not have been placed in that position. She had trusted him by coming and he had let her down. He dozed briefly which eased the ache in his head a bit. As the train approached Rotterdam, he stared out the window. *What now?*

The clerk at the shipping office peered at him from beneath a green eyeshade.

"May I help you, sir?"

"Meisen. Alex Meisen. I'm trying to locate a young lady who may have already booked our passage to America. Her name is

Katharina Thannen. Perhaps, you could check your records?"

The passenger agent frowned.

"It's against company policy to give out passenger names. Is she a relative?"

"My fiancée. I was unavoidably detained and we were separated. She must be waiting at a nearby hotel, probably frantic with worry."

Alex pulled some schillings from his pocket and laid them on the counter.

"Well, I don't see the harm."

The man opened a large ledger, its pages covering the coins.

"The Holland-America Line has vessels departing for America."

He pointed to a bench.

"If you care to wait, I'll scan the passenger lists as I'm able."

"Most obliged."

Alex perched on the edge of the splintery bench. With growing impatience, he watched as people straggled up to the window and occupied the agent's attention. Fifteen minutes elapsed before the agent summoned him back.

"I believe I've found what you were looking for. Her ship sailed November 11. Here it is."

He traced the line with his finger.

"Katharina Thannen. Third class passage on the Maarsdam."

"Impossible."

Alex reached across the desk and grabbed the man by the front of his shirt.

"You've made a mistake."

People turned to stare.

"Please, you'll get me in trouble," the man begged.

He turned the book for Alex to look.

"Here, see for yourself."

"I'm sorry," Alex murmured as he released the man's shirt and backed away, truly ashamed.

He looked where the man pointed. Katy's signature accompanied the entry. She had gone on without him. *Why?*

His head began to pound again.

Almost in a whisper, he asked, "When does the next boat sail for America?"

The clerk consulted his lists and answered, "Next Thursday."

"Thursday? That's almost a week from now."

"Ships leave less often as it grows later in the season."

"Never mind, book me on the next one . . . Third class."

Alex placed the ticket in his wallet and wandered out the door. He did not care where he went. What he did the next six days held no importance. Only one thing mattered: Katy had sailed without him . . . in steerage. *Well, I'll do the same.*

He sat on a bench and held his face in both hands. People passed by and glanced at him, curious. An elderly couple stopped to ask if he was ill. He did not answer.

• • •

The cheap boardinghouse offered shelter and bad food. Alex ate little and slept the better part of four days. Then—his headache finally gone—he methodically repacked his suitcases and laid out his purchases. He had a pair of homespun pants, a woolen shirt, and a warm jacket. Beside them he placed heavy socks and sturdy boots.

He removed items of his college wardrobe to make room. He also considered leaving his grandfather's rifle behind, but changed his mind. It would be his job to protect Katy; he knew not what dangers they might face.

Then, he took paper and pen, and began to write:

Dear Mother,

> *I'm posting this from Rotterdam where I'm waiting for a boat to sail for America. Katy has gone ahead and I'll join her there.*

> *I know I've caused you much sorrow, but, perhaps, if anyone can understand, it's you. I must find my way, discover who I am. So far I've botched things badly, but I intend to make amends even if it takes the rest of my life.*

For one thing, I vow to repay every cent I owe Father. I know he'll find it hard to believe, but I hope you'll have faith in my word. Please forgive me, Mother, and pray for me.

Your loving son.

When at last the ship sailed, Alex welcomed the disgusting conditions as penance for having put Katy through the same experience. He only hoped the swearing and loathsome sounds of hacking, spitting, and farting with resultant discord was less common among women than men.

Driving rain and a heaving sea produced a fiendish frenzy which tossed the ship like a glass bottle. Alex endured the nausea, swallowed bile repeatedly in a stoic refusal to exhibit frailty.

He ate little and forced himself to exercise daily on the foredeck. He stayed apart from the other men and willed himself to remain active, physically and mentally.

A young man near his age occupied the lower bunk across the cabin from his. Alex regarded him with suspicion, although he did not know why.

The fellow appeared immune to seasickness. He ministered daily to those who suffered from it, and exhibited a calm cheerfulness which irritated Alex.

Sometimes he read from a small, black book. He thumbed back and forth between its pages—hardly the sign of a serious scholar.

His stomach stabled, at last, and Alex dug into his satchel for his book—one about American history. He had purchased it his last day in Rotterdam.

Unable to concentrate, Alex thumbed the pages. Then, he slammed the book shut in irritation and tossed it aside on his bunk. The young man looked up and smiled; the line of his jaw strong and firm, his dark blue eyes warm.

"Feeling better?"

Alex frowned and looked away.

"I'm fine."

"I'm Samuel Schneider. Folks call me Sam."

The young man swung his legs off the bunk and crossed the cabin to offer his hand. He was not tall, but he had an athletic build and a direct approach.

"You speak German, I see."

Alex nodded and shook his hand.

"Alex Meisen. Austrian."

"Ah, such a beautiful country. I'm Swiss, but I've spent the past four years in Heidelberg as a student at the university."

"I, too, am a university graduate. Innsbruck."

"Excellent. Your course of study?"

"History."

He could not help, but to ask, "And yours?"

"Philosophy. We could have interesting discussions."

Never one to be rude, Alex found himself being rude.

"You appear to have trouble concentrating on your book."

Sam looked perplexed. He held out the book, a finger held his place.

"You mean this?"

His expression mirrored his surprise.

"You read the Bible?"

Sam laughed.

"It's not a book to read straight through, although I have. I find it a book to study and cross-reference. Some days I need to read certain passages, but on other days I let the pages fall open."

"As a philosopher, I imagine you find its conflict with other philosophies quite unsettling."

Sam shook his head as he sat down on the edge of his bunk and replied, "Not at all. My study of other philosophers led me to delve into the Bible in the first place."

Alex could not resist the urge to ask, "How so?"

"Have you read the Gospels?"

"I'm Catholic. I don't have to read them to know their contents."

"I see. Well, I come from no religious tradition myself. My parents were agnostics, so I was raised believing the Bible to be a collection of myths and legends. I wanted to see for myself what made Christ the central figure."

Interesting, Alex thought.

The free thinkers he had known at the university rebelled against authority. Yet, he detected nothing strident in Sam's demeanor. Instead, the young man appeared friendly and sincere.

"I find some of the stories hard to believe," Alex admitted, as much to himself as to Sam. "I'm afraid I'm not particularly strong in the faith. I, however, believe in God as Creator and in His commandments as a moral guide."

"Exactly, but beyond that, does belief in Christ make a difference in life's daily living? In how we think and act? Those were the answers I sought."

Alex fingered his crusader's ring.

"I'm not sure of those answers myself, but this much I do know: I abide by the teachings of the Roman Catholic Church as far as I'm able. I may not be devout, but I believe in the equality of man and doing good to others. What more can God expect of mortal men?"

Without waiting for an answer, Alex jumped down from his bunk, and headed for the door and his daily exercise on the deck.

CHAPTER 12

The sighting of land brought most every passenger to the rail of the ship, even those who could not stand without support. While some cheered, others voiced apprehension. Like Katy, some passengers showed no outward emotion at all.

Nearby ships plowed the waters close by, their decks crowded with onlookers. As the ship pushed through the headlands of the bay where land bordered both sides of the ship, anxious eyes probed the mist. The uneven rooftops of tall buildings stenciled the skyline, hazed by morning fog.

A man shouted, "There she is!"

Some wept, some fell to their knees. Others had no knowledge of what the copper-clad statue represented. Katy knew the woman symbolized the immigrant dream, but the sight reminded her of a different statue beside an altar and a wave of homesickness swept over her.

The engines stopped. As he walked briskly down the steps to the foredeck, a ship's officer dressed in crisp whites shouted through a megaphone: "All immigrants prepare to depart ship. A ferry will come alongside to take you to the Barge Office Station for processing."

A barrage of questions bombarded him. He raised his hand to cut them off.

"One at a time," he ordered.

A woman in peasant garb asked, "Why aren't we docking at Ellis Island?"

The monstrous landmark loomed in the distance and had already caused a flurry of comment.

"My cousin docked at Ellis Island," the woman continued. "He told me all about what to expect."

"A fire destroyed several buildings two years ago and repairs aren't completed. The Barge Station is being used in the meantime. Please collect your belongings and form a line on deck."

The grumbling continued. Katy had never heard of Ellis Island, but apparently others had. They faced another unknown.

Another questioned, "Why are we stopping here at all? The fancies in first class are loading on the ferry, pretty as you please."

As Katy surveyed the crowded deck, she saw the new mother being carried from the hold. The young husband had crossed hands with another man and grasped wrists to form a chair for her. To Katy's surprise, the old woman who followed behind and cradled the newborn in her arms was none other than the old crone who occupied the bunk above hers.

The men lowered the young woman to her feet. Pale, but radiant, she thanked them and with great tenderness took the baby from the old woman's arms.

"Thank you again for your wise words when they were sorely needed."

She shifted the baby in her arms to wipe away a tear.

"I'll never forget them."

"Didn't know you'd take 'em to heart that way," the woman muttered as she blushed and ducked her head.

"Being reminded of God's presence is always a blessing."

The young woman planted a kiss on the wrinkled cheek. The bundle between them squirmed, and the two women bent their heads together over the tiny face.

Katy felt tears prick her eyelids. Loneliness swept over her and she longed to have someone at her side—Sofie, Father Kaspar, even her mother. She knew no one; had no one.

It was afternoon, and the passengers were cold and hungry. Children cried as the wind whipped around them. The ferry drew close to the pier and the captain cut its engine as it docked at Battery Park.

"Two lines please—women on the left, men on the right."

The man on the pier spoke through a bullhorn, giving directions in English, but motioning as he spoke so everyone straggled into place. In a single line, the women inched across the hard-packed earth toward the wooden doors of the Old Barge Office.

"Step up, please. Deutsche?"

Katy nodded and the man beckoned to an interpreter who asked a question in German.

"Katharina Elisabeth Thannen," Katy answered.

"Place of birth?"

"Bregenz, Austria."

"Age?"

"Nineteen," Katy lied.

The clean-shaven clerk peered over half-moon spectacles and asked, "Single?"

"Yes."

"Living arrangements?"

With shaking hands, Katy dug into her purse and produced the letter Father Kaspar had given her. She thrust it toward the man. He peered at the paper.

"See that you go there," he said sternly. "New York is no place for women alone. How do you intend to eat?"

"I'll find work."

Katy dug her fingers into her sweating palms.

"Doing what?"

Katy's mind went blank, but then she remembered the letter.

"This woman will have work for me. We have a mutual friend—a priest."

"Money?"

The interpreter translated when Katy did not answer.

"Schillings?"

Katy produced the remaining dollars she had exchanged in Rotterdam, about forty in all, and spread them out on the counter. They seemed enough because the man nodded approval. He handed her some papers and waved her on.

A woman doctor motioned for Katy to walk across the room and back, taking notes as she watched.

An interpreter asked, "Do you read and write? What is the date today?"

The second doctor, another woman, held a stethoscope to Katy's chest. Then, she moved it to her stomach. Katy flinched. *Is it possible to hear a heartbeat this early?*

Again the interpreter: "Heartburn . . . Stomach problems . . . Pregnancy?"

Katy shook her head to all the questions.

The doctor put her hands on both sides of Katy's head and tipped it forward. She separated the hair with her fingers and probed under the coiled braid. *She's looking for lice!*

Katy cringed with embarrassment.

The doctor dipped her fingers in a basin of rubbing alcohol, picked up the stethoscope, and dismissed Katy by turning to the next person in line.

The eye man was last. He rolled each eyelid inside out with an instrument like a button hook, and then dropped the instrument into a bowl of disinfectant and dipped his fingers in as well. He motioned for Katy to move on.

Katy noticed doctors made a mark with chalk on some of the women's shoulders. Not knowing what it meant, she feared it happening to her. At last, she reached the end of the line.

The young Jewish mother sat behind a wire partition, the swaddled Moses on her lap. Chalk marks striped the shoulders of her shawl and Katy felt a surge of concern as their eyes met.

"Don't worry," the young woman reassured her. "I'm marked for the hospital . . . to be checked over, just in case. We're both fine, I'm sure. See? He's perfect."

She pulled back the edge of the blanket to reveal a tiny, wizened face.

"I saw you many times on the boat, of course, but, well . . . You kept to yourself, you know. We never met. I'm Hannah Silverstein and this is Moses."

"I'm Katy Thannen."

"It's nice to meet you, Katy. If you see my husband, will you please tell him where I am, and ask him to wait by the door until they bring us out? I'm afraid he's frantic by now."

"All right."

Katy hesitated. Hannah rocked the baby in her arms and crooned tunelessly.

"Was it bad?" Katy asked; her eyes focused on the infant.

"What? Oh, the birth you mean? Yes, it hurt quite a lot, but just look at him . . . So beautiful."

"Well, good luck," Katy stammered, unable to think of anything else to say.

At the exit, a man took her papers and stamped them. Then, he motioned across the outside yard, stomped bare of grass by many feet, to a platform where men piled suitcases unloaded from wagons.

Sure enough, the young husband stood nearby. He shifted nervously from one foot to the other, luggage piled beside him, never taking his eyes from the door through which Katy had walked.

She hesitated, but she had promised.

"I saw your wife and baby," she said as she approached him. "They're waiting to be taken to a hospital to be checked over. She said to tell you it's routine and nothing to worry about. You're to wait here for them."

A huge grin split the wide breadth of his homely features.

"Thank God. I was so worried. I'm a new father, you see."

The words seemed to startle him, as if they remained a fresh revelation. He tugged off a wool mitten and stuck out a roughened hand.

"Hiram Silverstein. They both could've died, you know. It was the hand of God."

Plus, the hands of a good nurse, Katy thought dryly.

"I'm Katy Thannen."

He studied her face and asked, "Have you family here?"

"Of course," she lied, as she knew the truth only led to more questions.

"I'm on my way to meet them now."

The aroma of grilled sausage wafted their way. Katy's stomach growled and she realized she was ravenous. Customers surrounded a nearby food stand, almost hiding it.

On an impulse, she asked, "Would you like something to eat?"

Hiram blushed deep into the collar of his thin jacket.

"It smells delicious," he admitted. "It's just that I'm Jewish, you see."

Katy felt foolish. With a curt nod, she walked toward the stand. When her turn came, she pointed to a sausage roll and held up one finger. Then, she motioned back toward Hiram, shrugged her shoulders, and raised her eyebrows.

The vendor looked over at Hiram with his side curls, and then grinned his understanding and pointed to a pile of sliced meat.

"Kosher," he said.

Katy nodded. Then, the vendor made a sandwich and handed it to Katy with the sausage roll. As she carried both back across the yard, she wondered why she did so.

Hiram beamed and took the sandwich from her hand with his.

"I can't refuse a gift from an angel. And you must be an angel."

Katy laughed. It felt good.

"I'm afraid it'll take more than one sandwich to make me that."

She devoured the roll, and then wiped her mouth with the paper it came in.

"I must go now. Good luck."

"Shalom, Katy Thannen. We'll pray for you."

• • •

Wagons waited for their fares. Katy found her suitcases on the dock and showed the driver the address on the envelope. He loaded her suitcases on the back of the open cart and helped her climb onto the seat. The horses had not gone far before they turned onto the cobblestones of State Street.

The driver motioned toward a graceful white mansion with a pillared entrance and a balcony over the roof of the portico. The wagon stopped and he climbed down.

The mansion was fronted by a black, wrought-iron fence. Attached to the gate, a sign read: HOME FOR IMMIGRANT GIRLS – MISSION OF OUR LADY OF THE ROSARY. Katy, however, was not able to read it.

She wished for more time to assimilate the fact she had reached her destination. It was all so overwhelming, and she felt so unprepared. *Am I dressed right? How does my hair look? Does anyone here speak German?*

The driver unloaded her suitcases, climbed back onto the cart, and waited. He seemed impatient as he tapped the toe of one boot.

Katy walked through the gate and up the walk, but still hesitated before ringing the bell.

"What am I getting myself into?"

A handsome woman in her sixties opened the door. She asked in German, "May I help you, fraulein?"

Katy supposed the dirndl under her open coat gave her away, but she found the familiar tongue a great relief. She held out the well-worn envelope.

"I'm Katy Thannen. Father Kaspar sent me."

"Father Kaspar. Bless his dear heart. I'm Agnes Voorhees. Mrs., not Frau . . . and you'll be Miss, not Fraulein. How much did you pay the driver?"

Katy turned back toward the waiting driver, who now drummed his fingers on seat of the wagon, and said, "I haven't paid him, yet."

"Goot."

Agnes Voorhees motioned for him to bring Katy's suitcases to the steps, and then asked him his fare.

"Too much . . . ," she scolded, "shame on you."

Reaching into her apron pocket, she handed the driver coins he grudgingly pocketed. Then, she helped Katy carry her suitcases inside.

"Leave them here in the foyer," the tall, regal woman told Katy as she put hers down and led the way to the parlor.

Katy admired her upswept hairdo and the perfect posture with which she walked.

She motioned Katy to a chair and said, "You must be exhausted."

Katy's eyes filled with tears.

Mrs. Voorhees clucked her tongue and said, "Wait here while I tell Cora to put out another plate for supper."

Katy waited until she left the room, and then sank back in the comfortable wing chair. She contemplated how things had worked out for her to stay in a place so fine.

A fire blazed in the fireplace and she realized she was very sleepy. *I could stay here forever*, she thought.

When Agnes Voorhees re-entered, Katy was almost asleep.

"Poor dear," she said when Katy sat up with a start.

"I'll take you right up to your room so you can have a proper nap. We can talk later. You'll be rooming with Baylie Root. How our Blessed Lord does provide. Her roommate moved out only this morning. Baylie speaks German and English, although you may have some trouble understanding her accent. Sixteen girls stay here at any one time, so you'll hear several different languages and dialects."

Katy was thoroughly confused, but she also felt a great sense of relief. Off the upstairs hall, Mrs. Voorhees ushered her into a sunny room. A large bay window faced the docks. Two beds, two dressers, a desk, and two chairs—one straight, the other a rocker—furnished the space. Rose-colored drapes hung at the window and a pink braided rug lay on the hardwood floor.

"Someone will wake you for supper."

Mrs. Voorhees patted Katy's shoulder.

"I'll have your luggage sent up later. Rest now, my dear."

It was a touch she had seldom received from her mother. Tears filled Katy's eyes, but she was asleep before they fell.

• • •

She awoke and squinted as lamp light flooded the room. A thick-set girl with piercing brown eyes and straight brown hair, cut into a short bob, set a tray on the bedside table. She looked to be in her early twenties.

"Baylie's my name. Dutchy sent this up instead of you comin' down. That bed's mine. Yourn's the other."

Katy jumped up and turned to smooth the coverlet.

"Sorry. Who's Dutchy?"

"The old lady."

Katy strained to catch Baylie's accent. Her broad face remained sober, unreadable. The sandwich and soup looked delicious . . . and a dumpling as well!

"How long you been here?" Katy asked as she carried the tray to the desk to eat.

"Three weeks. I'm an orphan. Only child . . . mother Belgian, father Cockney. That's why I sound like working class London with a Dutch accent. My ma and pa were done in by a runaway carriage in Antwerp."

Baylie's monologue was delivered without change in expression or tone.

"A farmer in the south of Belgium took me on as a hand. That's why I speak German. When he took it into his head to bring his family to America, I had wages put away to come along. 'Course they're on their own now and so am I."

The warm dumpling tasted so delicious Katy could hardly pause to chew.

"The Im'grant's Aid Society sent me here."

Baylie flopped down on the bed Katy had left and swung her heavy oxford shoes onto the coverlet.

"Figure it was due to CATHOLIC written on the farmer's papers. I'm not Catholic, but guess they thought I must be. How 'bout you?"

"A friend gave me this address."

Katy wiped her mouth with the napkin. She hoped her answer would end Baylie's questions.

"So, why did you come to America?"

Something about Baylie made it hard to evade her questions. Maybe it was her flat tone of voice and the rather menacing way she leaned into the conversation, even with her head on the pillow.

"To start a new life," Katy said as she crumpled her napkin and pushed the tray away in what she meant to be a dismissive gesture.

Baylie's derisive laugh came out almost a growl.

"Didn't we all? Well, you'll get your chance soon enough. They let you stay here a month, more or less. Then, you move on to make room for someone else."

Katy knew it was too good to be true. *Why had I been so naive to think I had found a safe haven?*

"I might already have a job," Baylie said as her mouth curved in a smug smile.

"Found it by myself."

She got up to strip her blouse over her head and throw it onto a chair.

"Hot in here. Dutchy must have cranked up the heat again."

Katy reached for her napkin and mopped her face with it.

"Saw what I thought might be a HELP NEEDED note tacked to a fence," she continued. "Asked a bobby at the corner to read it for me. Not much of a job—hard work, but I'm used to that. Besides, who can be picky? Got to eat, right?"

Katy nodded.

The girl was tough, Katy recognized it. Bregenz had plenty of those—dock workers, barmaids, and such.

Baylie sat down hard on the bed again and propped herself up against the headboard. She kicked off her sturdy oxfords and stretched out. Her thick ankles were encased in coarse cotton socks.

"By the way, the old lady's bringing up hot water for your bath. It's not even Saturday, but seems you're special. She's really tetched sometimes."

Katy unpacked a nightgown, the first clean one since that night in Frankfort when her only worry had been finding the hotel. She found the bathroom at the end of the hall where Mrs. Voorhees had poured hot water into the tub.

Surely nothing had ever felt so good. With eyes closed, the sweet warmth soaked away the knotted tension in Katy's body. Sights and sounds, even the smells of the past few weeks began to fade. A friend, who so obviously admired Father Kaspar, took such special pains to find her a job and a safe place to live. *Maybe things will work out after all.*

When Katy returned to the bedroom, Baylie was snoring.

CHAPTER 13

Sister Anne waited in the parlor. Katy learned from Agnes Voorhees that Sister Anne would be the one to assist her in finding proper employment and a place to live. She had counted on Mrs. Voorhees to help her.

"What do nuns know about the real world?" she muttered.

Fiftyish, Sister Anne sat on the settee and fanned herself with her prayer book. A white habit framed her round face. Her forehead bulged above close-set eyes.

"My, such a warm turn for late autumn. Please sit down, Katharina. You've been assigned to me because I speak German. Let's begin by you telling me about your background."

Katy took a deep breath.

"I was born and raised in Bregenz, Austria where I attended convent school."

That should impress her, Katy thought.

"Because of my studies, I didn't hold a fulltime position, but I worked several hours a week in the household of the governor of Voralberg."

"Hmm . . . ,"

Sister Anne slowed the fan and pursed her lips.

"Do you type?"

"No. But I take dictation. I had planned to apply for an office position in Innsbruck, but then . . . ," Katy's voice trailed.

"I suppose you transcribe in German rather than English?"

"Well . . . Yes."

Katy realized Sister Anne preferred a different answer.

"Unfortunate unless we can find a German employer. Most want typing skills. Another source would be domestic help, of course, but so many apply for those positions they're harder to come by. We'll just have to see. Where you live will depend on where you work, so finding suitable employment comes first. Take today to collect yourself and pray for God's wisdom. Father Vanderhoof says Mass at ten o'clock."

She clutched the prayer book and stood with effort, as if her knees hurt.

"And don't worry. Something always turns up. God provides."

• • •

Behind the mansion, a sanctuary of flowers and shrubbery contained a stone grotto that served as a small chapel: comfortably cool for the handful of worshippers who attended mid-morning Mass. Katy followed the familiar Latin liturgy. When it ended, Father Vanderhoof singled her out.

"You're new here, my child?"

His black eyebrows arched.

"I'll be glad to hear your confession."

Katy longed to escape, but she followed meekly and seated herself on one side of the curtain. She pictured the long face of the priest, the eyebrows lowered. *What can I confess?*

If she revealed the big sin: she carried a child, they would probably kick her out as beyond hope. Her mind raced.

"I'm waiting, my child."

Katy crossed herself, took a deep breath, and then confessed, "Forgive me, Father, for I have committed the sin of anger. I also lied about my age and showed disrespect to an old woman on the boat."

The priest waited, but Katy said no more. As soon as she received her penance, she fled to the privacy of her bedroom and shut the door. She stared out the window toward the harbor and took stock of her situation.

Already, the waistline of her skirt felt tight. *What should I do?*

She twisted the folds of her skirt into a tight knot. Then, she stood and paced the floor.

As the dinner hour neared, Katy trudged to the dining room.

Her assignment was to set the table. As she placed silverware beside the twelve plates, Baylie clumped into the room.

"There you are . . . been looking all over for you."

She pulled out a chair from the table.

"How much money do you have?"

Katy frowned and asked, "What business is that of yours?"

"Oh don't be so high and mighty."

Baylie reached over to pluck a grape from the fruit bowl that served as a centerpiece.

"I got reason for asking.'"

"Well I'm not completely lacking."

"Good. Been thinking maybe we could share a flat—split the rent—if I can talk Blanche Maloney into hiring both of us that is."

"Who?"

"My new boss; she takes in laundry. Has her kids helping now, and they ain't worth spit."

Laundry—a job Katy hated.

"Well, I don't know . . . ," she hedged. "Sister Anne—"

"Look, Miss High and Mighty. You have a pretty face and all, and I heard tell you read and write, but first off you got to learn the new ways and how to speak English. You can't afford to be choosy."

Baylie had some rough edges, yet Katy was impressed. Baylie had found her job on her own. Weeks might go by before Sister Anne found something for her. She did not have long before her secret was out.

However, when she told Sister Anne about a job through Baylie which she had considered, the Sister frowned and said, "It's different for Baylie. She has no education. She doesn't even have the comfort of the church, although she probably thinks we don't know that."

"But—"

"Please listen, Katy. Mrs. Voorhees feels a special obligation for your welfare and Baylie Root's no proper companion for you. You'll see. Something suitable will come along. You just got here— patience, my child, patience. You have plenty of time."

No I don't. Maybe Baylie's right. Best find a job . . . Any job. I can better myself later on, after . . . but better not to think too far ahead.

• • •

Katy clapped her hands over her ears. As the approaching train roared along the track high above her head, its wheels hissed. Baylie bought their tickets, and then shoved Katy toward the covered stairway. They emerged on the cold, breezy platform just as their train rumbled into the station.

Katy forgot her vow to emulate Baylie's nonchalance and perched on the edge of her seat. To her right, the colorful sails and flags of clipper ships dominated the East River, and on her left, lower Manhattan spread out in a maze of buildings and streets crowded with people and horse-drawn wagons and carriages. The steel arches of the Brooklyn Bridge soared ahead.

As the train lurched around a steep curve inland, Katy felt Baylie jostle her elbow.

She yelled into Katy's ear, "We get off at the next stop!"

The intersection of Bowery and Grand Street was a dizzying melee of sound. Elevated trains ran on both sides while the tracks of a cable railroad ran down the middle. A mail wagon, drays, garbage carts, various hacks and carriages, and numerous pedestrians criss-crossed the streets in all directions, wherever space allowed. Above them, telephone and power lines intersected everywhere.

Katy pivoted in circles and tried to take in everything.

"Come on," Baylie ordered as she tugged at Katy's coat sleeve. "You can lollygag later. We haven't all day."

As they turned the corner onto Canal Street, Baylie led the way. The large houses evoked the impression of a once elegant neighborhood. Weeds and broken glass littered the yards, now, and the sidewalks were crumbled.

Baylie stopped in front of a ramshackle, two-story dwelling. Chunks of mortar were missing from the stone walls, and slates which had fallen from the roof lay broken in the dirt yard.

With the cocky air of one knowing her way around, Baylie

climbed the sagging steps and pounded on the splintered door. There was no response, but when Katy turned to leave, Baylie caught her sleeve.

"She's here all right. Where she be goin' on a week day? Just takin' her time."

When the door opened, at last, a large-boned Irish woman gave Baylie a nod and stepped back to admit them. Her frizzy hair was gathered into a careless topknot from which floated long, blowzy wisps the same color as her red-chapped hands.

"Mrs. Maloney, this here's Katy Thannen."

Baylie pushed Katy forward.

"She needs a job."

The door slammed shut behind them.

"Begorrah, that wind's cold!"

Blanche Maloney planted her hands on her wide hips. The sleeves of her navy shirtwaist, though pushed to the elbows, were dark with moisture at the cuffs.

"What am I to do with two of you?"

A child began to cry and Mrs. Maloney shooed Katy and Baylie toward the kitchen. She motioned them to straight-backed chairs beside a large rectangular table crudely covered with tin. After she sank into a large, complaining rocker, Mrs. Maloney placed the squalling toddler onto her lap.

Two other children ran in from a back porch—an older girl and young boy with a runny nose. Both were barefoot in spite of the cold. Through the open door, Katy saw a maze of clotheslines which crisscrossed the expanse of a large backyard bare of any grass or foliage.

The children grouped behind their mother and stared at her visitors.

The woman asked, "Your friend got a tongue?"

"She don't speak English," Baylie replied.

"Another reason I don't need her."

Baylie eyed the mounds of dirty clothes and the Maloney children.

"I s'pose they're all the help you need?"

Blanche hooted and swatted at the one closest her.

"These brats? They never pay me no mind. Spill the wash water and get underfoot every minute of the day. Worthless as their father. Be better off farming them out to the factories."

The children giggled and ducked away.

"If you had more help, you could stay ahead."

Baylie's tone was firm and persuasive.

"Even take in more laundry."

Blanche wrinkled her brow, bit her lower lip, and agreed, "Saints preserve me, you might have a point. I s'pose I could give it a go long as she pulls her weight."

She reached to take two long, threadbare aprons off hooks, and handed them to Baylie who tied one on Katy. It was then Katy realized she had the job.

What had probably once been the parlor had bare, splintered floors. Any furnishings had been removed to make room for laundry tubs and washboards. The room beyond, perhaps once a formal dining room, held a long table stacked with folded clothes.

A rickety ironing board with a flatiron resting on it stood in one corner. At the windows, tired drapes of rich brocade hinted of better days.

Baylie showed Katy how to fill the wooden washtubs from kettles of hot water on the coal-burning stove. She swished the bar of lye soap to make suds, and then put in a batch of clothes and scrubbed them on the washboard.

Next, she used a cut-off broom handle to fish out an item and transfer it to a neighboring tub to rinse before she fed it through wooden rollers, and turned the handle of the wringer to squeeze the water back into the tub. At last, the item dropped into a bushel basket to be hauled to the clothesline when the basket was full.

"Nothing to it," Baylie muttered as they started to work. "Beats sloppin' hogs and pitchin' hay."

• • •

The strong soap stung Katy's hands and arms up to her elbows. Her back ached from scrubbing, even before she picked up the first heavy basket to carry outside.

Blanche shoveled more coal into the cook stove. She continued to harangue her children while she sprinkled water from a jar onto shirts and ironed them dry.

At noon, a girl of twelve or so addressed as Rosie by her mother, dished up stew served with a plate of black bread. They ate on the tin tabletop in spaces cleared between more stacks of clothes. The stew lacked seasoning and the bread came plain without butter or jam.

Back at work again, Katy pushed her hair out of her eyes with a wet forearm. It seemed the day would never end.

At last, Blanche shooed the children out of the kitchen and strained to reach a jar from a top shelf in one of the cupboards. Extracting a drawstring bag from it, she drew forth a handful of coins she had counted out on the table in two separate piles. She scooped up one pile and handed the coins to Katy, and then patted her on the shoulder.

"You do fine. Tomorrow . . . Eight sharp."

Katy did not understand the words, but when she counted the coins, she felt her stomach drop. *So little for so much.*

By the time they took the train back to the mission house, almost nothing was left. When the door closed behind them, she said as much, but Baylie brushed her comment aside.

"We won't be spending money on train fare. Come, I'll show you."

Instead of heading back to the train station, she walked in the opposite direction. Katy stumbled after her, too tired to argue.

In the December twilight, the neighborhoods grew even shabbier. At last, they came upon a huddled group of dingy storefronts.

"Where are we going?" Katy asked through clenched teeth.

"We're here."

Baylie stopped in front of one of the stores.

Katy looked in the window and said, "This is a butcher shop."

"Upstairs, silly, that sign says: FLAT FOR RENT."

Katy tipped her head back and saw the sign taped inside a second-story window.

"I canvassed the neighborhood last weekend."

Baylie reached up and rang the bell over the door. A skinny man with bad teeth and stringy hair hung over one eye came out of the shop; he wiped his hands on a blood-stained apron.

He curiously growled, his accent thick, "What'cha want?"

Baylie pointed to the sign, and then at her and Katy. The man pulled a ring of keys from his pocket and opened the door. Katy trailed behind as they followed him up the steep flight of stairs. The narrow steps had no railing and fallen plaster littered the steps.

The butcher motioned them into the room, but stayed out in the hallway. The room was filthy. Spider webs draped the corners of the cracked ceiling and mice droppings were scattered over the floor. A rusted iron stove which appeared to serve for cooking and heating stood out away from the wall, its stovepipe heavy with soot. Two dented pans and a chipped enamel coffee pot sat on the stove lids.

A battered table, covered with faded oilcloth, occupied one corner. Above it, rough boards served as shelves for a few chipped plates and cups. In the opposite corner, an iron bedstead—its paint badly chipped—held a bumpy, blue-striped mattress. A chamber pot with a cracked lid sat beneath it. Water dripped into a cast iron sink where it created a thick comma of rust.

Katy cleared her throat and admitted, "I can't live here."

"And why not? It's real cheap and we can walk to work."

Katy glanced toward the hallway and said in a lowered voice, "But it's just too awful."

"Oh, I see."

Baylie's face wore a sneer.

"Nice you can afford to be uppity, seeing as you're pregnant and all."

Katy gasped and flushed as red as Blanche Maloney's hands.

"How did you know?"

"You 'spect no one's guessed? Maybe you've hoodwinked the nuns and the crazy Dutch woman. They might not think it, you being Catholic and all, but I've spent enough time 'round brood sows to know when females have life in their bellies."

Baylie snorted a short, bitter laugh.

"How long 'til they get wise and kick you out? Thought about that, have you?"

She had money left. *But when it's gone, what then?* Katy fought back tears. *I hate you, Alex Meisen.*

The butcher cleared his throat.

"How much?" Katy asked.

Baylie told her and Katy opened her purse to count out her share of the rent. Baylie paid the rest. Neither spoke on the way back to State Street.

• • •

Determined to salvage what little pride she had left, Katy refused to give out her new address. She made Baylie promise to do the same, not that Baylie appeared to care.

Sister Anne and Agnes Voorhees pled with Katy, but she pressed her lips together, packed her things, and carried the suitcases downstairs.

"No point staying longer," she told the worried housemother. "I have a job and a place to stay. You've been most kind, but my leaving will make room for others."

"But Katy, why the secrecy? Your welfare is my concern."

Mrs. Voorhees followed Katy to the door and grabbed at the suitcases as if to take them out of her hands.

"Each young woman who crosses our threshold is someone God has entrusted to our care. Besides, there's Father Kaspar. I can't be letting him down."

Her last glimpse of Father Kaspar flickered in Katy's mind. She felt a great sadness. *Would he have understood? Can anyone understand?*

"The hack's here!" Baylie yelled from the front steps.

Katy pulled the suitcases free, moved toward the door, and then said, "Don't blame yourself, Mrs. Voorhees. It's a decision I must make myself."

As the wagon pulled away, she saw Sister Anne put her hand on the housemother's arm.

"It's that Baylie," she heard her say. "She's a bad influence. We must pray for her soul."

• • •

December was perpetually damp and cold. As they laundered clothes, steam streaked the windows. Items pinned on the clothes-lines froze and had to be spread around the rooms to dry. Little by little, Katy began to decipher Blanche's constant chatter.

Two of the Maloney children no longer ran underfoot. Blanche hired Rosie out to do piece work. She assembled dried flower arrangements in a crowded room of a nearby tenement house. Ten-year-old Eric joined a street cleaning crew, one of dozens which followed behind the many horse-drawn convey-ances with shovels. Nine-year-old Jenny was left to set food on the table and eight-year-old Ethel watched the two toddlers.

Blanche ironed beside the kitchen stove and used her foot to jiggle the baby's cradle.

"How far gone are you now?" Baylie quizzed in a whisper.

"Three months. I think she suspects."

"Prob'ly. That's the good luck of this here job. She won't care one way 'ter the other, long as your work gets done."

Using a broomstick, Baylie hefted a sopping mass of cloth out of the tub into the rinse water and asked, "But what about after? You don't want to end up like her, do you?"

Katy stopped scrubbing to look at Baylie.

"There's a man at the pub," Baylie began.

Katy made a face and scrubbed harder on the washboard.

Baylie let the stick fall into the tub where it splashed water on the floor and sneered, "Oh, I know, you're too fine to climb on a stool and down a pint. You'd rather hide away in our fancy digs, making a cover for that cracked window, trying somehow to turn a sow's ear into a silk purse. Well, this here man knows a doctor. In Harlem. Ten dollars up front."

Katy let the soap slip from her hand and float to the bottom of the tub.

"Oh no, I couldn't."

"So, don't then!"

With a snort, Baylie turned her back. The muscles rippled in her upper arms as she cranked the handle on the wringer.

"Maybe Blanche will let you tie the brat on your breast so it can suck while you scrub."

Katy did not sleep that night. She no longer jumped at the rustlings in the walls, and she had grown accustomed to Baylie's snoring and the way she hogged the bedclothes. She had even learned to ignore the hacking cough of the old man in the flat next door.

No, Baylie's words were what repeated in her head.

"She's right," Katy admitted softly as she stared at the ceiling in the dim light of the street lamp on the corner.

What will I do with a child? No one cares . . . least of all Baylie. My mother would die of humiliation if she knew.

It had been different for the Virgin Mary. She had her cousin, Elizabeth. Katy tried to picture the tranquil smile on the blessed face by the altar, but the thought of it only drove her to deeper shame.

Her situation seemed hopeless. Baylie was no Elizabeth, and if God stayed near, as the Lutheran lady on the train said he did, He sure kept Himself hidden.

Ridding herself of the baby meant committing murder, a terrible sin. She had a long list of sins already. *Will one more matter? If only Sofie was here.*

Thoughts of her friend created a deep longing. Katy turned and wept bitter tears into her pillow.

At daybreak, Baylie rolled over and stretched. The bed springs creaked.

Katy asked, "How can I find that doctor in Harlem?"

CHAPTER 14

Alex wrestled his blanket. The snores and snorts of other men, the fetid smells of the close quarters, and the steady throb of the ship's engines kept him awake. Ghostly shadows, cast by oil lamps which swung from hooks on the ceiling, danced like the dark thoughts which tormented him.

What horrors had Katy experienced on her ocean crossing? She must've decided I'd changed my mind or she never would've gone on alone. She must not have known about the train wreck. When I find her—if I find her—will she hate me, or will she only feel contempt which will be even worse. At the very least, she's bound to be angry.

A strangled voice broke into delirium. It sent almost visible shock waves through the cabin before the demented sounds muffled.

Another man screamed, "He's in convulsions . . . Must be the typhus!"

The room erupted as men threw off blankets and jumped to their feet. They began shouting and cursing.

The old man below Alex wailed, "We're all sure to die!"

Across the aisle, Sam's voice remained steady.

"Take courage, my friend, God will not forsake those who call on Him."

"But we could suffer terrible deaths," the man's voice insisted.

"It's true we could die. We all die sometime. However, death holds no fear for those who believe."

"Fanatic," the man mumbled.

At dawn, deckhands roped off the stairs which led down to steerage and posted quarantine signs. Crew members with bull-horns warned men not to mingle with women passengers, but to stay at their end of the ship.

The ship's doctor attended to the sick man and warned others to keep their distance. He sent down a deckhand with a bucket of coal tar and instructions to rub it into hairy parts of the passenger's bodies to prevent the spread of lice, a known carrier of the disease.

The deckhand also brought a folding screen to isolate the sick man. The poor soul in the bunk below took his bedroll and slept on the floor at the opposite end of the room.

Alex paced the deck and fought to control his fears. Until then, he had dwelled on the moment he found Katy and dreaded the predicament he had left her in and her reaction to it. However, now, he was tortured by the thought he might not live to see her again.

Sam's words rang mockingly in his head . . . "Take courage."

His thumb twisted the crusader ring round and round his finger. He had lost weight and the ring felt loose.

"Pray for the courage to hold to your convictions," his grandfather had told him.

Yet, without Katy, life had no meaning. He felt helpless, desperate, and anything, but brave.

"Face facts," he told himself. "You're a coward. You're afraid to face the future and even more afraid of dying."

Sam Schneider fell in step beside him as he walked.

"Sometimes it helps just to talk," he told Alex, "to encourage one another."

Something about Sam helped Alex calm his thoughts.

"So talk," he told him.

The two men sat down on coils of rope, their heads inclined toward one another. Sometimes Sam bent over the worn black book. His lips moved as he read aloud. Other times they walked and swung their arms to warm themselves.

"Only in Jesus can we find courage to face hardships," Sam said.

"I thought you said it's God who sustains us," Alex reminded with a tinged of sarcasm.

"True, but Martin Luther said, 'Take hold of Jesus as a man, and you will discover that He is God.' Because Jesus lived on earth as a man, then cared enough to die for us on the cross, and was resurrected, He confirmed His claim to be God's son. We can count on Him to plead our case with the Father—to be our friend."

"You make him sound more human than divine."

"He's both. His character demonstrates the goodness of God and His love for us. God sent His only Son to free us from temptation and the awful burden of our sinful natures."

"But those very things trap us no matter how hard we try," Alex insisted. "As a young boy I went to Mass daily, prayed the rosary, made confession, and I still did wrong. All my efforts only made me feel worse."

"Exactly; St. Augustine said God created us for Himself and our hearts are restless until they find rest in Him."

"Rest?"

"Inner peace . . . ceasing our own striving to attain a noble calling, moral integrity, goodness and virtue, or however you label it."

"And how do we attain this magical peace?" Alex asked sarcastically.

His heart, however, yearned for the answer at the same time.

"It's not magic," Sam answered. "God's plan requires only simple faith."

He flipped the worn pages and pointed to the words: "But as many as received him, to them gave he power to become the sons of God, even to them that believe on his name."[1]

"We can't earn his goodness."

Sam rubbed his chin.

"We must accept it as His free gift."

"I've been in the church all my life, but it's as if I've never heard any of this," Alex admitted.

Sam thrust the book into Alex's hands.

"It's all here. Start with the Gospel according to John."

At first, Alex felt uneasy reading the words himself, but soon he was unable to lay the book down. He strained to see in the flickering light and read on into the night until, with great excitement, he came upon the passage—the vision his grandfather had created for him of the crusading knight.

---

1   John 1:12, King James Version (KJV)

"Put on the whole armour of God, that ye may be able to stand against the wiles of the devil."[2]

A scream pierced the still cabin followed by an anguished cry which filled the cabin with a tumult of terror.

"He's dead. The poor bloke's dead!"

Panic gripped Alex.

"Father in heaven," he prayed, "I have no courage of my own. Please give me enough faith to trust in Your armor. I want Jesus as my Savior."

Amazed, he felt fear ebb away. It was replaced with a wonderful comfort, not unlike what he felt as a child when his mother placed her cool hand on his fevered brow and assured him all would be well.

Alex placed his face into his pillow. He sobbed with relief and awed gratitude.

• • •

The next morning the man's remains were wrapped in his blanket and placed on the foredeck. Crew members secured the blanket with ropes and tied weights to it, and then consigned the corpse to the sea.

Buckets of lye were brought into the cabin to scrub down the dead man's bunk and other wood surfaces. Men stayed to themselves, afraid of contagion by transmitted words. In the next two days, another man took sick, and then another.

Alex and Sam stuck close to each other. The bond forged between them now made the time short for all they had to share.

"Will you live in New York?" Alex asked.

"Not me. I plan to head west. I can make a living as a carpenter . . . Worked my way through university as a cabinet maker."

"Really?"

Alex admired people like his grandfather who worked with their hands.

---

2   Ephesians 6:11, KJV

"My burning desire is to become one of John Calvin's reformers. Calvin applied the gospel message to all of society, making it the basis for a new form of civilization. New York is full of corruption, but people heading west seek a fresh start. I believe many will respond to the gospel message. How about you? What are your plans?"

Alex had poured out his heart to Sam. His new friend had listened with great compassion.

"I'll stay in New York to search for Katy," Alex told him. "I haven't thought beyond that."

"I'm sure you'll find her," Sam assured him. "God will go with you."

"I know that," Alex answered, aware of a new dimension in his search. "I won't give up, no matter how long it takes."

Because of the quarantine, the men in steerage class found themselves herded onto a separate ferry to be processed at the Barge Office, and then isolated and examined at a hospital on Staten Island. Alex chafed against the further delay, but also relished the extra time it gave him with Sam.

Sam was the first real friend he had ever known. He dreaded their parting and the prospect of finding himself alone again.

"A threefold cord is not quickly broken,"[3] Sam quoted. "We now have the bond of Christ's love between us and distance won't change that. Somehow, I feel certain our paths will cross again."

At last, the two men boarded the boat which granted them passage across the bay. They leaned on the rail and gazed across the harbor at the Manhattan skyline.

"I guess you'll be leaving soon," Alex said.

"Yes, I'm afraid so. No use wasting time and money. I'm headed for Grand Central Station, but you'll be in my thoughts and prayers always, my friend. I pray you'll soon find your Katy."

As they walked off the pier, Alex awkwardly offered his hand in farewell. Sam embraced him instead. When he pulled away, both men took out handkerchiefs and wiped their eyes. Then, Sam reached into his breast pocket and pulled out the worn black book.

---

3   Ecclesiastes 4:12, KJV

"This is for you," he said. "Remember, God is our refuge and strength, a very present help in trouble."[4]

Alex swallowed hard and stared at the gilt-edged pages. He reverently fingered the leather cover.

"I'll remember."

He embraced his friend once more.

"Take care of yourself and don't get shot by some wild Indian."

Sam laughed and reassured Alex, "I won't. But I might convert a few."

The two men lingered, silent and unmoving—how people delay when they hope to suspend a moment in time. Then, Sam turned away.

"God bless you, my friend."

• • •

Alex decided his first plan of action. During the processing procedure at the Barge Office, he noticed a desk marked: IMMIGRANT'S AID SOCIETY.

As alone and desperate as Katy must've felt, might not she have been drawn to this sign?

Alex waited in line.

"Yes?"

The woman looked up from the tall desk, and placed her forefinger to mark her place on the paper before her. Perspiration beaded her forehead, and she used her other hand to mop it with a wadded white handkerchief.

"I'm looking for a young woman who arrived in New York alone several weeks ago. If she made inquiries here, where might you have directed her?"

"Inquiries about what . . . relatives, lodging, employment . . .?"

Alex hesitated and answered, "Lodging first, probably."

"Did she have money?"

"Some, but she would be in need of making it last," Alex answered.

The woman frowned, tapped her pencil on the counter top, and then said, "Well, the mission home on State Street might be a possibility. If they had room, it would've been our first recommendation for a woman traveling alone."

"Why is that?" Alex inquired.

"The housemother, a Mrs. Voorhees, is exceptionally kind and understanding. The nuns work hard to find employment for the girls. I'll write down the address, as well as that of the nearest settlement house."

"Settlement house?"

The woman adjusted the tiny glasses on the bridge of her nose and wrote as she talked. Then, she handed him the paper.

"Charity organizations located in the poorer neighborhoods give aid to destitute families and single women who have nowhere else to turn."

"Thank you. Thank you very much."

The woman had already turned to a woman who shouldered her way past Alex to be next in line.

Outside, the aroma of cooking meat drew Alex to a nearby food stand. He purchased a sausage roll and devoured it in a few bites.

"Katy had surely passed this way, but where is she now?"

CHAPTER 15

Anton Adler immigrated to America after his wife begged to follow her parents' crossing three years earlier. At first, the young doctor resisted her pleas; he had no desire to uproot his prosperous practice in Hamburg.

Then, the unfortunate death of a young patient caused talk and blemished his reputation so he became more open to the move. When a clipping—sent by his mother-in-law—stated the need for German-speaking doctors, Anton Adler was convinced.

Settled in Brooklyn, he purchased acreage to include a commodious house and moved his wife's parents out of their east side tenement. He convinced his father-in-law to plant fruits and vegetables on the land as a way to provide their support. The long hours it took to establish a practice kept him conveniently away.

To a large extent, his practice in Germany had derived from his skill in terminating pregnancies. Although public advertising for abortion services was banned in New York, word-of-mouth spread and brought clients to his waiting room. Thus, Anton Adler established a livelihood in Harlem.

However, things changed a few years later. The American Medical Association closed ranks in order to maintain its exclusive reputation. Its members were disdainful and distrusting of the immigrant practitioners whose competition encroached on their lucrative practices.

When they lobbied the U.S. Congress for stricter licensing laws, many members found it expedient to embrace the moral outcry that made the killing of unborn babies a criminal offense.

Thus, Adler lost his physician's license. However, he did not lose the demand for his services. Under his title of medical practitioner, he dispensed harmless remedies for female ailments while he continued to accommodate the referrals of desperate women. His lifestyle suffered not at all.

• • •

Katy knew none of this when the physician called for her turn and she entered the examining room. He introduced himself, but she avoided his piercing eyes magnified behind thick lenses.

Without further ado, he appraised her belly and declared her more than three months pregnant. She felt her insides quake and feared she might vomit.

He inquired, "How did you obtain my name and address?"

Katy stammered the name of Baylie's acquaintance at the pub. He gave a short nod of recognition. His direct stare continued to study her face. She told herself he was not unkind, only straightforward.

"Cash, in ten dollar bills," he told her.

"I know. I have it with me."

"In that case, I can perform the procedure now."

He plucked a white, starched gown from a pile stacked on an enameled table and handed it to her. Then, he motioned to a screen in the corner of the room, put on rubber gloves, and began to arrange items on his instrument tray.

Katy experienced a sudden panic. Things were happening too fast. She had expected to meet the doctor and perhaps ask some questions to return later if she decided to do so.

"Just as well now as later," the doctor said as if he had read her mind.

Katy studied his profile and found the unremarkable features somehow comforting. The man was not a person to her, only someone who could relieve her of a bothersome inconvenience, the same as a dentist removes an aching tooth.

She moved toward the screen, but once behind it panic seized her again. She had shut her mother from her thoughts, but now Helga's face floated into her consciousness, stern and reproving . . . and the nuns.

Over and over they had made their students recite the Ten Commandments; Thou shalt not kill. She threw the gown on the floor and grabbed her purse.

"Please hurry," the doctor called. "I have another patient waiting."

Katy hesitated. She could say she had changed her mind. He would not stop her. *But then what would I do? Soon everyone will know my secret. Where can I go . . . Back to the mission home?*

Her shame would be too great. So, with a mighty effort of self-control, Katy set down her purse, retrieved the gown, and seated herself on the folding chair to take off her shoes.

The injection left her light-headed and dizzy. She cringed from the cold steel instruments and found the dilation and scraping repulsive. Yet, she experienced little pain and the procedure was soon over. *Shouldn't it have taken longer? After all . . .*

Dr. Adler's nondescript face came into her line of vision.

"That's it," he told her. "Rest now, I'll be back to check on you." *He's a good person, almost fatherly.*

Occasional snatches of conversation drifted from the adjoining room as Dr. Adler talked with another patient. Katy had no idea how much time had elapsed before his return. She worked hard to keep her mind blank.

"You can dress now. Leave the packing in until tomorrow morning. Then, remove it carefully. You'll be fine, but take a cab home and don't do much walking for a day or two."

He helped her sit up and get down from the table. She felt a little wobbly, but, otherwise, quite normal. Once more behind the screen, she put on her clothes, buttoned her coat, and came back out. Then, to her chagrin, she began to weep.

The doctor regarded her without expression.

"Tears are a normal aftermath," he stated flatly, "an emotional release from tension. Remember, my dear, I have as much at stake here as you do. My skill protects me as well as you. I don't make mistakes."

Katy nodded and counted the bills from her purse without speaking. She wiped her eyes and stumbled outside the door where she took the stairs down one step at a time. Acutely aware of her flat belly and the full feeling below it, she grasped the railing for support.

• • •

Once back on the street, Katy paid a driver to transport her back to the sordid flat above the butcher shop so she could collect her belongings. It did not take long to do so. She knew not where she was going; only she could not live there and work for Blanche Maloney any longer. After she scribbled a note to Baylie, she tore it up, and left some bills on the table instead.

At last, she boarded a streetcar headed south. She had learned from the German-speaking girls at Mrs. Voorhees' boarding house many German immigrants settled in Brooklyn.

What money she had left was not going to last long. She was unable to think of another plan. *Does it matter? God will surely punish me regardless.*

She disembarked at Canal Street, and judged correctly it was still early afternoon. The odors of fried onions, peppers, and sausages from nearby pushcarts nauseated and enticed her.

At last, hunger won out and she crossed the street toward a cart whose vendor faced the other way. When he turned, she found herself face-to-face with Hiram Silverstein.

They stared at each other for a long moment.

"Katy?"

Hiram's face broke into a giant grin.

"It took me a moment. What a surprise!"

"Hello."

Katy started to turn away, and then turned back, her dismay vied with relief to find someone she knew.

"How are Hannah and the baby?"

"Fine . . . Fine. Little Moses grows like a weed."

Katy forced a smile.

"And here you are, selling your own sausages."

Hiram threw his head back and laughed.

"Not sausages. However, seeing the vendor that day at the Barge Office gave me the idea. My cousin came to America a little less than a year ago and opened a small grocery. Now, he cuts extra meat in our kitchen. His wife and Hannah bake the bread, and his two sons and I go out to sell sandwiches. It's a living, and what we can't sell, we eat."

The simple story, combined with Hiram's smile and unquenchable optimism, overcame Katy so completely tears poured from her eyes. Hiram hurried from behind the cart.

"Oh, please forgive me. I've been talking about myself and haven't asked about your family at all."

His voice revealed his great consternation.

"My family?"

"At the docks . . . You said you had family waiting for you."

Katy remembered and confessed, "I have no family here."

"You're all alone? But that's terrible. Everyone needs family. Have you work?"

Katy shook her head. She told Hiram about Mrs. Maloney, Baylie, and the miserable flat—everything, but the events of her terrible day.

Hiram gathered meat into a fresh roll and handed her the sandwich.

"This is on me," he offered. "I owe you one, remember?"

With a wan smile, Katy took it and thanked him. It tasted delicious and she realized it was the only thing she had eaten all day.

"I'm not good with words. Come home with me and see Hannah. We live only a few blocks away. She'll know what to do."

Katy did not argue. She remembered Hannah's kindness and felt great relief to be enveloped by Hiram's goodness. Recalling the doctor's instructions, she walked carefully as Hiram pushed the cart over the cobblestones.

"It's not much," he told her. "Three rooms for the seven of us, counting the baby. But it's a roof over our heads and no more fear of horsemen burning our village in the night."

"Horsemen?"

They were at the door where Hannah greeted her with joy and disbelief.

"Katy! I don't believe it. Come in, come in."

Hiram told her about their meeting.

"It's a miracle. God brought you to our doorstep."

She cradled baby Moses in one arm, and then thrust him toward Katy.

"See how much he's grown. Isn't he beautiful?"

Katy shrank back.

"I think he's wet."

"Isn't he always?"

Hannah laughed, but then she sobered as she studied Katy's face.

"Things aren't good with you."

Katy burst into tears. She poured out the story of the dismal job and the horrid flat she shared with Baylie. Again, she left out mention of what lay most heavy on her conscience.

Hannah guided Katy to a chair and sat down opposite her.

"You must stay with us."

"Oh no, I couldn't. You have so little room as it is."

Katy turned to Hiram for confirmation, but he nodded in agreement with his wife.

"You helped us in our time of need," he said. "God requires we do the same. Wait here."

His tone left no room for argument. Hannah and Katy sat in awkward silence while he conversed with someone in the adjoining room. When he returned, he wore a broad smile.

"It's all set. My cousin and his wife agree with me. We'll have to make your bed on the floor, Katy, but you're welcome to stay as long as it takes you to find a suitable job and a decent place to live."

Katy fought to hold back tears. She was overwhelmed by their generosity. *What makes these quaint people so unselfish, so content with so little?*

At dinner, she met Myron Silverstein; his wife, Gerta; and their two young sons. Then, Hannah made a thick pallet of blankets on the floor and gave Katy a nightgown to wear. Exhausted, she fell asleep in an instant.

• • •

Early the next morning, while the others still slept, Katy locked herself in the small bathroom and gingerly pulled out the stained packing. It left a stretched, empty feeling. She recalled how the nurse on the ship had torn strips from a sheet for Hannah's packing, but Hannah had her child to show for it.

The realization of what she had done enveloped her like a shroud. *What can ever atone for such a terrible sin?*

She ripped off a strip of her petticoat and wrapped the bloody gauze into a tight package. Then, she poured water from the bucket, scrubbed her hands with the strong soap beside the wash pan, and rubbed them hard with the rough towel. At last, she crept into the hallway, ran down the back stairs to the street, and stuffed the bundle deep inside a nearby ash can.

"That's that," she told herself.

Nothing was able to change what had happened. She had to put it out of her mind and find a job. That was the important thing.

She did not want to impose on Hiram's and Hannah's hospitality any longer than absolutely necessary. Somehow, she had to be on her own as soon as possible.

After breakfast, when Gerta Silverstein had left for her job as a seamstress, Katy helped Hannah with the breakfast dishes. Then, she rode the train uptown and studied women workers as they left and entered office buildings or ran errands on the busy sidewalks.

She noted their hair styled in upswept rolls, black skirts with long-sleeved white blouses, and high-buttoned shoes. That night she loosened her thick coil of braids and held handfuls of lustrous black hair in different positions as she stood in front of the mirror and studied the effect. Hannah watched.

"Cut it," Katy instructed.

"Oh no," Hannah protested. "It's so long, so beautiful!"

The baby cuddled in her arms began to wail.

"See . . . A male opinion," Hannah commented with a laugh.

"His opinion doesn't count unless he's offering me a job," Katy countered.

With a deep sigh, Hannah put the baby back in his cradle, clutched a bunch of Katy's hair in one hand, and cut it off at shoulder length with Cousin Myron's butcher shears. Tears rolled down her cheeks as she laid the luxurious swatch on the table and gathered up another handful.

Although Katy felt no remorse, Hannah's emotion moved her. She had never shared such an intimate moment with anyone, not even Sofie. She wished she was able to somehow reciprocate. The natural way was to share Hannah's love for little Moses, but, in truth, she wanted as little to do with him as possible. In fact, being near him repulsed her.

• • •

Katy twisted the remaining hair into a coil at the back of her neck and went shopping for suitable clothes. She spent a good portion of her dwindling funds to outfit herself in the proper fashion. Then, she bought a paper from a vendor at a newsstand.

She asked him, "Can you please read aloud the HELP WANTED ads for women workers?"

"Guess I've nothing else to do," he obliged.

By closing time, Katy emerged from the New York Central Realty Company with a simple, but paying job running errands and filing papers written in German.

"You have sufficient schooling," Herr Jaeger told her, "but you'll need to speak English before dealing with customers. If you attend night school, I'll give you more responsibility and better pay."

"Oh yes, I can do that."

Katy did not know what night school was, but she knew she had to find out. Once back on Canal Street, she took what felt like her first deep breath in days.

When she left that morning, the activity had appeared almost frenetic. Housewives hurried between sidewalk stands, and stepped into the cobblestone street to inspect pushcarts which displayed every kind of food from eggs to onions.

A stiff breeze flapped laundry draped over the railings of balconies. Smoke rolled from rooftop chimneys as Hannah began to bake bread for the Sabbath meal.

Hannah greeted Katy when she returned home that evening. A white tablecloth and candles adorned the table, and Myron's and Hannah's young children waited beside their chairs to take their places. Their faces were scrubbed shiny above the collars of their homespun shirts.

"Hurry, Katy. Shabbat is about to begin."

Myron Silverstein sat at one end of the long table, and his wife at the other with a shawl draped over her head. As Katy took her place, the older woman stood to light the candles.

Although, Katy did not understand the Yiddish prayers and songs, she soon sensed the fervent devotion and strong bond of fellowship which encircled the table.

Myron stood to place his hands on the heads of his sons. He stooped to place his lips gently on their foreheads. As unexpected tears sprang to Katy's eyes, she looked away. A deep longing surged within her; for what she did not know, but she acknowledged the ache.

Hannah motioned for her to join them when she raised her glass of wine. She demonstrated how to hold it in the palm of the right hand with the five fingers curled upward.

"This is the Kiddush, the prayer of sanctification. The full cup symbolizes overflowing joy and bounty. Our fingers are like the petals of a rose, the symbol of perfection reaching upward in longing for God."

They passed a bowl and towel round the table for the ritual washing of hands. Then, Myron blessed, broke, and distributed the Shabbat bread to each person as the meal began . . . and what a meal it was. The women hoarded all week for the courses they proudly displayed.

Talk and laughter swirled round the table although Katy said little. She felt welcome, yet separate. The bond between family members came from long standing, like the bond evident between them and their God. She felt a bond to no one—not her family and certainly not Alex.

That night Katy hunted for her rosary among her belongings. Her lips moved as she stumbled over the long-neglected phrases, but her beloved Mary seemed far away and disapproving.

"My sins are too many," Katy grieved. "I don't deserve to be loved."

CHAPTER 16

Alex read the sign on the gate: IMMIGRANT HOME FOR GIRLS. A tall, middle-aged woman answered the doorbell. Her regal bearing reminded Alex of a duchess or queen.

He inquired, "Mrs. Voorhees?"

"Yes, how may I help you?"

"I'm looking for a young lady named Katharina Thannen. She's a friend of mine from Austria. By any chance might she be here?"

He held his breath as he awaited her answer.

The woman caught her hand to her throat and studied his face. "Do come in, please."

She stepped back and opened the door wide.

"How do you know Katy?"

The conversation continued in the parlor where Alex poured out the story of their separation. His voice shook as he gripped his hat in his hands and turned it round and round.

"I wish I could be of help," the matron sighed. "You see, I only knew Katharina briefly. She was a lovely, intelligent young woman. Her abrupt departure disturbed me greatly. Partly, because of Father Kaspar's concern for her."

"Who is Father Kaspar? Where is Katy now?"

Agnes Voorhees went on to explain, "When I lived in Holland before coming to the States, Father Kaspar was a good friend of mine. He made Katy's acquaintance on the Rhine boat trip and gave her my name as someone who would help her."

She fingered the crocheted cover on the arm of the chair and sighed again.

"I'm afraid I failed him. We begged her to stay until we could find her a better position, but she insisted on leaving with Baylie Root. With all my heart I wish I had never assigned them as roommates.

Baylie is rough and unsophisticated. Not her fault. She's lived a hard life and I'm sure she's had to be tough to survive, but she became a wrong influence for Katy."

"Katy's not easily influenced," Alex argued. "In my experience, she thinks for herself."

He placed his elbow on the arm of the chair and covered his eyes with his hand.

"You'll have to excuse me. I find it hard to believe I came so close, only to lose her again."

He took a moment to collect himself, and then said, "Tell me about this Baylie person."

"Well, she arrived a short time before Katy, and learned her way around in a very short time. Baylie found some menial position—laundry work, if I remember correctly. Completely unsuitable for someone of Katy's education and presence, but Baylie talked her into going to see about the job. When they returned, they packed their bags and left. It all happened so fast."

Agnes Voorhees leaned forward and spread her hands as if in supplication.

"I did my best—begged her not to act so hastily. She did call once to thank me and say she was all right—said she owed that to Father Kaspar. However, she wouldn't give me an address. Why only last week, Sister Anne learned of an opening for a clerk's position for a German banker; would've been perfect for Katy, so I tried my best to find her. I remembered the name . . . a Mrs. Maloney on Canal Street. Wonder of wonders, I obtained a phone listing and called, but a woman with an Irish brogue told me Katy no longer worked there. She just didn't show up one day."

"And Baylie?" Alex probed.

Agnes shook her head, frowned, and said, "The woman put Baylie on the phone, but she was very sullen and defensive . . . Wouldn't tell me anything."

"Do you have an address for this Mrs. Maloney?"

"Yes I do. I'd forgotten. The operator gave it to me and I wrote it down."

Agnes stood and crossed the room to a small writing desk where she hunted in one of its drawers.

"Here it is. I don't know why I kept it, except the whole thing bothered me so much and I felt I'd failed Katy and Father Kaspar as well."

She extended the paper to Alex and offered, "You're welcome to take it, though I don't know what good it'll do you."

A Dutch priest? Laundry work?

It was all so confusing, but at least it gave him somewhere to start. He stood to leave.

"Thank you, Mrs. Voorhees, you've been most kind."

"God go with you. I pray you find her."

"I won't stop until I do."

Alex twisted his hat in his hands.

"We were to be married. I can't go on without her."

"Then, make your petitions known to God, young man. God answers prayer."

"Yes."

Tears stung Alex's eyes.

"I'm learning that."

• • •

Afternoon shadows gathered by the time Alex reached Canal Street. A cold wind whipped the leaves on the sidewalk, and he feared Baylie had already left work.

He walked faster and searched out the house numbers. *This must be the right block.*

Ahead, a stout young woman emerged from the last house on the corner. Short and stout, she wore a thin brown coat and heavy oxfords. Alex met her on the broken sidewalk.

"Excuse me," he began.

She pursed her lips and turned her cheeks into fat dumplings. Then, she barreled toward him so he had to jump aside.

"Stop!" he ordered as he regained his footing to block her path. "Are you Baylie Root? I'm Alex Meisen, a friend of Katy Thannen."

The girl's stare started at his feet and ended, unblinking, eye-to-eye. Alex felt a flush rise from his neck.

"So, you're the famous Alex."

The girl gave a scornful snort. Alex's heart thudded in his chest.

"She told you about me?"

"Well, she had to talk to someone. You sure weren't around to do her no good."

Alex looked away from her punishing stare.

"I know well I let her down. I have to find her."

Baylie snorted again.

"Good luck. Left me high and dry, she did. Month's rent was due and I with barely enough to pay it. Let alone eat!"

"Left? When? Why?"

The pitch of his voice rose higher with each question like a schoolgirl's. A smirk crossed her sullen face.

"Kind of late to be worried, ain't it? Nothin' you can do, anyway. I gave her the doctor's name and that's when she took off . . . Haven't seen her since."

Blood pounded in his ears. Alex forced himself to concentrate, to glean from her every word.

"'Course I made sure I got more pay here," Baylie went on. "The old lady can't do without me."

She jerked her thumb over her shoulder toward the house she had left.

"But I still need a roommate . . . Got me a lead at the pub."

Alex gripped her shoulder. His fingers dug into the cloth.

"You said something about a doctor? Was she ill? Tell me!"

Baylie wrenched out of his grasp and pushed him away with both hands. Alex staggered to maintain his balance.

"Look here, Mister. I don't have to tell you nothin'!"

Alex fought for control. He pulled his wallet from his pocket and took out a crisp bill.

"I'm sorry. I really am. I know you befriended Katy; helped her find work."

He held the bill out toward Baylie.

"I'm indebted to you for that. Maybe I could help with your rent in return for the doctor's name."

Baylie eyed the money, her eyes narrowed.

"Well, I did do her a big favor, you know . . . for almost no thanks. Stuck my neck out. Lied to Mrs. Maloney . . . Told her Katy was sick that day. All so Katy could look up that quack. Then, I come home, dead tired, of course, to an empty room and a few bills on the table. How's that for thanks? And after all I did for her. What a sneaky coward . . . Couldn't even tell me to my face! Well, I don't owe Miss Uppity a dime."

She snatched the money from Alex's hand and stuffed it inside the threadbare coat, deep down into the cleft of her bosom. Her large teeth protruded from lips pulled back in a taunting grin.

She taunted, "Want to find her pretty bad, huh?"

Alex clenched his fists to his sides to keep from shaking her.

"I made you a deal," he said as he raised his voice.

"All right. Name's Adler . . . Somewhere in Harlem. That's all I know."

"And why did she need a doctor?"

"Hey, I told you what you asked for, do your own detective work."

Baylie pushed past him.

"Men are so stupid, specially the good-lookin' ones. You're prob'ly better off not finding her. This doc ain't exactly on the up and up . . . Could mean trouble."

As Baylie walked away, she turned her head to look back.

"Good luck, Mister," she mocked.

Anger and despair threatened to overwhelm him. The chilly wind rustled trash against the curb. Alex pulled his coat collar close about his neck. The low rays of the sun cast his shadow on the sidewalk. It was too late to do any more.

With slow steps, he walked back to the main street where he hailed a carriage, aware of how weary he had grown.

The driver asked, "Where to?"

"A hotel," Alex answered, "something cheap."

"A few blocks over, twenty-five cents to take you there."
"Fine."
Alex leaned back and closed his eyes.

CHAPTER 17

Street vendors began shouting their wares at an early hour. Alex woke from an exhausted sleep and hurried to dress. He was anxious to be on his way even though he realized the doctor's office would not yet be open. He wondered how far it was to Harlem.

Alex repeated the name again, as he had countless times, "Adler, Adler."

As he stepped out onto the sidewalk, he saw a food vendor approach with his cart. The odors of fresh-baked bread, smoked salmon, and pungent cheese triggered a growling in his stomach, and the recognition he felt starved. He had not inhaled those aromas since leaving the valley of Egg.

The young man had a pleasant face and a wide smile.

"Guten Morgen. Breakfast?"

"Yes. I'll take some of each."

"Splendid."

The vendor laughed his delight and hurried to oblige. He tilted his head back toward the hotel.

"New here?"

"Yes. Last week."

Alex noted the skullcap and wondered what part of Europe the young man came from. He spoke German, but most inhabitants of Brooklyn did as well.

"Myself? A little over a month. Name's Hiram. This here's my cousin's cart. He's been here a year."

"Pleased to meet you."

Alex paid for the food and edged away. He was unable to eat and talk at the same time. The small loaf laden with salmon and cheese made his mouth water.

"Good day," he called over his shoulder, "and good luck."

The young man doffed his cap.

"Shalom," he called back, "till we meet again."

At the corner pharmacy, Alex put coins in the pay telephone and dialed the operator.

"I need the Harlem address for a Dr. Adler, please."

"One moment, please. There's an Anton Adler in Harlem, but he's not listed as a physician."

Alex wrote down the address she gave him.

"Thank you," he told her. "Thanks very much."

Strange a doctor doesn't advertise himself as such. How do patients find him? What difference does it make? He has to be the right man.

Alex hardly believed his good fortune—he found Mrs. Voorhees, then Baylie, and, now, this doctor in such a short span of time. It was miraculous. *I'll be reunited with Katy in no time at all; perhaps, this very day.*

He ran the distance to the elevated train, bought a ticket, and bounded up the stairs.

The ride north would have fascinated Alex under other circumstances. He had seen large cities before, but the mystique of this gateway to the New World provoked endless curiosity for immigrants, rich and poor. Today, however, Alex's thoughts rested elsewhere.

How he longed to put his arms around his precious Katy, explain what had happened, and assure her of his love. He believed everything would be all right, he felt certain of it. When he obtained her address, he planned to buy flowers . . . a mixed bouquet of bright colors to convey his happiness.

Why had she left the immigrant home in such haste? Why did she need to see a doctor? Could she be in a hospital?

The thought terrified him. Then, he recalled Baylie saying Katy returned to the flat to get her things and relief flooded through him because he realized it could not have been anything serious.

The conductor announced, "Harlem!"

Alex got off at a busy intersection where streetcar wires crisscrossed overhead. A hack stood at the curb; the driver scratched his whiskered chin as he lounged on the seat.

Alex showed him the scribbled address.

"Yeah, these are my streets."

The driver sat up straight and pulled on the points of his plaid vest to straighten it.

"That there address lies over a piece. Be glad to take you there."

"No thanks," Alex said, "I prefer to walk if you could give me directions."

He took some coins from his pocket and held them out.

"Obliged," the man muttered.

The fare was more, but the driver gave Alex the directions needed.

Once Alex took a wrong turn, but retraced his steps and came out at the right street. Shops lined the sidewalks. Above them the lettering on second-story windows announced the presence of various professions: attorney, dentist, palm reader, and tailor. *There it is: Anton T. Adler, Medical Practitioner. Female Complaints.*

Alex hesitated and reassured himself, "It was probably a delicate, private concern, but how else can I find her?"

He opened the door and climbed the flight of stairs. Along the hallway, black lettering on frosted glass panels spelled out names on office doors.

Alex found the office he sought and turned the door's porcelain knob. Two women sat on folding chairs in the sparsely-furnished waiting room and looked up from their magazines. He saw no receptionist.

"Is Dr. Adler in?" Alex asked no one in particular.

One of the women jerked her thumb toward a closed door.

"In there," she mumbled.

Alex sat down in one of the empty chairs. Both women stared at him, but then turned back to their magazines. The silence twitched only when one of them turned a page. Although both women wore coats, Alex felt perspiration break out on his forehead.

He started to remove his coat, but then the inner office door opened. A young girl—followed by a graying, stoop-shouldered man—came through it.

"Good day, Miss Brown," the man said to her back.

His spectacles glittered.

"You'll be fine."

The girl nodded and hurried out the door.

Alex jumped to his feet.

"Dr. Adler? Excuse me, sir . . . I need a word with you. It'll only take a minute."

The man peered at him through thick lenses.

"Do I know you?"

"No, but I'm trying to find someone who may have been your patient. It's very important."

The spectacles flashed and Alex fought an impulse to step backward. The doctor spoke in a frigid tone.

"Information concerning clients is privileged, sir."

"Of course, but she's my fiancée. Her name is—"

"Stop."

The man put up his hand, palm out like a policeman stopping traffic.

"I won't allow further conversation unless the young lady is present."

He turned away in dismissal.

"Mrs. Schneidert, I'm ready for you now."

The woman folded the corner on a page of the *Woman's Home Companion*, to make a neat triangle. She stood, magazine in hand.

"Wait!"

Alex reached out, but the man grabbed the woman's elbow, guided her ahead of him, and then shut the door in Alex's face.

Alex banged his fist on the wooden panel. The other woman in the waiting room jumped up and fled into the hallway. Alex heard her heels clatter down the bare floorboards. The inner door remained shut and Alex pounded on it again with both fists.

"Dr. Adler! Please listen. I can explain."

Still no answer.

Alex's heart raced as he emerged onto the sidewalk without knowing how he got there. The sky had clouded over and a cold mist found its way under his collar; it chilled the sweat against his skin.

He shivered, his anger spent, but with a deep hollow in his chest. Not knowing nor caring which direction to follow, he stuck his hands deep in his coat pockets and started to walk.

CHAPTER 18

Alex remained at the hotel and reasoned Katy was most likely somewhere on New York's Lower East Side where German-speaking immigrants shared the bond of their common language. For weeks he walked aimlessly, too worried to think clearly, and made hundreds of inquiries in shops or with people on the street. *If only I had a likeness of Katy to show people.*

Sometimes even the image of her which he carried in his head seemed to be fading. It made him even more desperate to find her.

Alex wrote to his mother at least once a week and checked the post office often for her letters of encouragement. They were a solace to his soul.

Each night he reached for the Bible Sam had given him and searched the scriptures for the strength to go on another day. He kept a bookmark at the book of Matthew which read "Come unto me, all ye that labor and are heavy laden, and I will give you rest."[5]

He also prayed. At first, he felt awkward and inadequate, as he often did around people. *Why do my thoughts form clearly in my mind, but come out hesitant and self-conscious when I try to voice them? If only Sam was here to instruct me.*

However, Sam was gone and Alex had nowhere else to turn. So, he persisted and cried out from his heart.

"Why Lord, why?"

Even when no answer came, he repeatedly returned to the Bible to seek an answer. Late one night, weary and broken-hearted, he fell to his knees and wept tears of frustration and despair. Almost as if a hand rested on his shoulder, he sensed Someone understood. Not only understood, but cared.

---

5   Matthew 11:28, KJV

A great tenderness and compassion enveloped him. He slept a deep sleep and awoke comforted and renewed. Except for the brief time with Sam, Alex had never known a companion he truly counted on. Thus, he discovered the Christ of the gospels—the One who knew his thoughts in the lonely darkness was one and the same. Jesus had become his friend.

Aware he needed a better plan, Alex did two things. He placed an ad in the PERSONALS section of the newspaper with the hope Katy might see it. He also searched the paper for part-time employment to allow him to continue looking for her.

Instead of further depleting his funds, he vowed to save money to begin their life together. Never once did he allow himself to think he was not able to find her.

An opening for a tutoring position caught his attention. It required someone who spoke German to help a young student perfect his English. With the first stirring of hope he had known in weeks, Alex made the telephone call. That same afternoon, he sat down with a German businessman and presented his qualifications.

Herr Jaeger made his living buying and selling property. He had arrived in America only a few years previous and his business had prospered. He lived with his wife and eleven-year-old son in a fine home in Brooklyn Heights. Roland was his only child and Herr Jaeger desired the boy's education be the best possible.

"My son attends private school in the mornings," he told Alex. "In the afternoons you'd oversee his homework and perfect his English."

He paused.

"One thing more, do you believe in Christ as your savior?"

"Yes, I do."

The answer came swift and sure.

"Splendid. I look forward to sharing our faith during the dinner hours."

Alex swallowed hard and confessed, "Herr Jaeger, I know the notice stated live-in accommodations, but it's important I continue to live where I am now. I hope that isn't a problem. I can be at your house for whatever hours you wish."

Herr Jaeger frowned and fingered his short, pointed beard.

"I'd prefer for you to be a part of our household, but I suppose you have your reasons."

He paused and ran his fingers through the thin hair combed back from his high forehead.

"Perhaps you would have dinner with us once or twice a week?"

"I'd be delighted."

"Good. Plan to meet my wife and son tomorrow night—six-thirty."

With a firm handshake, he showed Alex to the door.

As Alex left the realty company, he caught a fleeting glimpse of a young woman who walked through the outer reception room. Something about her walk and build reminded him of Katy. His blood rushed to his head as he started to call out, but stopped himself. *Surely, my mind's playing tricks on me. Katy neither dresses nor wears her hair in that fashion.*

He had almost made a fool of himself. He shuddered to think what Herr Jaeger would have thought.

• • •

A warm friendship developed between Alex and the Jaeger family. Roland proved to be a likeable young man and an able student. Their hours together passed pleasantly.

After weeks of loneliness and isolation, Alex looked forward to the twice-weekly dinners and lively discussions that followed. The questions and insights gave him an even greater hunger to study God's Word. In the lonely nights, he often did so.

His notice in the PERSONALS section went unanswered. He posted a description of Katy in public buildings and shop windows. The flyer read: MISSING PERSON and noted his telephone number for contact.

On Christmas day, Franz Jaeger lit the last advent candle and read the beautiful account from Luke of the birth of Jesus. Alex felt his heart stir, yet no holiday mood came upon him. *Where's Katy this day? Will I ever find her?*

• • •

In February, ruthless winds whipped snow into deep drifts and halted traffic as surely as freshly-poured concrete. Office workers stayed home and the Brooklyn Bridge closed to traffic.

Katy used the time to do assignments for her night class, but the confines of her rented room closed in on her. She made her way back to Hiram's and Hannah's apartment instead.

Over time, she had poured out her story to Hannah, minus the part about the pregnancy and what had happened in the doctor's office. The two of them looked out the window at the whirling snowflakes.

Hannah said, "I still can't believe Alex deserted you. Something happened. As I've said before, I think he followed you to America and is in the city right now, searching for you."

"That's all very romantic," Katy answered, "but, if so, I'm not sure I want him to find me. In fact, I'm not sure of anything anymore."

"Don't say that," Hannah admonished. "Be sure of the God of Abraham. He led Moses out of the wilderness. He can lead Alex to you. Nothing is too great for Jehovah."

Katy felt torn. Yes, she wanted to know what had happened to Alex, but so much had changed. She had killed their child. She could never expect him to forgive her. *After what I've done, how can I be a good wife?*

• • •

A fierce snowstorm confined Alex to his hotel room. As long as he continued his search, he managed to feel somewhat in control, yet the gloomy landscape only darkened his despair.

When, at last, the blizzard abated and brigades of men and boys began shoveling the snow into horse-drawn wagons, Alex ventured onto Canal Street. He took in gulps of the frosty air; glad to be outside, he walked for blocks.

Up ahead he saw a street vendor. The striped awning on the cart somehow lifted his spirits.

"Hello there."

Hiram rubbed his hands together and cupped them to blow on his fingers.

"Still around, I see."

The unexpected greeting startled Alex until he recognized the cheerful little man who had fixed him a sandwich so many weeks ago.

"I'm afraid so," he answered. "I'm searching for someone."

"And who might that be, if I don't mind me asking?"

Stories of separation circulated often among Jewish immigrants. Many sent wives and children on ahead, and then searched them out upon arrival.

"Her name is Katy. Katharina Thannen."

Hiram's eyes grew wide and his mouth fell open.

With more assertion, Alex asked, "Do you know her?"

He reached across the cart to grab Hiram by the arm and pull him close.

"Know her!"

Hannah had told him every detail of Katy's story.

"Are you Alex?"

• • •

Hannah invited Katy to stay for Shabbat and Katy accepted. She loved the warm family feeling of the Friday ritual. Hannah lifted the braided Challah bread from the oven while Katy peeled potatoes, an ordinary scene until Hiram burst through the door.

"You're home early," Hannah remarked.

Hiram put a finger to his lips and pointed over his shoulder to the stranger behind him.

The awkward silence caused Katy to turn and see Alex in the doorway. The potato fell from her hand and rolled across the floor.

Baby Moses reached for it and squealed with delight. With one arm, Hiram scooped him up. With the other, he propelled a sputtering Hannah into the next room and closed the door behind them.

He's a total stranger, Katy thought.

Her vision blurred and noise intensified—the baby's wails and the distant clang of streetcars seemed deafening. A stream of cold sweat ran down her back. She resisted falling by reaching both hands behind her to grip the edge of the counter.

For a brief moment, she allowed herself the luxury of overwhelming relief, a dropping of her great burden of desperation and loneliness. Then, hurt and pride resurfaced. Although her hands shook, she turned her back to him and picked up another potato.

"Where have you been all these months?" she asked, her tone flat.

"Katy, darling!"

Alex started toward her, but stopped short as if some invisible barrier stood between them. Katy turned toward him once again.

He's changed. Premature gray edge his temples and his clothes hang on his bony frame. Even his eyes are different, sunk deeper in their sockets, perhaps from the ordeal of the crossing; but no, it's deeper than that, as if his suffering has been refined while mine has not.

Of course, that's what money and position do for a person. It insulates him from the desperation I've known these many months. He probably made the crossing in first class, found a good job. An educated person from a good family can always meet the right people, find the best opportunities. Perhaps, he did feel some guilt and remorse, but I don't need his pity.

The thoughts jumbled in her mind.

• • •

Alex catalogued the changes—the unfamiliar clothes and hairstyle, loss of weight, and peculiar mix of rage and panic in her wide eyes. They held him back from rushing to embrace her as he had so often dreamed of doing.

Yes, she's the same girl I'd seen at Herr Jaeger's place of business.

"Katy," he sighed heavily.

He reached out for her, but withdrew his hand when she turned away.

"You've got to listen to me. There was a train wreck . . . Near Frankfurt. I was in a coma for three days. When I finally made it to

Rotterdam, you'd already sailed. I took the next boat and I've been searching for you ever since."

"Train wreck?" Katy asked and frowned. "Oh what does it matter? It's too late, anyway."

Too late? Alex thought in disbelief.

"Oh no, Katy, don't say that."

Panic caused his voice to rise.

"I love you. I want us to be married as soon as possible. Don't you understand?"

He studied her face and made no further move to touch her, as if he saw into her mind and sensed its fragility.

"Katy," he slowly said and chose his next few words carefully, "my finding you is a miracle of God. I cried out to Him and He heard me. When I finally gave over my useless efforts, He placed my feet on the right path. It was no accident I ran into Hiram today."

His blue eyes blazed with such intensity they riveted hers to his.

"If anything, Katy, if anything, I love you with a deeper love than ever before. I have immense admiration for your bravery in going on alone; your tenacity in making a way for yourself. Now, I'm here to relieve you of that burden. I want to spend my lifetime ensuring your happiness."

• • •

He's the one who doesn't understand, Katy thought dully. *If only he'd found me sooner—before Dr. Adler. But would he have wanted a child so soon, before we even started the new life he had so carefully planned?*

No doubt his finding her involved some incredible coincidence, but she had never known Alex to talk about God. She knew Hannah said prayers for her. *But Alex?*

Yes, marriage to Alex was certain to solve a lot of her problems. She probably never had to worry about money at all. Alex always had plenty.

For some reason she thought of Father Kaspar and his reference to the "shipwreck" of wrong decisions. The decisions of the past few months had been forced upon her by her circumstances. Maybe now was the time to make one that gave her a new start.

"All right, Alex," she said. "I'll marry you."

Even to her, the words sounded cold and distant.

Alex rushed to her side and reached for her hand to press it to his lips. Then, he folded her into his arms. She yielded to his fierce, yet tender, kiss. Yet, she still felt lonely.

•   •   •

Hannah and Hiram were ecstatic. Hannah sparkled with plans for a festive celebration with food and dancing. Only with great reluctance did she reconcile to Katy's demand for a simple ceremony. Alex, however, did not mind . . . whatever Katy wanted, he wanted also.

The parish priest performed the sacrament with two nuns from his parish who served as witnesses. Hiram and Hannah, along with Cousin Myron and his wife, Gerta, sat in one pew and Herr Jaeger with his wife and son, Roland, were seated across the aisle.

"God works in mysterious ways," Alex observed.

He was in awe to find he and Katy had the same employer. Katy found it a coincidence almost too weird to contemplate.

Minutes before the ceremony began Agnes Voorhees slipped in and took a seat. Alex had thought to invite her. Katy said she did not mind. The woman had been kind to her at a most desperate time. Katy only hoped she refrained from asking questions.

"Alex Meisen," the priest began. "Do you promise to love and to cherish, for richer or poorer, in sickness and in health, to have and to hold, forsaking all others, 'till death do you part?"

Throughout her young life, Katy had dreamed of her wedding day—the white dress, the traditional crown atop her hair, music and dancing, and an admiring crowd of family and friends. Yet, she stood stiffly in the black skirt and white blouse of her working attire, her face without expression, and her answers wooden.

Dreams of adventure and romance had fallen by the wayside. Nothing had turned out the way she had pictured the day she sat on the pier and read Alex's letter.

With deep regret, Alex thought of his mother, who should have been there. However, he stayed intent on every word, determined to impress each vow upon his heart as sacred. With God's help, he was going to be a good husband and show Katy faith surmounted any problem.

She needed time to get over the hurt, time to be assured of his love, time to trust in their future together. Then, everything was assured to fall into place—they were going to have a wonderful life.

PART TWO

CHAPTER 19

Morning light filtered between the lacy patterns of the curtain. Alex stirred, and then lay still again with his back to her.

Is he asleep? Katy wondered

She had hardly slept at all. Once Alex had turned over and reached for her. He whispered her name, but she feigned sleep, so he settled back under the luxurious comforter.

She knew their wedding night disappointed him. Alex told her as much, and then hastened to acknowledge it as the expected result of such an eventful day. Yet, she knew differently.

The seed of desire which had sprouted so joyous in the forest glen had withered into a stony pit. She was only seventeen, but she felt dried up, as dead inside as the dust baked into the ornate plaster of Paris molding which edged the ceiling above.

When Alex roused and turned over, his ruffled hair gave him a boyish appearance that belied his twenty-five years.

"I knew you'd look beautiful in the mornings," he told her.

Katy eluded his grasp and reached for her robe.

"Let's get dressed," she said. "I'm starving."

Yet, Alex lingered and crossed his arms behind his head.

"It's so nice here," he called after Katy as she disappeared into the bathroom. "Let's stay until we settle into the house in Brooklyn Heights that Herr Jaeger promised to help us find."

• • •

Some things Alex knew he was not able to recapture. He was never going to greet Katy with flowers at the boat dock, be married by the ship's captain, nor carry her over the threshold of a well-appointed cabin in first class quarters. Perhaps, a longer stay in this extravagant suite was one way to convince her of his determination to make up for the past.

The previous night had proved a poor beginning. During the past months, he had relived their rendezvous in the mountain glen many times, and anticipated the joy of their reunion.

He told himself it was going to take time to erase the months of worry and hardship. Time and patience on his part, patience he owed his young bride. He recalled the night onboard ship when the epidemic broke out—Sam told him of the courage and comfort to be found in Christ. He longed to share this knowledge with Katy, but he needed to wait. She was not yet ready to hear it.

He called room service, ordered coffee and poached eggs with ham and biscuits, and watched as Katy ate every last morsel.

"Words can't express my thanks to God for bringing us together again," he told her.

She kept her eyes on her plate.

"I thought it was Hiram."

"Hiram was the instrument, but the Spirit of God guides us when we ask for direction."

"Honestly, Alex, I don't know what you're talking about. You've changed with all your talk of religion. It makes me uncomfortable."

Alex reached for her hand, kissed the finger tips, and said, "Well, you haven't changed. You're as enchanting as ever, although I still mourn the loss of your beautiful tresses."

"Bosh."

Katy had picked up the expression from girls in the office.

"It's the latest style. Besides, it's much easier."

"But long hair is a woman's glory."

"Says who?" Katy asked tartly. "I'll bet it was a man."

"You're right . . . The apostle Paul, in fact."

Katy gave him a piercing glance and asked, "Are you studying with a priest?"

"No. Why?"

"Then, you're getting all that from reading the Bible on your own. Trying to be holier than the Pope, Alex, or just holier than me?"

"Neither, love. Come, let's change the subject."

•   •   •

A bright sun greeted them as they left the hotel. The doorman made a deep bow.

"Good day, Mr. and Mrs. Meisen."

"Thank you. Same to you," Alex replied.

Katy walked several steps ahead.

"Let's go shopping," she said over her shoulder. "We should buy something to take to Hannah and Hiram when we go to their place for dinner tonight. It's only good manners."

"A great idea!"

Alex was delighted by her unexpected thoughtfulness. If only his mother had heard, she would no longer worry about Katy measuring up.

"We owe them so much," he added. "How about a crib? Moses is fast outgrowing the dresser drawer. We could have it delivered this afternoon."

Katy studied her gloves.

"I suppose so. I had candy in mind, or flowers, but I've never given anyone such an expensive gift. It would be worth it to see their faces."

"Then, let's do it."

They found a furniture store where Katy fancied an expensive maple crib on rockers. The corpulent sales clerk gave Alex a broad wink.

"You'll rock many a babe in this 'fore it wears out," he boomed in a loud voice.

Katy scowled, but Alex stepped in to reply, "We intend to."

He knew he had made a mistake when Katy shot him a furious look. Seconds out of earshot, she turned on him, hands on her hips.

"You have no leave to make me feel like a brood mare in front of a total stranger."

"What did I say? I didn't mean—"

"Never mind what you meant. I just want to make myself clear."
Her bottom lip quivered. "I have no intention of bearing a passel of
'kinder,' and certainly not 'til we can well afford it."

Alex studied her face. He had no idea what caused the outburst.

"I agree we need a start first," he ventured. "But money isn't
everything and children will be a great blessing."

Katy set her mouth, but said no more. Instead, she asked to go
back to the hotel suite where they ordered sandwiches from room
service and she retired to the bedroom. Alex took his Bible to read
in the lobby, puzzled by the turn of events. *What had I said? Why
does she react so whenever I mention children?*

· · ·

The table held four place settings.

"It's just us," Hannah told them. "The cousins left to visit family.
But come and see."

She put her hands to her rosy cheeks. A beaming Hiram stood
behind her.

"There never was a more beautiful place for a baby to lay his head!"

Hannah's eyes shone as she led the way down the hall to
their bedroom.

"The store delivered it right after lunch. Must have cost a fortune."

She put a finger to her lips as she pried open the door. The
crib was wedged in the tight space beside their bed. Moses slept
on his stomach.

Hannah ducked her head, her voice barely above a whisper.

"Katy, I always knew you loved Moses more than you let on.
Sometimes I thought you blamed him for what I went through the
night he was born, but when you have a child of your own, you'll
understand how all that's forgotten. I'm just so grateful to discover
how much you truly care."

As Alex watched plain-faced Hannah and skinny Hiram, their
arms entwined as Hannah bent over the sleeping child, he experienced a wrenching stab of envy. The innocence of their kind
faces reflected their open hearts and the strong bond between

them, as well as that with their child. Katy had not told him about the baby's birth on the ship, but then she told him little of the months they were apart.

The round oak table was laid with Hannah's best linen. She had prepared a special dinner of dishes she knew to be Katy's favorites: leg of lamb, potato latkes, and cherry cobbler with its perfectly browned crust.

The conversation recalled the wedding—the guests, the beauty of the vows, the miracle Katy and Alex had found each other again. Katy said little.

They retired to nearby chairs. Hannah refused Katy's offer to help with the dishes. The baby awoke and Hannah brought him out from the bedroom and placed him in Katy's arms.

Katy sat upright in the chair, arms stiff around little Moses. Soon, she handed him back to Hannah who gave him to Alex. Hiram retrieved his zither and sat on a wooden stool to strum a lullaby while Alex held the child close and gazed upon his face.

Soon, Katy announced it was time to leave.

"I go back to work tomorrow," she told their hosts.

As they put on their coats, Hiram told them his news.

"I bought my own cart today."

His beaming face and straightened shoulders showed his evident pride. With an arm about her waist, he drew a blushing Hannah close.

"Soon, we can move to our own place. Then, we can fill another dresser drawer."

"Oh you!"

Hannah poked him in the ribs with her elbow.

"Best of all," she continued as she laughed, "we'll have room to entertain without putting relatives out of their home."

"That's wonderful news."

Alex turned to his wife.

"But it's our turn next. Isn't it, Katy?"

Katy stiffened.

"Of course," she replied.

Hannah hurried over and gave her a hug.

"Turns don't matter. Much more important is we're friends. We just want you to be as happy as we are."

• • •

When the door of Hiram's and Hannah's apartment closed behind them, Katy lashed out at Alex.

"I don't know how to cook fancy dishes and you're committing me to serve company? I could never make a meal like we had tonight and it's not fair for you to put me on the spot like that."

Alex took her arm and pulled her close.

"Oh, Katy, every new bride gets jitters the first time she entertains. We'll buy a cookbook and do it together."

Katy wanted none of it.

"It isn't just the cooking, Alex. It's the whole idea of being a wife and mother. I'm not ready for that."

"Of course, you're not," Alex said. "I know we need to get on our feet first, but we can dream about it. You'll be a wonderful mother when the time comes."

He wouldn't think so if he knew what I'd done.

Katy wrenched her arm free and kept space between them on the carriage ride back to the hotel. Once inside their hotel room, the bathroom door closed behind her and she stayed there until Alex went to bed and turned off the light.

The following week, Herr Jaeger showed them several houses in an affordable area, but Katy found something she did not like about each of them. Staying longer in the expensive room at the hotel was no longer an option, so, at last, they rented a furnished apartment.

Using her job as excuse, Katy convinced Alex to take their evening meals at a small neighborhood café, except for Sundays when they ate dinner with the Jaeger family.

Katy did not much like those occasions, but Herr Jaeger was her employer also, so she dared not refuse.

"Why must the subject always turn to religion?" Katy asked in complaint. "It makes me uncomfortable. Even young Roland discusses religious history and doctrine, whatever that is. I feel so out-of-place."

Alex hugged her close.

"I pray every day God will reveal Himself to you as He has to me, Katy."

"Whatever that means," she countered and twisted away.

The part she did like was the walk several blocks back to their apartment from the Jaeger home. She let Alex take her hand as she peered through lit windows of the houses they passed. She loved seeing how the rooms were decorated and imagined the day they might be prosperous enough to own such a dwelling.

She sat on the sofa, English book on her lap, and legs tucked beneath her as she worked on her assignment. She was proud of the progress she had achieved in her weekly night class.

Herr Jaeger praised her and said she was soon going to qualify to be the receptionist. The woman who held the position planned to leave in another month.

"Katy?"

Alex put down the newspaper and waited until she looked up from her book.

"I answered an ad in the Times yesterday."

"Humph."

Katy returned her eyes to the page. Alex gave her daily reports, but so far had not found the right fit for another position.

Alex got up and crossed the room to sit at the other end of the sofa. When he spoke, his tone was so earnest she, at last, gave him her full attention.

"Katy, listen to me. The ad I saw promoted land in Iowa at bargain prices."

Katy frowned.

"Just when I think I know the city, there's a new neighborhood. Iowa. Is that in Queens?"

Alex pressed his lips together to stifle his laughter.

"No, my sweet, Iowa is a state . . . A thousand miles west of here."

He waited until she looked up and he knew he had her full attention.

"It has some of the richest farm land in the world and this is a good time to buy. The railroads have opened up the way to world markets and overall farm conditions have improved. But the '90s' were hard times. Some farmers couldn't make it. They're forced to sell and banks are ready to make the loans."

"Alex Meisen!" Katy's tone held an ominous inflection. "Do you have some romantic notion about heading west in a covered wagon? To live in a log cabin, and fight bears and wild Indians?"

She swung her feet to the floor.

"If you do, think again!"

When Alex saw her fierce expression, he turned the Crusader ring round his finger with his thumb and chose his words with care.

"We'd go by train," he told her. "Iowa's no longer a frontier. Over three hundred thousand people live there. It's nearly the size of England and almost all of it is under cultivation."

Katy expression mirrored her skepticism; she asked, "How do you know so much?"

"I told you. I answered the ad, talked to the people who sell reclaimed land. They gave me a booklet published by the Iowa Board of Immigration with all kinds of useful information."

He placed his hand on the back of the sofa to lean close, his face only inches from hers.

"Katy," he said, "I saw the ad, and then yesterday something happened I saw as a sign from God."

"No doubt the clouds spelled out Iowa."

This time Alex's expression remained intent.

"No, I got a letter from Sam. Samuel Schneider, the friend I made on the crossing."

Katy swung her feet to the floor and nodded as if to hurry him along.

"When we went our separate ways," Alex continued, "Sam said he'd write me at General Delivery so we'd stay in touch. I check at the main post office every other week or so, and last week I received a letter.

"He's preaching on a circuit through the Middle States and he mentioned Iowa in particular. Said a large number of German-speaking immigrants are settling there and building fine communities. I trust Sam to tell the truth."

"So?" Katy countered. "German immigrants have prospered here as well. Look at the Jaegers."

How can I make her understand?

"I'm not interested in riches, Katy. I'm talking about freedom to own land without being born to it. A future for our children limited only by a man's willingness to put in honest toil among people who subscribe to Christian values."

Katy turned back to her lesson.

"Do we have to talk about this now? I have class tomorrow night."

Alex stood. His shoulders slumped and his voice reflected his discouragement.

"All right, darling. We'll talk later."

• • •

On Saturday, Alex brought the subject up once again. Katy realized he meant to pursue it. The spring morning burst with sunshine and fresh air as they walked home from Mass. Katy wore a new hat with a perky white feather, her dark hair curled in soft layers beneath it.

"The land agent showed me a map," Alex began.

He held her hand in the crook of his arm and pressed it to his side as he stopped walking and turned to face her.

"We can buy one hundred and sixty acres for three dollars an acre near a town called Lake City in the north central part of the state."

Katy frowned in her effort to multiply in English.

"That's almost five hundred dollars."

"Four hundred and eighty to be exact which includes a team and wagon, a plow, and a cultivator and harrow with some other implements thrown in. And listen to this, Katy, the owners even left furniture in the house."

Katy adjusted her hat and continued walking.

"Furniture, why would anyone leave furniture?"

Alex hurried on and explained, "There's a house and barn.

Separate buildings—not one on top of the other like in Austria."

"You mean people live right on their land?"

In Austria, crops filled the fertile valleys. Farmers clustered their homes in hillside villages and drove wagons out to their fields.

"We'd have neighbors close by."

Katy did not make sense of it. Over time, she believed life in the city might be bearable. They each had steady jobs, and they were studying to become citizens. Alex seemed to want to throw it all away.

"But an even better opportunity might turn up here," she persisted.

Alex turned the key in the lock of their apartment door.

"This land won't be available long. Someone else will snap it up. Besides, if we leave for Iowa next month, we'll still have time to plant spring crops."

"Next month? That's impossible."

Katy's eyelids pinked, close to tears.

"We'll talk about it later," Alex conceded as they entered the apartment. "Just think about it. That's all I ask."

Katy, however, knew he had made up his mind. Already, she counted the losses. In addition to her job, they continued to see Hiram and Hannah. She also had several new friends at work. As she rode the trolley home, she often thought back to Blanche Maloney's laundry tubs and how far she had come since those days.

A familiar routine had developed which she had never thought possible a year ago. She and Alex still had their ups and downs, but they had started to forge a new life together.

Most of the time, she pushed what she had done out of her mind. The familiar routine helped. Now, they would be starting all over again.

She removed the hatpin and laid her hat on the foyer table.

"Why would you want to live like a peasant?"

"Not a peasant, Katy, a landowner."

"You don't know a thing about farming."

She took off her gloves and flung them beside the hat.

"I can learn. Please try to understand, Katy. When I lived with my cousins in Egg, I came to appreciate the rural way of life. It's such a simple, honest way to earn a living . . . A partnership with God to subdue and replenish His creation."

"I have a headache," Katy told him.

She turned her back and went into the bedroom where she closed the door behind her.

• • •

Hannah poured cups of tea and set a plate of cupcakes on the table.

"Men can be infuriating . . . No doubt about it. Yet, God made women to be a helpmate to their husbands. Sometimes it's well to defer to their decisions and trust God has granted them wisdom. Besides, it's different for you. People like Hiram and me immigrate to American cities to band together with other people of our faith and carry out our traditions. You can go anywhere and be accepted."

Katy studied the plain face of this precious friend who had been so good to her. *What she's saying is probably true.*

"Still," she replied, "no one is going to make up my mind for me. I'll have my say."

In the days ahead, however, Alex continued his persuasions. When they sat at the breakfast table or walked home from the Jaeger's, he quoted the land agent's glowing descriptions. At night he read aloud from the journals of early settlers whose words described hard-won accomplishments with satisfaction and pride.

"Katy, I hear what you're saying. You've worked hard and accomplished so much. I, however, am responsible for our future and this is a decision I must make. It would just be so much better if you trusted me to do the right thing."

• • •

At last, Katy gave in. She had on her nightgown and was ready for bed.

"After all, you have the money," she said with considerable heat. "If you're that determined, what choice do I have?"

"No, Katy, darling, the money is ours together, but we must be good stewards of what God provides. I have a strong conviction this is the future God has prepared for us."

He grasped her hands in his, brought them to his lips, and held them tightly while he kissed her fingers one by one.

"This is a new beginning for us, my precious. With God as my witness, I won't let you down again."

"Words," Katy huffed to herself.

How can he make such a promise?

She pulled her hands away and turned off the light.

"Lake City," she repeated the town's name to herself.

Not very imaginative, but a lake's a lake. Not the Bodensee for sure, but a lake will help.

CHAPTER 20

Leaving Hiram and Hannah proved to be hard. Katy and Hannah cried, and Katy spent the afternoon on the train in silence. She took back her hand when Alex sought to hold it and closed her eyes to shut out the wooded hills of Pennsylvania, poignant reminders of her beloved Bregenzerwald.

Alex had spent money to ride in a sleeping car in order to make the trip more comfortable. After the porter made up their bunks, Katy lay awake a long time, watched for each station's red signal lantern, and listened for the train's whistle as it rounded the curves. The sound was as lonely as the thoughts which spilled tears on her pillow.

If only Alex had found me before I went to see Dr. Adler; if only I had Sofie to confide in or, at least, had written down her address to write; if only . . .

The train passed through Ohio during the night. It reached Indiana the next morning, where greening grass spread to the horizons and orderly towns appeared. The pointed church spires and tidy clapboard houses granted a sense of permanence and orderliness which continued in the crisscross of surfaced roads. Red barns, and black and white dairy cows dotted the countryside.

Alex and Katy ate in the dining car. At stops, they stepped out on the depot platforms to stretch their legs before the conductor's call returned them to the train.

The next day they rode through Illinois. Katy expressed relief at seeing a city the size of Chicago.

"Look, Alex. There's one of those carriages that run without horses."

"Iowa is next," Alex told her. "On the other side of the Mississippi River . . . It's not far now."

Just as the sun set, the train crossed the river bridge and the town of Dubuque spread over the opposite river bank. Quaint Victorian houses perched on the shadowed bluffs.

Katy placed her hands on the windowpane and leaned up close.

She asked with a breathy voice, "Is that it? Is that Iowa?"

Alex reached for her hand and squeezed it.

"The Indians named it: the Beautiful Land."

Cathedral spires poked into the sky and a riverboat with a large paddle wheel laid at anchor.

"Dubuque!" The conductor called.

"Sounds French," Alex commented, "charming."

Katy's spirits rose, but when they awoke the next morning, the countryside spread flat again and stretched out to the horizon. During breakfast in the dining car, a steady drizzle streaked the train windows and deepened the gloom. Katy kept her eyes shut, tapped her foot, and drummed her fingers on the arm of her seat.

The land was flat—miles and miles of it. After lunch, Katy dozed. Then, at last, the conductor announced their stop. He called off the names of several towns, including Lake City. Alex stood to collect their things from the overhead rack.

A middle-aged couple seated across the aisle also prepared to leave the train.

The man asked, "First trip out?"

"Yes," Alex replied. "We've purchased land near Lake City."

"Good. We're the Kirks . . . From Lake View. Been back to Chicago selling hogs and ordering furniture at Sears Roebuck."

Katy perked up.

"Did you say Lake View?"

"That's right, it's a few miles on west."

"So, your town has a lake as well."

Mrs. Kirk looked puzzled, and then broke into a hearty laugh.

"There's no lake in Lake City. It's named after someone named Lake, although I've heard it did have a lake some fifty years ago. Pond Grove Lake, I believe they called it. Good-sized, so they say . . . drained off years ago. Come over to Lake View if you like to fish. Bullheads the biggest you've ever seen."

Katy turned away to collect her purse and hide her disappointment, but Alex hurried to reply, "Thanks, we'll do that."

• • •

They stepped off the train which soon departed. Wet cinders patterned the lonely platform. An unpainted two-story depot stood stark against the gray sky with flat prairie fanning out in all directions.

In a wagon nearby, a man sat holding the reins of a sturdy work horse.

"There's Albert Junior. Come get our bags, son!" Mrs. Kirk called. "Is someone meeting you folks?"

"Yes," Alex answered. "That must be him now."

A tall boy of fifteen or so walked toward them. He wore overalls, a flannel shirt, and a slouch-brimmed cap. As if to balance the stiff gait of his heavy work shoes, he swung his arms—one hand held a furled umbrella.

"Good. We'll be off then . . . Godspeed."

Mrs. Kirk hiked up her long skirt and Mr. Kirk tipped his hat as they hurried toward the waiting wagon.

"Mr. Meisen?"

Alex extended his hand to the boy and confirmed, "I'm Alex Meisen. This is my wife, Katy."

"Thad Heim, your neighbor's son."

He took Alex's hand in a brief grip, and then lifted the cap and pushed a thatch of straight brown hair from his eyes. He nodded at Katy.

"Here, ma'am, Ma sent this along. The wagon's open."

His voice trailed off when he saw Katy already held an umbrella.

"Oh well," he shrugged and handed it to Alex instead. "You'll need one, too."

"Thanks," Alex replied, "most thoughtful. Did the land man send you?"

"He wrote a letter to my dad . . . Should've told you that right off, I guess. My real name's Thaddeus. Folks call me Thad. My dad's been boardin' your team. Guess you owe him for hay."

"Yes, of course."

"Wagon's out back."

Thad picked up two suitcases and Alex took the others. Katy lagged behind.

Alex boosted her onto the front seat. The wagon, a long flat box made of weathered boards, had iron wheels and a long wooden tongue pulled by horses. Thad untied the reins from the hitching post and held them as he climbed up beside Katy. Alex took the springboard seat in the rear.

"Is this the team?" Alex asked from the back with registered surprise.

"Jake and Jed are ornery and stubborn as any pair could be."

"What kind of horses are they?"

Katy was bewildered as she stared at their long pointed ears and broad backs.

"They ain't horses. They're mules, ma'am. Cross between a donkey and a horse."

He held the reins loose and let the animals plod ahead at their own pace.

"Fewer of 'em 'round here now than years back when everybody was usin' either mules or oxen for bustin' sod."

"Oxen?"

Alex leaned forward as if not to miss a word.

"Yeah. You've heard the expression, 'strong as an ox'? Virgin prairie grass has roots in rock-hard soil. Takes either an ox or an ass to plow it up. Mules stand heat and hard work better'n horses, and got more common sense, too. A horse'll go 'til he drops, but a mule quits when he's had enough. And when he's too hot, he won't drink his fill. Lots of farmers own both, for different jobs. My dad does."

"I have so much to learn," Alex admitted. "I assumed by team you meant horses."

"Yeah, well, a pair of good plow horses are fine, but once you get 'em goin', critters like these can be a lot more abidin'. They'll stay in the field long after a horse is back in the barn."

A general store and a brick building with CREAMERY painted in red on the side were the only buildings near the depot. Flat countryside spread before them as far as Katy was able to see.

"Surely this isn't Lake City!"

"No, ma'am. Yetter. Lake City's five miles south. Illinois Central brought the line here a year ago. Serves several towns."

Five miles, she thought as her chin dropped.

Puddles lined both sides of the road.

"Been wet," Thad offered. "Need a dry spell to get the crops in."

"The land agent said Iowa has good drainage," Alex offered.

He leaned forward like an eager schoolboy.

"Progress every year," Thad acknowledged. "My grandfather says the county was one big swamp when he came fifty years ago, fit for nothin', but muskrats, coyotes, frogs, and mosquitoes. Said a person lookin' out from the home place saw land so boggy if you jumped up and down on one corner, water'd squash up on the opposite."

Thad chuckled at his joke.

"Needed fires built at night so cows were able to stand in the smoke to rest from flickin' off skeeters. If settlers like my grandpa hadn't dug drainage ditches, there'd still be nothin', but field mice and bullfrogs in these here parts. Now, farmers bury tile underground. We've buried miles of it on our place."

The mud made smacking sounds as the mules slogged through it. The one Thad called Jake relieved himself—muck mixed with manure as the wheels mashed the two together.

Katy covered her nose with her hand. Alex pointed out stands of trees surrounding the homesteads they passed.

"Good windbreak," Thad said. "As you can tell, you don't have to travel far to find a neighbor . . . Not like Kansas or the Dakotas. Soil so rich a man's got his hands full with fewer acres. He builds him a house and a half mile away another man does the same."

"I told you so, Katy," Alex said, relieved to find it true. "It won't be lonesome at all."

Katy did not answer nor give any sign she heard.

Thad adjusted his cap and pulled the brim down lower.

"Don't have far to go to get grain milled or horses shod. 'Course some towns are dying that ain't near the rail line. Farmers want grain elevators and livestock yards near the depots, so they can get the best prices in Omaha or Sioux City."

"Makes sense to me."

Alex settled against the seat.

A long silence followed, broken only by the sucking sound of the mules' hooves and the animals' occasional snorts. Here and there the road—more or less—disappeared, but the mules seemed to find their way regardless.

"Did we keep you out of school today?" Alex asked.

Thad shook his head and replied, "No, I ain't been this year . . . Finished sixth grade, though. Pa only went through third. He and Ma are strong for book learnin', but I've had enough. Good farmers learn by doin'."

He jerked the reins to turn left, but the animals ignored him.

"Haw, you jackasses!" Thad yelled and they stopped in their tracks.

Katy almost fell off the seat and Alex reached to steady her.

"S'cuse me, ma'am," Thad said. "They make me powerful mad sometimes . . . Used to rile Pete, too."

As the mules began a slow curve to the left, Thad put both reins in his left hand, took off his cap, and scratched his head.

"Pete?" Alex questioned.

"Pete Gregg's the fella that quit your farm."

A clump of cottonwoods laid ahead.

"Quit, you say?"

"Yeah. Had a wife and three little girls. Mary died givin' birth to the last. That's when Pete left and went back East. 'Course they'd barely made it 'fore that, anyways."

Alex saw the rigid set of Katy's shoulders and feared the worst. Her mouth was more than likely set in the hard line he had come to dread. He saw a barn behind the trees—a red structure, weathered gray. Then, he spotted the house and his shoulders sagged.

No more than a small cabin, the dwelling was built of horizontal boards to which only a few flakes of paint still adhered. A narrow plank door sat atop a high threshold and tar paper covered a roof topped by a brick chimney circled with a tin collar.

"That's the house?"

Katy's tone said it all.

Thad nodded and asked, "Not much, huh?"

Alex looked beyond the cabin to the marshy land along the creek bed. Not a temporary pond caused by too much rain, but long-standing water surrounded by swamp grass.

Thad pointed north.

"There's your good cropland. This here needs dirt fill and tile. Too low to drain itself off. Pete never had the cash to do it. Take it you got the place pretty cheap?"

Alex swallowed and replied, "I guess so."

"We thought as much. What . . . Three, four dollars an acre?"

Alex nodded. He knew by the flush on Katy's neck she resented Thad's questions, but of course, land prices were of interest, the sale likely registered at the courthouse. Public knowledge—the way things were done in a government by the people. He did not want to have it otherwise.

The wagon stopped and Alex jumped down. He offered his hand to Katy, but she ignored it to climb down from the seat herself and march through the wet weeds to the door. As she touched the latch, the door swung open on its own.

Concerned, she questioned, "Why isn't it locked?"

Thad snickered and answered, "Nobody locks their doors. Doubt if there's even a key for it."

"What about Indians?"

This time Thad laughed out loud.

"Ain't been no Indians for years. Though my dad recalls a few trappin' and fishin' along the creek before I was born."

• • •

Katy crossed the cabin threshold with her head held high. She shivered and hugged herself, but it was not just the damp air causing a chill. It was as if she trespassed where someone else lived.

The room bore witness to thoughtful care. On a wall above the iron bedstead, a framed sampler read: A MOTHER'S PRAYER in rich embroidery and a cushion done in needlepoint rested on a cane-backed rocking chair. A braided rug made from colorful scraps of cloth laid on splintered floorboards. In one corner Katy spied an iron cook stove near a roughly-hewn table and two chairs. An open bare cupboard stood beyond.

She strolled into the bedroom where she found a double bed and a chest of drawers made of pine. Pink ribbons tied back the muslin curtains and in one corner a wicker crib stood embellished with a frill of crocheted lace. In an alcove beyond, brightly-colored patchwork quilts topped bunk beds.

Thad Heim cleared his throat and scuffed the toe of his heavy boot on the bare floor.

"Pete left sudden-like. Couldn't take much on the train, I reckon."

"How could anyone leave behind keepsakes like that sampler and cushion?" Katy probed.

Her dark eyes flashed as she pointed to the crib.

"It's indecent . . . and that . . . I won't abide leaving that in here."

"I understand," Alex answered, although his puzzled expression showed he did not. "I'll take care of it."

He turned to Thad.

"Thanks for coming after us. I'll take you home and settle up with your father for the hay."

"It's only half a mile," Thad replied. "I'd as soon walk. Oh, I almost forgot."

He went outside and returned with an oilcloth-covered basket which was in the rear of the wagon box.

"Ma sent this food for your supper, seein' as how you wouldn't have supplies laid in yet."

"That's very kind," Alex said and extended his hand. "Please thank her for us."

"Neighbors got to help neighbors, my dad always says. Just pull the wagon inside the barn and take the harness off Jake and Jed. I pitched some hay in the stalls 'fore I left this mornin'."

"Thanks," Alex stammered, embarrassed by his obvious need for instruction.

"Don't mention it."

The door closed behind Thad.

• • •

"There's no bathroom," Katy announced.

She still held the umbrella. Water dripped in a small puddle at her feet.

"I saw a privy out back."

"Privy?"

"An outhouse."

Alex went to the window. The narrow shack stood fifty feet or so from the house, between the barn and the chicken house.

He pictured the board seat with the stench coming up through the open hole. Likely Katy's family had used something similar and he had brought her half-way round the world to nothing better.

He tried to put his arms around her, but she twisted away.

"Katy, Katy," he pleaded. "It won't be for long. I promise. I'll start on a new house just as soon as the crops are in."

Katy opened the food basket and started taking out the contents. When she spoke, her voice was as cold and flat as the expression she wore on her face.

"We haven't eaten since breakfast," she stated.

They still wore their coats.

"I'll get some wood," Alex replied.

Behind the house, canvas covered a stack of kindling. Alex carried an armload inside and started a fire in the cook stove. A cast iron washtub hung from a peg on the wall.

"I'll fetch water from the well for baths," he told Katy.

She did not answer so he left to prod Jake and Jed toward the barn. As he struggled to unhitch the wagon and remove the bridles, he felt as inept as he was exhausted. He leaned his forehead against Jake's back and whispered a prayer.

"Dear God, did I hear You wrong? Did I misunderstand what You had in mind? Please help me."

•   •   •

Katy stood the umbrella near the stove, took off her coat, and hung it on one of the wooden pegs beside the door. She did not wait for Alex, but emptied the contents of the basket, removed the bone from a piece of chicken, and slipped the meat between thick slices of homemade bread. She held the sandwich in her hands and ate it in just a few bites. She ignored the apple pie, and then made up the double bed with blankets packed in one of their suitcases.

By the time Alex returned from the barn, Katy was on her way to the outhouse. Once inside the putrid necessary, she let the tears come and swiped at them with the heels of her hands. When she returned to the cabin, Alex had a fire started to heat water for bathing.

Katy went directly to the bedroom to unpack her flannel nightgown. Then, she asked Alex to tack a blanket across a corner of the room where she washed and undressed behind it.

She saw how his shoulders drooped, yet she stiffened her resolve. Alex had brought her to this place and she needed to make it clear how much she hated it.

She blew out the candle on the nightstand and climbed under the covers, only to slide to the middle of the sagging mattress. She clutched the edge and moved back to her side where she pretended to sleep while Alex sat at the table to eat his sandwich and a large piece of the pie.

The kerosene lamp flickered shadows against the wall. His shadow loomed large among them.

At last, he undressed and put on his nightshirt. Then, he banked the fire by heaping the glowing ashes, and closed the dampers of the iron stove. Katy watched. *Where did Alex learn to do that? There are still so many things about him I don't know.*

When he blew out the lamp, Katy expected him to climb into bed. Instead, she felt only a slight movement of the mattress as he knelt to pray. The shadow of his bent head loomed large on the wall.

Maybe he's as scared as I am, she thought, yet when Alex climbed under the covers, she hung one arm over the edge to prevent her body from rolling toward him.

• • •

Sun streamed in the window to awaken them, their bodies curved together, spoon fashion. Not fully awake, Katy felt cozy and comforted. Then, Alex moved away.

"I saw some boards in the barn I can cut to brace up the mattress," he said, "will make it firmer. Meanwhile, I'll add some wood to the fire and boil water for coffee."

Katy stayed under the covers until the strong aroma lured her out of bed where she faced the west window. In Mary Gregg's garden plot, patches of strawberries and rhubarb poked up from the untended dirt. Raspberry bushes formed a hedge along one side and hollyhock vines climbed up the broken fence.

Beyond the wild grasses, prairie violets and buttercups peeped out, beyond that willow trees lined the bank of the creek. When she raised the window, bird songs reached her ears. She stretched her arms above her head and turned back toward Alex.

"The coffee smells good."

Alex smiled; his face registered his relief as he took down a china cup from the cupboard.

"Here, sleepyhead, have some. Coffee is all I can offer until we go to town this morning. I'll put that crib in the barn and we can stop by the Heim place to return the picnic basket and ask Mrs. Heim what to do with the sampler and cushion."

Katy made no comment. Somehow, Mary Gregg's things did not matter so much this morning. She sat down at the table and drank the coffee, and then cradled the cup in her hands.

"I made a list of staples," Alex said and placed the list in front of her. "Look it over and add whatever else you think we'll need."

Katy read through the long list.

"I suppose we could plant some vegetable seeds," she commented.

His raised eyebrows registered his surprise.

"Good girl. Write it down."

Alex disappeared into bedroom. He reappeared with the folded crib under his arm. As he crossed the room and carried it out the door, his back was straight, his step brisk.

CHAPTER 21

The government brochure indicated the town of Lake City had two thousand residents due to the arrival of the railroad. This population justified two banks, a post office, a newspaper, several churches, two school buildings, numerous mercantile establishments, and a substantial number of dwellings on both sides of the rail lines.

The town boasted its own water system and fire department and, only recently, a two- story high school had replaced one which burned down. When Alex and Katy arrived at the town square mid-morning, two workmen labored to install another street lamp beside the plank sidewalk encircling it.

Alex halted Jake and Jed in front of the general store. It had taken some doing to bridle the team and hitch them to the wagon, but he had done so. He watched for Katy's reaction to the town.

As she sat beside him on the wagon seat, he took pride in her appearance—a plaid shawl over the white blouse and black skirt of her office days. A black taffeta bow held back the unruly tumble of dark curls that grew long again.

• • •

She allowed Alex to hand her down from the wagon and surveyed the local establishments. The bank building commanded the most respect. It stood on the corner and occupied a fourth of one side of the square. Its brick exterior had a classic design which rivaled many structures she had seen in New York. Ornate decoration adorned the top corners and cement arches framed the tall windows on the first floor.

Storefronts bordered the rest of the square in a variety of styles; some were more imposing than others. Grass and flowers surrounded a bandstand gazebo in the center, and carriages were parked along the sidewalks, their horses tied to hitching posts.

A bell tinkled as they entered the general store. Fred Blair, the storekeeper who wore garters which gripped the sleeves of his white shirt, came forward to greet them. While he and Alex filled their order, Katy browsed the aisles of merchandise.

Two young women stood with their heads bent together as they appeared to inspect a display of hat pins. They stopped talking as she neared.

The tall redhead asked, "Good day, new in town?"

The other girl twisted the cuffs of her long-sleeved shirtwaist. Her gaze rested on Katy's out-of-fashion, high-buttoned shoes.

"We bought the Gregg farm," Katy answered.

The girl dropped her hand and looked up with sudden interest. A knowing look passed between her and the redhead.

"Pete Gregg's place?"

"You poor thing," the redhead said sympathetically.

Katy felt heat on her neck.

"What do you mean, 'poor thing'?"

Katy's tone was indignant.

"The farm needs some work, but it has good cropland. Thaddeus Heim told us so."

"Sure. Thad Heim and Pete Gregg were thick as thieves. Everyone knows half the land is under water and poor Mary never had a decent roof over her head."

Warmth rushed through Katy's entire body.

"The land may need draining and the house may not be much, but my husband intends to build a new house right away."

"With plantin' coming on? Oh, don't get me wrong. Mary Gregg was a saint. Broke her back carin' for them children and doin' for the church, bringing in fresh vegetables for needy folk—if you can imagine anyone more needy than her. And every Sunday, flowers for the altar. But that good-for-nothin' Pete was good for nuttin', but gettin' drunk and keepin' poor Mary pregnant."

The other girl gasped. The redhead turned and gave her a look.

"Oh, don't act so shocked, Rosalia. The word's in the dictionary. When he did come to church, at Easter and Christmas, Pete preened like a peacock, acting like he owned the place, walking on ahead of poor Mary, leaving her to watch the little ones. Heaven help those children now."

"I must go," Katy muttered and backed down the aisle. "My husband's waiting."

"I'm Maggie Tate!" The redhead called after her, "and this here's Rosalia Bottrop!"

The bell jangled as Katy hurried outside where Alex stood loading their purchases into the wagon.

He asked as she approached, "What's the matter?"

"Nothing."

Katy climbed up onto the seat.

"Just hurry up. Did you get garden seeds?"

"No, I waited for you to pick them out."

"Never mind. I need to ask Thad's mother what kinds to buy. Hopefully, she has more sense than her son."

"Thad?" Alex blurted curiously. "Why do you say that?"

"It's not important. Just hurry."

Alex dropped the subject. As they rode, he commented on the broad, tree-lined avenue and the stately residences fronting it.

"Why must we live way out in the country?" Katy asked once again.

Alex sighed, "It's the way it's done here, Katy. If we intend to farm the land, we must live on it."

"You're as smart as any of the people who live here, Alex Meisen . . . Probably smarter. You could live in town and do any number of things besides farming."

"We've bought the land, Katy, and I intend to succeed at farming it. But that doesn't mean we can't take part in the life of the community."

"It's not the same and you know it."

Katy squeezed to the far side of the seat.

The sun beat down hot on the rough road. Alex pointed at

jackrabbits as they scampered across the road, and a quail which flew out of the grasses. However, Katy held onto her brooding silence.

• • •

At length, Alex turned the mules into a long lane which led up to the Heim farmyard. White-washed fence posts and a wire fence surrounded the well-tended yard of a two-story farmhouse fronted by a broad porch. Chickens pecked the ground nearby and pigs squealed somewhere distant.

Alex pulled on the reins to stop the mules at the farmyard gate. A lean brown dog bounded round the corner of the house and barked furiously.

"Bowser, stop that!"

The screen door slapped shut and a string bean of a woman— judged by Katy to be at least seventy—called out to them.

"Don't mind that dog. Wouldn't hurt a flea, though I'm glad when strangers don't know that. I'm Beulah Heim, and you must be the Meisens."

Alex jumped down from the wagon.

"Yes. Alex and Katy."

Bony fingers gripped first his hand, and then reached up for Katy's.

"Welcome!"

Close up, Katy changed her mind about the woman's age. Her brown hair had only a few streaks of gray and the deeply lined face held clear blue eyes. Katy reached for the picnic basket at her feet and extended it.

"We appreciated the food."

Her words sounded stiff and formal.

"Most generous of you."

Beulah took the basket.

"Now, what are neighbors for? Felix—that's my husband—and Thad are out in the field, but won't you come in? The coffee pot's on."

"Next time," Alex replied. "We have a lot to do today. Besides, we just came from town, and have butter and eggs to put away. Don't know how we'll keep them when we do get them home though."

"Put them in the root cave."

"Root cave?"

"Sure, every place has a dirt cellar for shelter in storms, if nothing else. I know Mary stored potatoes and vegetables in theirs, as well as any other perishables."

"That reminds me," Katy said, "what kinds of vegetables grow here?"

"Wait."

Beulah Heim ran lightly up the concrete steps and back into the house. The screen door slammed behind her.

"What did I say?" Katy asked Alex.

He shrugged, but Beulah soon reappeared with a tattered copy of the *Henry Field's* seed catalog in her hand.

"Newly germinated," she said. "Not hidden away on Fred Blair's shelves for heaven knows how long."

She handed the catalog to Katy and said, "The seeds I plant are marked. I've already mailed my order, so you're welcome to keep the catalog. There's another order blank inside."

"Thank you."

Katy fingered the colorful pages and realized she had committed herself. *I'll actually be expected to grow a garden.*

Alex reached to the back of the wagon for the blanket-wrapped bundle.

"This is sort of awkward, Mrs. Heim—"

"Call me Beulah."

"All right."

He cleared his throat.

"You see, Beulah, the former owners left some personal items in the cabin and we don't know what to do with them."

Alex unfolded the blanket and Beulah Heim's mouth twisted as she fingered the sampler and cushion.

"Pete seldom thought of others. 'Specially his kin. If it's all right with you, I'll keep these to send on for the children if I ever hear of their whereabouts. Very thoughtful of you to save them."

Katy remembered the redhead's remark about Pete and Thad. She suspected it somehow explained the bitter inflection in Beulah's voice.

On the way home, she told Alex about the conversation with Maggie and Rosalie. A muscle twitched in his cheek.

"Gossip is a tool of Satan, Katy. We mustn't abide slanderous talk about people we don't even know."

"I didn't abide it. I walked out, didn't I?"

"I didn't mean it the way it sounded," Alex added. "It's just that we're fortunate to have good neighbors and if they've had trouble . . . Well, it's their business."

"You don't have to lecture me. Besides, they slandered us as well—hinting at what a poor place we bought . . . How dare they!"

●   ●   ●

The next morning Katy copied her neighbor's selection to fill out her seed order. Alex leaned over, kissed her bent head, and inhaled the sweet scent of her soap-scrubbed hair.

"I appreciate how you're plunging right in like this," he told her. "Anything we produce ourselves will be a big help."

"I'll show those two smart alecks."

She licked the stamp and attached it firmly to the envelope.

"We'll have the best farm around, 'specially when the new house gets built."

CHAPTER 22

Spring became summer as Alex and Katy molded a marriage out of exhaustion and isolation.

"Anything you need in town?" Alex asked.

"You're going to town today? This isn't Friday."

"I'm going to the bank to apply for a loan." *There, I said it.*

Katy looked up from the table where she stemmed strawberries in a blue granite basin.

"A loan? Why do we need a loan, for heaven's sake?"

"Because we don't have enough money to last until we sell the crops."

Yes, he knew he had not been forthright concerning their finances. Whenever Katy needed cash for something, he gave it to her. Still, she had to be aware of the expense— groceries, seed, a cow, chickens . . .

Katy glanced around the room.

"Of course, we do need a great many things," she mused, "even before you start building the house."

How can I tell her?

"Katy, I'm afraid the house will have to wait. Now, that the crops have been planted, the pond must be drained, fence built . . . We need more cows and chickens. Besides, the money we must pay back to my father."

"What do you mean, 'pay back'? You're intending to pay back money that's rightfully yours? The inheritance your mean, tight-fisted father kept from you so you'd have to do what he wanted? And especially now, after the way he's treated you?"

Her voice rose in pitch. She crossed her arms to hug herself as a shudder went through her body.

Alex's mother had written his father not only forbade the family to speak Alex's name, but had also stricken all reference to him from family records.

I hope with all my heart to see you again one day, his mother wrote, *but, tragically, for your father you don't exist.*

Alex berated himself for not spelling out the truth of their circumstances before. He had just assumed Katy had felt as he did—his actions came about as a desperate measure and must someday be rectified.

"Katy, what I did amounted to stealing."

"Stealing?"

She dropped her arms and stamped her foot.

"From your inheritance?"

"Yes, at least the way I went about it. I've had to repent, ask God and my mother to forgive me."

"I knew it."

She clutched the edge of the table and leaned toward him.

"You're sorry we ran away together."

"That's not true, darling. I love you. I could never be sorry I found you, at last; however, perhaps if I'd been more patient, earned some money of my own first."

"Patient? Where does patience get a person?"

Katy dropped her hands and began to pace back and forth in the small room.

"I agreed to your plan 'cause I thought it daring and exciting; I saw you as different from the dull boys I grew up around."

Has she ever loved me?

He dared not ask.

"Katy," Alex started as he fought to keep the tremor from his voice, "I need to go, now. We'll talk about this later."

• • •

Beulah Heim directed Alex to the barn where Thad and his father were ringing pigs to prevent their rooting under the fence. Alex had never heard of such a practice until Felix explained it. He watched, fascinated as Thad wrestled a squealing shoat onto a high bench where Felix deftly clamped the ring through its snout. His movements were efficient and humane.

The task completed, Thad went off to do other chores while Felix considered Alex's needs. Since his calving season had been productive—producing two sets of twins—Felix wanted to sell Alex another cow at a fair price. Three young pigs were also up for purchase, and later, the Heim boar was to be loaned to breed them.

Alex made a mental note to read up on farrowing—a term Felix used for producing a litter of pigs. Beulah parted with some of her brooder chicks and, most helpful of all, Felix offered a suggestion to drain the slough.

"At least twenty acres on this end of your land slopes toward my drainage tiles—you could dig ditches to intersect with mine for run-off to the creek. I tried to talk Pete into it, but he didn't have the inclination . . . or the ambition."

Felix Heim sighed and drew his hand down over his face. It was a gesture of frustration, or resignation perhaps; Alex could not tell which.

"Some folks you can help, some you can't."

Felix closed the barnyard gate and turned toward the house.

"Prob'ly be late this fall time you get that land drained and plowed, but you could still get in a crop of winter wheat. Meanwhile, you ought to cut those grasses during dry spells. Makes breaking sod that much easier and will fill your haymow in the meantime. Knowing Pete, the haymow's likely empty."

Alex wondered if Thad appreciated his father's wisdom. He doubted it from Thad's attitude which bordered insolence toward Felix. If his father had been willing to sit down and talk instead of issuing ultimatums, Alex might still be his father's son.

He found each day blurred into the next as he milked cows, mended fences, and cut the slough grasses for hay. In the evenings, he fished in the creek for bullheads and catfish. After dark, he studied copies of *Capper's Weekly* as well as pamphlets on agriculture put out by the state college.

In late summer, he started digging the ditches, and expended hours of exhausting labor to lay even a few feet of tile. At mid-morning and mid-afternoon, Katy went out to the well to fill a fresh jug of cold water for him—one of the few favors she granted.

He knew Katy's chores loomed equally unending: cooking, washing, tending and harvesting the garden, skimming cream off the milk to make butter as Beulah Heim had taught her, scattering corn for the hens, and hunting for their precious eggs.

Alex observed the tight set of her face as she went about her work. He tried to find ways to compliment and encourage her, but she warned him not to patronize her.

"We're both new at this," she said.

Cherries ripened on wild fruit trees, and raspberries grew on the bushes in the garden. When the chokecherries were ripe for picking, Katy labored over a strudel and rolled a crust from her precious store of flour.

When the bottom crust burned, Alex told her the filling was fine. Regardless, she threw the whole thing into the barnyard for the chickens to peck on.

"This ancient stove is impossible!" she raged. "Strudel and wie-nerschnitzel are two things your mother taught me to make. Now, I've ruined the strudel . . . and when I asked the butcher for veal, he looked at me as if I was crazy."

Alex laughed.

"Probably so. How about me bagging a deer? After the first bite, I'll bet you can't tell the difference."

"Don't try to humor me, Alex. Besides, I haven't seen any deer."

Alex did, however, supplement their diet with rabbits, quail, and pheasants. As long as he cleaned the game, Katy cooked it.

• • •

Every Friday, Alex harnessed the mules for the ride to town, and traded butter and eggs for staples like salt and sugar. They stopped at the mill for flour and the post office where they some-times found a letter from Alex's mother or Hannah Silverstein.

Alex also hoped for a letter from Sam in response to the one written to Sam's last known address.

"The townspeople seem so standoffish," Katy complained.

"Like who?"

"Those two I met in the store, the ones who gossiped about Pete Gregg and Thad."

She told Alex about how Maggie Tate and Rosalia Bottrop always crossed the street or ducked into the newspaper office to avoid her.

"You can't judge the whole town by two people," Alex told her. "We need to be friendly ourselves for others to respond."

"Why?" Katy protested. "We're the new people. Isn't it their job to make us feel welcome?"

Alex did not answer. As far as he was concerned, folks treated them fine.

"Anyway, don't talk to me about overlooking the actions of others, Alex Meisen. Maybe it makes you feel noble to plan on paying your father back, but you can't hide from me how you really feel about him. Can you honestly say you've forgiven him for the way he's treated you?"

The barb hit home. Alex turned away so Katy did not see how accurately she had aimed it. He avoided the issue, even with God, because he found forgiving his father an empty gesture.

• • •

When not completely exhausted, Katy longed for some kind of diversion from the everyday sameness. Sometimes, she tagged along on the rare evenings Alex had energy left to go fishing along the creek. She explored the sloping banks, picked ripe apples to eat, and one evening ventured downstream and made an amazing find.

Around a bend of the creek, and partially hidden by tall weeds and hollyhocks, a sod dugout faced the creek. Built into the high dirt bank, the front wall consisted of stones cemented together and centered with a rough plank door. The door creaked on rusty hinges when Katy pushed it open.

Lit only by two small windows on either side of the door, the shadowy interior contained an earthy smell. As she stepped inside, she found it cool and surprisingly spacious.

"Reminds me of peasant huts high up in the Alps!" Katy exclaimed when she retrieved Alex to show him her find. "Did someone actually live here, you think?"

"Must've . . . probably until they cut down trees and built the cabin."

The excitement and intimacy of their shared discovery stayed with Katy as they walked back to the cabin. She watched the rising moon, listened to the chirp of crickets, and felt as if she shared a bond with those who struggled before them. When Alex put his hand on her arm, her breath quickened and her flesh tingled.

"Let's not light the lamp tonight."

His voice was low, urgent as he pulled her to him. Katy amazed herself with her ardent response. Later she lay within her husband's arms as the moonlight streamed through the window and painted a bold stripe across the floor. Alex stroked her hair.

"I love you, Katy Meisen," he whispered.

"I know you do," Katy answered.

She was ashamed she was unable to answer with the words he wanted to hear. She propped herself on one elbow to plump the pillow, and then settled back down to sleep. *What would he think of me if he knew the terrible thing I'd done—the secret thing I never told anyone?*

• • •

The next morning, a dry hot wind swept up from the south and threatened to make the late August day all but unbearable. The mood of the previous night had vanished.

Katy trudged down the hard dirt path to the outhouse, and brushed away honeybees which buzzed at the door. She wrinkled her nose at the stench which had already risen with the heat.

After breakfast, she washed the dishes, tossed the dishwater into the yard, and draped the wet towel over a fence post. She lingered outside the cabin door, and looked past the garden to where coneflowers and prairie phlox grew wild along the creek.

Alex had already left to dig his infernal ditches. She had awakened to a nagging fear of what might result from their reckless passion. She pushed the thought aside and made a hasty decision.

Before she could change her mind, she untied her apron and hurried to change clothes.

"Alex can be sweaty and stodgy if he must—grasshoppers and toads are his constant companions. I'm going to town."

She struggled with the harnesses and wagon hitch, but she had watched Alex often enough. She finally mastered them and made haste to lead the mules out of the barn, lest Alex saw her and talked her out of going.

That's silly, I'm not a prisoner here, she thought; although, she often felt like one.

She hurried to the barn to grab a gunny sack and pail. Then, she ran to the chicken coop to gather a dozen fresh eggs. She wrapped them carefully in the sack, deposited the sack in the milk pail, and placed the pail in the wagon before darting back into the house.

After writing a note to leave on the table, she reached under the new mattress ordered from the Sears and Roebuck catalog. Alex felt it was her money as much as his, but he kept it and made decisions about how to spend it. She vowed to someday again earn money— hers alone to spend. *Meanwhile, how can he begrudge me two dollars?*

• • •

Beulah Heim stood hoeing her garden as Katy passed. She looked up and waved, but Katy pretended not to see her. She kept her eyes on the road and covered her nose with her handkerchief to keep from choking on the dust the mules kicked up.

Billowing clouds piled up massive towers in the sky behind her, but Katy faced a vaulted horizon which held no hint of gray. *A sprinkle or two would be nice, in fact.*

She had no umbrella, but it did not look to her as if she needed one. The sun glared down and wilted sunflowers along the fence rows. Heat from the burned earth quivered in the dry atmosphere.

The wagon rattled past other homesteads. Katy speculated on the occupants she had not met. The houses hid behind stands of trees and rows of corn stretched endlessly beyond.

The horseflies were savage. Jake and Jed suffered their bites and broke stride as they switched their tails and kicked in the traces. Katy found it better to loosen the reins and let the team manage themselves while she swatted at the flies.

When Alex drove, he sometimes sang hymns, inspired by what he described as the awe and wonder of nature. Katy saw nothing poetic about corn and grass. The pioneer spirit may have captivated Alex, but the day-to-day sameness wore her down.

•   •   •

Inside the town limits, Katy took her favorite route past nice homes set back from the street on spacious lawns and the Bellflower Hotel, a red brick structure fronted with white pillars. More carriages than usual filled the streets.

In the town square, a crowd of people milled about, spread blankets on the ground, and unpacked picnic lunches. Others occupied benches in front of the bandstand. Katy wondered what caused all the commotion.

She walked into the general store and felt as if she entered the mouth of a tunnel. Once past the front windows, the light grew dimmer and the air cooler as she progressed down the aisle of wooden floorboards.

While she waited for the stoop-shouldered storekeeper to finish with a customer, Katy held the heavy pail of eggs in front of her. She clutched the handle with both hands.

Merchandise either mounted the walls on long shelves, or resided in glassed-in cases accessed only when the storekeeper slid open a panel and reached in. The hat resided in one of these cases, alone as if placed there to tempt her.

An array of ostrich feathers curved over one side of the brim, black with a single white plume in the center. Katy had never seen anything so smart—a startling contrast to the everyday items one expected to find.

The hat seemed to call to her the way Father Felder told her the Lorelei of the Rhine beckoned to sailors. She giggled at the thought, and then set the pail down on the floor and leaned on the counter for a better look. Fred Blair appeared at her side. He leaned to see where she pointed.

"Three dollars," he said. "I don't generally stock hats like that, but a woman heading to Colorado traded it for bullets. Said she and her husband had more need for protection than frills; claimed she bought it on Fifth Avenue . . . Comes with a hatbox."

Katy did some fast figuring. Mr. Blair should give her at least a dollar for her eggs. With the two dollars in her pocket, she would have just enough.

"Hate to hurry you," the proprietor said as he adjusted the garters on his sleeves. "Store's closing in five minutes."

Katy glanced at the Seth Thomas clock which ticked away on the wall above their heads. The hands edged toward eleven.

She asked, "Why so?"

"Haven't you heard?"

He fingered the pencil behind his ear.

"There's a political rally today. Albert Cummins is running for senator."

Katy turned to look out the front windows. Men in their Sunday best were mounting the steps of the bandstand gazebo.

"Please wait," she told him. "I'll be right back."

She hurried down the street to the hatchery and sold her eggs and ran back. Transaction completed, she hurried out to stow the empty pail in the wagon, but returned to the square carrying the hatbox, as proud to show off the NEW YORK label as she was if she wore the hat. All the benches were taken, so she stood with others at the edge of the crowd.

The banner above the bandstand read: CUMMINS FOR SENATOR '02. Someday she and Alex were to take the oath of allegiance to become United States citizens, eligible to vote in upcoming elections. Here was a candidate for office right before her eyes.

Albert Cummins proved to be an accomplished speaker. Katy found he had interesting things to say concerning the needs of the state; however, the apparent disinterest of the townspeople caused her to frown.

Women talked behind fans which advertised the funeral home, children ran around the perimeter of the park, and only once, when Mr. Cummins touted trade tariffs, did the audience grant him a smattering of applause. A few men went forward after the speech to shake the candidate's hand, but the women quickly moved away.

Katy wanted to grab them by the arm and shake them. Many were immigrants like her and ought to care more. After all, this was not New York City . . . A vote more than likely made a difference here. *Maybe I ought to start reading the Lake City Graphic Alex brings back when he makes trips into town. Then, I can form an opinion on matters, one way or the other.*

She surprised herself with such thoughts, but she had never had occasion to form them before. The common people did not have a vote in Austria.

A few sprinkles of rain and a sudden burst of cool air hurried her back to the wagon. An angry bank of clouds spread over the southwestern sky. She secured her hatbox under the wagon seat and headed for home. Besides, she was hungry and had spent all her money.

· · ·

By the time she reached the edge of town, raindrops came faster and thunder rolled. Katy took the empty gunny sack out of the pail and spread it over the hat box, and then placed the box between her feet. She covered it with her skirt, and slapped the reins in an effort to hurry the mules. They, however, continued their slow plod, heads down.

Her thin cotton blouse and skirt soon soaked through. The skirt clung to her knees and water ran down her face and off her chin. The blue sky became a leaden dome with thunder reverberating within.

The first hailstones were small and scarce, almost imperceptible. Then, a cold wind swirled around the wagon and the pellets began to sting. They increased in size and intensity as they rained down harder and became a ferocious bombardment. Katy tucked the reins between her knees and covered her head with crossed arms which proved to not be enough.

She grabbed the empty tin pail and held it over her head with both hands. The noise was deafening. At least, she was able to open her eyes, but the hailstones bit into her hands and beat on her huddled shoulders.

She saw a flash of fire and heard a crash as lightning hit a nearby tree. The mules sloshed through water so deep it splashed up to the hubs of the wheels.

The sides of the pail obscured the sight of familiar landmarks. *Am I even on the right road? Do the mules know where to go?*

Although they plodded on, it seemed hours before she tipped the pail and sighted the cabin in the far distance. She never dreamed to be so glad to see it nor find the glow of lanterns so welcoming. As for Alex, she realized she would be relieved to see him.

About half a mile from home, the hail stopped. Katy lifted the pail and saw three figures holding lanterns by the end of the lane. They were huddled together under one large umbrella, but Alex broke away and ran to meet her.

"Katy! Are you all right?"

She nodded. Alex's worried look broke into laughter.

"What a sight you are! You look like Don Quixote with that pail over your head."

When he grabbed her round the waist and swung her to the ground, she dropped the pail and flung her arms about his neck.

"Oh Alex, I'm so sorry!" She wailed and pointed to the sodden gunny sack. "I spent three dollars on a new hat and now it's ruined."

"A hat? Well, never mind, there's someone you must meet, at last!"

He gestured toward the couple which hurried to catch up with them.

"Sam and Susannah Schneider. I still can't believe they're really here."

Katy failed to reply, but Alex did not appear to notice. He was intent on making introductions. As the couple drew near, he waited no longer.

"Sam and Susannah, meet my Katy."

CHAPTER 23

The rain slowed to a drizzle and the hail never reached the farm. Sam Schneider closed his umbrella and reached for Katy's hand which he squeezed with his.

"I feel I know you already, Katy, having spent so much time listening to this fella talk about you."

He paused for her response. When none came, he continued.

"Please forgive us for arriving unannounced. The temptation to surprise you and see Alex's face when I introduced Susannah as my wife was just too great, I'm afraid."

He let go of her hand and gave Alex an affectionate punch on the shoulder. Alex smiled, but kept his eyes on Katy.

Susannah Schneider stepped into the circle of her husband's arm where her head reached his shoulder. With one hand, she pushed blond ringlets of wet hair from her forehead.

"I tried to tell him it wasn't a good idea," she said with a nervous laugh. "But men can be so stubborn."

Katy had yet to speak.

• • •

So, this is Sam, the paragon Alex admires so much.

Katy judged him to be at least four inches shorter than Alex and not nearly as good-looking. Although, the dark eyes and curly hair fit his athletic physique, as did the deep voice. In contrast, Susannah was a wisp—a fairy nymph. Katy felt somehow diminished by her.

How am I supposed to respond to their unexpected arrival?

Alex cleared his throat and said, "Of course, it was a good idea . . . A wonderful idea. Right now, we'd better change into some dry clothes. I'll unhitch the mules and be right in. We have much to catch up on."

Katy followed Alex as he took the reins to lead the mules toward the barn. She ignored his questioning stare and turned back to Sam and Susannah.

"You can change first," she told them and gestured toward the cabin.

"As I'm sure you saw, we have almost no extra room. I assume you have other clothes with you?"

Susannah's blue eyes sobered, but Sam was quick to reply.

"Yes, we do. Thank you, Katy."

•   •   •

Alex strode through puddles toward the barn, his knuckles white on the harness strap. He looped the reins around the top board of the stall and jerked them into a tight knot. Then, he turned to face his wife, eyes dark with hurt and anger.

"That was extremely rude, Katy."

"I don't care."

Her hands balled into fists as she set them on her hipbones.

"What right do they have to barge in on us? Where are we going to put them?"

Alex fought to keep his voice down.

"You don't *put* guests anywhere, especially good friends like Sam. You invite them to make themselves at home, give them your bed, if necessary."

"Well that's easy for you to say, Alex Meisen. You don't have to cook, clean, and put up with them underfoot. You and Sam can always go off and dig your ditches. How long did they say they're staying?"

"I didn't ask."

He jerked a currycomb off a shelf and hurried to rub down the mules, his jaw set.

"They arrived only a few minutes ahead of the storm."

He sighed and pulled back his shoulders.

"I know you've been through an ordeal today and Sam is a stranger to you."

He reached to hug her close.

"Don't worry," he told her. "Everything will work out fine."

Katy did not answer. She stiffened in his embrace, the frown remaining. Alex forked some hay into Jed's stall and leaned the pitchfork against the partition. In the next stall, a mare snorted and sidled against the boards. Katy jumped.

"It's their horse," Alex told her.

She did not respond and Alex tried again.

"Katy, you've been saying how alone you feel when I'm in the fields, and how unfriendly some people are to you—"

"We can't all be like you, Mr. Perfect."

"I'm not saying this to criticize, Katy. You've had good reason to feel the way you do. But now we have opportunity to extend hospitality to others. Sam and Susannah can become lifetime friends, if given the chance."

"What makes you think so? Preaching like he does . . . Traveling all over the country. We probably won't even see them again. They're just taking advantage."

Alex sighed, his shoulders sagged.

"Sam's not like that. And I know he wouldn't choose a wife who didn't share his values."

"And maybe you did?"

Her words hung like icicles between them.

"I suppose she reads the Bible every day like you do."

"Maybe."

For months, he had allowed guilt to sidestep him from honest speech. However, the ease he witnessed between Sam and his wife made him impatient with the strain of screening every word he said to Katy.

He grabbed the soggy hat box and shoved it into Katy's hands. Then, he walked out ahead of her and looped the leather strap over the wooden peg to fasten the barn door. Finally, he turned toward the house.

"Give her a chance, Katy."

• • •

Susannah removed a parcel from one of their saddlebags and placed it on the table. She laid out a loaf of home-baked bread, thick slices of cured rabbit meat, and four rosy peaches.

"God always provides," she told Katy. "He gave Sam hands to build things and words to reach men's hearts. In return, people are generous to us."

Katy had used the small bedroom to gather her thoughts. As she changed into dry clothes and redid her hair, she knew her mother would scold her, tell her she was being rude and should be polite to visitors in her home.

She asked, "Your husband builds things?"

"Yes, Sam's a carpenter, a very good carpenter."

Susannah motioned toward the sodden bundle Katy had dumped on the sideboard.

"I'm sorry about your hat."

Alex and Sam remained engrossed in conversation as Katy reached in to gingerly pull the water-marked hat box from the wet burlap. *Three dollars wasted on a ruined hat. Susannah probably never indulged in anything so frivolous.*

Katy pried up the lid and peeked inside. She was surprised the tissues still looked dry. She plunged her hands deep inside the box and lifted an undamaged hat from papers that floated down to settle on the floor.

"Ooh," Susannah cooed. "It's breathtaking."

She stood on her tiptoes, tapped her fingertips together excitedly, and squealed, "Please, Katy, put it on."

Katy crossed the room to the oval mirror—Mary Gregg's mirror—and carefully lowered the hat atop her dark curls. Even she was not able to deny the effect. Her cheeks turned rosy and her dark eyes danced above a delighted smile.

In three long strides, Alex crossed the room to appear in the mirror, put his hands on her shoulders, and lean to kiss her on the cheek. Susannah begged to try on the hat, and they all laughed as it slid down over her ears. The laughter came easy.

"Remember the Bible story about the woman and the alabaster box?" Sam asked in retrospect. "Beauty to feed the soul is often more important than nourishment for the body."

•   •   •

Alex said the blessing.

"Thank you, God, for good friends and good food. Amen."

Amazing, he thought. *God used a hat to answer prayer.*

They ate the food Sam and Susannah provided to which Katy had added lettuce and radishes from the garden. At first, Katy turned up her nose at the rabbit meat, but discovered she liked it after all.

"Not that different from chicken," she observed.

While Katy and Susannah washed and dried the dishes, the men went outside to sit on the stone stoop. Talk came as easy as if the two men had been apart a month instead of a year. Letters helped, but the bond went beyond that.

"Have you found a church?" Sam asked.

"We attend Mass in Lake City on Sundays," Alex told him. "Father Felder is very kind and welcoming, but the congregation is small and made up mainly of older people."

"Why am I so self-righteous?"

Alex continued, changing the subject.

"I love Katy dearly, but sometimes I'm disappointed when she doesn't respond the way I want her to. I know the months before I found her were difficult, but she has shared so little about that time, I can't help, but feel shut out . . . as if she's keeping something from me. "

"We're human, Alex. We all let pride stand in our way at times, especially in regard to those who matter most to us . . . because of the very fact they do matter most. Only by remaining in right standing with God, seeking His help to love and forgive one another, can we grow to be more like Him."

"Speaking of forgiveness . . . ,"

Alex told Sam about his mother's letter, and the hurt and anger which kept him from forgiving his father.

"Have you asked your father to forgive you?"

"Not directly. But I did explain everything in letters to my mother and promised to pay back every penny . . . and, of course, I confessed my transgression to God."

"I think you know that's not enough, Alex. We all sin and fall short. God forgives, but He also requires us to seek forgiveness from those we sin against."

Katy and Susannah joined the men in the twilight. The night air was cool after the rain, but noisy with crickets which chirped down by the creek.

Alex and Sam gave up their seats on the stone threshold. Each stretched out nearby on a blanket spread over the damp grass, crossed their arms behind their heads, and gazed at the canopy of stars above.

They talked of many things. Born in North Dakota to Swedish immigrants, Susannah still lived at home when Sam came to town. He asked permission from a farmer to set up a tent in his field; the farmer proved to be Susannah's father.

"He swept me clean off my feet," Susannah recalled.

She theatrically drew the back of her hand across her forehead like a rescued maiden in a melodrama.

"Tent?" Katy questioned.

"Sometimes towns own a tent for circus events, county fairs, and the like," Sam explained. "If not, I post notices announcing a meeting in the park, a field, or a vacant lot. People gather and I preach under the stars."

He tipped his head back and swept his arm toward the canopy above.

"Like these. Susannah rides with me."

"But you have only the one mare," Katy remarked.

"Mollie? Yeah, I kind of like Susannah riding sidesaddle in front of me. Sort of like a circuit rider on the old frontier with his mail-order bride."

"Oh, you," Susannah protested.

"What about your belongings?"

"We don't need much. The Bible, my tools, a few clothes . . . What fits in a couple of saddlebags."

Sam explained he built furniture to provide a living, even a small house in Kansas.

"When I was single, I could always find a spare room or a haymow to sleep in. Now, it's more complicated, especially since . . ."

His voice trailed off, but even in the dark, the upward inflection of his voice hinted at a smile on his face. Susannah laughed.

"Sam, you tease. You can say it. We're going to have a baby."

Alex raised his body on one elbow.

"That's wonderful!"

He wished he could see Katy's reaction, but the sky had grown too dark.

"When?"

"Sometime in February . . . That's why we're aiming to settle in one place for a while. Susannah and I alone don't need much, but now—"

Alex scrambled to his feet, and paced back and forth. His hands were linked behind his back.

"Maybe we can help."

"Oh no," Sam stammered. "I wasn't implying—"

Alex feared how Katy might react, but he plunged ahead anyway.

"It's God's provision or, at least, I hope it is, and I'm not just being selfish."

He could hardly contain his excitement.

"When we arrived here, I came to realize I knew nothing and God had to teach me everything. I felt so scared and lonely; I cried out to Him for help. Now, you're here. Don't you see? God heard my prayer."

Alex strained to see Sam's face in the darkness. He wondered why it took so long for Sam to grasp his meaning.

"Don't you see, Sam? We need a decent house so we can start a family ourselves. You could help me build it, do some carpentry work for other folks perhaps. Why just the other day Felix Heim mentioned he needed some new hog pens. We could fix up the sod house for you and Susannah to live in, and share food from the garden. There's plenty of wild game around. The previous owner left some traps in the barn. We could trap for muskrat, fox, even mink—"

"Whoa," Sam protested. "You've lost me."

Alex herded them all back into the house

"Light the lamp, Katy. We have much to discuss."

• • •

Their sentences toppled each other during their spirited discussion.

"I'll have to finish the ditches first," Alex said.

"I can help," Sam offered.

"That's not fair," Alex protested.

"Sure it is . . . Part of the rent. By the way, how do you manage those mules?"

"I'll show you. How do you draw up plans for a house?"

Meanwhile, Katy and Susannah held a separate discussion.

"Wait 'til you see how the willows grow right down to the bank of the river," Katy said.

"I love to cook," Susannah offered. "Do you mind if I cook a big meal for all of us sometimes?"

Katy's eyes widened and she blurted, "Mind . . . Do you honestly mean it?"

"Oh yes, I do! Imagine me being a real housewife. I'd love it."

Katy paused, and then ventured on, "And perhaps I could get a real job . . . In town."

Alex heard the last and realized with a jolt Katy meant what she said. She sounded as if she had already given the idea considerable thought.

"Then, why don't you?" Susannah asked as if the idea made perfect sense.

"Maybe I will."

Sam raised his hands in surrender and suggested, "I don't know about you, but I'm about to cave in. How about sleep? We can talk in the morning."

Sam and Susannah insisted on sleeping in the bunk beds. Long after Sam began a soft snore, Alex lay awake as his thoughts swirled as in a whirlwind. One minute, he thanked God for sending Sam and Susannah. The next minute he panicked.

Surely, I'd be little or no help to Sam in return for what he might do for us. And Katy, talking about a job in town, leaving the cooking to Susannah. It'd be wonderful if Katy and Susannah were friends, but won't we be using these good people . . . taking advantage of them while giving little back?

At last, he closed his eyes and asked God for wisdom. He was determined to rely solely on His guidance and help. As he fell asleep, he began to mentally compose a letter to his father.

CHAPTER 24

The following week Alex helped Felix plant sorghum in the areas where the hail ruined his corn crop. He gave thanks to God the hail stopped before it reached their farm.

Sam went into town to fetch lumber he needed to frame larger windows in the rock front of the sod house. He took along a note of introduction from Alex to show the postmistress. When he returned, he brought back a letter for Katy from Hannah Silverstein.

Katy and Susannah were sweeping out the sod house when he drove up in the wagon.

"Take a break so you can read your letter," Susannah urged. "I could use a breather myself."

So, Katy sat down on the ground with her back against a huge cottonwood tree while Susannah stretched out beside her. Susannah's pregnancy weighed down her small frame, and she told Katy the hard ground felt good.

Hannah's cramped penmanship detailed the achievements of one-year-old Moses and announced Hiram and Cousin Myron had opened their delicatessen on Canal Street. She wrote:

> I can still hardly believe it. It could only happen in America.

Katy scanned to the last paragraph.

> I've saved the best news for last. Moses will have a brother or sister come next May. Isn't it wonderful? The doctor told me to be extra careful since my first delivery was difficult, but I'm feeling fine. Of course, Hiram is busting his buttons, handing out cigars already.

Katy dropped the letter onto her lap and leaned her head against the trunk of the tree. She closed her eyes and relived the memory of that terrible night onboard ship.

How can Hannah be excited about another terrible ordeal? What strength do Hannah and Susannah possess which I lack? And what about Mary Gregg . . . What good did it do her to be such a saint?

For several weeks, Katy had pushed the signs away and refused to believe she might be expecting another child. She thought she had carefully timed her monthlies, and had yielded to her husband's desires when she thought it safe. *How could I have been so stupid?*

As before, she kept the sure knowledge concealed in an icy reserve deep within her. Once again neither father nor future child had earned a voice or a viewpoint. She dared not risk their meddling.

After all, Dr. Adler required no second opinion, only cash money. It had been less than two years since the day she fled his office, relieved of worry and fear, only to acquire a burden of guilt and shame not so easily dismissed.

She had deceived herself into thinking the doctor was kind and concerned that morning, his long face with the thick spectacles almost fatherly. She wondered how she could have been so naive.

She had recently suffered a nightmare in which a man with a rat-like face peered into her eyes while instruments scraped at what felt like her very soul. The sharp teeth gnawed off each accusing word: *you made your choice, your choice, your choice . . .*

Katy shut her eyes. This time she needed to find another way out. *But what?*

Her sob came from deep down inside. Susannah noticed and struggled to sit up.

"Katy, what is it . . . Bad news?"

Startled, Katy's eyes flew open.

"No, of course not," she answered and struggled to her feet. "I'm just hot, that's all."

"But you were crying," Susannah insisted.

"You're imagining things. Hannah's letter grew tiresome, actually. She went on and on about how happy she is to be expecting another baby."

"Well, of course, she is."

Susannah circled her hand around the mound beneath her apron.

"How wonderful!"

"She forgets the ordeal she suffered delivering her first."

"That doesn't mean it'll be like that again. Besides, they say one soon forgets the pain in the joy of—"

"It's time to fix supper," Katy snapped as she stuffed the letter inside her apron pocket and scrambled to her feet.

"My goodness, so it is."

Susannah got to her knees and braced her hand against the trunk of the tree to help her to stand. Then, she hurried to catch up. She skipped now and then to keep up with Katy's long stride.

"Thanks for your help with the curtains, Katy. You were right. The colors bring out the shades in the fireplace stone."

"You're welcome."

"You have a gift," Susannah added. "Like Sam does when he looks at a piece of wood and turns it into a chair or a table."

She glanced sideways at Katy's unyielding profile.

"I never get tired of watching him work," she added with a nervous giggle. "Besides, it gives me an excuse to rub his back at night."

Still no response.

"Please forgive me, Katy," Susannah burst out, at last. "I can't stand it if I've hurt you some way."

"How could you hurt me?"

Katy stopped in the path and Susannah almost tripped over her.

"You never do anything to hurt anyone. You probably never have."

"But that's not true! Except by God's grace—"

"Oh hush, Susannah. I used to hear the priest use those words back home in Bregenz, in the church with the statue of Mary. But I never knew what they meant and I still don't. I know you and Sam are big on God, so is Alex, I guess. But I don't know what I believe. Maybe I believe in America and that's my faith—what America is and what people here can become. Like Hannah said, 'Only in America.'"

They reached the house where Katy busied herself rattling pans and gave Susannah no opportunity to respond. That night Susannah repeated the conversation to Sam.

"We must pray for her," he said. "Something's wrong, but she's not ready to say what it is."

• • •

Katy saw the ad in the *Lake City Graphic*. WANTED: Part time typesetter. Man or woman. Must be sober and reliable. No experience necessary. Apply at newspaper office.

She asked Alex, "What's a typesetter?"

Alex thought a minute and said, "Let's see, how can I explain it? A typesetter places metal letters called type into a frame to spell out words. Then, the type is inked and printed on newsprint to make up the articles in the newspaper."

"Would that person need to know how to spell in English?"

"Probably not. I imagine a typesetter works off a copy. Why are you asking?"

"Just curious."

A week later, Katy landed the job. At first, Alex tried to talk her out of it. His mother had never worked outside their home. He liked knowing Katy was there when he came up to the house, even when she seemed distant and preoccupied.

Katy, however, persisted. After all, she was scheduled to work only three days a week, she reminded him.

"We could use the money, and besides," she added, "Susannah likes being alone in the kitchen."

That part was true. Susannah appeared to thrive on domestic chores. She sang as she worked and never seemed to tire, even as her pregnancy advanced. When she did sit down, she worked on a rag rug for their bedroom. She braided it from scraps Beulah Heim had given her.

Perhaps this is a God-given opportunity, after all. It'll give Katy a chance to try her wings. Then, perhaps she'll be content to stay home once we have children of our own.

Alex hoped it was soon.

That first week on the farm, he had discovered an old, broken-down buggy in the weeds behind the barn. Off and on, as time and money allowed, Alex replaced the rotting floor boards and the cracked canvas seat.

Katy told him it was a waste of money. Yet, when Alex presented it to her with a new coat of black paint, she hugged his neck.

"Oh Alex! For me? But we don't have a horse."

Alex glowed to see her pleasure.

"Felix says he has a gentle old nag he's kept around. Says he should've sent her to the glue factory long ago, but he didn't have the heart. Told me we'd be doing him a favor just by feeding her. Name's Nellie."

So, the morning arrived when Alex hitched Nellie to the refurbished buggy and Katy left for her new job at the newspaper office. Alex saw her off, and then walked down to the sod house, and lingered with Sam and Susannah over his morning coffee.

"You've been a tremendous help, Sam, and now we're imposing on you, Susannah, just when you should be taking it easier."

"Nonsense."

Susannah pushed Sam's head forward to position the scissors at his hairline.

"I'm as strong as our faithful Mollie, and this might be just what Katy needs. She'll make some new friends and maybe find the job something she really enjoys. I happen to love keeping house and tending garden. People with different talents have different needs."

"That's right."

Sam reached up to brush hair from his neck.

"Katy needs to find her stride."

Alex frowned.

"I'm sure you've noticed how jumpy and irritable she's become. I suggested she see Doc Owens, but the idea set her off even more. I've wanted to believe nothing's wrong, so I haven't pushed. I thought for sure the plans for the house would spark her interest but, as you know, Sam, Katy's left all the decisions to me. For a while, things seemed better between us. Now, she's so distant again. I don't know how to reach her."

Susannah put down the scissors and came round the table. She reached up and put both hands on his shoulders.

"I know it must be disappointing, Alex, but Katy is a good person. We need to be patient and, in time, I'm sure she'll open up and tell you what's wrong."

Sam gathered the towel from his shoulders and opened the screen door to shake out the clippings.

"I have a few ideas for the house that might capture her interest. You know, 'catching flies with honey'?"

CHAPTER 25

Katy jolted upright in bed, sweat-drenched by the dreaded nightmare. As usual, it concerned the familiar neighbor woman writing in the bed clothes. She feared she would never forget that night.

"She shouldn't be bearin' yet," Katy's mother announced. *"I'm goin' for the midwife."*

Helga ran out the door into the black night.

"If you leave her," she called back, *"she'll die and you'll be to blame."*

Yet, her current dream included something else. Her mother's words still echoed in Katy's head.

"She did it to herself," Helga added, *"by eating the aloe, the aloe, the aloe . . ."*

Katy lay back down, clutched the blanket, and listened to Alex's regular breathing. She repeated the words in her mind and wondered what they meant.

• • •

Housed in the basement of the bank building, the newspaper office remained cool during the summer, but warm in the winter when the coal furnace fired up. Katy found it another world, one of purpose and importance, even a certain amount of glamour.

As she laid the news type, she strived to read the words she spelled out—stories of McKinley's presidency, the economic future of Cuba, the scarcity of farm hands in rural communities.

The thick dictionary remained open on an oak lectern. Katy used it often to check spelling as the editor taught her to do. She ran her finger down the column of As and found aloe: a bitter, purgative drug obtained from the juices of several species of aloe plant.

As she flipped more pages, she found purgative: a medicine having the quality of purging. All at once the dream became clear to her. The ignorant neighbor woman tried to avoid giving birth by chewing on the leaves of an aloe plant. It was not the leaves, but the juice.

Katy felt a great sense of relief. She simply had to drink the juice and have a simple miscarriage. It was not a baby, yet. She was not doing what Dr. Adler had done. *But where can I find an aloe plant?*

Then, she remembered. Beulah Heim kept one on her window sill. That very afternoon, she stopped at the Heim's place.

"The juice is the best thing for burns," Beulah told her. "I'll break off some leaves for you to start your plant."

Even before Katy arrived back home, she knew she was not able to do it. She was still going to commit a terrible sin. Better to die than be further damned to hell.

• • •

Young Thad seemed at ease with a hammer. Indeed, he proved himself to be a big help as Alex and Sam raced to enclose the new house before harvest.

"It's very generous of your father to give up your help," Alex commented.

"Oh, he don't mind," Thad answered. "Long as he approves the company I'm in."

"Then, I'm glad we're approved," Sam said.

"You kiddin'? A preacher and a greenhorn neighbor who hangs on his every word of advice? What better keepers could he ask for?"

Sam moved on to a new subject.

"Soon as this roof's on, we'll start work inside."

Thad showed up every day to help. Sam taught him to fashion moldings for the ceilings and construct the kitchen cabinets. Indeed, Thad proved himself to be a big help as Alex and Sam raced to finish the house before winter.

• • •

Enticed by a bay window Sam had inserted in the frame-work, Katy made one of her rare inspections. As she entered the partially-completed farmhouse, she heard Sam talking.

"Someday, I'm going to preach a sermon and call it 'The Parable of the Neighbors.' I'll use you to illustrate the good neighbor."

"Really?" Thad probed,

He sounded pleased.

Katy studied the oak floor and the intricate cornices in the archway of the parlor.

"It's beautiful," she gasped

"Thank you," Sam replied. "Thad did a lot of the work."

"From Sam's patterns," Thad hurried to add.

He hunched over a sawhorse, and used a curved knife to carve scallops along an edge of a long, thin board.

"Where will that go?" Katy asked.

"Outside."

Katy looked to Sam.

"Victorian, milady . . . under the edge of the roof."

"Victorian?" Katy quizzed with a gasp. "How did you know I love Victorian houses?"

"Alex mentioned it. But I'll admit the fact I had to study up on them."

Through the archway into the parlor, Katy saw Alex perched on a stepladder, his back to her. She felt ashamed. *Why do I treat him as I do? He's often thoughtful of me and I seldom acknowledged it.*

"Could there perhaps be a leaded pane above the parlor window?" Katy asked as excitement took hold of her.

Sam grinned and answered, "We're way ahead of you. It's al-ready ordered."

"And later, if we add a porch, maybe some spindles in the railing?"

"My, seems you've made quite a study," Sam observed.

Katy blushed and hurried on to inspect what was to be the kitchen.

"The paper runs a column on household hints," she said over her shoulder.

Alex put down his hammer and grinned at Sam.

"Like flies to honey. Good thing those traps you found in the barn are bringing in extra income. It's helped pay for the fineries. If it makes Katy happy here, it'll be worth it."

•   •   •

Katy made daily visits to inspect the progress. She and Alex were due to move into the new house before Christmas. Then, Susannah and Sam could leave the sod house to occupy the cabin.

When the two couples shared the evening meal together, Katy tried her best to help. Susannah was so tiny and her pregnancy was already so huge—a constant reminder to Katy of what laid ahead for her.

"I'll miss our little sod house," Susannah said. "It's been like a honeymoon cottage—so secluded and peaceful. But with cold weather approaching, there's the baby to think of. The dirt floor does stay damp whereas this cabin is cozy and dry, just perfect for the three of us."

Katy stood at the sink and peeled potatoes as Susannah plunged ahead.

"Katy," she ventured, "are you keeping a secret?"

Sobs burst forth and shook Katy's shoulders. She dropped the knife with a loud clatter and buried her face in her hands.

Susannah rushed to her side and pulled Katy's head down onto her shoulder.

"You're expecting a child, aren't you?"

"Oh, dear God. Alex mustn't know. Please, Susannah, don't tell him!"

Katy's wail seemed to rise out of a deep chasm.

"But why not, for heaven's sake? He'll know soon of his own accord. And he'll be thrilled. He's told me many times how much he wants a family."

"Men." Katy spat the word as if she regained control by summoning contempt. "They talk as if they birth babies themselves."

"Is that it, Katy? Are you afraid of childbearing?"

"Of course, I'm afraid. And why aren't you, Susannah Schneider? Are you crazy, or what? I mean, just look at you . . . so tiny, and that *thing*!"

The word jangled between them, like the twang of a broken banjo string.

"I'm not going to die, if that's what you mean." Susannah's tone hardened and her blue eyes snapped. "This 'thing' is a baby and women have birthed babies for thousands of years. It's the natural plan of God."

Katy swiped fiercely at her eyes and shot back, "Oh, I know all about that—procreation and being fruitful, multiplying the earth. But priests don't have babies, neither do nuns, and the Bible says women will have pain in childbirth because of Eve's sin. You see, Susannah, you're not the only one who knows the Bible."

Alex's and Sam's voices carried to her as they approached the house. She grabbed Susannah by both arms and dug her fingernails into her flesh.

"Promise me! Don't tell anyone. Not a soul."

Alex walked through the door before Susannah was able to answer. Katy dropped Susannah's arms and turned away.

• • •

In only a few more weeks, Alex guessed what Katy had kept from him. He tried to express his mixture of joy and hurt. Joy at the miracle life God had created; hurt Katy had kept the news to herself.

"It's wonderful news, Katy. Why couldn't you tell me yourself?"

"It's my body, not yours," Katy answered and froze further conversation into icy silence.

A deep ache lodged in his heart. *Is this punishment for those awful weeks before I found her . . . Weeks she won't talk about? Will having a child draw us closer or drive us further apart?*

CHAPTER 26

To announce the weekly hymn sings, Thad posted notices on fence posts and tree trunks along the roads. When the weather proved mild, people sat on blankets under the trees, and when it rained they assembled in the barn. Sam and Alex had scrubbed out empty stalls, removed partitions between three of them, and placed peach crates for use as benches.

"I'll attend because it's our farm and it wouldn't look right if I didn't," Katy told Alex. "I know Sam and Susannah have good intentions, but shouldn't worship take place inside a church?"

"I can't find that in the Bible," Alex teased. "Besides, Sam says your soprano, especially when Susannah joins you in harmony, is a real drawing card."

Sam read from the scriptures and explained their meaning so simply Katy wondered if it was blasphemy to take away so much of the mystery. On one occasion, Sam used Thad as an example of a good neighbor to illustrate the story of the Good Samaritan. However, later, when Sam told the story of the prodigal son, Thad took issue with it.

"Fathers don't act that way," Thad told Sam. "At least mine don't. He hated the company I kept and how I lived my life. Put me to work. Might as well have locked me up. Couldn't even ride my horse 'til I started comin' over here to help you and Alex."

Sam put his hand on his young friend's shoulder.

"The father in the parable represents our Heavenly Father. Sometimes, we need to prove ourselves to our earthly fathers to earn back their trust, but when we're truly sorry and turn to our Heavenly Father, He loves us without any conditions and forgives our sins that instant, no matter how bad they seem to us."

Katy overheard the conversation.

"Not always," she muttered to herself. "Some sins are too bad to be forgiven."

She ran from the barn and stopped only when she reached the garden gate. Dusk gathered and neighbors prepared to leave as Alex caught up with her and grasped her arm.

"What's wrong, Katy? Are you sick? It scared me when you ran out like that."

"Yes, I'm sick. Sick of hearing Sam talk about God like a friend. Aren't we supposed to fear God, and bow down to Him? Kneel in front of an altar and take communion to receive His forgiveness?"

"People can worship God anywhere in many ways," Alex told her. "Folks in this little group come from different backgrounds. They come together simply as Christians—the name the book of Acts gives all believers in Christ."

He reached for her hand, tucked it inside the crook of his arm, and said, "I wish you could be happy, Katy—in your faith, and about the baby and all."

His vague way of saying how he felt pricked her conscience. She knew she made life miserable for him. It hurt Alex when she did not share his enthusiasm concerning the future. *Isn't it best not to count on a future for myself?*

Not that she wanted to hurt him. Alex worked so hard to make her happy, but in the very core of her being she sustained a life which would soon insist on coming forth. She thought of little else.

After the baby was born dead, as she had decided would happen as punishment for the great sin she had committed, she was to surely die as well. *So, why get involved in things that won't include me? Better to leave Alex to make a fresh start.*

• • •

After the corn was picked and stored in the crib at the back of the barn, Alex took the township teaching position. The present teacher, Miss Marley, had given notice when her father died. She said she wanted to move back East to take care of her mother. The clapboard school building stood on the corner of the section of land adjoining their farm.

With his first paycheck, Alex bought a horse.

"Next spring I can finish laying tile to have more land to put into corn," he told Katy. "In the meantime, this job will give us some extra income."

Felix Heim had recommended Alex to the county superintendent. He cited the over qualification of Alex's university background. The eight students, ages six to fourteen, proved to be well-behaved and respectful, if uninspired. Alex was dedicated to finding the spark to kindle the love for learning he possessed.

He toiled to inspire each child. It provided a welcome escape from the worry he feared was going to otherwise obsess, and perhaps, consume him.

Katy still seemed a world apart. When he locked the schoolhouse door and turned his horse toward home, his shoulders slumped over the reins.

• • •

Felix Heim had served many years as township director.

"Too bad his youngest turned out to be the rotten apple," one father remarked in conversation. "Felix has served the community well."

"Are you speaking of Thad? Why would you say that?" Alex asked.

He was tired of the oblique references and insinuations concerning his neighbor's son.

The father, a neighbor who attended the hymn sings, hung his head as if embarrassed.

"Maybe I put it too strong. But hang it all, Felix and Beulah Heim are good folk, and that boy gave them a load of grief. 'Course Pete Gregg proved to be the real scoundrel, leavin' his wife and young'uns at home and buyin' beer for Thad so he'd join him on a toot now and then. Felix put his foot down. The boy warn't more'n fifteen or so. But the boy idolized Pete and snuck off to town with him.

"Things came to a head when young Mary went into labor at home," he continued. "All alone, 'cept for her two little ones, . . . no one to help her. It's a downright miracle the baby lived, but by the time Pete got home, it was too late for poor Mary. She died 'fore Doc got there.

"Thad's the one that rode for Doc Owens. Doc later testified the kid's breath 'bout knocked him over—that Thad could barely stay in the saddle. The whole affair caused a big uproar. The sheriff arrested Pete for buyin' liquor for a minor. Pete jumped the bail Felix put up, took the kids and the new baby, and left in the middle of the night. No one's heard from him since. May heaven have mercy."

• • •

Alex had asked Felix and Beulah if Thad could come back to school.

"With harvest over, I thought you might be able to spare him," he said.

"Sparing him isn't the problem," Felix answered. "When I bought that forty acres last spring, added to my cattle herd and hired on another hand, I never stopped Thad even one day from working on your new house. First time he's taken a real interest for quite a spell."

"Broke my heart when he quit school," Beulah Heim chimed in. "Our other three sons graduated from high school and the oldest went through college."

"Why did Thad quit?"

Alex hated to pry, but if he knew the story, maybe he could help.

Felix's straight shoulders slumped.

"Maybe for the same reasons we quit going to church. False pride, shame, bein' discouraged, and givin' up. Right, Beulah?"

His wife nodded with tears in her eyes.

Alex placed his hand on his neighbor's shoulder.

"Mind if I talk with him?"

"We'd be mighty pleased if you can get through to him."

• • •

Sam puttied the last pane in the window frames. Friday was set as moving day. School dismissed for Thanksgiving, and Katy had the week off from the newspaper.

Alex shot a wild turkey which Susannah stuffed with cornbread dressing, and served with green beans and tomatoes canned from the garden. The aroma of her sourdough bread wafted from its basket and fresh apple jelly jiggled in its dish as both were passed around the table. Sam said grace and gave heartfelt thanks for the many blessings granted them.

"Next year we'll have potatoes for Thanksgiving," Alex said as he carved the turkey. "Felix says the lowland peat bogs make great ground for spuds as he calls them."

He turned to his wife and hoped she joined the conversation, for once.

"How does that sound, Katy?"

As usual, Katy had nothing to say. Helpful to Susannah and polite to them all, she behaved like a paying guest. Conversation circled around her and she spoke only when necessary.

Susannah changed the subject.

"After we get moved, let's go shopping for some flannel, Katy. I saw the cutest pattern to make gowns for the babies."

Katy kept her eyes on the meat she cut with her knife.

"I don't sew. If necessary, we'll purchase through the catalog."

What does she mean by 'if necessary'? Alex thought bitterly. *Of course, it'll be necessary.*

Alex wondered if this way of speaking had become the lifelong patchwork of their marriage.

No, he assured himself. *Our baby will change things.*

Other husbands joked about the moods and whims of their pregnant wives. He supposed it normal for Katy to dread the first birth. Susannah, however, did not seem at all anxious. In fact, she grew more radiant as she became more awkward. At almost seven months, her girth caused her to waddle like a duck in order to balance her small frame.

Yet, her complexion took on a soft glow, like down, and her bright eyes reflected the relish with which she appeared to greet each morning. *Forgive me, Lord, but why can't Katy be more like Susannah?*

• • •

Susannah knocked on the cabin door while Katy and Alex were still seated at breakfast.

"I didn't mean to rush you," she apologized as she deposited an armful of blankets on the floor in the corner, and pushed back the wool cap corralling her mass of golden curls. "It's just that I couldn't wait to get started, so I carried up this pile of bedding. Sam will hardly let me lift anything heavier than a feather."

She placed her hand at the small of her back to arch her spine and smiled as she looked out the window.

"It's truly a day the Lord has made. Would you just look at how the sunshine sparkles on the snow?"

"Silly for you to carry anything at all," Katy said, her voice cross. "You might have fallen. Alex plans to drive the wagon down to get your things."

Susannah's smile faded.

"I knew you'd have everything organized," she told Katy. "I was just so excited, I didn't think."

Alex took his felt hat from its peg on the wall and shrugged into his heavy jacket.

"I'll hitch up the team and get started."

The door closed behind them. Katy was alone in the cabin. Susannah was her friend and she had not meant to hurt her feelings. *But how can Susannah remain so unconcerned, so eager for each new day when she has to know what lay ahead?*

Of course, Susannah had not sinned as she had. As far as Katy was able to tell, Susannah never sinned.

• • •

The move into the new house took only half the morning. The fancy new cook stove was already installed as well as a pot-bellied stove in the parlor. Best of all, was a housewarming gift— a fine, sturdy bed Sam had constructed with a tight framework of ropes to support the mattress.

The rooms still lacked furniture, but when Alex laid down Mary Gregg's rag rug, and placed her rocking chair beside the pot-bellied stove, Susannah clapped her hands in delight.

"Oh Katy, I can just picture you here rocking your baby, all cozy-like. Sam has promised to make me a chair just like it."

Katy crossed the room and lifted the chair from the floor.

"Here. Take this one. I don't want it."

Susannah's hands flew to her mouth.

"Katy! Why would you?"

She turned to Alex, but he also stared at Katy in disbelief.

"I'm so sorry," Susannah cried as she fled the room.

Katy's shoulders slumped as she set the chair back down and turned to open a crate of dishes. Alex started toward her, but then turned and followed Susannah.

Left alone, Katy let the tears come. She had not meant to hurt Susannah again. Mary Gregg's chair had served as a reminder of what had happened to Mary and her baby when Thad and Pete Gregg had failed to come home in time.

She trailed her hand over the smooth walnut frame of the new bedstead. Alex worked so hard to please her. *What thanks have I given him?*

She felt so ashamed.

• • •

Alex caught up with Susannah as she hurried in awkward, duck-like fashion back to the sod house.

"Susannah!" he exclaimed and grabbed her arm. "For heaven's sake, stop!"

Susannah obeyed and swiped at her tear-streaked face with both hands.

"Oh Alex, what can we do? She won't let anyone help her."

"I know."

"Sam says to put her in God's hands, but it's so hard. I just want so much to be her friend."

She dried the last of her tears as Sam rode up on Mollie.

"Bout time," Alex chided as he forced a light-hearted tone. "This wife of yours can't reach her toes, let alone heft your belongings."

Sam swung himself down to the ground.

"She'd better not try, either. Although, from the looks of things, that bundle she's totin' could lift them himself."

Susannah put her hands on her hips and a smile on her face.

"Him? And what if it's a girl?"

"Then, she could lift them as well."

Sam stopped the banter when he saw Alex's sober face.

"By the way, I brought something for you. Stopped to pick up the mail after collecting the money Fred Blair owed me for building those new shelves in the store."

He took an envelope from his coat pocket and handed it to his friend. Then, he turned to Susannah.

"Come, wife, time to take down the curtains and say farewell to our former abode."

•   •   •

Alex took the letter with him to the barn. In an empty stall, he sat down on an overturned nail keg and thumbed open the envelope. The letter began:

My Dear Son,

First of all, I must tell you how thrilled I'll be to have a grandchild. Please give my very best to Katy. I'll be eagerly awaiting the announcement of its birth.

But now, I have some less happy news. Your father died very suddenly from a bad heart. He died without speaking your name although he received your letter at least two weeks before. I found it in his desk. I'm so sorry, Alex. I wish I could tell you he forgave you, as you asked him to do in your letter, but if he did, he didn't share that with me. He was a good man, but a hard man. It means much to me that you forgave him. I hope it brings you peace.

The letter continued with news of his sisters and his mother's plans to remain in the house. She also asked if Katy knew she had a baby sister, born the previous summer. Anna Meisen wrote:

I didn't know myself until I met Helga Thannen in the market square one day. Strangely enough, our paths seldom cross.

She closed by writing:

Now, since your father is gone, I hope you'll come back to Austria for a visit. It'd give me such joy to see you again and meet my grandchild. I hope you'll make the journey as soon as the infant is old enough to travel. Your father left you no inheritance, but the money belongs to me now and I can do with it as I please. I'm enclosing a bank draft. If you insist on paying back whatever you feel you owed your father, I'll respect your wishes and regard them as admirable.

Just don't wait too long. Life's unpredictable, as your father's death proves. I love you very much and I now speak your name often.

Mother.

For the first time since the dark day he learned Katy had left for America without him, Alex wept. He wept as the child whose father had never understood him and as the youth who longed for a conversation that mattered, an opinion that counted, an emotion he dared display without risk of embarrassment. As a man, he also wept for his father and the lonely isolation which characterized his life.

He made no attempt to restrain the flow of tears and, at last, a healing calm came over him. Even though he was never to know the answer in his father's heart, he had accomplished what God required of him.

As he put the letter back in its envelope, he saw the bank draft. The amount was generous, indeed.

Love for his mother engulfed him, but not because of the money. Her last words had been a sweet balm for the lonely ache he experienced these days: *I now speak your name often.*

CHAPTER 27

The news her mother had given birth to another baby so late in life proved unimaginable to Katy. She supposed it was a good thing which granted her mother someone else to provide for and worry over, as she had for Katy.

Katy knew she never missed her mother the way she should. On rare occasions her family came to mind, Katy recalled few vivid memories—a haze of daily routines which faded into sameness. She recalled feeling her mother's disapproval more than her love, and as for her father and brothers, it seemed they were always at work. Therefore, they were absent most of the time.

As for a trip back to Austria—provided she survived the birth of the child—it would be wonderful to see her native land again.

Who do I really want to see? Sofie, of course.

She experienced guilt over leaving Sofie the way she did. *Besides, hadn't I promised to take her a present?*

Then, there was the money. That came as a huge surprise. It caused Katy to reassess her feelings of resentment toward Anna Meisen, and remember how fairly Anna treated her when she worked in the Meisen household.

Even if Alex persisted in returning the amount he took from the cheese factory, life was going to be easier. They were able to add onto the house, if need be, and buy more farm equipment, even make the sea voyage in comfort if they did go back for a visit. *If, always if.*

Sam finished Susannah's rocking chair and fashioned a cradle. When Katy looked across the yard and saw lamps flickering late into the night, she imagined the teasing banter between husband and wife, or perhaps the give and take of serious conversation. When she looked across the room to where Alex sat reading his farm journals, she thought of nothing to say.

Her heart ached with longing for what Sam and Susannah shared. If she were able to define it, perhaps she might somehow imitate it. The depth of the bond between them went beyond romantic feelings described in novels, or even the respect and affection between Hiram and Hannah.

Alex probably envied it as much as she did. She saw it in his eyes when he watched them together.

A small congregation which held services at the schoolhouse asked Sam to be its pastor and he accepted. Felix Heim gave him a check to buy an organ.

"Because you've been a good friend to Thad," he said.

The gift appeared to touch Sam deeply.

"I hope both of you will come to hear it played," he told Felix. "Susannah will be in 'seventh heaven' the minute she pumps air into its bellows."

• • •

After school dismissed on Wednesdays, Alex cut wood and cleaned the school building as required by his contract. He stayed on for Sam's midweek prayer meeting, and then milked the cows when he got home after dark. He offered to come back for Katy, but she always declined. Sam and Susannah accepted the excuse of her condition and did not press the matter.

In truth, Katy hated the long evenings alone. She was wary of the stillness in the house and the darkened windows of the cabin across the yard. She tried reading, but nothing held her interest for long, and she had no interest in the knitting and sewing Susannah relished.

Sometimes, she accompanied Alex to the barn after he came home to hold the lantern while he milked. They had little to say to one another, but one night Alex ventured to tell her how the service often became a sharing time—how each person gave reasons for being thankful.

His forehead pressed into Betsy's side.

"I gave thanks for our abundant corn crop." His voice became shy, tentative, as if gathering courage. "I also thanked God for bringing Sam and Susannah into our lives, and for the coming baby."

The streams of milk hissed against the sides of the tin pail. Katy did not comment . . . She had nothing to say. She welcomed the dark because she was unable to see his eyes.

"Katy . . . ," Alex began again with great weariness in his voice. "I can't make you talk about what's bothering you, and you can't keep me from praying for you . . . and giving thanks."

He stood, poured the milk into the tall metal can, and jammed the lid on tightly. Then, he took the lantern from her and left the barn.

Katy felt like a small child as she trailed his yellow-lit shadow up the narrow path.

• • •

The weather was warm for December. Brown leaves clung stubbornly to tree branches and the ground, gray with frost, felt spongy underfoot. Sam prepared to leave at dawn on Monday to travel the thirty miles to Fort Dodge to bring back a load of coal. He wanted to make sure of a good supply before the baby came.

"The snows will come sooner or later," he told Susannah, "and coal's much cheaper when purchased directly from the mine instead of being delivered."

"I hate to be gone overnight," he told Alex as he hitched up the mules, "but it gets dark too early now to make it there and back the same day. I have a preacher friend in Fort Dodge who'll take me in, but you'd be doing me a big favor if you'd keep an eye on Susannah."

"You know we will."

Alex watched from the barn as Sam and Susannah embraced in the cabin doorway. When Susannah reached up to touch Sam's cheek, Sam bent down to cup her chin and tilt her face up to his.

Unable to tear his eyes away, Alex felt such bitter longing in his gut it almost made him nauseous. Susannah waved until Sam was far down the road.

When he returned to the house, he found Katy sitting at the kitchen table. Her chin rested in her hand, and one finger loosely hooked the handle of her coffee mug. Dark circles shadowed her eyes against sallow skin.

"Since Sam's gone," Alex asked, "would you mind inviting Susannah over for the day? Keep an eye on her? I promised Sam we would."

"I don't have to," Katy answered without looking up. "She invited herself to bake Christmas cookies. Our oven is more reliable."

When she shrugged, her old bathrobe fell off one shoulder.

"It's all right. Helps pass the time."

Alex lifted her hair to kiss the back of her neck, walked out the door, and rode off to the schoolhouse. *Perhaps, Susannah's sunny disposition will lift Katy's mood.*

The sky contained a violet cast and wet tree branches arched over the road. He supposed it was the aftermath of a light frost.

By the time he reached the schoolhouse, a mist fell—unusual this late in the year.

$$\bullet \quad \bullet \quad \bullet$$

Susannah hung her blue jacket and wooly cap on a hook beside the door, and shook out her curls.

"It's starting to rain!" she exclaimed. "Can you believe it . . . In December?"

The fire crackled under the stove lid as they rolled out cookie dough on the kitchen table. In spite of herself, Katy warmed to the festive atmosphere.

She had never baked Christmas cookies before, so she watched closely as Susannah traced bells, angels, and Christmas trees onto brown paper. Susannah showed her how to trim the dough away from the shapes and sprinkle the cutouts with colored sugar.

When six dozen cookies cooled on racks, Susannah wiped off the table and sank onto a chair with a satisfied sigh.

"Please pour some coffee, Katy dear. Me thinks it's time for cooks treat."

Katy set out mugs and arranged some warm cookies on a plate. They did look good and she was pleased with herself.

"My, it's hot and steamy in here," she said. "I'll crack a window open."

However, the handles did not budge.

"The window's frozen shut," she told Susannah as she crossed the room to open the door instead.

"Susannah, come here!"

The wind had shifted direction from south to northwest, and hard crystals of snow flashed white from gray clouds which slanted downward in parallel lines. Susannah shivered in the cold blast of air.

"Oh dear, I wish Sam hadn't left."

Katy pushed the door shut.

"Now, don't start fretting. Jake and Jed find their way in any weather. I can testify to that. Remember, the hail storm?"

Susannah laughed.

"You're right, of course. How well I remember my first sight of you with that pail on your head."

Katy smiled at the memory and wished she felt as assured as she tried to portray. She closed the door and prevented Susannah from seeing the layer of ice which coated the ground. Wind howled down the chimney, and she wished Alex home as well.

• • •

As the day wore on, Alex watched the weather from the tall windows at school. *If conditions worsened, will parents come after their children?*

He put more wood in the coal stove and drilled the students on their lessons. Their attention wandered, however, and they grew more restless as the sky grew darker, and sleet froze on the window panes.

Sure enough, parents arrived one-by-one. Shortly after noon, Alex locked up the building and turned his horse into the wind. As he headed home, he decided to cut across fields where corn stubble provided better traction than the road.

A glaze soon coated his clothes like stiff armor, and frozen crystals glued his eyelashes together. When the mare neared clumps of
trees, Alex saw branches bent almost to their breaking point.

At each fence gate he dismounted and used a rock to knock
ice off the latch so the gate opened. The going was slow and
treacherous, the sleet slanted down with increasing fervor. He
thanked God Katy and Susannah were safe at home. Sam was able
to take care of himself.

• • •

As time passed, it was Susannah who calmed Katy. The rafters
creaked under the icy weight and Susannah chattered on to distract
Katy from the eerie sound.

"I remember one Christmas in North Dakota," she told her,
"sleet came down all night and the next morning it looked like a
fairyland. The trees and grass, everything sparkled with ice and—"

She stopped midsentence and doubled over in her chair. She
circled her belly with her arms and sweat broke out on her forehead.

"What's wrong, Susannah?" Katy inquired of her.

She jumped up and almost knocked over her chair.

"Oh, please, no. It isn't time yet."

Susannah straightened with effort and smiled weakly.

"Prob'ly just too many cookies. We've eaten the whole plate full."

She moved toward the kitchen counter.

"I'll just put the rest in the cookie jar, away from temptation."

She stopped and clutched her belly again and stood very still.

"Katy," she whispered, wide-eyed, "my water broke."

Katy heard herself cry out a long wail.

"No, it can't be, Susannah, it just can't be. It's way too early."

Alex burst through the door and stamped his feet on the threshold.

"What is it? What's wrong?"

Katy fell into his arms, unmindful of his ice-encrusted coat.

"Oh, Alex, I'm so glad to see you. I'm so glad you're home."

Susannah clutched the edge of the counter, her teeth clenched.

"Susannah!" Alex exclaimed. "Is it time?"

"Yes," she gasped with a weak smile.

Alex unwrapped Katy's arms from his neck.

"I'll ride for Doc Owens," he told her. "Get her to bed and don't leave her."

Katy paled. She staggered backwards as if Alex had struck her.

"Katy!" Alex spoke with authority and grabbed her arm.

"Pull yourself together. Susannah needs you."

•   •   •

The exhausted mare balked at leaving the barn so soon after entering it. Alex coaxed her gently and led her partway down the lane before he put one foot in the stirrup and swung his body over her back. He leaned close to her ear and talked to her. The loosened reins allowed horse and rider to close their eyes against the sleet and drift forward with the wind.

When almost upon the Heims place, he became aware of a bizarre occurrence. Black smoke curled close to the ground and twisted through the eerie grove of ice-coated trees.

Alex straightened in the saddle and breathed the acrid scent. Ahead, he saw a rider turn out of a lane and punish his horse down the road ahead of him. He recognized the broad-brimmed hat. *Thad.*

Thad's appearance had a wild, desperate look as he whipped the horse's flanks on one side, and then the other. Alex saw him dig in his heels in a useless attempt to force the horse into a gallop, something Alex knew the horse was unable to do on the icy terrain.

"Thad!" Alex called. "What is it? What's happened?"

Thad turned and pulled back on the reins. The animal slid sideways, and horse and rider almost fell, but Thad seemed not to notice. His words came in gasps as Alex rode alongside.

"Dad started a fire in the fireplace and went back to bed. Not feeling well . . . Didn't check the flue . . . Mom tendin' her chickens . . . Saw smoke . . . Yelled for me in the barn . . . Had to crawl on my hands and knees to find him. They're safe in the barn now, but Dad's unconscious."

He gulped for air, tightened the reins on the skittish horse, and said, "I'm ridin' to fetch Doc."

The stallion reared off its front legs. Fighting for control, Thad miraculously brought him back down.

"Oh Alex, if anything happens—"

"Thad, you stay with your parents. I'm on the way to get Doc myself. Sam's gone and Susannah's started her labor."

"Oh no. Not like Mary Gregg. Please, Alex, all the more reason it should be me who goes."

Alex searched the pleading young face. Thad was right.

"Go then," he said, "but use sense, boy. Slow down. You won't get there at all if that horse breaks a leg. Bring Doc to your father first. We'll manage somehow until he gets to our place."

CHAPTER 28

Katy's hands shook as she stripped off the bedding and threw a clean sheet across the mattress. They continued to shake as she helped Susannah into one of her nightgowns and rolled up the sleeves to free her hands. Thank heavens for the downstairs bedroom.

Even while in pain, Susannah appeared excited—cheeks pink and eyes bright. *Is she delirious?*

Once again, the dream of the neighbor woman's labor and Hannah's ordeal on the ship flashed across Katy's mind. *Will Susannah suffer the same?*

"Thank you, Katy," Susannah said as she slipped under the blanket.

She continued to reassure Katy even as her breath came in gasps. She grabbed hold of the spindles on the headboard and strained against them.

"Everything will be fine," she promised as she reached for Katy's hand. "God is with me. Just hold my hand . . . tight."

"Will God deliver the baby?"

Katy dropped the words like stones. *Why pretend?*

"In His own way, He will," Susannah replied. "Just having you here with me is a great comfort."

Me? Katy thought. *I'm useless, totally useless.*

It seemed like hours before Alex burst into the room. Katy sobbed with relief when she saw him. He suddenly seemed very dear to her.

Alex was soaking wet. "Did you fetch Doc Owens . . . Where is he?"

"He's coming."

Alex moved to the bedside. Susannah grabbed his arm as another contraction gripped her.

"Thank you, dear Alex," she whispered. "I wish Sam was here."

"Of course, you do, but we'll manage. What can I do?"

"Pray," Susannah pleaded. "Pray for this little one who's coming too soon."

Alex reached for her hand and knelt by the bedside.

"Dear Lord. We trust you and we know you can deliver this child safe and perfect. Please be with Susannah and bring Sam home to her soon."

As he stood, he tried to reassure her.

"I'm sure Doc will be here soon. Until then, we'll take care of you."

Katy twisted her skirt in her hands.

How can Alex make such a promise? What do we know about birthing babies?

Susannah was so tiny. *She'll surely die and the baby as well.*

She tried to collect her thoughts, to remember what the nurse had done for Hannah on the ship, but her mind remained numb with fear. It was Alex who timed the pains as Susannah said Doc Owens had instructed her to do when her labor started. He bathed her face with a cool cloth, and put another pillow behind her head as well as a smaller one under her lower back.

By late afternoon, the storm abated and darkness engulfed the house. Alex lit the lamps and put more coal in the stove. He was careful to check the stovepipe to avoid a catastrophe like the Heims had experienced.

Katy felt utterly helpless. *How can Alex remain so calm? Where did he get the strength?*

Alex had no more experience than she, but she witnessed him take on the unlikely role as if Someone looked over his shoulder and gave directions.

I'm a woman, Susannah's my friend. I'm the one who should be of help.

She roused herself and rallied to gather towels, heat water, and tear cloth strips from an old sheet the way she remembered her mother had done for the neighbor woman. She told Susannah Doc Owens would arrive soon, although she raged inwardly because he was not there already, let alone Sam.

Yet, the time arrived when any thought fled before Susannah's pain. Katy and Alex braced themselves on either side of the bed and let Susannah clutch their arms as the contractions arrived with increasing ferocity. Katy felt of little use, but Susannah thanked her profusely.

Alex continued his calm reassurances as he told Susannah God would see her through. Katy saw it brought Susannah comfort although she saw no reason why. The pains grew even worse.

Thirty minutes passed before Susannah's clenched eyelids opened wide.

"The baby's coming!" she blurted as excitement filled her voice. "Dear God, please help him!"

Katy peeked under the sheet and froze as the baby's pick scalp emerged. She lifted the sheet for Alex to see.

"It's here!" she cried. "What should we do? Where's Doc Owens?"

Alex moved forward to cup his hands on either side of the head, and guided the squalling wee babe into the world.

"It's a boy," he told Susannah. "Tiny, but perfect."

Katy let out the breath she held, still unable to move.

"Katy, hand me a clean towel!" Alex demanded.

At last, Katy roused herself to do so. Alex tenderly swaddled the baby and placed Susannah's son in his mother's arms.

"Isn't he beautiful?" Susannah insisted as the tiny mite screwed up his red face and gave a series of short yelps.

"Just like a runt pig," Alex said with a nervous laugh, but his face mirrored the awe Katy felt herself as they watched the bluish skin turn a vibrant pink.

"Oh you . . . ," Susannah admonished as the baby continued to wail. "He's perfect."

• • •

Alex gazed at the new mother's face. After all she had been through Susannah was the one who was beautiful. Her eyes shone with pride and her sweat-drenched face held an aura of radiance. Wet ringlets of hair framed the joy reflected therein.

Alex spoke barely above a whisper, "Just now, before you saw him . . . How did you know it was a boy?"

"I don't know. I just knew."

Alex was scarcely able to tear his eyes from mother and child. When he did turn to Katy, he expected to share the moment with her as well, yet her face was stark white.

"Katy? What's wrong?"

Her long hair had come loose from its coil. It framed her face as she leaned forward, arms crossed over her unborn child. She moaned as she rocked back and forth.

"Nothing . . . Everything."

Katy broke into sobs and ran from the room.

Alex turned to Susannah, but Susannah shook her head.

"First, help me cut the cord, Alex. Doc Owens told me how, just in case."

Alex found scissors and gripped the handles with a folded towel. He lifted a lid on the stove and held the blades briefly in the fire as Susannah instructed. Then, he returned to the bedroom to cut the cord and bind the babe's abdomen with the strips of cloth Katy had torn.

He cradled the infant as if carrying fine china and wrapped him in a large bath towel before he placed him in Susannah's arms.

"You did just fine," Susannah told him.

She gazed at her son and stroked the tiny cheek with her fingers.

"You're a dear man, Alex. Now, go to Katy. She needs you."

• • •

Alex pulled Katy to him.

"Hush, darling," he soothed as he stroked her back. "Everything's all right now. It's over."

"But it's *not* over. Not for me!" She cried as she pulled away. "It'll never be over, Alex. Don't you understand? I killed it."

Her voice thickened with tears. She backed up to a chair, and sat down, and then put her face in her hands and broke into sobs.

"It was a real baby and I killed it."

Alex shook his head, as if to clear away a dense fog.

"What on earth are you talking about?"

Katy dropped her hands back into her lap. *What's the use? What difference does it make now?*

Yet, the full knowledge of what she had done seared her through and through. Between sobs, she spoke in a monotone.

"I'm not talking about Susannah's baby. It was *my* baby . . . *Our* baby. I never saw it . . . Never knew what it looked like, but it must've had real fingers and toes, eyes and a mouth . . . a breathing child, not just some nameless object."

The sobs choked her now, and tears streamed down her face unchecked as Alex dropped to his knees. He rocked her back and forth in his arms and she let him.

"I could have kept it. Mrs. Voorhees would've helped me—I know she would've," Katy shuddered, "But it was my choice, don't you see? God will never forgive me. Nor should you, Alex."

Alex stilled, as if he focused every thought in his effort to understand.

"Tell me, Katy," he murmured. "Tell me everything."

The words spewed forth in a jagged rush, like rocks bursting through a dam. She confessed the terror of being stranded in Rotterdam without knowledge of what had happened to him, wondering if he'd changed his mind or what? Then, something Father Kaspar said made her face the fact she was carrying a child.

She recounted Hannah's ordeal giving birth on the ship and her own fears brought on by the childhood experience of being left with the neighbor in labor. She described how alone she felt in New York and how Baylie had told her she was unable to raise a child alone.

As she talked, she avoided looking at Alex.

"I didn't see any other way out," she sobbed. "Baylie knew about this doctor . . . Dr. Adler."

Alex stiffened at the name.

Katy's voice took on a hollow quality as she continued, "I thought he cared, but afterward it seemed so evil."

She writhed on her chair as if reliving the moment.

"It's as if I can still feel the scraping, even though Dr. Adler gave me something so I wouldn't feel it."

Alex dropped his arms. He pulled back and stared at his wife. Katy lifted her eyes to look at him.

"Go ahead, Alex, hate me. I deserve it. I swore I'd never get pregnant again. That's why I've treated you so awful, even when you tried so hard to please me. I couldn't stand it that you, Sam, and Susannah had such peace of mind while I was scared to death. Before you found me in New York, I thought of myself as the strong one. It was the one thing that kept me going."

She stood, and paced back and forth.

"That's not all."

She took a deep breath.

"When I found out I was pregnant again, I considered getting rid of this new life, but I didn't have the courage. God will surely let me die when the baby's born, as my well-deserved punishment."

She was completely spent—calm and dry-eyed.

• • •

Alex sat stunned, unable to form any words. While Susannah crooned softly in the bedroom, he recalled his search for Katy in Brooklyn, the climb to the second floor office, the arrogant doctor and how angry he had been when the door slammed in his face.

How would I have reacted if I'd learned the truth then? Would I still have married Katy, brought her with me to Iowa?

He found it impossible to grasp he had fathered a child and never knew it. Katy kept it from him, made the decision on her own to destroy their child's life. *How could she?*

Yet, how did he know her state of mind, her terror at the thought of raising a child alone? He remembered the bitter Baylie and how convincing she was. *Still . . .*

Outside, a commotion erupted. Thad burst into the room with Doc Owens right behind, black bag in hand. Their faces looked stiff, almost frozen.

"Sorry, we didn't knock," Thad said.

His breath came fast.

"Susannah?"

He forced the name out as if fearful of saying it.

"She's fine."

Alex went to the bedroom door, and motioned toward mother and child.

"The baby, too. A boy."

Doc Owens threw his hat in a corner and hurried past Alex to Susannah's side.

"Leave us alone, now," he ordered. "Wait outside."

Thad sank to his knees.

"Thank God. Oh, thank God. If Susannah had died, like Mary did . . . ," his voice broke. "Well, I just couldn't take it. My father's fine, now. We stopped there on the way back."

His hand raked through his hair.

"I've been a terrible son . . . Thought my father too hard on me. But when I thought he might die, I wanted a second chance, even though I don't deserve it."

Thad took some deep gulps of air.

"When I came back with Doc, my father hugged me, told me he loved me."

Thad stopped again to regain his composure.

"Don't you see? I'm like the prodigal son in the story."

Tears ran down his cheeks and admitted, "I don't deserve it, but I've been given a second chance."

Katy stood near, but her voice sounded far away, small, and timid.

"A second chance?"

Alex inhaled a ragged breath, as if Thad's words rescued him from drowning. The certainty of Thad's words penetrated the fog of his inner turmoil. *Who am I to judge Katy when I stole from my father and broke my mother's heart?*

He reached for Katy's hand and explained, "Yes, a second chance. Like the calm God gave me the night typhus broke out on the ship. Like the peace He gave me when I wrote the letter asking forgiveness from my father."

He pulled Katy to him and took her face in his hands.

"God sent His son to die on the cross so those who repent of wrongdoing can be forgiven and live as His child forever . . . Even when we don't deserve it. God never stops loving us."

Katy's eyes met his.

"I need Him to forgive me . . . ," she sobbed, "to give me a second chance."

"He's waiting," Alex said.

He gathered Katy close and kissed her forehead.

"He's waiting for all of us to know the wonders of His love."

Alex pulled Katy down beside him as he knelt beside Thad.

"Let's pray."

• • •

Doc Owens closed the bedroom door behind him. He carried the baby in the crook of his arm.

"S'cuse me, folks," he said, "Susannah tells me you have one of those new-fangled stoves. This fine lad's had a bit to eat and now we'll store him in the warming oven until he grows a mite."

The three rose from their knees and wiped tears from their eyes.

"Do you mean it?" Alex asked.

His tone conveyed how incredulous he thought the idea was. They followed Doc Owens into the kitchen and stared in disbelief as he opened the metal box above the stove, and placed the swaddled babe inside its snug interior. He shut the door, but left it slightly ajar.

"He really means it!" Thad exclaimed.

Doc Owens threw back his head and hooted at their amazed expressions.

"You bet. Just like those new-fangled incubators . . . Maybe better. If you folks don't mind, I'll spend the night right here. One of the few good things about bein' a widower . . . Don't have anyone at home worryin' 'bout me."

Alex made up a cot for Doc Owens in the kitchen, close to the makeshift incubator and Susannah. Then, Alex, Katy, and Thad talked far into the night.

Thad told them about the night of drinking with Pete—how it made him feel grown, important. It had been well after midnight when the two of them returned to the cabin to find the two children crying in their bunks and Mary in hard labor.

"I rode for Doc that night as well," he told them, "but it was too late. Mary died and so did the baby."

A lump in his throat choked his voice. He took deep gulps of air and swallowed hard before he continued.

"The baby never slept in that crib Mary made the cover for."

Alex slipped beside Thad and put an arm around his shoulders.

"Scripture tells us all have sinned and come short, but God forgives us when we ask with true repentance. He gives us the chance to start over."

They heard the closure of the warming-oven door. Doc's steps crossed the linoleum to the bedroom.

"I must get home," Thad said. "My parents will be worried."

He reached for Alex's hand.

"Thank you, friend, it's like a huge weight rolled off my shoulders."

"Read your Bible," Alex told him. "It'll change your life, as it has mine."

When the kitchen door closed, Katy turned back to Alex. Fresh tears slid down her cheeks.

"I hated you for a time. I'm so sorry."

Alex wrapped her in his arms and replied, "And I'm sorry for all those months I didn't understand. I was jealous of what Sam and Susannah had, but we didn't. Please forgive me."

Katy rested her head on his shoulder.

"I'm not afraid, anymore, Alex. It's a miracle."

Alex wished Sam were there to say it better.

"The Bible says . . . ," he began and stumbled for the right words.

Warmth filled his being as he pressed Katy closer.

"God's peace fills our hearts and minds. It goes beyond anything we can figure out for ourselves. We don't have to understand it. Just accept it."

. . .

Alex and Katy waited for the service to begin. Katy squirmed on the hard bench, not comfortable anywhere as her pregnancy progressed. She stole a sideways glance at her husband's strong profile and took comfort again to know Alex was going to be by her side when her time came. Doc Owens had promised.

She watched Alex finger the crusader ring his grandfather gave him, it was an endearing habit. *Why hadn't I always loved him?*

Perhaps, she was no longer the self-centered girl who told Sofie goodbye on that morning long ago. Nor was Alex the lovesick college student who flattered her with his romantic proposal. Katy still had many questions concerning her new-found faith, but they had their lifetime together to search out the answers.

Susannah pumped away at the organ, her rapt face flushed. Sam stood at the schoolhouse door and greeted parishioners with baby Daniel cradled in the crook of his elbow.

Felix and Beulah Heim—with Thad at their side—paused to greet Alex and Katy. Alex leaned to whisper in Katy's ear.

"Thad's going back to school next fall . . . Told me he wants to be a doctor."

"That's wonderful," Katy replied. "Do you want our baby to be a boy?"

"Only if he looks like you," Alex teased with a sideways grin. "Otherwise, a girl will do just fine."

Little Daniel was to be baptized that morning. Sam and Susannah had asked Alex and Katy to be his godparents. As Sam came down the aisle, he handed the baby to Katy and walked into the pulpit. Alex linked his arm in hers as the room quieted.

Katy was beginning to realize being a Christian made room for a variety of ways of doing things. A priest conducted a different form of worship, but God looked on hearts. This insight made her smile as she recalled the scripture they had read together that morning: "It is of the LORD's mercies that we are not consumed, because his compassions fail not. They are new every morning: great is thy faithfulness."[6]

Susannah's fingers caressed the organ keys as she played the first hymn. Her face tilted upward with a rapt expression.

As they stood to sing, Katy juggled little Daniel in her arms and leaned toward Alex once more.

She whispered, "You know that crib you stored away in the barn? The one Mary Gregg made the cover for?"

Alex nodded.

"I've been thinking. We'll need it for the baby."

PART THREE

CHAPTER 29

Katy felt her chest tighten as their train pulled into New York City. She held Hilda Rose in the crook of one arm and gathered a fistful of her plaid skirt and petticoat in the other. She stepped down to the platform, grateful for the porter's assistance.

Luggage carts rattled past Katy on the rough cobblestones. Coal smoke from the engine's smokestack settled on her gray cape.

"I don't see them."

Alex searched the crowd for Hiram and Hannah.

"There they are."

Katy detoured around a cluster of men who wore bowler hats and dark, vested suits. Her intent to reach their precious friends—who also hurried toward them—was quite obvious.

Hannah Silverstein, perhaps a bit more round in cheek and chin, but with the same radiant exuberance, reached Katy first. Her embrace was so vigorous Katy's wide-brimmed hat pulled free from its hatpin and fell to the ground.

"Katy! Oh, Katy! I can't believe you're really here."

Hannah gripped Katy's arm as if reluctant to ever let go.

"And this must be Hilda Rose. Let me have a look at you, darling girl. Aren't you the sweet one? Just look at that silky blond hair—like her daddy's."

A small boy stooped to retrieve Katy's hat. As he handed it back to her, his eyes remained fastened on the white egret plumes which topped a gray felt brim faced in pink satin. Round-eyed and solemn, he held the hat in his hands as he offered it up to its owner.

Katy transferred Hilda Rose to Alex and stooped to thank the child. She took the hat from his hands and cupped the child's upturned chin with her free hand.

"You must be Moses . . . My, how you've grown."

Alex and Hiram exchanged hearty handshakes.

"You've put on weight," Alex said. "It suits you."

"I do declare," Katy exclaimed and playfully pulled at Hiram's full beard. "You look like a rabbi."

Hiram's burst of laughter caused a passersby to stop and turn. Little Moses grabbed his father's leg and buried his face in his father's pin-striped trousers.

"Just a grocer, I'm afraid, but a happy one."

"And who's this?" Katy asked.

Hiram jostled the bundle in his arms and extended the sleeping child for inspection.

"Meet little Morey. Two boys . . . God is good. Both will be my partners one day . . . SILVERSTEIN AND SONS," he announced and swept his arm in an arc across the sky as if he envisioned the storefront shingle.

"Ah, America. Such a land."

"Don't get him started," Hannah laughed. "We'll be here all day. Come now, let's collect your luggage. We have a driver waiting."

"Oh, you shouldn't—"

"Nonsense. What's money for?"

Hiram led the way. His short legs almost danced on the platform.

"Later though, you must take the child on the new electric streetcar. Moses loves them. They run almost everywhere now. And they're still digging the underground railway, miles and miles of it. Supposed to take, at least, another year to finish. Can you imagine such a thing? Seemed to us the whole city would just cave in. I hope they know what they're doing."

Their carriage rattled across the Brooklyn Bridge and soon stopped before an attractive brownstone. Trees shaded the broad sidewalk on which two young girls turned a rope for a third to jump.

Katy marveled at the air of stability the neighborhood possessed. *Does Hannah miss the voices of the pushcart peddlers on Hester Street? Or the aroma of baking bread as it floated up the fire escape?*

Having read Hannah's letters, Katy still pictured Hannah skimping all week to save for Shabbat and guarding conversation within paper-thin walls. Of course, Hannah would be equally surprised by their farm in Iowa. But Iowa seemed a million miles away, and Katy felt an unexpected twinge of disappointment to find so much had changed.

"We have the second floor apartment," Hiram announced. "Not a bad climb."

Not bad, indeed, Katy thought as they stepped into the square entrance hall with its broad staircase. *Hiram's business must be doing well.*

A handsome, middle-aged woman, who wore a boldly-flowered blue dress, descended the stairs. She carried a cloth shopping bag over one arm.

"Ah, your goyim friends have arrived."

Katy had often heard the term when she lived with the Silversteins. She had taken it as an insult until Susannah told her the phrase simply meant non-Jewish.

"I'm Sylvia Shom," the woman continued "a neighbor."

She stuck out her hand in greeting.

"Welcome to Brooklyn."

"Thank you."

Alex shook her hand and responded with his usual openness.

"We're Katy and Alex Meisen," he told her. "This is our daughter, Hilda Rose."

"Would you look at her . . . Such a darlink!"

"When we were first married, we lived in Brooklyn."

"Then you should've stayed," Mrs. Shom said with fervor. "I hear you went west to settle among the Indians."

"I've told you," Hannah reminded her, "Katy and Alex have a farm in Iowa. They've never mentioned Indians."

"And why would they? It isn't the sort of thing you put in letters to friends who worry about your safety."

Alex threw back his head and laughed.

"Well, Mrs. Shom," he said, "I hate to disillusion you, but our scalps are quite safe. Hail and tornados? Yes. Indians? No."

"Speaking of the weather—" Sylvia continued, leaning against the wall.

She crossed both arms and ankles, as if ready for a long exchange.

"A lovely day it is," Hiram interjected as he pulled a ring of keys from his pocket and steered around her.

"Shalom, Mrs. Shom. Remain in good health."

"As God wills," she called after him.

Then, she turned to Katy.

"How long will you be staying? After all, you've come so far—"

"Only a few days, and then we're sailing for Austria . . . To visit relatives."

"God in heaven! To get back on the boat . . . I should live so long. Of course, you're young . . . Probably left family behind. Now, my family—"

"Nice to have met you, Mrs. Shom," Alex cut in.

He patted Hilda Rose on the back as her head nodded against his shoulder.

"We'll see you again, I'm sure."

"Enjoy!"

The word echoed up the staircase and trailed them down the hall.

Hilda Rose had fallen asleep by the time they were inside the apartment. Katy and Alex followed Hannah into the nursery.

Hannah motioned for him to place the child in the crib which Alex and Katy had purchased for Moses two years earlier. It stood sturdy and tall on its wooden rockers.

As Alex eased the child onto the mattress, Hannah turned to Katy.

"Remember how we took turns rocking it that first night?"

Her dark eyes shone with the memory.

"I had never seen anything so beautiful."

"But isn't it the baby's bed now?"

"Oh, he sleeps anywhere. He'll drop off right on the floor or wherever he gets sleepy."

Alex left the room, but Hannah and Katy stood and looked down at the sleeping child. A sudden shyness rose between them.

"Her name surprised me," Hannah admitted. "I figured you'd choose something more in fashion. But I've decided I like it. It has certain stability to it."

Katy studied the face of the open, caring woman who befriended her without question at a time of desperate need. She wondered if she was ever going to tell Hannah the whole truth, as she had Susannah. *Probably not.*

The taking of life broke one of the Ten Commandments given to Moses, tenants of Jewish faith. Besides, Hannah might be hurt Katy had kept the secret while she lived with them.

Susannah, on the other hand, understood the forgiveness of sin bought by Christ with his death on the cross. Not that Hannah would have turned her out—she was much too kind—but it would have caused her great sadness.

Hannah's voice broke into Katy's thoughts.

"Come, I'll show you to your room. You can rest while Hilda Rose sleeps."

As they passed the parlor, Katy noted a new table replaced the scarred one where she shared the family's Passover. Yet, the familiar rocking chair had Hannah's shawl draped over the back and the zither still leaned against the wall.

She asked Hannah, "How's Cousin Myron's family?"

"They're doing fine. Still on Hester Street, but with plenty of room now that we've moved out. We wanted them to move here, to Brooklyn, but Cousin Myron likes being able to walk to work. So, they stay, only now he prepares meat in the store instead of his kitchen. Come, you must be exhausted."

Hannah spread back the quilt on the double bed. Katy reached to squeeze her shoulder.

"Dear Hannah," she said as Hannah hugged her in return. "It's good to be back."

Tears sprang to Hannah's eyes.

"Rest well," she whispered.

Katy pulled the quilt up to her chin and relaxed against the soft featherbed. She savored the way it cushioned her. In the hazy interval between sleep and wakefulness, she recalled Hannah's comment concerning Hilda Rose's name. She had called it "stable" and "not in fashion".

She was awake as she remembered. Actually, Alex felt the same way. She knew they were both right.

She had surprised herself. She knew it was neither a name expected of her nor one she would have chosen ahead of time. Before the birth, she fancied the name Annabelle which she had typeset in the POETRY section for Poe's "Annabelle Lee."

It was one of the things she liked best about her job at the newspaper. She was able to work and read at the same time.

Alex had favored the name Elisabeth.

"I've always loved your given name—Katharina Elisabeth," he said. "Besides, Elisabeth is a variation of Elizabeth—a good biblical name."

"But it's so old-country," Katy protested.

Anyway, she believed their child was to be a boy. So, she had not given the matter much thought.

She had, however, agonized over the decision Alex had left up to her—whether or not to tell Doc Owens about the abortion. Because she feared the procedure might have done something to jeopardize the baby's delivery, she finally stammered out her story.

• • •

"I was terrified," she, at last, confessed to the kindly physician.

Her eyes had focused on the floor, but when she looked up, she saw Doc Owens nod.

"Alex and I weren't married and I was alone. I just want to make sure this child has every chance."

The country physician took off his spectacles and rubbed the bridge of his nose between his thumb and finger. He then placed his hand on hers.

"Katy, you're as healthy as a brood mare."

Katy winced, but she knew he meant the homely phrase as a compliment.

"As far as I can tell," he continued, "everything's fine. You should have no problems whatsoever."

He was right; she had not experienced any problems. In fact,

Katy marveled at how easily the child arrived. Oh yes, there was pain, but, as Doc Owens had promised, Alex was at her side and held her hand.

At the baby's first wail, his chest heaved a mighty sob. Tears ran down his face.

"It's a girl," he told her.

"No heavyweight," Doc Owens said, "but she's got a filly's start in length. What's the name?"

Katy had taken the baby into her arms and laughed at the red, screwed-up face. All arms and legs, the baby did not look like an Annabelle.

"I'm not sure," she answered.

Alex registered surprise, but the old doctor chuckled and pushed his spectacles onto his forehead.

"After all this time? Well, no hurry. When you make up your mind, let me know so I can record it at the courthouse."

• • •

Katy turned onto her side and plumped the pillow. She felt sleepy, but her mind kept working. Daniel was several weeks old when Sam and Susannah had him baptized, but their Catholic upbringing had prompted Alex and Katy to contact Father Felder to set a date.

Beulah Heim brought home a book of names from the library. Alex read the feminine names aloud while Katy listened, the baby motionless at her breast, except for the steady pumping of the tiny cheeks. She stopped Alex in the middle of the Hs.

"That's it. Hilda."

"Hil-da?"

Alex hyphenated the word as if it stuck on his tongue.

"My grandmother's name."

"Hilda?"

Alex consulted the book.

"Derives from Brunhild—the heroine of Wagnerian opera."

His raised eyebrows caused Katy to giggle.

"And you thought Elisabeth was old-country."

"Well, somehow it fits her," Katy replied.

Alex continued to read, "It means breastplate."

His thumb twisted his ring.

"Grandfather wished for me to be strong and of good courage, and I tried so hard to be those things. When Sam introduced me to the scriptures, I learned I could rely on the armor of God's faithfulness. Our little girl will need that assurance."

Katy's brow remained puckered in thought as she placed the sleeping babe inside the cradle.

"Hilda Rose sounds nice. Wasn't Rose your grandmother's name?"

"Rosina. My sister, Rosa, was named for her."

Alex trailed his finger down the columns of names.

"Rose means simply that—a rose. What could be sweeter?"

Alex closed the book and reached across the cradle to place a kiss on the tip of Katy's nose.

"Katy, if it's the name you want for her, Hilda Rose it'll be—a child of sweet courage."

Katy returned his affection with an absent-minded smile. Then, she touched the cradle with her toe and set it in motion.

"I'll let Doc know for the records," Alex told her as he bent over the cradle to study the baby's wee, wizened face.

"I believe she favors my father's side of the family. Still," he chuckled and looked up at Katy with a twinkle in his eye, "I prefer Hilda Rose over Thomassina."

Katy frowned.

"The dead deserve respect," she told him, "but I'd never give any child of mine your father's name. Thomas Meisen was a domineering, disagreeable man."

As she teetered on the edge of sleep in Hannah's bed, Katy still worried if the name Hilda Rose suited their child. She remembered she had voiced the notion to Sofie that names wait and form themselves around people. She prided herself on her name: Katharina Elizabeth, and secretly hoped she personified its beauty.

Does the name Hilda Rose do my child a disservice? Oh, will I ever be more like Susannah, or Hannah for that matter, so calm and self-assured?

Her newfound happiness still felt fragile, and needed to be closely guarded.

What awaits us in our homeland?

At last, Katy drifted off, determined to leave her worries in the hands of the One she was learning to trust.

CHAPTER 30

A breeze ruffled the bright-colored flags atop masts fore and aft the ship's smokestacks. It carried a whiff of ocean air and left a taste of salt on Katy's tongue before it dissipated among the odors which still bound them to the docks. Fetid fumes from factory chimneys mingled with horse manure, fireplace smoke, and the human sweat of dockworkers who loaded luggage and other cargo into the hold.

"But no steerage," Katy whispered and breathed a prayer of thanksgiving.

Bound for the French harbor of Le Havre, she felt immensely grateful funds from the inheritance allowed them to book passage on a first class travel steamship.

As the ship moved away from shore, Hiram and Hannah faded into tiny dots. Then, the Lady of the Harbor came into view and Katy's attention turned to Hilda Rose. The child was only fourteen months old, and was far too young to understand. Yet, Katy pointed out the statue just the same, and hoped someday she might remember.

· · ·

Katy and Hilda Rose napped in their stateroom while Alex lounged in a deck chair under a blanket pulled up to his chin. Hilda Rose's little face shimmered in his thoughts. Katy thought her plain. He reproached her and pointed out the serenity of Hilda Rose's nature, her obvious intelligence and trusting gray eyes. Most of all, he delighted in the way the child responded to him.

"You're biased," Katy told him. "After all, *Daddy* is her first and only word. Is that normal, I ask you? Whatever happened to *Mama*?"

Yet, Hilda Rose did light up when she saw him and held out her arms to give him a big, juicy kiss. He was hardly able to wait for his mother to see her. Only through forgiveness was the thought of reunion so sweet.

A steward dressed in crisp whites broke into his reverie. The silver tray in his hands held several white china mugs and two teapots, steam rising from their thick cozies.

"Excuse me, sir. Would you care for some tea or hot chocolate?"

Alex reached for one of the cups and felt as cosseted as the cozy carafes.

"Chocolate, please . . . How thoughtful."

The steward kept his eyes on the tray.

"No trouble, sir. It's teatime."

So, the pleasant days passed. Alex and Katy pushed Hilda Rose round the deck in a rented baby carriage. Its hood shielded her small face against the brisk breezes. Meals were served in the dining salon on long, linen-covered tables lined by mahogany chairs.

In the evenings, strains of orchestra music reached them from the grand salon. Katy envisioned the rosewood paneling, velvet draperies, gilded mirrors, and circular bull's eye windows.

"I wish I was there," she told Alex. "I remember hearing the music from steerage and seeing the women in their fine gowns. Now, I can hire a nurse and be among them . . . If only you liked to dance."

Alex teased, "I never would've rescued you at the street festival if I hadn't been standing on the sidelines."

"Yes, I remember, but I wish you'd, at least, try to learn."

At last, the ship slipped into the English Channel and docked at Le Havre. From there, a train was to carry them across the French countryside, through Switzerland, and along the banks of the Bodensee to Bregenz. Alex cabled ahead so Anna knew when to expect them.

At the first sight of their beloved Alps, Alex and Katy held Hilda Rose up to the window of their compartment and pointed out Switzerland's majestic monarchs. The fabled forests of Bregenzerwald laid only a border away.

When, at last, the vast lake came into view—its waters an opaque washtub blue—tears sprang to Katy's eyes. Alex squeezed her hand.

"I didn't know how much I'd missed it," she told him.

• • •

Anna Meisen searched the faces behind each window as the squares flicked by. The train ground to a halt and trailed a haze of coal smoke the length of the cars. *Will he look the same?*

Her daughters stood beside her, unmoved and oddly stiff—one stout, one slim. Both pressed hankies to their noses to shield away the engine fumes. Anna regarded them nervously.

She twisted her handkerchief in her hands and thought, *When had they become such strangers? Why had I insisted they come to meet his train?*

Neither Rosa nor Maria had never been close to their older brother and openly resented him because of the inheritance. Once again, Anna had tried to squeeze fantasy into the frame of reality and failed.

Lately, she found herself fearing her entire life had been a fraud. Her adored father was an idealist and fostered her imagination as a child. He weaved fanciful stories for her at his workbench as he sculpted stone into objects of art.

Against her father's advice, she married Thomas, a humorless pragmatic. She then turned her talents to flower arrangements, culinary creations, a well-managed household, family outings, and devout Catholicism. As she reached middle age, all those things seemed insignificant, except for her faith. *What will I do with the rest of my life?*

Alex appeared on the platform of the last car. A small child rode in the crook of his arm. *My first grandchild!*

Anna felt as if her heart was going to burst.

Alex looked more wonderful than she had dared hope. His hairline had receded a bit and he was deeply tanned, but some deep-seated difference changed his countenance. It replaced the hesitation which so often shadowed his sensitive nature in the past. Yet, in no way did it remind her of his father's arrogance.

"Mutter!"

The greeting gripped and squeezed her heart. Alex stepped off the train and held the child out to her. Anna's tears commingled with the precious fruits of her womb as she embraced them.

"Meet Hilda Rose," Alex said.

His sisters remained silent, unmoved. They allowed Alex to kiss them on both cheeks; yet, they spoke no words of welcome. Anna frowned, but they avoided her eyes. She turned away to embrace Katy.

As pretty as ever, but different somehow. A scattering of freckles sprinkled her nose and cheeks, and her chin still had its spunky tilt, but her countenance seemed softer, more relaxed.

Helga Thannen came alone. She stood to one side. Katy approached and embraced her mother's rigid form, and then looked into the gaunt, unsmiling face. Traces of the beauty Katy inherited were reduced to a skeletal framework of high cheek-bones and almond-shaped eyes.

"Hello, Mutter."

Katy's voice was almost a whisper.

"I got to get home," Helga murmured. "Maybe you come by the house?"

"Of course," Katy replied. "Tomorrow morning . . . or will you be at work?"

"Work? Oh no, I've quit work. At my age, keepin' up with the young'un takes all the starch out of me."

"Then, I'll be by with Hilda Rose. I look forward to also seeing Father, Horst, and Frederick, of course."

• • •

It was a short walk to where two carriages waited. Alex, Katy, and Anna—who held Hilda Rose—rode in the first. The sisters followed in the second with luggage piled on the back. Helga refused Anna's offer and walked in the opposite direction.

However, as the driver picked up the reins, Katy shouted, "Wait!" She jumped down from her seat.

"Sofie!"

She picked up her skirts and ran toward a young woman who stood at the end of the platform.

"Wonderful to see you . . . and how pretty you are!"

Sofie took a step back as if to gauge the sincerity of Katy's greeting. Then, she moved into Katy's arms.

"It's really you, isn't it? I scarce believed when I heard you were coming."

"I bought you a gift, just as I promised."

Katy bit her lip. She heard her words as those said to a child. This trim young woman with upswept coiffure no longer fit her memory of the self-conscious schoolmate who trailed behind her and did her bidding. She hurried to bridge the awkward moment.

"We've so much catching up to do. How soon can we have some time together?"

"Tomorrow morning? By the fountain in the market square?"

Katy giggled with delight.

"Our old meeting place. Perfect. Eleven? I need to see my family first, but eleven should be fine."

"See you there . . . and Katy? Welcome back."

• • •

Anna invited her daughters to stay for lunch. She then regretted not taking them to an eating place instead to lessen the need for conversation because Maria gave a tedious account of her charity work at the hospital, and Rosa described her recent wedding in minute detail.

"Of course, if Father were alive," Rosa went on, "the wedding would've been even grander."

Why do I lapse into fantasies of fixing things, wishing occasions to turn out better than before? Anna thought.

She folded her arms across her chest and gave Alex such a malevolent look Anna shuddered.

"But then, of course," Rosa continued, "the money wouldn't have been wrongly divided. Father made it very clear you no longer belonged to this family and would have no inheritance."

"Rosa!"

"It's all right, Mutter," Alex said quietly. "I understand Rosa's resentment. I sinned against all of you when I left as I did. I beg your forgiveness, Rosa."

"That's for a priest to do," Rosa shot back. "Besides, I don't see you wearing sackcloth and ashes."

"Repentance is an attitude of the heart," Alex replied. "Scripture tells us to forgive one another and set things right between us. We need no go-between, save Jesus, who made forgiveness possible by his death on the cross."

Rosa's voice rose to a shrill pitch.

"My, aren't you the mealy-mouthed hypocrite?"

Anna saw her son's hands clench in his lap and pushed her chair back from the table which scraped the legs on the polished wood floor.

"That's enough. Either you apologize to your brother and sister-in-law or leave my table."

Rosa stood and faced her mother. Her color was high and her eyes flashed.

"I have my own home now, thank you, and my own inheritance. Alex has always been your favorite, Mother. Anyone could see that."

She wadded the linen napkin, flung it beside her plate, and stalked from the room. Her back was rigid and her long neck was beet red.

• • •

Katy welcomed the excuse to take Hilda Rose and leave the house to visit her family as well as Sofie. She had not slept well. Alex said they needed to pray for his sisters and put it in God's hands. Yet, the scene at the table repeated in Katy's mind.

Even before Rosa's outburst, she felt out-of-place, as if she was supposed to serve the meal instead of eat it. Not that Frau Meisen treated her with anything, except warmth and consideration, but Katy wondered what her mother-in-law really thought of her.

Does she naturally think me beneath Alex, unworthy of him? Because of me, Alex left. What reason does Anna have to believe her former maid deserved her son's love, or his money for that matter? Will the difference in our ages and education forever influence Frau Meisen's opinion of me?

She seated Hilda Rose in the old wicker pram Anna retrieved from the attic and wheeled it out the door. After all, they only came for a visit. She was going to make the best of it.

Hilda Rose sat up very straight and patted the padded leather seat with her small hands. Anna offered Katy a driver and carriage, but Katy insisted on walking—the bright sun and refreshing breeze off the lake were a welcome distraction. She started off at a brisk pace as they trundled downhill toward the village square.

As she neared the walls of the convent school, bells in the cupola tolled the hour. They chimed in tandem with other bells across the city. Tears came to Katy's eyes at the well-remembered sound.

As she passed the iron gates, she wondered how the nuns remembered her. Of course, they heard the village gossip—rumors must have flown. Her father and brothers seldom went to Mass, but her mother probably bore the shame of the whispered conversations.

A sudden impulse caused her to detour in the direction of the parish church. Morning Mass was over and the oak doors stood open. Katy looked straight down the aisle to the altar and the painted frescos which adorned the wall behind it. Close beside the altar stood the statue of the Blessed Virgin.

Katy stopped to regard the sweet features meant to portray attributes of Mary's character. She shuddered as she recalled how she pretended to be pious while memorizing Mary's expression to use for her selfish purposes.

"Please forgive me, Holy Mother," she whispered.

CHAPTER 31

When, at last, she maneuvered the cobblestones to arrive at the familiar dwelling, Helga opened at the kitchen door before Katy knocked.

"I never figured you'd walk," her mother said.

Helga smoothed down her drab brown dress, and patted the bun which drew back her thin hair.

"Why not?"

Katy despised her defensive reaction, but there it was.

"I used to walk home every day from the Meisen house. Besides, life on a farm makes for lots of exercise."

Helga led the way into the front room. She had yet to acknowledge Hilda Rose.

"That's another thing I can't picture," she said. "You livin' in the country. Just like my beginnings . . . Not that being the wife of a blacksmith took me very far away."

The clock on the wall ticked loudly. Hilda Rose slept in the pram, her little head lolled to one side.

"Your sister's asleep as well. You can peek at her if you want."

Helga gestured toward the hallway which led to the bedrooms.

Katy was unable to account for her panic.

"Is Papa home . . . and Horst and Frederick?"

"Of course," her mother's tone flattened, "back in the shop, like always."

"Then, I'll see them first."

Katy avoided her mother's eyes. She questioned her reaction.

Am I punishing Mother for bearing another daughter? That's ridiculous.

Helga shrugged her shoulders and said, "Have it your way. You always did."

Nothing unfolded as Katy had hoped. Helga followed at a distance as Katy wheeled the pram down the dirt path to the shed. Smoke bellowed from its tin chimney.

Walter Thannen wiped his hands on his soiled leather apron and pecked his daughter on the cheek. He smelled of sweat and horsehide. Then, he bent over with his hands on his knees and acknowledged his sleeping granddaughter.

"She ain't as purty as you."

Katy knew he meant it as a compliment and took it as such. Her brothers crowded alongside and angled awkwardly for a look.

Katy always thought of her brothers as more or less interchangeable, although Frederick was taller. Perhaps, because their faces were always dark with soot or she seldom really looked at them.

"Hi, Sis," they both said, almost in unison.

The thought struck Katy she never really knew her brothers. Guilt tugged at her heart.

"You happy, Katharina?"

The question caught her by surprise since it came from a father who seldom spoke, and never of feelings. A father who ate, slept, left the house, and came back to do the same again. The question and his use of her given name brought quick tears to her eyes.

"Yes, I'm happy, Papa. And you?"

His eyes squinted into hers, as if he appraised her sincerity. Then, he turned back to the fire and his bellows, and answered with his back to her.

"Business good. What more can a body ask? Right, boys?"

"Ja, Father," both brothers agreed as one voice.

"Are there smithies in America?" Horst asked.

"Oh my goodness, yes."

Katy smiled at her brothers, glad to address a safe subject.

"It's an important trade. New York City alone has thousands of horses and they all need shoes. Plus, every farmer in Iowa counts on the blacksmith to keep his beasts shod and his tools sharpened."

"That's goot," Horst said.

He swiped a dirty rag across his sweaty brow which left a white streak like a bandage across his forehead. Katy resisted a sudden desire to touch it with her hand, as one did to soothe a child.

Horst and Frederick looked at each other, and then at Katy. Horst kicked at straw near his foot.

Katy filled the awkward silence and suggested, "I don't want to keep you from your work. We'll come back soon."

"Ja," her father answered as the three men returned to work.

Back in the kitchen, Helga poured steaming coffee into two thick mugs and added clotted cream to hers. She motioned Katy to the kitchen table.

"Might as well sit a spell," she said. "You staying for lunch?"

"No, thank you. I'm meeting Sofie."

Katy pulled out the hand-made wooden chair which had been hers. As Helga placed the mug on the table, Katy noticed her knotted knuckles, the split nails. She calculated for the first time ever her mother's age.

She can't be much past her middle forties.

"Never figured you for country life what with all your grand ideas," Helga repeated. "Nor Alex Meisen as a farmer, for that matter. Most of all, I can't take in us both havin' babies nigh 'bout the same time . . . seems unnatural."

"Ma . . . ,"

Katy wondered how to bridge the hurt, the unasked questions.

"Ja?"

"Maybe it's a blessing—God giving us something in common."

"Something in common? Now, that's a strange thing to say. Blood ties don't mean nothin'? Seems you bein' my flesh should count for somethin'."

"Of course, it does."

Katy pushed her cup aside.

Could nothing go right?

"What I meant—"

"Is that why you borrowed my mother's name for your young'un? Thinkin' it would set things right 'tween us?"

Helga stood, clattered her cup into the tin sink, and then pushed hard on the pump handle. Katy felt a flush spread up from her neck and struggled to keep her voice even.

"Mutter, I know how much it must've hurt you when I left without saying goodbye. I never expressed any gratitude for how hard you worked to send me to convent school and buy me nice things."

Hilda Rose stirred in the carriage and Katy hurried on.

"I've learned many lessons since then. I hope . . . ,"

She stopped to swallow back tears.

"I hope I've changed."

Helga rested the palms of her hands on the sink board and leaned into it. Katy stared at her bony back and tried again.

"It's hard to explain, but when I heard I had a baby sister, at first I was jealous. I also hoped you having her would help make up for my leaving."

Her mother remained silent. Katy fought against spilling forth her frustrations—so long bottled up—the need for a mother at home after school, someone to listen to her instead of pointing out her faults. She swallowed hard and kept "a civil tongue" as her mother put it.

"I'm not sure why I named our baby Hilda Rose. Now, that I live so far away, maybe I needed a link to my roots."

Helga straightened her shoulders and pumped more water into the pail.

"Name's fine. And puttin' Rose after it sounds right pretty."

She turned from the sink.

"Come, I hear mine fussin' and look at your'n—wide awake with nary a peep, her ears perked up to everything we say. Let's put 'em together and see how they make out."

Katy knew it was the best she would get from her mother. She turned her attention to the small child Helga brought before her— her sister. It seemed so strange to call her such—she resembled their father. Katy had no idea what she expected, but little Angelika was like any other child to her. Eighteen years separated them . . . and thousands of miles.

The babies stared at each other. Hilda Rose sucked her thumb.

When the cuckoo clock struck the half hour, Katy knew it was time to go. She promised to return for other visits, lifted Hilda Rose from the floor into the pram, and trundled down the street toward the market square. She had taken Angelika on her lap, but her mother had not touched her granddaughter.

• • •

Above the stone relief sculptures which bordered the roof of the government building, Austria's black and yellow flag flapped in the breeze. Over the entrance, the emblem stared downward with the fierce eyes of an eagle. Katy wondered who replaced Thomas Meisen as the provincial governor.

As she trundled the pram over the cobblestones, she allowed herself to see her birthplace as a stranger. In the far distance, a mighty tower marked the remains of a medieval fortification and stone arches supported a bridge dating from Roman times. Katy made out carts which trundled over it and marveled at how old this homeland was compared to her new one.

She remembered how the nuns taught about the different empires which dominated Austria and their influence on it. The red tiles of Turkish turrets dotted distant mountain trails which led away from the city. Along the way, ruins of crude shrines dated back to Celtic superstition.

Austrians, as a whole, were friendly people known for welcoming strangers and making them feel at home. History forced the accommodation of many different peoples within a relatively small area.

It was a new thought to Katy, and one she tried out in her mind on America—a vast land which mingled many cultures. *Over time, will America have a similar attitude of acceptance? Or does it encompass too much territory for a similar need?*

• • •

The sight of Sofie waiting on a stone bench in the village square banished all serious reflection. She almost tipped over the pram in her hurry to cross the uneven roadway.

"Poor child," Sofie laughed and moved over to give Katy room on the bench.

As naturally as if she had done it every day, Sofie plucked Hilda Rose from her seat and placed her on her lap. Her voice was low and musical, so different from the strained, self-conscious quality Katy recalled.

"I sat thinking of the last time we met here. You told me about the letter from Alex. It had all the ingredients of a fairy tale. I guess it still seems that way to me."

"Well, in some ways it was a fairy tale."

Katy smoothed her skirt before pleating the cloth between her fingers. *Why am I suddenly the shy one?*

"Things have a way of turning out different in real life."

"I know."

Sofie turned her head and waited for Katy to look up.

"I thought you would write," she said. "What news I've had, I've heard from Helga."

"I'm so sorry," Katy said as she lowered her eyes again. *Sofie is so well-spoken, so different than I remember.*

"If you recall," Sofie continued, "I was the one who had to tell your mother of your departure."

Katy nodded without looking up.

"I've kept in touch with her," Sofie continued. "I think she never forgave me for keeping your secret until you were gone."

She uttered the words without rancor, but the hurt registered with Katy. She raised her eyes to meet her friend's.

"It's a long story, Sofie. So much happened—I was just too wrapped up in myself, too overwhelmed by what Alex proposed. Please forgive me."

Tears welled in Sofie's eyes and Katy hurried on.

"While I'm here, I hope we can spend time together."

Hilda Rose grasped Sofie's bodice to pull up to a standing position. She then reached a chubby hand to touch Sofie's face.

"Hilda Rose knows who she likes," Katy told her friend.

She looked into Sofie's eyes and saw a lovely, self-assured young woman. With a true sense of shame, Katy realized she had always regarded Sofie as inferior to herself. Yet, Sofie became the confident one.

"I don't wonder she's attracted to you," Katy said. "You must know how much you've changed."

Sofie's laugh came natural, not in the least offended. She bounced Hilda Rose on her knee and Hilda Rose squealed with delight.

"I'm married," she said. "I think you might remember him . . . Johann Rehm, the baker's son. He still helps his father in the shop, but he also paints. In fact, he's sold some of his paintings as far away as Innsbruck."

"That's wonderful. It's easy to see you're happy."

Sofie glowed.

"Oh yes, I am. Johann is a wonderful man. You've changed as well, you know. Your hair is shorter, and neither of us wears dirndls any more, but it's more than that. Maybe it's motherhood that's softened you. I worried you might start off bossing me around again."

Katy's fit of girlish giggles caused an older lady crossing the square to turn and look their way. Katy felt herself relax. Sofie's candor stripped away pretense.

As she caught her breath, Katy admitted, "I did a lot of that, didn't I?"

She leaned over to kiss away Hilda Rose's concerned expression.

"No, I'm afraid it took more than motherhood to turn me around. I hope to tell you all about it."

After the noon lunch hour, shops reopened and the square began to fill with people. Vendors uncovered their stands and merchants rolled up the curtains on their shop windows. Katy and Sofie bought fruit and frankfurters, and took them to the shade of a tree near the lake where they spread their skirts and took off their hats while Hilda Rose slept in the pram.

Katy reached into her satchel and retrieved the beaded purse she had purchased at Macy & Company.

"It's lovely!" Sofie exclaimed. "I'll prize it always."

With a stab of sadness, Katy realized she knew almost nothing about this dear soul who had been her loyal friend so many months ago. She might have little use for a fancy purse.

"Sofie—" she started as tears came to her eyes.

Sofie reached to cover Katy's hand with hers.

"It's all right, Katy. Let me show you something."

From her pocket, she retrieved a clipping from an Innsbruck newspaper. A photo showed the town mayor at a local art show presenting a first place ribbon to a thin, earnest-looking young man.

"It's Johann," Sofie said, her voice shy, but proud. "He's an artist."

"Really?"

Katy was impressed.

"What kind of art?"

"Mostly landscapes—he does commercial printing for many of the Bregenz merchants. He's beginning to sell more of the ones he renders and hopes to open a shop someday."

"That's wonderful!"

In turn, Katy told Sofie about her job at the newspaper office. Soon late afternoon shadows slanted across the square.

"I can't wait to meet Johann," Katy said as they parted.

"I think Alex will like him," Sofie answered.

"Of course, he will. As will I."

Hilda Rose was now asleep on Katy's lap. Katy placed her back in the carriage and hugged Sofie goodbye before concentrating on the steep climb back up the hill. Her eyes feasted on the stupendous progression of mountains which marched eastward. Fog rolled off the lake and collected round the base of the Pfander which stood its contemplative guard over the town of her youth.

Anna was expecting her for supper. Her time with Sofie had flown by and she must hurry.

CHAPTER 32

Over the next several weeks, Katy spent much of the time with her parents and brothers, but Helga continued to keep a certain distance. Perhaps, because Katy was also a mother, Helga treated her as an adult, but certain topics remained off limits.

As long as Katy described events—the crossing, the immigrant processing station, the squalid flat she shared with Baylie Root, Blanch Morrissey's laundry work, and the train trip west—Helga listened with apparent interest and asked numerous questions: Was the trip across the ocean as bad as everyone said? What are streetcars? Are trains in America as good as in Austria?

In turn, Katy bounced Angelika on her knee and inquired about people and places she remembered. However, if a conversation turned to any topic of a serious nature or revealed the slightest emotion, Helga jumped up to fix tea or played a game of peekaboo with Hilda Rose.

Only once, as Helga busied herself with dressing Angelika, did her tone take on an intensity which caused Katy to look up. She noticed her tightened lips and the jerky way Helga pulled on the baby's clothes and waited for what came next.

"Katy . . . ," Helga started and cleared her throat, "I have something I feel I must confess to you."

Her words gained momentum as if she willed herself to say them.

"I could've sworn you ran off because you were in a family way. I guess I was wrong."

Katy took a deep breath. Their future relationship possibly hinged on her answer.

"And if I had been?"

The silence lasted so long Katy decided her mother was unable to answer. Then, Helga turned to her as tears misted the weary eyes sunk deep inside their sockets.

"I would've said prayers that you be forgiven . . . lit a candle at the altar, but I would've understood you sparing us the disgrace."

So, that was it, Katy pondered.

The deepest hurt rested in Katy's sudden departure with no excuse to blame it on. Katy knew she must spare her mother the whole truth. Mention of the awful day in Dr. Adler's office was only going to widen the chasm between them.

"Your prayers are important to me, Mutter," she said.

She chose her next words with care.

"I'm very grateful for my upbringing in the church. God's Word tells us to train up our children in the way they should go and when they are grown they will not depart from the teachings."

Helga's eyes searched her daughter's face and she asked, "Are you still a Catholic, Katy?"

"Yes, I am," Katy answered, "but I've gone beyond the ritual and doctrine to grow in faith."

"Some things shouldn't be questioned."

Helga's tone had firmed again. She placed Angelika in the wooden high chair.

"But I'm pleased you, at least, think I did something right. You've turned out pretty well at that."

"Thank you, Mother. I'm glad you think so."

The conversation would have ended there, but Katy wedged in a question. Earlier that day she had come upon her mother as Helga took a brown medicine bottle from the sideboard, unscrewed the lid, and tipped the contents to her lips. Then, perhaps sensing Katy's presence, Helga screwed the cap back on the bottle and buried it beneath Grandmother Hilda's crocheted tablecloth. When Katy stopped and cleared her throat, her mother quickly shut the drawer.

"Mutter? Are you feeling well?" Katy ventured to ask.

Helga's hand flew to her throat, and then asked, "Why do you ask?"

"I've seen you press your hand to your stomach as if it pains you."

"Indigestion . . . Started when I was carrying the baby. As you now know, being in the family way ain't easy."

"Have you seen a doctor?"

"Course I have. Now, don't be sayin' nothin' to your father."

Katy found her mother's answer inadequate, but she knew the subject was closed.

• • •

When Katy and Alex took Hilda Rose with them to spend evenings with Katy's family, Walter Thannen sucked on his pipe and said little. He asked a few questions about farming methods in the new land and listened to the answers, but he appeared to be in awe of Alex, as were Katy's brothers and their wives.

In contrast, Alex and Katy felt at ease with Sofie and Johann in their snug cottage. The walls displayed Johann's artwork: delicate landscapes and a few whimsical renderings of animals.

Alex was drawn repeatedly to a small oil painting of dairy cows which loped down an Alpine mountainside. Cowbells swung from the cow's necks as their fat udders swayed side-to-side. Johann had captured the exact shades of approaching dusk. Alex almost heard the tinkling echoes through the valley.

He finally asked, "Is it for sale? It so reminds me of the Valley of Egg."

"No, it's not for sale—" Johann stated.

Then, he broke into laughter at the crestfallen look on his new friend's face.

"—but it's yours . . . My gift, so you won't forget your homeland, or us."

Alex was deeply touched. He went on to describe his cousin's family and his time spent with them.

"Listen," he exclaimed. "Let's go on a picnic. I've meant to take Katy to visit my cousins and you can meet them as well . . . See the cheese factory. We'll take the painting along. They'll love it. Cousin Alois knows every cow on the mountain by name."

Katy stole a quick glance at Sofie and recalled the fateful picnic when she had so rudely dismissed her friend in order to be alone with Alex. Sofie met her eyes with a smile which said she also remembered, but forgave the hurt it caused. Katy reached to squeeze her hand, but the memory brought a flush to her cheeks.

● ● ●

Late summer sunshine filtered through the trees on the day set aside for their outing. As the carriage entered the forest, a sheepherder's voice echoed in some far recess, and from another direction dull thuds of an ax fell in steady rhythm.

Alex welcomed the distractions. As they neared the valley, he wondered what to expect. After taking the money, he left Alois to break the news to his father. Not only had it required a trip down the mountain, but Alex only imagined the scene with his father.

How will Alois feel about seeing me again . . . Will we be welcome?

Alex had not thought about those things before he issued the invitation; however, he need not have worried. Alois Meisen embraced him in a mighty hug and Therese's scrubbed face glowed as her rough hands clasped his. Even Grandmother Emma revealed her toothless smile.

"I just knew she'd be that pretty," she said of Katy.

"You told us enough times," Alois teased and slapped Alex on the back.

Squat glasses came out of the cupboard and Alois poured schnapps all round. Alois' young sons neared their teens. They took turns giving Hilda Rose piggyback rides around the yard while Alois gave the adults a tour of the cheese factory. If either Alois or Therese harbored any ill feelings, they did not show.

At last, Alex found a moment alone with his cousin.

"I did you a terrible disservice, Cousin, leaving you to find the money missing and take the news to my father. It took real courage, courage I didn't have. Please forgive me."

Alois nodded his head.

"Your father wasn't an easy man with good news, let alone bad, but Therese and I talk often of the good times that summer. It's wonderful to see you again. And now that I've seen Katy, I don't wonder you were so lovesick."

• • •

On their way back down the mountain, the two young couples settled on a spot shaded by an old, abandoned inn, its painted designs still vivid against the peeling whitewash. They spread a cloth on the ground, poured the wine, and prepared to eat their simple lunch of cheese, fruit, and cold chicken. Before they ate, Alex prayed and thanked God for good friends and His glorious creation.

"You sound like you're on a first name basis with God," Johann commented. "Isn't that a bit presumptuous?"

"Not when you know His Son," Alex answered. "Do you?"

So, a lively discussion began which lasted into the afternoon shadows. At first, Katy fidgeted and picked at blades of grass. She worried what Sofie was thinking, but Sofie paid close attention and seemed not the least offended by anything Alex said.

Katy relaxed and listened as well. While Hilda Rose napped on a blanket in the shade of a large oak, Katy found she was, in fact, learning, too. Alex made the gospel message so clear. Unlike her, he did not appear to feel his throat close and his palms perspire when he talked about God to people who might turn away from what he said.

Sofie and Johann interrupted each other in their eagerness to ask questions.

"What did it mean to be saved? Wasn't the crucifixion more important than an empty tomb?"

"Christ died on the cross for our sins, once for all, to bring us to God," Alex explained. "The empty tomb proves God raised him from the dead. He's alive today as our living Lord and Savior."

To Katy's amazement, by the time they gathered up their things and started back down the mountain, all of them shared an eternal bond of faith. As Johann helped Sofie into the carriage, Katy hung back to squeeze her husband's arm.

"Thank you," she whispered as she leaned her head against his shoulder. "What a present for Sofie . . . Far better than the beaded purse."

• • •

In just the few short weeks since her son's return, Anna felt years younger. She delighted for every moment spent with Hilda Rose, and was captivated by the intense expressions on her little face. She studied every nuance of her grandchild's personality against the moment Alex and Katy left.

What a fine man Alex has become, so calm and confident, so rich in character. As for Katy, she has a depth no longer reminiscent of the self-absorbed, coquettish lass I remember.

Not all of her qualms vanished, however. Katy's straight-forward speech and obvious intelligence and resourcefulness impressed her. Katy was a good mother and anyone saw Alex adored her. Yet, Anna sensed a reserve in Katy toward her. In truth, Anna knew she also held back from Katy as well.

On long walks with Alex, her arm linked in his, Anna gathered courage to ask him to forgive her part in sending him away that summer. She gazed out over the placid lake, her eyes the clear blue of its reflection.

"It wasn't because Katy worked as a maid in our household," she told him. "I hope you know that, Alex. I was afraid you were infatuated with her beauty and thought spending time away from her would lend some perspective."

She paused and questioned the honesty of her words. *Are they the actual truth . . . Are my reservations deeper than that? Do I judge Katy as not equal to my son?*

"Nevertheless," she continued, "you were an adult. Your father and I acted too hastily, without regard for your feelings."

Alex gazed upon his mother's still youthful countenance, the white widow's peak in her dark hair accentuating the high, unlined forehead, and the deep sockets of her expressive eyes. She often outpaced him as they walked.

"You never judged people by their station, Mother; I knew that. You weren't too wrong. I was as lovesick as they come . . . stubborn, too. When Father said I couldn't marry Katy, I became obsessed with finding a way. So much has happened since then. Katy and I are different people than we were then."

"Yes, you are. It makes your leaving that much harder."

Alex stopped in the path and turned to face her. He put his hand over Anna's as it rested on his arm. Her chin began to tremble.

"As you know, Mother," he began. "We need to return to Iowa to harvest the crops. Thad Heim, our neighbor's son, promised to look after the chores, but his father will soon need him at home. Katy and I want you to come back to America with us."

Anna's heart lurched in her chest. She had not dared hope, yet she had. Oh, she knew what she had told herself: Austria was her home and her daughters needed her, However, that internal argument grew weaker, especially after Rosa's outburst.

She indulged vague daydreams concerning a new life, a new start. Then, she berated herself for her foolishness. *After all, I'm, fifty years old—too late to start over, but is fifty really so old? What possible use can I be if I go?*

She felt she must have a purpose, make a useful contribution. She did not want to take advantage of her son's soft heart. She was able to cook and help out around the house, but she did not want Katy to see it as competing or interfering.

Sometimes, she bit her tongue when Katy was cross with Hilda Rose. *Won't it only be natural for Katy—mistress of her household—to sometimes clash with the way I do things?*

"Dearest Alex," Anna began. "You'll never know what your invitation means to me. But I'm afraid I must decline . . . It just wouldn't work."

Alex chuckled and said, "Oh, I know you, Mother. You picture yourself put out to pasture—sitting in a rocking chair crocheting doilies the rest of your life."

He waggled his finger at her and Anna laughed. He knew he had perceived at least a part of the truth.

"I know you're always one to keep busy. Even with maids to help, you always worked alongside. But you don't know what it's like to live on an Iowa farm."

He guided her to sit beside him on a low stone wall which bordered a small park. Children's voices wafted toward them from the nearby playground.

"Now that Susannah and Sam have moved to town for Sam to pastor a church, I know Katy must be lonesome with just Hilda Rose for company while I'm working in the fields, laying tile, or tending the livestock."

He looked out over the park and took her hand in his.

"Katy loved her job at the newspaper office and the editor appeared very satisfied with her work. If you helped with the baby, perhaps, she can go back to work a few hours a week. You'd be wonderful with Hilda Rose."

• • •

He never revealed Katy's initial response.

"Are you crazy, Alex Meisen? It's not as if your mother is old and feeble, and needs our care. She'd be as miserable as I would."

However, after giving it thought, Katy had changed her mind.

"I'd like going back part-time, Alex. Perhaps, it could work after all."

• • •

"You wouldn't object to Katy working?" Alex's mother asked, stunned.

Anna's eyes widened. She had heard her son argue a mother's place was with her child.

"I'm just saying having you at home with Hilda Rose would be different than anyone else . . . Maybe for just a few hours a week."

Alex stood and offered Anna his arm.

"Promise to think about it, Mother. If you do decide to come back with us to America, it'd make me very happy."

• • •

Anna struggled to arrive at a decision. She was going to miss her homeland. *What about Rosa and Maria . . . Wouldn't I abandon them? And the church . . . Mass is a source of daily spiritual comfort. The farm is too far away from a church.*

Rosa came to her mother's house reluctantly, at Anna's request. She had not been back since her outburst at the dinner table. They gathered in the parlor where Rosa chose a chair on the opposite side of the room.

"It just proves you don't love us," Maria whined.

"I will always love you," Anna told her.

She was relieved to find in her heart she truly meant what she said.

"If you really loved us, you wouldn't leave," Rosa accused.

She smoothed her upswept hair off her neck and drummed her long, tapered fingers on the polished table beside her chair.

Anna smoothed one hand over the other, and willed to stay calm.

"Life is a series of choices, my dears, and even the best choices often have painful aspects. I only know I have the rest of my life to live and I want to remain as productive as possible. Besides, I do have enough money to return for visits."

She paused, but neither daughter spoke.

"In America, I can be helpful to Alex and Katy. You're both adults now and will eventually have your own families . . . and each other, of course."

Maria burst into tears. She dabbed at her eyes with a lace handkerchief.

"Rosa's married, but this house is my home. How could you?"

Anna sighed.

"I was getting to that."

She spread out several papers on the low table in front of her.

"I'm giving you both this property. I signed the papers today."

It pained her to see the change in their reactions—widened eyes and animated expressions which passed between them.

"It's your business how you work it out," she continued. "I see no reason why you couldn't continue to live here, Maria, and run the house."

"I've never understood you, Mother."

Rosa pressed her lips together.

"That's not unusual," Anna replied. "Your father understood both of you better than I did. I'm sorry for that, but I did my best. Now, you're grown women and have your destinies to pursue. You'll have my blessing always, and my prayers."

Rosa opened her month as if to speak, and then shut it again.

Maria looked down at her hands and moved the toe of her shoe back and forth on the carpet.

"Maybe you're right," Rosa said, at last. "Maybe it's better this way."

CHAPTER 33

Alex wired ahead so Hiram and Hannah were able to meet the ship at the dock and welcome back their friends. Alex introduced them to Anna and promised a full account of the trip over lunch. He sensed their initial reserve with his mother, but they soon warmed to her smile and frank admission she had been curious to see why Alex and Katy thought of them so highly.

This time, however, Alex had reservations at a hotel in the heart of the city. He explained to Hiram and Hannah he wanted his mother to see the sights of New York before their return trip to Iowa.

So, the next day, guidebook in hand, Alex and Anna took a streetcar to the Lower East Side. Anna knew America was described as a melting pot and after meeting Hiram and Hannah, she began to understand. Jews and other minority groups generally kept to themselves in Europe, but in America, Alex explained, they retained customs with those of like background, but also embraced the company of others.

Alex pointed out the hotel where he had stayed while he searched for Katy, and the tenement house on Hester Street where Katy had lived with Hiram and Hannah. Although Anna expressed dismay at the crowded conditions, Alex knew she had no real grasp of what either he or Katy had experienced.

They toured Manhattan, even saw a play on Broadway. Anna expressed awe at the ongoing construction of skyscrapers—as people called them, the clang of streetcars, and the bustle of so many people.

While Anna and Alex took in the sights, Katy enjoyed visits with Hannah. She also window-shopped along Madison Avenue as she pushed Hilda Rose in the pram Hannah insisted she borrow.

· · ·

On their last day in the city, Anna awoke at dawn. No certain plans were made. She reached for the well-worn guide-book and skimmed through its pages. She might never have another opportunity to see all she wanted to see.

"Harlem," the book's entry read: "an interesting mix of fine homes and retail establishments."

Why not go alone—give Alex and Katy a day to themselves?

She wanted to poke around the shops and, perhaps, find some small items to interest Hilda Rose on the train trip west. This was a good opportunity to show some independence.

The bell captain tipped his hat.

"Good morning, Mrs. Meisen. May I be of service?"

"Good morning. Perhaps, you can recommend a nearby bakery or coffee shop?"

"The hotel restaurant is excellent, Madam."

"Yes, I know. We've dined there several times. But today I feel like a morning stroll."

"Then, I recommend the cafeteria. Two blocks left, on this side of the avenue. The entrees are hot and they have a good selection."

"Excellent."

She extracted a coin from her purse, pressed it into his gloved hand.

"You've been most helpful."

He bowed from the waist and endowed her with an admiring look as he watched her depart.

She found the cafeteria a perfect choice. No one thought twice at seeing an unescorted matron. She carried her tray to a table by the window and ate every bite of the omelet and croissant while she sipped from the steaming cup of coffee the waitress was quick to refill.

Still wary of the electric cars with crackling cables which threw sparks on the turns, Anna boarded a horse-drawn streetcar instead. In no hurry whatsoever, she enjoyed the slow pace through neigh-borhoods as they came to life in the warm morning sunshine.

Her map showed the approach of the neighborhood she sought, named by Dutch settlers who retained its name from their native Haarlem. Pastures and small cottages had transformed into grand avenues with townhouses and apartment buildings which accommodated immigrants from all over Europe.

Up ahead, Anna saw a group of business establishments. She decided to step off the streetcar at the next stop. Shopkeepers unlocked their doors, cranked out store awnings, and greeted her as she passed.

"Mornin' ma'am. Beautiful day."

"Another scorcher, I think."

Anna felt at home. All morning she browsed up and down the tree-lined streets. She stopped here and there to buy a trinket to put in her shopping bag for Hilda Rose. Then, she stepped inside the gilded foyer of the Harlem Opera House and studied the playbills at the New Orpheum Theatre.

Over a chicken sandwich and ice-cold lemonade in a cozy tearoom, Anna decided to visit just one or two more shops before she boarded a streetcar for the return trip. She wanted to get back early as promised in the note left for Alex and Katy.

The next shop displayed an array of exquisite music boxes. Anna discovered with delight the merchant came from Vienna. After he carefully wrapped her selection in tissue paper, they enjoyed a pleasant chat. By the time she left the store, it was mid-afternoon.

She moved hastily and returned to the main thoroughfare to board the first streetcar that came along. It was one of the new electric ones. Anna hesitated, but her guilt at being gone so long urged her to put her fears aside.

She sank onto the shiny oak bench and paid scant attention as landmarks passed, this time in rapid succession. She braced her feet against the sway of the car, and rearranged the items in her shopping bag. She wrapped and rewrapped the delicate glass music box.

When, at last, Anna looked up, the surroundings appeared unfamiliar. She grabbed the brass handles on the seat backs to maintain her balance and stood to make her way to the front of the car.

"Where are we?" she asked the motorman.

"Approaching the Bowery, ma'am."

Panic rose in Anna's voice as she demanded, "Let me off, please. I've come too far."

"But ma'am, wait—"

"Now! Do you hear me?"

The motorman applied the brakes. The electric streetcar wheels screeched as sparks shot from the overhead wires. Passengers lurched forward and shouted in protest. Anna fairly flew out the door and down the steps.

"Be careful, lady. Are you sure you want off here?"

Anna did not reply. She was only focused on heading back.

"How could I have been so stupid?" she mumbled.

Dry weeds caught at her skirt and clods of dirt caused her to stumble. Buildings clustered in the distance, but she had disembarked in an open field.

Sweat broke through the dark blue serge of her dress and stained her bodice. *Why hadn't I thought to carry a parasol?*

Without a brim, her hat was useless against the hot sun. She pulled it off to fan herself instead. Wisps of hair strayed down her neck from the loosened pins, which made her feel much hotter.

By the time she reached the buildings, shadows crept across the field. Hot and thirsty, it was all she was able to do to keep her mind on finding some form of public transportation.

A glass bottle smashed to the ground at her feet and rolled away. Anna jumped back, her throat constricted. Propped against a wooden barrel, a drunken vagrant sprawled in the grass.

"S'empty, ma'am," he slurred. "Din't see ya. Sorry."

Anna began to run, but the toe of her shoe caught on some object in the weeds; she toppled to the ground. Behind her, the derelict's cackle caused a shiver to run up her spine.

She grabbed the shopping bag and scrambled to her feet. The sound of broken glass jangled within it. As Anna hobbled ahead, her twisted ankle sent stabs of pain up her leg.

At last, she reached an alley between two crumbling brick buildings and emerged onto a narrow street. Shadows began to deepen.

Anna had never seen such squalor and filth. Trash littered the street and many store windows were either boarded or broken. Ash cans and garbage spilled over everywhere. A rag picker rattled by with his cart. When he saw her sudden appearance out of nowhere, his face mirrored her startled expression.

Raucous music poured forth from an open tavern door where it mingled with drunken shouts and curse words. Anna shrank back as a dirty long-haired beggar—she was unable to tell whether male or female—dangled a battered tin cup under her nose.

When she reached for her purse, icy horror spread through her like a slow-moving glacier. She must have dropped it in the field when she fell. Instinctively, she turned back. Hot tears of fear and frustration stung her cheeks.

"What'cha got there, lady?"

A sharp tug on the shopping bag jerked her arm.

"Let go!"

Anna clung to the bag with one hand and desperately clawed at the man's grasp with the other. His body odor assaulted her and she wanted nothing more than to get away.

The heavy-set drunk focused his watery eyes upon her with obvious lust.

"Wanna play games, huh? I'll take you and this here bag as well, if you please."

Anna screamed. A man burst through the tavern door. Before Anna knew what was happening, her assailant lay sprawled on the broken sidewalk.

• • •

Alex grabbed the ringing telephone. He had been pacing the hotel room since early afternoon. The hotel operator connected the call.

"Alex Meisen? Got your ma here, mate."

Alex heard loud music and voices in the background. His forehead creased.

"What do you mean? Who is this?"

"She's a mite shook up. H'aint no money on her neither. The bar-keep took pity to let me make this here call." *This has to be a mistake.*

"What's this woman's name?" Alex inquired.

Voices muddled over the crackling telephone wire.

"Anna . . . Anna Meisen. Don't know yur own mum, man? For shame."

"Where are you?"

"Burn's Barroom. Five Points. By Chatham Square. No place for a lady."

"I'll be right there. Please stay with her. I'll make it worth your while."

The voice snapped, "Who ya think ya talkin' to, bub? I saved her life."

• • •

Anna took a bath and put on her robe. The hotel doctor ban-daged the sprained ankle and elevated it on a bag of ice. Though calmer, Anna felt no less humiliated.

Katy stood nearby as she held Hilda Rose who sucked her thumb in her usual way to show concern.

What must Katy be thinking? Anna wondered. *I've made such a fool of myself.*

Alex pulled a chair up beside her bed and took Anna's hand. She pulled it away.

"Alex, dear," she said. "Don't treat me like a child just because I acted like one. If you want to be helpful, please dispose of those."

She pointed to the mound of clothing on the floor.

"I never want to see them again. And please take Hilda Rose with you. I want some time alone with Katy."

A worried frown wrinkled her son's forehead. Katy's eyes widened.

Oh no, Anna thought. *I'm doing this all wrong.*

Alex picked up the clothes and laid them over one arm.

"Of course, Mother . . . if you say so."

Anna cringed at his obvious attempt to humor her, but was grateful when Alex obeyed and took the child from Katy. Hilda

Rose started to fuss, and looked back and forth between her father and grandmother.

Anna called after her, "Granny's fine, sweetheart. We'll read a story later."

The door shut and Anna turned to Katy. *I must do this before I lose my nerve, while this traumatic experience is fresh and painful in my mind.*

"Katy, please sit down. I have something to say."

She motioned to an armchair nearby. Katy obeyed, eyebrows raised and expression turned cautious.

Oh dear, Anna thought, *she thinks I'm going to lecture her. Please let me do this right.*

"Katy," she said as she drew a deep breath, "my experience today caused me to realize some of what you must've gone through those months before Alex found you. Oh, I know you weren't as foolish as I was. I'm sure you stayed far away from places like the Bowery. But you must've felt terribly afraid and alone—like you could die and no one would ever know how it happened."

Katy's eyes brimmed with tears. Anna hurried, afraid she had somehow insulted Katy or invaded her privacy.

"I just want to apologize for being insensitive. Please don't think I mean you'd do anything foolish—"

"But I did."

Katy hesitated as if startled to hear her words, but then they came in a flood, propelled by Anna's unexpected compassion, so unmistakably sincere.

"It could've happened exactly as you said." Katy's words tumbled out and tears streaked her face. "I could've died there in Harlem and no one would've known when or where. Then, Hiram came along. Sort of like that cockney sailor did today. Like a miraculous intervention."

"Hiram Silverstein?"

Katy poured out the story. As she told it, Anna reached for Katy's hand and took it in hers. Katy's face paled and the tears flowed faster as she relieved the days working for Blanch Morrissey, and the squalid apartment she shared with Baylie Root. Then, almost as if not aware of what she said, she told of finding Dr. Adler in Harlem where she had gotten rid of the baby.

Anna's expression reflected her shock. *Katy pregnant before they married? An abortion? A deadly sin, to be sure.*

Yet, when Katy spoke of her agony of guilt and the feeling she was never to be forgiven, Anna reached to embrace her.

"But then Alex found you," she soothed.

"Yes and I blamed him for not finding me sooner," Katy sobbed. "It wasn't until I was expecting Hilda Rose and watched Susannah deliver Daniel when I cried out to God and received His forgiveness. It was like a big stone lifted off my chest."

Anna barely took it all in, and then asked, "Did you confess to a priest?"

"Yes. Father Felder granted me absolution, but God had already forgiven me."

Anna reached to take Katy in her arms. She rocked back and forth as her tears flowed.

"I had no idea," she murmured.

Her hand stroked Katy's hair.

"Your faith has made you strong, my dear . . . Much stronger than I was today. I admire that very much."

"Only by the grace of God," Katy whispered.

Dark shadows beneath her beautiful eyes revealed the toll extracted by the telling. Alex found them lying side-by-side, asleep. Katy's head rested in the crook of Anna's arm.

CHAPTER 34

Even though Alex explained how American farming differed from the Austrian tradition, Anna still found it strange farmhouses were so distant and apart from each other. Nevertheless, she admired the house Alex and his friend had built, so sturdy and comfortable. Impressed by the craftsmanship, she looked forward to the trip into Lake City to meet this Sam whom her son so admired.

Sam pastored a church in Lake City where the couple lived in a rented house. Anna looked forward to making the trip. Thad Heim met them at the railroad station, but she was so weary from the long train ride Anna only vaguely recalled the endless fields and occasional farm buildings. She needed to establish her bearings.

Anna still grappled with the fact her son was a farmer. Likewise, she had trouble conceiving of a pastor who supported his family as a carpenter. Yet, she respected men of intellectual ability who did not find it beneath them to work with their hands—Saint Paul made tents to provide his support and Christ had been a carpenter's son.

But do educated men still follow that path today?

Thanks to her son's thoughtfulness, Father Felder, the local priest, knew of her arrival and came to the farm in his horse and buggy to welcome her to his parish. Anna appreciated the priest's visit and looked forward to attending Mass. She hoped to feel welcome in his parish, but she could not help but wonder what Father Felder thought of Sam, a preacher of a different cloth.

When Katy pulled the rig to a stop in front of the cottage, Susannah ran out to greet them. She embraced Katy with a mighty hug.

"I thought you'd never get back!"

Anna took to Susannah right away. With her diminutive frame and fine features, Sam's wife hardly looked old enough to have a child. Wispy curls escaped from the thick braids wound round her small head and Dresden blue eyes reflected an innocence that sprang, not only from her sheltered upbringing, but from her view of people. Katy told Anna Susannah always found only the best in others.

What a rare quality, Anna thought.

As Susannah set a plate of date-filled cookies on the table and poured steaming hot tea into china cups, her sturdy and obviously strong-willed son, Daniel, stood in his high chair and reached for the pot of geraniums on the window sill. When he plunged both hands deep into the soil, the pot tipped over the edge and crashed onto the floor.

As if it were a common occurrence, Susannah plucked the toddler from his seat and carried him to the sink.

"I think Daniel has my father's inclinations," she sighed as she trapped the thrashing body against her side.

She clasped his muddy hands together as she pumped water over them from the cistern below.

"He's forever attracted to God's creation. My father would leave his plowing to bring wildflowers to the house or retrieve a fallen robin's nest so he wouldn't turn it under."

She giggled as she set the child down on the floor.

"Perhaps, Daniel will be another John Audubon, or a famous botanist."

Anna smiled. She liked this plucky pastor's wife.

Katy licked two fingers and plastered down Hilda Rose's cowlick. It popped back up again like silky milkweed. Hilda Rose sat on her lap and regarded Daniel with a placid expression.

"If we have another child, I hope it's another girl," she said with emphasis.

Susannah laughed.

"And deprive Hilda Rose of a brother to dote on? She will, you know. It's her nature."

A staccato of sharp taps on the frame of the screen door interrupted their conversation. With outstretched palms, Daniel ran headlong into the screen panel and caused the screen to sag a bit more than it did already.

"Daddy, Daddy!"

The compact, muscular man did not at all fit Anna's image of an aesthetic philosopher. His firm jutting jaw and the friendly appraisal which returned hers, defined him as a man who had set his course. Yet, his manner was easy.

"Welcome to Iowa, Mrs. Meissen," he said in a booming voice. "What do you think of our little town?"

Anna took his outstretched hand.

"I'm so pleased to meet you, but you must call me Anna. As for the town, it's hard to say. This is my first visit."

Sam threw back his head and laughed.

"Now, that's a diplomatic reply if I ever heard one."

He swung the clamoring Daniel up and onto his shoulder.

"Actually, Lake City's a fair little burg . . . plenty of good folk. You'll feel at home in no time, especially since you already speak English."

Anna gave thanks for having learned English from Alex when he studied at the university. She had urged him to converse with her in the language at home. Marriage to an authoritative husband never suppressed her innate curiosity and the excitement of a challenge. Yet, in no way had she dreamed to someday live where a real need existed to speak it every day.

●   ●   ●

A routine evolved. On Sunday they all attended Mass together, but on Wednesday nights, Anna stayed home with Hilda Rose when Katy and Alex rode off to Sam's Wednesday night prayer meeting.

"I like Sam," Anna assured Alex. "I'm sure he's a man of God. It's just I'd rather keep to the faith of my youth."

"I understand, Mother," Alex replied.

"Besides, you and Katy need some time alone and I'm perfectly happy to stay here with Hilda Rose. We'll eat leftovers and you two should try the new café in town."

They did. Katy admired the white tablecloths, black and white tiled floors, and the porcelain light fixtures which hung on long chains from the high ceiling.

Mondays were wash days. Alex went about his work in the fields as Katy and Anna filled the laundry tubs. On Tuesdays and Thursdays, Katy worked at the newspaper office. Anna harvested vegetables from the garden and performed other chores as she watched Hilda Rose. Alex often worked into the night to mend harness or work on the farm accounts.

Anna marveled at the competent efficiency with which her daughter-in-law accomplished daily chores. In Austria, Katy's performance as a maid had been adequate, at best. Their reversal of roles felt awkward at first, but soon she settled into a comfortable routine.

Anna admired the give and take between Alex and Katy; they loved and respected each other. That observation made her happiest of all.

Survival depended upon completing work while the sun shone. It did not shine every day and clouds brought rain, sometimes too much or too little. Anna realized townsfolk, as well, existed at the mercy of the weather, and whether or not the farmer had money to spend.

Anna respected lives governed by nature, the acceptance of which coincided with acceptance of God—acknowledged dependence upon Him and necessitated submission to His will. Perhaps, this accounted for the fact almost everyone in the community attended a church.

Still, at times she wondered if she had made the right decision. She did not quite feel entirely at home. For one thing, few in the community were of the Catholic faith and daily attendance at Mass was out of the question for most. She suspected Father Felder often conducted the celebration alone.

How will Rosa and Maria remember me?

Their sparse letters were stiffly worded.

When will I see them again?

Oh, how she missed her mountains. Surely, on a calm day even the Bodensee laid less level than these horizontal plains. Sometimes, she squinted at fluffy clouds on the horizon, and summoned a vision of mountain peaks to appease her longing.

While Katy was away at work and Hilda Rose napped, Anna usually took up some sewing or set up the ironing board. As the house seemed to snuggle around her, she felt contented and expectant. As a grandmother, she took delight in each facet of Hilda Rose's development without a parent's burden of credit or blame.

One afternoon she tiptoed past the crib where the child napped and felt an urge to stoop and kiss her fisted hand. Hilda Rose opened one eye and grinned with her whole face. Then, she snuggled down and went back to sleep.

If she never has a pretty face, Anna thought, *she'll be lovely when she smiles.*

It seemed to her Alex never got enough of his daughter, nor she of him. Often not a word passed between them as Alex amused her with silent finger games and nuzzled her face against his. Yet, when necessary, he was firm with the two-year-old, and the child instantly obeyed.

When the weather turned bad Alex tended the animals, and then came back to the house. Often he sat in the rocking chair and read from his farm journals.

On one such day, Anna took up her knitting and settled nearby, needles flying.

"Have you given up all thoughts of teaching? You used to have such ambition in that direction."

Alex put down his pencil and rubbed his chin.

"I don't know," he replied. "I do miss it. I filled out one term, you remember, the year Katy was expecting Hilda Rose. They wanted me back, but I didn't want to leave Katy alone with the baby after Sam and Susannah moved into town."

He turned his head and gazed out the window in the direction of the schoolhouse.

"Maybe someday . . ."

CHAPTER 35

Katy added flour to the bowl and began to knead it into the dough.

"Dynamite? Isn't that dangerous?"

"Not if you're careful and respect it," Alex told her. "I've hunted with a rifle all my life and dynamite is no more dangerous than gunpowder."

"Well, I don't like guns either."

Katy nodded toward the young child seated in the high chair.

"Besides, the noise will terrify Hilda Rose."

Alex laughed.

"She'll love it. Remember how she clapped her hands when they shot off the Civil War cannon on Decoration Day?"

"That's because you held your hands over her ears and she liked the puffs of smoke."

"Well, you can watch from the window and do the same thing. Or go to town and visit Susannah that day. When you get home, the stumps will be gone and we can plant potatoes next spring."

"All right, you win."

She dumped the dough onto the floured counter and punched it with her fist.

"But I still don't like it. Don't make me say I told you so."

• • •

Alex hired Thad to help. They cut down the willows near the creek with axes and used a scythe to clear away the underbrush. Only the stumps were left.

Alex ordered the dynamite and delivered it home from the lumber yard. He opened the wooden box on the kitchen table to show

Katy the ten sticks buried in sawdust. About an inch and a half in diameter and eight inches in length, each stick stood vertical, wrapped in a strip of brown paper coated with paraffin to keep dry. Alex pulled out a stick for her inspection.

"Looks like a long cigar," she commented.

"And about as harmless," Alex assured her.

Felix Heim insisted on setting the charges.

"A finer man there never was," Alex told Katy and Anna, "but he can be an old fuddy-duddy. Sometimes, I can see why Thad developed a defiant streak."

Anna smiled.

"There's an old saying: a child becomes an adult, but a parent remains a parent all his life. I'm sure Felix means well."

"Of course, he does. I wouldn't have made it this far without my good neighbor's advice and assistance. Don't worry, I won't offend him, but it doesn't take a genius to follow directions on a crate of dynamite sticks."

"Maybe he knows something you don't," Katy replied.

She plunged her arms into the wooden laundry tub and doused the garments against the washboard. As she continued to scrub, she watched in the distance when Alex set down the box near Felix and Thad.

Anna took Hilda Rose with her to the clothesline. The child carried the clothespin bag and placed pins on the wire fence surrounding the garden.

Katy sighed and thought: *She indulged the child. Now, Anna will have to collect the pins.*

When Anna came back with the empty basket, Hilda Rose followed. She clutched onto Anna's long skirt while she attempted to fasten a clothespin to its folds.

"She's a determined one," Anna laughed.

The first blast rattled the window panes. Katy stiffened and placed her hands over Hilda Rose's ears. She could not cast off the feeling of dread. *You're being silly,* she scolded herself. *Why am I being such a coward?*

• • •

With growing satisfaction, Alex watched the stumps up-root. More often than not, farm labor exacted its toll. One stick of dynamite—two tied together if the stump measured wide across—and wood pulp flew in all directions which left only splinters to dig out.

Two stumps remained. Alex glanced toward the house and hoped Katy took time to explain the noise to Hilda Rose. *No matter. I'll recount the event tonight, take Hilda Rose down to the creek to see the results, and explain to her how it made room to plant potatoes.*

He wanted them to make the boom sounds together. *She'll laugh and clap her hands.*

Felix helped Alex check the blasting caps. He laid out the fuses and inserted one in each stick of dynamite before he twisted the ends of the fuses together. Felix and Thad walked away and left Alex to strike the wooden match and light the fuses. Alex turned, poised for flight the second the flame caught.

At the first hint of sizzle from the fuse, he started to run. Clods of dirt flew around him as he trampled the tall grass. Then, the toe of his boot appeared to strike something hard and he stumbled.

As he flailed his arms and fought for balance, Alex's foot twisted as he landed on his back. The ground trembled beneath him and the explosion echoed down what seemed to be a black tunnel into which he fell.

Far away, he heard Felix and Thad yell his name. The smoke made it hard to breathe and their voices faded.

• • •

Katy went inside the house to fetch a fresh bar of laundry soap. She shuddered against yet another blast. *Surely, they're about finished.*

Then, she heard Felix yelling—a shrill note in a voice she never knew as anything, but calm and measured. She flung open the back door and flew down the path. Alex lay unconscious. His foot was twisted in an unnatural position beneath a hunk of broken tile.

Thad swore.

"When we were doing the tiling, I just flung the old tiles toward the river. Never gave it a thought."

Katy found blood spread in a widening splotch on Alex's pant leg. Felix dug into his hip pocket for his jackknife, split the cuff, and used both hands to rip the fabric.

Blood coursed in a jagged wound, like rapids in a rocky riverbed. Katy clasped both hands to her mouth to keep from screaming.

Felix tore off his denim shirt, tied the sleeves round Alex's thigh, and then groped in the grass for a stick he used to make a tourniquet. Then, he felt for a pulse in Alex's neck.

"Get a blanket, Katy," he ordered. "He's going into shock. Bring two. I'll stay with him. Thad, ride for Doc. Hurry!"

Anna stood rigid by the clothesline. She held Hilda Rose tightly in her arms.

"He's unconscious," Katy gasped as she ran past her into the house and up the stairs to the hall linen closet. She pulled blankets from the top shelf and grabbed two from the pile which fell onto the floor.

Anna caught Katy's sleeve at the bottom of the stairs. Hilda Rose remained in her arms and sucked furiously on her thumb.

"How bad?" Anna asked firmly.

"I don't know."

•   •   •

Alex was conscious when the doctor arrived, but kept his eyes tightly closed. His teeth chattered in spite of the blanket and the warm October sun. Felix had fashioned a stretcher from the second blanket and two fallen tree limbs. He bound it with leather straps pulled from Jed's harness.

"Prob'ly saved his life."

Doc Owens nodded toward the tourniquet as he inspected the leg.

"Gangrene's the next worry. Let's get him up to the house. I'll have to operate."

"Operate?"

Katy searched the doctor's familiar face, lined by relentless fatigue and other people's pain.

"His leg?"

"Don't know, yet. Ankle's broken. Kneecap's shattered. We'll see."

Katy raged in silence, *why has God allowed this to happen? What'll we do now? If only Alex had listened to me.*

Thad ran to the barn for a board. Felix slid it under Alex's leg and lifted him onto the makeshift stretcher. Katy trailed them into the house where they transferred Alex onto the dining room table. She asked Doc Owens about his dilated pupils.

"Shock and concussion," Doc Owens answered. "Makes usin' ether touchy. Gonna try whiskey instead."

"But Alex—"

"Medicinal," the doctor answered gruffly.

He took a bottle from his bag and held it to Alex's lips.

"Numbs the pain. Now, leave us."

• • •

Katy sank down on the parlor sofa. Anna sat in the rocking chair and held Hilda Rose who continued to suck her thumb with her eyes shut.

"How is he?"

Anna's voice was strained, but low for Hilda Rose's sake.

"I don't know. Doc Owens is operating on his knee . . . sent me away. I knew something like this was going to happen. Alex wouldn't listen to me and now look."

Katy stood to pace back and forth on the rose-patterned carpet.

"It was an accident, Katy."

"Of course, it was an accident. But why did it have to happen? He's worked so hard, Frau Meisen. It isn't fair."

Her hands fisted at her sides.

"It's time you called me Anna, Katy. You're right. Life isn't fair, but God is merciful. He never gives us more than we can bear."

Katy pondered Anna's statement in silence broken only by the creaking sound the rocking made. Secretly, she sometimes judged her mother-in-law and thought Anna lacked real faith because she did not study the Bible for herself like Sam had convinced them to do. Yet, Alex's mother was right. Perhaps, her wisdom came from Anna's experience.

"Thank you for reminding me, Anna." she said, at last. "I needed to hear that."

Hilda Rose pulled harder on her thumb. Katy thought, *she hasn't done that in a long time.*

Anna's lips moved as she silently worked the beads of her rosary through the thumb and forefinger of her right hand.

On the wall, the Seth Thomas clock's tick was loud and constant. Katy recalled verses she had memorized:

"My grace is sufficient for thee[7] . . . The steps of a good man are ordered by the Lord[8] . . . Be careful for nothing; but in every thing by prayer and supplication with thanksgiving let your requests be made known unto God.[9]—"

Gradually her breathing steadied. At last, the parlor door opened. Doc Owens strode across the room and rolled down his shirtsleeves to fasten the cuffs.

"We've put Alex to bed," he said. "Thanks to Felix's quick thinking with the tourniquet, he didn't lose a lot of blood and the circulation is returning. I've set the ankle in a splint, cleaned out the knee, and poured in plenty of sulfa before I bandaged it. Now, we wait and see. Keep him quiet."

Katy tried to be patient, but it did not stop her from worrying. *Alex can be laid up for weeks, even months. How will we manage?*

As word spread, neighbors rallied to pick the corn. Farm wives Katy had never met before arrived with food and expressed their concern. Thad Heim rode over morning and night to milk the cows and slop the hogs.

Anna took her knitting and sat by her son's bedside. Some days

7   2 Corinthians 12:9, KJV

8   Psalm 37:23, KJV

9   Philippians 4:6, KJV

NO TURNING BACK

she read aloud from the newspapers Sam Schneider had delivered. She leaned close when she needed to show Alex words she had not yet learned to pronounce.

Alex washed from a basin and pulled the chamber pot from under the bed. He raised his upper body by pulling on the rope Thad had looped over a peg installed atop the high headboard. Katy brought his meals on a tray.

Alex demanded Hilda Rose be allowed on his bed at any time. She carefully steered clear of his *hurts*, as she called them. If her movements caused him pain, he never showed it. They made up games with checkers and built towers with wooden spools. The days dragged by.

Katy changed Alex's bandages and swabbed the edges of his wound with alcohol, sprinkling in more sulfa as Doc Owens had shown her. She knew Alex suffered pain, but steeled himself against it.

Gradually, the carnage appeared less gruesome as new flesh inched into raw crevices. Still, Katy did not know what to expect. No one mentioned the possible loss. There was no need. The strain showed on their faces.

Sometimes, Alex and Katy prayed together. Sam came almost daily and Katy knew Alex drew strength from his visits. She often found him reading his Bible after Sam left.

Felix was also a faithful visitor. One day Alex asked him about Jeremy Parker, the Civil War veteran with the legless torso. His wife pushed him to the town park on pleasant days and left him sitting under a shade tree in his high-backed wooden wheelchair.

"Cannonball," Felix answered brusquely.

"I'm fortunate," Alex remarked. "It could've been so much worse."

• • •

At last, the day arrived for Doc Owens to remove the ankle splints and inspect his knee. Tension became an almost tangible presence as Doc Owens took scissors from his scarred leather satchel, cut away the bandages, and removed the splints.

Katy held her breath when Doc Owens held Alex's ankle and maneuvered his foot. Alex winced a little, but then grinned and wiggled his hairy toes.

"A little stiff, maybe, but see . . . It works."

Without comment, the white-haired physician moved to the knee, lifted the dressing, and probed the wound. Katy watched and wished he was gentler. Alex set his mouth and the silence continued.

"No poison. . . . far as I can tell. Katy's done a good job. With a wound like this one, you're a lucky man, for sure. Lots of damage though; you'll walk stiff-legged the rest of your life."

"But I'll walk. Thank God, I'll walk."

Katy flew to the bed and hugged her husband's neck. Anna pulled her handkerchief from her pocket and Hilda Rose reached for her daddy's hand. Doc Owens smiled down at the little girl as he replaced the instruments and snapped his bag shut.

"She's a kind one, for bein' so small. I always say look at the contents, not the bottle."

Katy winced at the homely description, but Alex beamed and patted the bed where the child climbed up beside him.

"Oh, she's a fine one all right," he agreed.

• • •

Within weeks, Alex walked the land with a cane. He had to swing out the rigid leg to take the next step. Every night he labored to bend it, determined to regain as much motion as possible.

"God's plan for my life may have taken a different turn," he said, "but His plan remains. Hiram Silverstein has a saying, 'What was, was. What is, is.'"

"Is that a Hebrew maxim?" Anna asked.

"Yiddish, I believe. Hiram came from Eastern Europe."

"I never knew any Jews before the Silversteins. To tell you the truth, I didn't feel at ease around Hiram and Hannah. I'm ashamed of myself because I know they're fine people. I guess I didn't know quite what to make of their ways. But there's real wisdom in Hiram's words . . . For any of us."

CHAPTER 36

It was Sam who helped Alex look to the future. Every week he rode his faithful mare, Mollie, out to the farm on missions of encouragement.

"God will open doors," he reassured his friend. "Make your requests known to Him."

"I thank Him daily for my recovery," Alex answered. "I also ask forgiveness for my times of self-pity and pray His blessing on all the good neighbors who have helped us."

"As you should."

Sam spread his hands as was his habit.

"But God wants us to be specific with our needs so our faith will grow as we see those needs fulfilled. When we've struggled to build our congregation and minister to our flock, I've had to learn this lesson again and again."

Alex determined to pray more, as his good friend suggested. He and Katy cherished their friendship with Sam and Susannah. They attended Sunday Mass with Anna, but made every effort to be at Sam's Wednesday night prayer service as well.

At first, some of the parishioners had shunned them, but Sam soon set that straight.

"Alex and Katy are born-again believers, same as you," he told them. "According to Matthew 22:16, God is no respecter of persons."

Susannah often invited Katy for lunch on days Katy worked at the *Lake City Graphic*. She and Sam lived only two blocks off the town square.

"How's everything?" Susannah asked one day.

"Fine . . . Anna is so good with Hilda Rose, although that child is easy to love. Sometimes, I feel guilty for being away, but

Hilda Rose always runs and greets me with a big kiss when I come home."

"I know you don't neglect her, Katy, and I know it's not Anna's intention to take your place. Do you think about having another?"

"We do . . . In God's timing. Our marriage is so strong now, Susannah. The accident brought us even closer, realizing what could've happened and how God brought us through."

•   •   •

When Alex went to town on an errand, he often stopped by the small white, clapboard church to see if he could catch Sam. If Sam had the time, they talked.

"Is the church growing?" Alex asked Sam one morning.

"Day by day, week by week," Sam replied. "Faith is a growing process, I've learned. That little mustard seed Jesus talked about has to be watered. Read and pray, pray and read. That's the answer."

Alex read his Bible daily. His prayers included the need for a hired hand—temporary help while his leg continued to heal. Perhaps, a down-on-his-luck drifter heading west, as many did these days.

He had a clear picture of the man—old enough to be steady, yet young enough to do hard work. He must be God-fearing so as to be trusted around Hilda Rose, not wrongly influence her. He was, of course, a bachelor so he was able to sleep in the spare bedroom and not require a high wage.

As Alex moved around the farm with his cane to fix fence or drop seed potato cuttings into furrows, he watched the road for a stranger to turn up the lane.

A quiet Christmas came and went. Then, as they sat at breakfast one morning, a tap came on the kitchen door.

"Word has it you're lookin' for a hand."

The man's work-worn fingers worried the brim of a sweat-stained felt hat. A white band across his forehead separated weathered skin like rusted iron from the fringe of grizzled hair which encircled his bald head. A deep cleft in his chin grew a thatch of black bristles, and muscular arms stretched the sleeves of a blue denim shirt the same color as the man's eyes.

Alex looked past him to a woman seated in a weathered buck-board wagon. Two young boys sat on the wagon floor behind her with a flushed, sleepy look on their freckled faces. A roll of canvas draped over the back of the wagon.

Alex felt the frown on his forehead and struggled to remove it. The man was all wrong for the job, but that was not the man's fault. He shook the outstretched hand and felt the calluses rub against his own.

"Had breakfast?"

The man nodded, but the widened eyes of the solemn children told a different story. Alex swung the screen door wide.

"Come on in."

• • •

Karl and Edna Grothe moved into the cabin by the creek. Karl helped Alex move the lumber stored there to the aban-doned sod house, and Edna voiced no complaints about lack of space. She soon had it looking like a home again. Starched curtains hung at the windows and, on Mondays, clothes hung on the line.

"The boys love the bunk beds," she told Katy. "Everything will work out fine."

In spite of her no-nonsense manner and whirlwind efficiency, Edna possessed a kind Christian heart. As for Karl, his steady, plodding ways relieved Alex of much anxiety. As he worked alone or with Alex, Karl took pride in a job well done . . . The same as if he owned the farm.

Lithuanian by birth, Karl and Edna had carried their dreams to Missouri, only to have the crops on their rented acreage drowned out the previous summer. Karl worked at odd jobs to keep the oldest young'un in school. At last, they migrated north and counted on Karl's strong back and work experience to land him a permanent position elsewhere.

The children were endowed with Edna's bronze-colored hair and ample freckling, yet she was slight and they had the sturdy build of their father. The oldest was seven, and the younger one had just turned four.

Unaccustomed to the daily company of other children, little Hilda Rose, who had just turned three, viewed the brothers with awe. She followed after them whenever she was able.

Alex told Karl, "That first morning after breakfast when I said we'd give it a try, I must admit I had a younger, single man in mind."

"I hankered after a couple lookin' to retire, who'd picture us young," Karl told him.

Both men chuckled.

"God's ways are not our ways," Alex observed.

"Amen to that," Karl replied.

• • •

With spring came news of Helga Thannen's death. Katy stood by the mailbox at the end of the lane and ripped open the envelope. The words blurred before her eyes.

Horst's wife, Julia, penned the letter. Katy realized probably neither her father nor her brothers were capable of composing the sentences. Oddly enough, the realization cut through her with almost as much force as word of her mother's passing.

Why had I been so vain, accepting convent schooling as my just due? Had I regarded my aptitude as deserving and my brothers as less able to learn?

When they quit school in the lower grades to work with their father in the blacksmith shop, she had thought nothing of it. It was just the way of things. *Was it what my brothers had wanted? Perhaps, they also had dreams.*

Julia's brief letter stated a stomach tumor took Helga's life. She wrote:

She suffered quite a lot, but the doctor's medicine made her sleep, and then she just slipped away. Angelika now lives with us and is a darling. Your father stays on at home, but takes turns eating at our house or Anton's.

Katy tried to explain to Alex the burden of guilt which consumed her.

"You asked forgiveness of your parents. But me? When I went to see my mother, I thought our babies would bring us together as something in common, but she said my being her daughter should be enough."

Tears caught in her throat.

"All the old feelings rose up and I didn't do a good job of it. And as for my father . . ."

Alex took her into his arms and pulled her forehead to his chest.

"We all fall short," he told her. "If you've asked God for forgiveness, you're forgiven. It was evident how proud your father is of you, and your brothers have good families of their own. Who's to say they're not happy?"

He put his hands on her shoulders and looked into her eyes.

"Besides, your father'll be pleased to hear he's to be a grandfather again."

Katy found comfort in his arms, but the sense of guilt lingered on. She wrote to Sofie and thanked her for staying in touch with Helga. She also wrote to Julia and Horst to commend them on their commitment to the child. She wrote: *Please tell Father I love him.*

• • •

The arrival of the Grothe family proved to be a blessing for Anna as well. She welcomed the thought of Edna nearby when Katy was at work and Alex was in the fields.

One morning when Alex came upon his mother scattering corn for the chickens, Anna brought up the subject of Katy's grief and her concern regarding it.

"It might help her if she took the new position George Colby offered."

"You may be right, Mother, but it means three days a week instead of two. Katy and I worry about you taking on more. You deserve time to yourself."

"I have that," Anna assured him. "There's the Altar Society once a month and Beulah Heim often takes me to neighborhood gatherings. I enjoy time spent with Edna as well. I'm even learning to quilt."

"I'm so glad."

"Don't worry about me, Alex, Hilda Rose's such a darling, and so little trouble. I like feeling needed. Talk it over with Katy."

• • •

Upon Katy's return from Austria, George Colby, owner and editor-in-chief of the *Lake City Graphic*, had hired her back as proofreader and folder.

"I'm probably stickin' my neck out," he told her. "You've proved yourself a good worker, but some folks don't cotton to a married woman with a small child holding down a job."

"I'm not neglecting her," Katy replied. "When I'm here she's in the capable hands of my mother-in-law."

"Of course, of course, it's just in a small town, people talk. Fact is though, it'll free me to get out and sell more advertising. The community's growing and our circulation is expanding, especially now with rural delivery."

"I'll work hard, Mr. Colby. You'll see. I want to learn everything there is to know about the newspaper business."

George Colby chuckled.

"I believe you do. Though why, I can't imagine. Hankerin' for my job, maybe?"

Katy's cheeks flushed.

"I have a good mind, Mr. Colby."

"Yes you do," Mr. Colby conceded.

So, the added responsibility became hers.

• • •

Alex purchased a used buggy and a black mare named Hero. Katy pointed out Heroine was correct, but the name given it by the former owner had stuck too long to change. When harnessed and hitched to the one-seater, Hero set off at a sprightly pace as if born between the reins.

Katy took pleasure in the proud head and sleek back—a sharp contrast to the rear view of plodding mules. Besides, it took her only one-third of the time to get to town.

She also relished the weather-beaten, but serviceable leather canopy which folded down behind the buggy seat and rose with little effort against the elements. After all this time, she still recalled the hail storm on the day she went to town and bought the hat which she still wore on special occasions.

To celebrate her promotion, they dined at their favorite restaurant with the black and white tiled floor. Hilda Rose went along as a special treat. Katy swelled with pride at how grown-up her child's manners were.

Right off, Katy demonstrated a talent for choosing the type, size, and face for the print to grant merchants the most for their money. She also made it her business to not only do the job assigned her, but also learn about advertising and the need for it.

Katy grew to realize advertisements kept the newspaper running. She had assumed the nickel people paid for a copy was all the income needed. She, however, soon learned church notices helped Sam's church grow, and the ADVERTISEMENT section informed Alex about where to find Hero and the buggy.

When her pregnancy was no longer concealed, Katy took several months off from work. She felt fine, but George Colby insisted it unseemly for customers to see an expectant mother working there. People talked.

"That's ridiculous," Katy told him, but he held firm.

"Not that I won't want you back," he told her.

• • •

It proved to be an easy birth. Katy looked forward to going back to work, but she worried two small children were too much for Anna.

Hilda Rose so adored her baby brother, however, she never moved far from his crib.

"As young as she is, Hilda Rose is exceptional help," Anna told Katy.

Alex never took the blessing of little Eduard for granted. He regarded his son's birth as redemption from the sin committed long-ago in the mountain glen and the trouble and grief which had resulted.

"Daily, I express my heartfelt gratitude to God," he said.

Without Katy, George Colby had been forced to do the advertising layouts himself so he was more than ready to welcome her back.

"You do have a knack with words," he told her. "People complained I'm too stodgy, whatever that is."

Once she set eyes on the bank building, Katy felt her day begin. She walked faster, and anticipated the reek of printer's ink and the blast of heat from the pot-bellied stove.

One bright morning as she neared the steps, her eyes rested on the sandwich board placed near the bank building door. It had been her idea. The sign read: JOB PRINTING EXECUTED ON SHORT NOTICE, INQUIRE DOWNSTAIRS AT LAKE CITY GRAPHIC. With a satisfied smile she ran down the steps, entered the print shop, pulled off her wool muffler, and shrugged out of her coat.

CHAPTER 37

Alex remained faithful to exercising his leg. Although he still limped, he got around well with the help of his cane.

He opened the narrow door of the schoolhouse stove and shoveled in coal to lay a fire. Mornings held a chill and mothers insisted on caps and jackets. Through the window, Alex saw the Baxter twins shed their outer garments and toss them onto the ground. Almost in unison, they picked up wooden bats and swung them in vicious arcs as they began the process of choosing up sides.

Actually, the Baxter boys became the reason for the vacancy. Their former teacher considered them incorrigible, not worth the aggravation.

"No one can control those two hellions . . . No one! I'll take my old-age pension and settle for some peace and quiet," she had informed the school board. "I've earned it."

Felix told Alex about the opening, and Alex decided to apply. At harvest time, school let out for the older children to help in the fields. Likewise, school dismissed for spring planting. So, Alex and the growing Grothe boys were home to help Karl when the work load picked up. Thad also helped out with planting when he came home from college on spring vacation, and his father did not need him.

The added income was also certain to come in handy to give Karl the raise he deserved. Relieved to find Karl and Edna content to stay on, Alex purchased lumber and Karl added two rooms onto the cabin.

Some parents expressed concern the accident might hinder Alex's ability to maintain control. He sensed others objected to his Catholicism. Few farmers were Catholic and Alex knew some viewed the Roman Catholic Church with the same suspicion other farmers viewed people who lived in town. They recognized a mutual dependence, but were wary of practices differing from theirs.

During his interview one board member stated, "School opens with prayer and scripture reading . . . Any objections?"

"None at all," Alex answered.

"My kids don't cross themselves . . . or nothin' like that."

Felix Heim slapped his farm cap against the leg of his overalls.

"Alex Meisen is a respected member of our community. I suggest you get his name on the contract before he changes his mind."

As a long-time township director, Felix's opinion was highly regarded. Besides, teachers by late summer were hard to come by.

Two years later, the Baxter twins were among his best students. Forewarned, he had watched them size him up that first morning. They weighed his advantage in height and authority against their perceived superiority in speed and flexibility.

Before recess, James zinged an apple toward the blackboard. Alex caught and cracked it with his cane which earned respect.

Alex credited the *National Geographic* with making the real difference. With the exception of the *McGuffey Reader*, it was the only textbook he employed. The Baxter boys, hard as they tried, were unable to restrain their interest.

The monthly issues provided spelling words, arithmetic story problems, map studies, and history and geography lessons. Even their art examples derived from the brilliant nature and wildlife illustrations which Alex placed above the blackboard with thumbtacks.

• • •

Alex completed his chores—laying out paper and pencils, and writing math problems on the blackboard. Then, he stepped outside to the schoolyard, and took his pitching position in time to hear Jimmy Baxter choose Hilda Rose last. Jimmy's tone of voice revealed he was not happy about it.

At age six, Hilda Rose was the youngest child in school, but Alex knew age was not the problem. While good at her studies, Hilda Rose showed no interest whatsoever in competitive contests, softball or otherwise. Relegated to the farthest outfield position, if a ball ever came her way, she ran from it. Then, collective groans arose, but no one—save Alex—ever chastised her.

Every child was the recipient of his daughter's inherent kindness. They all loved her without knowing it. The morning proved no different.

Joe Baxter slammed Alex's pitch toward left field. Hilda Rose ducked and protected her head with her arms.

"Hilda Rose!" Alex shouted. "You didn't even try."

"I'm sorry, Father," she called back. "It scares me when the ball comes so fast."

She ran toward him.

"I'd rather watch, anyway. Billy's here now."

James Baxter flashed his brother a victory sign and Alex willed himself to turn away. Sometimes when he heard his father's voice in his, he despised the sound of his words.

Isn't it my duty to hold her to a higher standard?

He loved Hilda Rose dearly, but wished at times she was able to show more spunk.

Eduard was going to be different, Alex saw the signs already. At age three and tall for his age, Eduard welcomed opportunities to prove himself. His mother had her hands full taking care of him while Katy worked, but Anna never complained.

When he rang the bell for classes to begin, Alex saw Hilda Rose link arms with an older girl who seldom smiled or talked.

"God forgive me," Alex sighed.

Last fall he had been offered a position teaching history at the Lake City High School. Though gratified by the offer, Alex declined. At one time he would have considered the offer a prize, but he valued the development of younger minds in all aspects of growth, and that, of course, included his daughter.

• • •

At last, Eduard gave in to a nap. Anna sighed with relief. The small boy had shadowed them all morning as she and Edna picked cherries off the trees behind the farmhouse. Her sturdy little grandson—dark eyes snapping and hair as black and curly as his mother's—would still be on the run if he had not worn himself out.

She sank into the rocking chair, thumbed through a magazine, and wondered aloud, "How can two offspring from the same parents be so different?"

Hilda Rose was so thoughtful and competent. She was content to look at books or play with dolls long after she outgrew her nap. Yet, Eduard put up such a fuss when she put him down, she needed a nap more than he did.

Then she thought of her daughters and how opposite of Alex they were as children.

Because his temperament is more closely matched with mine, did I favor Alex?

She had allowed Rosa and Maria to model themselves after their opinionated and self-centered father, liking them less at times because of it . . . *A terrible thought.*

Rosa had a child now, and Maria was engaged to be married. Maria begged Anna to return for the wedding. She wrote: *It won't look right for you not to be present.*

The thought of making the long trip alone was daunting, to say the least. *Do I have the courage and stamina to board the train alone and endure the long boat trip across the ocean and back? I'm not getting any younger.*

Still, the thought of seeing the Alps again, as well as taking Holy Communion in her beloved parish church, made the effort tempting. After more than five years in America, she still felt a foreigner in some respects.

She had read in the newspaper about Susan B. Anthony's death and had to ask Alex who she was. On the other hand, with interest she gleaned tidbits from her daughters' rare letters regarding Franz Joseph's struggle to hold the Austrian empire together.

As she roused herself to accomplish some ironing, a soft tap sounded on the kitchen door. It was Edna who had surmised Eduard was asleep.

"Sorry to bother you." Edna kept her voice low. "There's a gypsy wagon coming down the road and I thought you might want to keep the young'un inside. I'll buy some pins or something and send them on their way."

"Thanks, Edna dear. They do scare me, though I know 'tis silly. Come back for a cup of tea before Alex and Hilda Rose arrive home from school."

"Pleased to."

Anna shut the door and peeked through the kitchen curtain. Sure enough, a narrow wagon boxed by a tall wooden enclosure lumbered into the barnyard's circular drive. A man with dark, leathered skin drove the team of horses. He reined in the animals as Edna approached.

Through the canvas opening, a middle-aged woman with jet-black hair and dangling gold earrings poked her head out. She looked Anna's way.

Sometimes, a caravan camped down by the creek. Anna saw their campfire at night and heard snatches of their music. They were a rag-tag bunch whose children were said to be wild and liable to steal a chicken while their parents haggled with buyers over the price of a package of needles or a tin of spices.

Thank God for Edna.

One of the neighbor boys who believed the rumors were silly had hitched a ride with them for a mile or two down the road and scared his parents out of their wits. However, to her knowledge no child had ever been kidnapped as some had predicted.

She watched Edna climb into the wagon and hoped she made her purchase in a hurry. If Eduard woke up, there was no containing him.

Edna emerged and the wagon circled the barnyard. Then, it bounced down the lane. Anna sighed with relief as Edna waved and turned back toward the house. She hurried to the door to welcome her.

CHAPTER 38

Sam propped his elbows on the table and put his face in his hands. "Why is it never enough? All night I prayed with Tom as his wife grew weaker and her fever raged. She died before morning and Tom's grief was so terrible nothing brought him comfort."

"I'm sure you did your best," Susannah assured him. "God's Word will lodge in his spirit."

Sam stood, and paced back and forth.

"I felt I had no choice, but to bring their baby girl home with me. Another burden for you, Susannah, but I didn't know what else to do. With Anna in Austria, it's enough extra work for you to keep Eduard on the days Katy works, let alone corral Daniel. We know what a handful the two of them are."

"It's all right, Sam."

Susannah placed her hand on his shoulder.

"You know I love babies."

"Then, you should've had another of your own by now."

Susannah flinched and put her hands to her cheeks.

Sam's shoulders slumped. His face was red, eyes filled with shame. He started toward her, but a knock on the door held him back.

"Hate to bother you, Pastor," the man said, "but a pipe froze last night and the church basement's flooded."

Sam knew Fred Haydn well. So, when Fred failed to meet his eyes, Sam knew his raised voice had carried outside. He placed his hand on the man's shoulder.

"Come in, Brother Haydn. I'll get my coat."

A small boy streaked past them and twirled a rope in the air above his head. The seven-year-old let out a whoop.

"Daniel," Susannah implored, "you'll wake the baby."

"What baby?"

Daniel skidded to a stop. The rope fell to the floor and he stumbled into the table, upsetting the sugar bowl. Sugar spilled across the table and sifted onto the floor.

Sam picked up the rope and wound it into a coil.

"Sorry," he said.

"The boy meant no harm," Brother Haydn replied.

Sam turned to his son.

"Where did you get this, Daniel?"

"I found it, Papa, like you must've found the baby. Where is it? I want to see it," his voice echoed back as he ran from the room.

Sam called after him.

"Daniel!"

"I'll handle it," Susannah told him. "You go on. You're needed at the church."

• • •

The door shut behind the men and Susannah started after Daniel. She collided with him in the hallway.

"Its face is all red, Ma . . . and it stinks."

Susannah took the broom and dustpan from the corner, and went back to the kitchen to sweep up the sugar.

"Get your coat, Daniel. It's time you left for school. I'll explain all about the baby tonight."

• • •

The door slammed behind the boy and Susannah lifted the stove lid to empty the dustpan. Then, she carefully replaced it and stood the broom in the corner. When the baby cried, she changed its diaper and rocked it back to sleep. The house remained silent as she sat down, crossed her arms on the table, and laid her head upon them to pray.

•   •   •

Sam sloshed through ankle-deep water to locate the broken pipe. He needed to fetch a plumber. A sigh escaped his lips. *Who knows what this will cost?*

The men of his small congregation had been faithful to help him erect the church building, but he knew of none able to remedy this situation.

Brother Haydn followed behind him and offered, "There's gypsies in town. A sign by one of the wagons said: HANDYMAN. Mightn't trust them though."

"On the other hand, that might be God's provision. Thanks, Brother."

•   •   •

In a couple of hours the pipe was fixed and the water drained away. Sam had remained at the swarthy man's side and found him worthy of the payment he required, which was not much.

Brother Haydn rounded up parishioners to help with the cleanup. Soon, things were set to rights again.

Later that afternoon, he returned home to find Katy leaving his house with Eduard.

He asked, "Has Alex heard from his mother?"

"Anna sent a wire saying the wedding was lovely . . . No mention of her return, yet."

"All in God's timing," Sam told her.

"I think His clock's slow," Katy retorted and they laughed.

Sam found Susannah in the kitchen and told her what had happened at the church.

"Gypsies come to town and Brother Haydn finds that man at just the right time? It was God. How could I ever have doubted His ability to meet our needs in any situation? 'All things work together for good to them that love God, to those who are called according to His purpose,' Romans 8:28. He can bring good out of anything, even a broken pipe."

Susannah put her arms around her husband's neck.

"Yes, He can. Tom Payne stopped by to say he wired his widowed mother. She'll be here next week to care for the baby."

The following week, however, a new case of scarlet fever quarantined another family. Susannah undertook the care of another small child. It appeared the worst was not over.

"It's fortunate we have a good doctor like Doc Owens," Alex observed when he stopped by to deliver a casserole Katy had sent and ask if there was anything else they could do to be of help.

"This could've become a real epidemic, but there have been no new cases because of the quarantine. Doc Owens has too big a load, but when Thad finishes medical school next year, he'll have a partner."

Sam nodded.

"Doc's doing his part and God's doing His. People are seeing the need of prayer and helping each other. Every week brings more people to church."

"You've done so much to encourage Katy and me in the past," Alex said. "Now, we're praying for you."

Sam gripped his arm.

"'A friend loveth at all times,' Proverbs 13:17. You and Katy demonstrate love and we can't tell you what it means to us."

• • •

The following day brooded dark and cold as Katy arrived home from work after picking up Eduard at Sam's and Susannah's. She knew from the light in the barn Alex and Karl were still milking.

She wished she had been able to stay longer to talk with Susannah. *Or help her, for heaven's sake.*

Eduard had been an extra burden for Susannah. Although good buddies, he and Daniel were a handful. Yet, that was Susannah: thinking of others when she had cares of her own.

Their small congregation experienced steady growth, but, of course, there were always problems. Most of all, Sam and Susannah wanted another child . . . or two or three.

If ever a woman is meant to be a mother, it's Susannah.

"Hilda Rose," she called as she entered the house, "where are you?"

She tugged off her coat and jerked the wool scarf from her neck. Then, she herded Eduard ahead of her. He responded with a series of short hops.

"I'm in here, Mama."

As often happened, Katy felt reprimanded by the calm, sweet voice. As she tugged to remove one of the wool gloves knitted for her by Anna, she ripped a small hole in one of the finger seams.

"What are you doing?"

"Ninety-eight, ninety-nine, one-hundred. There, I'm finished."

Hilda Rose replaced the hairbrush on the dresser as her mother stepped into the doorway of her bedroom. *It seems downright unnatural for a child so young to be so self-disciplined.*

"Did you set the table?" Katy asked.

"Yes, Mama."

Hilda Rose smiled at her in the mirror.

"Thank you, daughter. You're a big help. Ever since your grandmother left for Austria, things have been all topsy-turvy."

Eduard jumped onto the bed and began to bounce on his knees.

"I'm hungry."

"Of course, you are. We'll eat when the oven heats the leftovers from the roast we had last night."

"But I'm hungry now."

"You'll have to wait."

Katy refused to look at the pout on his face.

Hilda Rose lifted her limp, honey-colored strands of hair to place them behind her ears.

"When's Granny coming home?"

"Soon."

"Hurray!"

Eduard stood and jumped atop the pillows.

"Come on, Eduard. I'll build blocks with you."

Hilda Rose took his hand and guided him from the bed to the floor.

Katy turned toward the kitchen.

"Soon can't come soon enough," she muttered to herself.

CHAPTER 39

M arie made a beautiful bride. Her hair was styled in ringlets and framed her face under a lace veil which extended down her back, above the long train of her satin gown. Seated alone in the front row across the aisle from the groom's parents, Anna dabbed at her eyes as the processional ended and the priest began Mass.

The Innsbruck Cathedral made a grand setting. Anna preferred the wedding be held in their parish church in Bregenz, but Marie was to live in Innsbruck where the groom's family retained vast holdings.

As matron of honor, Rosa stood tall and slim between her sister and the long row of bridesmaids. Gowned in purple satin, the color granted her a regal appearance. She had married a wealthy merchant and was welcomed into Innsbruck society. Her house was not going to be far from Maria's. It pleased Anna how her daughters had remained friends.

How foreign their lives seemed compared to Anna's simple life on the farm. Neither daughter expressed a desire to visit their mother in Iowa.

"New York, of course," Rosa had said, "but Iowa? What would we possibly do there?"

Anna did not judge them for it. Rosa's attitude saddened her, but she had chosen a different life for herself; it did not make her daughters' choices wrong.

As the familiar ritual continued, Anna thoughts drifted to Rosa's small son at home with his competent nanny. He was a bright, handsome child. She wrote letters, sent gifts, and stayed abreast of his interests as he grew. Yet, even if she returned another time, she was a stranger to him. That was the choice she had made . . . She had no part in his upbringing.

The thought saddened her. However, she hoped through her letters and gifts she sent on his birthdays and at Christmas, he always knew he had a grandmother who loved him, even though far away.

The priest's pronouncement of a final blessing returned her thoughts to the ceremony. As the bride and groom turned to recess down the long aisle, Maria's eyes met hers with a warm smile which brought tears to Anna's. She was very thankful she had come.

A catered reception followed the ceremony; it boasted a lavish buffet and an orchestra for dancing. The groom's parents were warm and gracious to Anna, and even Rosa and her husband made it a point to stop by her chair. All in all, it was more than she had expected.

Yet, sorrow gripped her heart to know the house in Bregenz was to be sold. It was the house to which she came as a bride and where she raised her children. It had remained a tie to her homeland, and now, the bond was to be severed.

• • •

In the days following the wedding, Anna visited Katy's father and brothers' families. She also spent time with Katy's little sister, Angelika. What a sweet, happy child. Katy will be pleased to know her family appeared happy and well.

One last errand remained. At the bottom of her largest steamer trunk, wrapped in soft flannel, were picture frames Katy and Alex wanted her to deliver to Sofie. Sam had fashioned them from walnut and carved the wood in an ornate, beveled design. They were truly lovely.

Anna knew Katy and Sofie exchanged letters which had surprised Anna. She remembered how upset Sofie was at Katy's departure, and how hurt she had been when she received no further word from Katy. At last, she had worked up the courage to come to the house and inquire. Although, at that time, Anna did not know Katy's whereabouts either.

When Katy and Alex returned to Bregenz, however, Anna knew they spent time with Sofie and Johann. Katy corresponded with her friend on a regular basis. Still, it was awkward.

She need not have worried. Sofie greeted her warmly and requested details concerning Hilda Rose, the Iowa farm, and Anna's impressions of America. As they lingered over tea and cakes, Johann arrived and Sofie introduced him to Anna.

Johann shook her hand.

"Ah . . . The mother of my brother in Christ," he exclaimed. "I'm deeply honored."

Anna was taken aback, but she recovered to retrieve the frames from her satchel.

"I've often admired your painting," she told Johann. "It hangs in my son's parlor."

"These beautiful frames will inspire me to paint others," Johann replied. "Katy and Alex are more to us than friends. Because of them, we have an even more perfect Friend."

"What do you mean?" Anna asked.

She took it as a compliment for Alex and Katy. But what does Johann mean by "perfect friend"?

"Why, Jesus Christ, of course. We knew about Him, but we didn't know Him until Alex explained who He is—not just a Being to revere, but Someone with whom to have a real relationship. What a difference."

Anna smiled and changed the subject. She made a mental note to remember to ask Alex what Johann meant—maybe Sam as well. Sam spoke of Christ the same way, as if he would know Him if they met on the street. At first, it had seemed almost blasphemous to her, but she knew Sam too well to think he dishonored the call God had placed on his life.

Sofie, Johann, and Anna went on to talk of other things such as Hilda Rose and Eduard, Anna's impressions of Iowa, and so on. Before she left, Sofie shyly shared within the year she and Johann were going to have a child.

"I wrote Katy the news just last week," she told Anna.

Anna reached out to clasp Sofie's hands in hers.

"Bless you," she said. "Katy and Alex will be thrilled to hear it."

As she rode back to her Bregenz home for the last time, she reflected on the breadth of Alex's and Kay's relationships—from Sofie and Johann in Bregenz to the Silversteins in New York to Sam and Susannah in Iowa.

She had agreed with her husband to send Alex to Egg long ago.

What a shock it was to discover Alex had stolen funds to run away with Katy to America!

Yet, God brought so much good out of all the heartache. She was ready to return. She missed Hilda Rose and Eduard, the straight back of Father Felder conducting Mass on Sunday, and even the seemingly endless rows of corn which stretched toward the horizon.

• • •

They waited on the platform as the train pulled in. Eduard jumped up and down, and Hilda Rose stood on her tiptoes, cheeks ablaze.

"I don't know how we managed without her," Katy remarked.

"You weren't working then," Alex reminded her.

"Yes, but it's more than her help. She's such a stable influence—good for the children and me."

Alex reached for her hand to squeeze it.

"I think she'd say it works both ways."

Anna fairly flew down the steps the moment the porter lowered them. She stooped and gathered the children into her arms. Tears flowed and she made no attempt to stop them.

Hilda Rose fairly burst to voice the news.

"Susannah's going to have a baby and I've decided to be a nurse when I grow up."

"But, of course."

Anna stood to embrace Alex and Katy.

"You'll make a wonderful nurse. And I'm so happy for Sam and Susannah. Another child. How wonderful."

"You'll never know how much you were missed," Alex told her.

Anna's eyes filled with tears. To be missed. What a blessing!

Yes, she belonged among ones she loved, who loved her in return.

CHAPTER 40

Iowa, 1908

The trip to Des Moines was a long-awaited occasion. Alex Meisen, Katharina Thannen Meisen, and Anna Meisen were scheduled to appear at the federal courthouse in order to take the Oath of Allegiance to the flag of the United States of America. At last, they were to be naturalized citizens of their adopted country.

As the three adults and two children boarded the train, the summer sun shone bright with just a hint of autumn's approach. Alex had insisted Hilda Rose and Eduard accompany them.

"Even though they're already citizens by birth, they deserve to be present because they studied the test questions along with us, and must understand the importance and dignity of what we endeavor to accomplish."

"That's right," eight-year-old Hilda Rose agreed. "You quizzed us over and over: What are the colors of the flag? What do the stars on the flag mean? What right is granted by the First Amendment?"

"Yes, darling," Alex interrupted. "We don't have time for all one-hundred questions, but you did very well . . . So did Eduard. When Mary Elizabeth is older, she'll learn the answers as well."

Sam stood to wave them off. They had left the baby behind in Susannah's loving care. Sam had obtained his citizenship five years ago, but Alex's accident, Katy's job, the birth of another child, and just daily busyness had delayed the event for Alex and Katy. The fact Anna joined them made the timing seem right.

"It's almost ten years to the day since you sailed to America," Alex told Katy.

NO TURNING BACK

"And you followed," she reminded him.

Hilda Rose and Eduard waved until Sam and Susannah faded out of sight. Nine-year-old Daniel ran beside the train until it picked up speed and left him behind.

Katy and Anna were dressed in their best, but Katy had made one concession.

"I'm wearing the feathered hat for good luck," she told them. "After all, it brought us Sam and Susannah."

She knew it was not luck. God had been with them all the way. Katy saw it. Even in the darkest hours, He never left nor ceased to remember them.

She reached her arm behind the children to squeeze her husband's shoulder. As he turned her way, she mouthed, "I love you."

"I love you, too," he answered. "God bless America."

The End

For more information about

JOANNE WILSON MEUSBURGER

&

NO TURNING BACK

please visit:

Twitter: @JMeusburger
Facebook: www.facebook.com/joanne.meusburger
Website: www.jmeusburger.com

For more information about

AMBASSADOR INTERNATIONAL

please visit:

www.ambassador-international.com
@AmbassadorIntl
www.facebook.com/AmbassadorIntl